Archie®

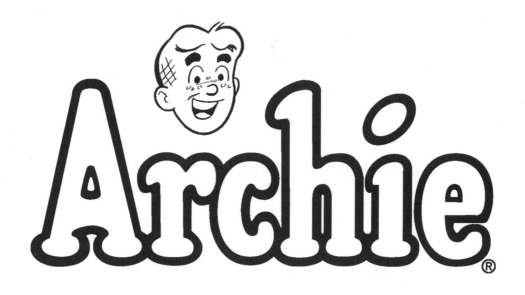

DAY BY DAY

ARCHIE DAY BY DAY, Volume 1, 2003. Printed in Canada. Published by Archie Comic Publications, Inc., 325 Fayette Avenue, Mamaroneck, New York 10543. Michael I. Silberkleit, Chairman and Co-Publisher. Richard H. Goldwater, President and Co-Publisher. ARCHIE characters created by John L. Goldwater. The likenesses of the original Archie characters were created by Bob Montana. The individual characters' names and likenesses are the exclusive trademarks of Archie Comic Publications, Inc.

ISBN 1-879794-16-0

www.archiecomics.com

Archie ®

DAY BY DAY

BY

HENRY SCARPELLI & CRAIG BOLDMAN

ARCHIE COMIC PUBLICATIONS, INC.

MAMARONECK, NY

RICK NEWCOMBE
PRESIDENT, CREATORS SYNDICATE

Archie is an American icon, as much a part of our culture as Coca-Cola, Kleenex and Corn Flakes.   When Bob Montana brought Archie and his Riverdale pals to life, little did he know that this redheaded character would become a symbol of America. The freckled-faced teenager made his first comic book appearance in December 1941, the same month Pearl Harbor was attacked.   Archie saw the young men of the Greatest Generation go off to war and return home to begin the Baby Boom.

I was one of the millions of Baby Boomers who grew up with Archie, Jughead, Betty and Veronica. Every Saturday during my pre-teen years, I bought the latest Archie comic book from the local five and dime store in our small Chicago suburb. I would ride my bike down to Lake Michigan, find a park bench and spend hours drinking Nesbit's orange soda and reading Archie. I had no idea that four decades later -- after I grew my hair long as part of the rebellious 1960s, later cut it, got married and had children of my own -- I would be syndicating the Archie comic strip to newspapers around the world.

All I knew was I liked Archie. I related to him. He goofed up like I did, but he was not lazy like Jughead. He was confident but not a know-it-all like Reggie. And, depending on which day of the week it was, I rooted for Archie to pick Betty over Veronica -- or Veronica over Betty.

"Which one would you pick if you could, Betty or Veronica?" What American boy from my generation didn't ask -- or get asked -- that question at least once? That question is one strand in the fabric of American culture. Archie arrived on the world stage shortly after the new art form of the comic book made its debut. But Archie was different from the others. Where they were dark and brooding, Archie was filled with humor and light. Where they were violent and cynical, Archie was cheerful and buoyant.

"Something I have really liked about Archie is that beyond the real basics of the characters, the comic strip doesn't concern itself that much with being overly topical or trying to teach lessons. It is really about the comedy and the character interactions, and it's not afraid to be a little far-fetched. There may be some life lessons to be learned in Archie, but that's not the first place I'd go to learn them," says Craig Boldman, current writer of the Archie Strip.

Therein lies the secret to Archie's success. He was never cynical. Having been spawned the same month America was thrust into World War II, Archie remained upbeat and optimistic during the war years and throughout the subsequent Cold War.   Even during the turbulent 1960s and the Watergate era, when pessimism and gloom pervaded the national sentiment, Archie remained fresh-faced and hopeful. Few characters created in the early days of comic books have survived the last half-century. Along with Superman and Batman, Archie Andrews is one of the few to have endured the test of time and become a comic book legend.   Archie hasn't merely survived; he's thrived.   Not only are millions of comic books and pieces of Archie-related merchandise sold each year, but the Archie comic strip still appears in hundreds of newspapers from India to Colombia, and from Malaysia to South Africa. As a popular part of newspapers in Pakistan and the United Arab Emirates, Archie is an unofficial American ambassador to the Middle East. And I'm proud to be a part of that.

Creators Syndicate began distributing the Archie comic strip in 1989, shortly after I started the company, and we have had a wonderful relationship with Archie Comics ever since. We distribute over a hundred features to thousands of newspapers around the world, and many of our columnists and cartoonists are world-renowned. Yet whenever I list our features, I always include Archie because of its immediate name recognition. And I always get the same response. People's faces light up, and they say, "Oh, yeah! I always read Archie when I was a kid!"

For the last 10 years, Henry Scarpelli and Craig Boldman have carried on the long-standing tradition of pitting Archie and Reggie against each other, letting Jughead eat too many hamburgers, allowing Archie to elude detention from Mr. Weatherbee, and, of course, giving Veronica's father the chance to kick Archie out of the house. Their work stands alongside the best of the Archie writers and artists.

Longtime comic book artist Henry Scarpelli's career has taken him to DC Comics, Marvel Comics, Dell Publishing's comic book division and now to Archie Comics. Scarpelli remembers his interest in cartooning starting with Milton Caniff's work and realistic adventure comics and then switching to humor-related cartoons. When he was 8 years old, one of his favorite occupations was to draw copies of the Little Orphan Annie and Dick Tracy comic strips as they appeared in the newspapers.

What did Craig Boldman do immediately after reading his first Archie comic book as a boy? He actually sat down and wrote and drew his own original Archie story.

"I remember the first Archie comic story I ever read. I just ran across it as a reprint and reread it. It was a very funny story about how to write a comic book. It was wordless -- no dialogue -- and explained step by step how to introduce the characters, create suspense and so on. It wasn't presented as information but was done as a gag, for entertainment."

Interestingly, when asked to name a favorite Archie character, both Boldman and Scarpelli say the same thing: Jughead.

"I see him as one of the all-time great comic book/comic strip characters," says Boldman. "I like all of the characters, but Jughead's non-conformist attitude appeals the most to me. Each of the other characters has a single, well-defined character trait: Reggie as the villain, Veronica as the stuck-up rich girl, Betty as the nice girl. Jughead has more options than the other characters."

Scarpelli says, "Jughead has great characteristics: He's aloof, lazy and an oddball character. He's different." Writers will often say that once they've created a character, the characters begin to write themselves. How much more evidence do we need for the truth of that than Archie? Many varied and talented men and women have lent a hand to bringing Archie to life over the last six decades, but Archie has a life of his own!

Archie's longevity is testimony to his universal appeal. Like me sitting on that park bench, millions of kids relate to him. And new generations are discovering him every day. The world has changed drastically since Archie first appeared, but he has remained steadfast. Archie may not be driving the old jalopy anymore (he's had a 1967 Ford Mustang since the '80s), but he's still dividing his time between Betty and Veronica. Betty may use e-mail now, but it's still to send a love letter to Archie. Veronica may use a cell phone, but she does so while shopping, spending her wealthy father's money.

Speaking of Archie's universal appeal, when I was in my 20s, I took a trip to Norway. This was before I was married, and I was talking with a couple of local girls I was trying to impress. I asked them what their idea of the average American male was. I'll never forget their response: "Like Archie!"

Henry Scarpelli – Artist

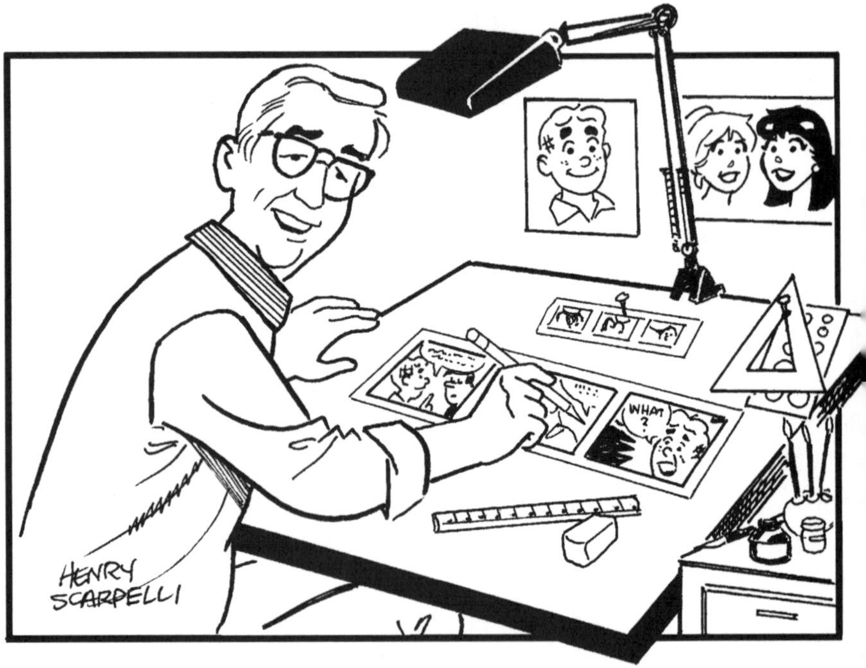
WHAT ?
HENRY SCARPELLI

After an art education at the School of Visual Arts in New York City, Henry Scarpelli received his first job offer from a newspaper syndicate designing sales brochures and ads for feature presentations.

An insider at the syndicate, he was presented with an opportunity to create "TV Tee-Hees," a cartoon humor panel feature appearing in 150 newspapers during the 60's and 70's.

Later, Scarpelli decided to explore career opportunities in comic books. He first worked at Dell Publishing as the artist for comic magazine versions of such TV shows as "The Beverly Hillbillies," "Bewitched," "Hogan's Heroes" and "Get Smart."

From there, Scarpelli moved on to major comic book publishers, such as DC, Marvel and Archie Comics. While at DC, he won two comic book "Shazam" awards and a National Cartoonists Society nomination for outstanding comic book humor cartoonist. After some years of doing comic book art for Archie comics, Scarpelli was offered the opportunity to do the Archie newspaper strip, both daily and Sunday.

Craig Boldman – Writer

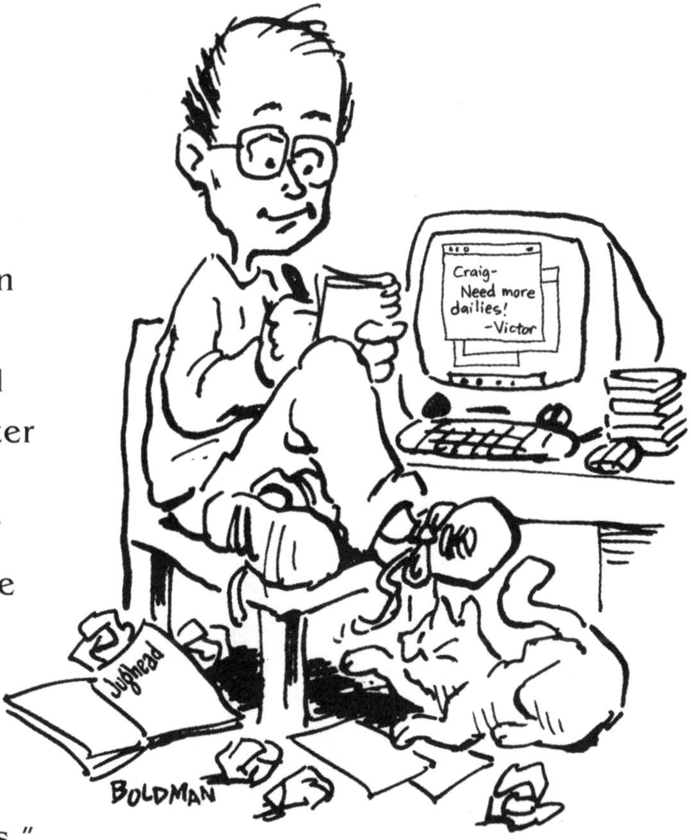
Craig-
Need more
dailies!
-Victor
Jughead
BOLDMAN

Craig Boldman has been a professional cartoonist since 1978. He has written and drawn over 10,000 greeting cards for such companies as Hallmark, American Greetings and Recycled Paper Products. He was a contract writer for Gibson Greetings for nearly a decade.

In 1985, Boldman wrote the *Adventures of Superman* for DC Comics, under the watchful eye of editor and living legend, Julius Schwartz. He has since written a variety of other well-known characters, including "Big Boy," "Bazooka Joe," and strips based on two Disney TV shows: "Disney's Doug," and "Disney's Recess."

Boldman currently writes the *Jughead* comic book for Archie Comic Publications, and has been writing the Archie newspaper strip since 1992, first in collaboration with artist Dan DeCarlo, and later with Henry Scarpelli, who continues drawing the strip today.

Boldman is the co-author/illustrator of a humor book from Andrews McMeel Publishing, "Every Excuse in the Book: 718 Ways to Say 'It's Not My Fault!'"

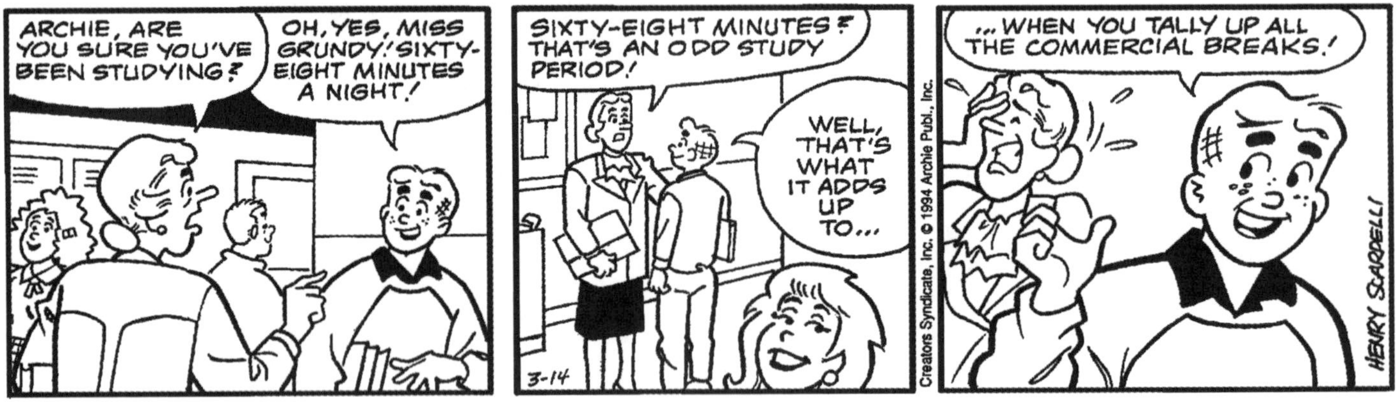
ARCHIE, ARE YOU SURE YOU'VE BEEN STUDYING?
OH, YES, MISS GRUNDY! SIXTY-EIGHT MINUTES A NIGHT!
SIXTY-EIGHT MINUTES? THAT'S AN ODD STUDY PERIOD!
WELL, THAT'S WHAT IT ADDS UP TO...
3-14
...WHEN YOU TALLY UP ALL THE COMMERCIAL BREAKS!
HENRY SCARPELLI
Creators Syndicate, Inc. © 1994 Archie Publ., Inc.

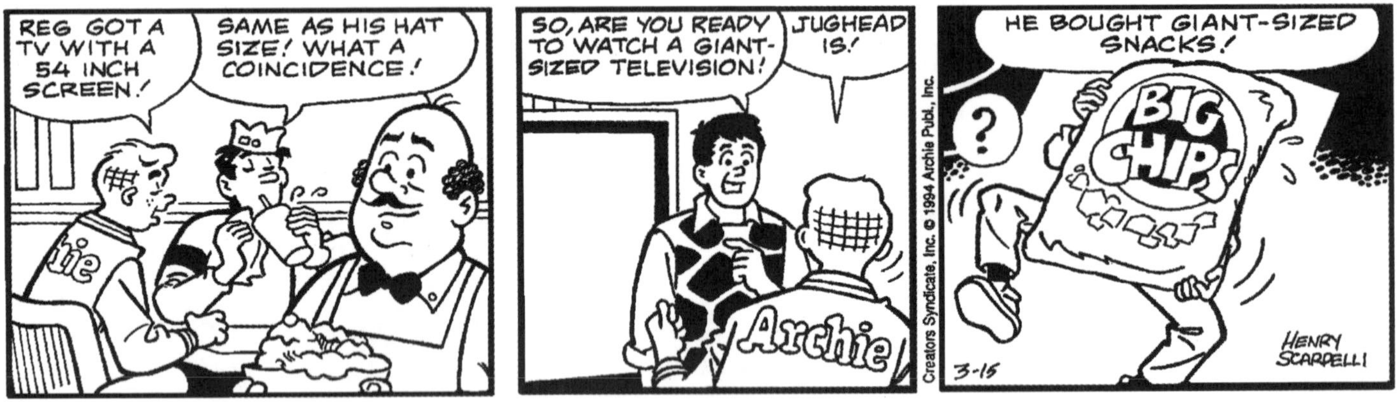
REG GOT A TV WITH A 54 INCH SCREEN!
SAME AS HIS HAT SIZE! WHAT A COINCIDENCE!
SO, ARE YOU READY TO WATCH A GIANT-SIZED TELEVISION!
JUGHEAD IS!
Archie
HE BOUGHT GIANT-SIZED SNACKS!
?
BIG CHIPS
3-15
HENRY SCARPELLI
Creators Syndicate, Inc. © 1994 Archie Publ., Inc.

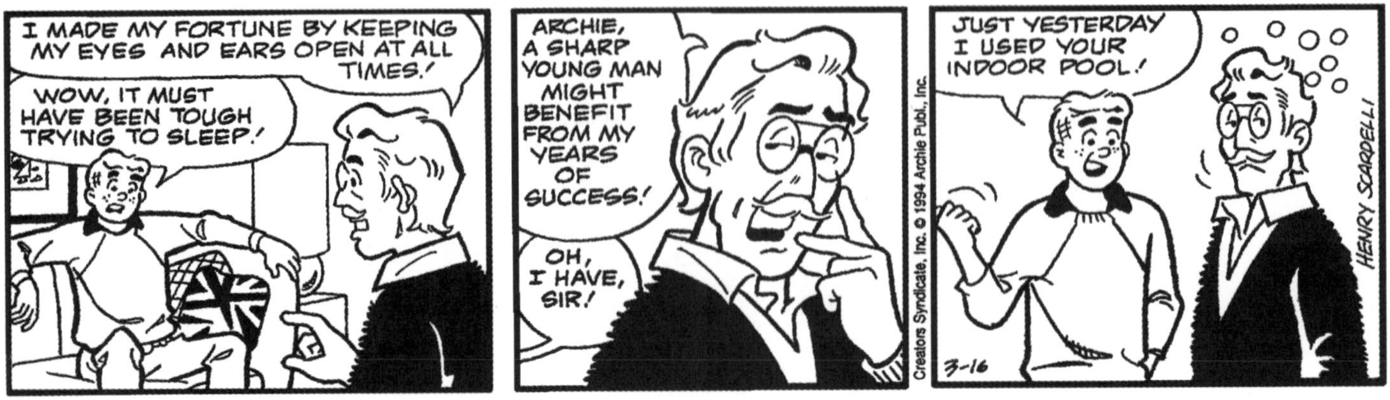
I MADE MY FORTUNE BY KEEPING MY EYES AND EARS OPEN AT ALL TIMES!
WOW, IT MUST HAVE BEEN TOUGH TRYING TO SLEEP!
ARCHIE, A SHARP YOUNG MAN MIGHT BENEFIT FROM MY YEARS OF SUCCESS!
OH, I HAVE, SIR!
JUST YESTERDAY I USED YOUR INDOOR POOL!
3-16
HENRY SCARPELLI
Creators Syndicate, Inc. © 1994 Archie Publ., Inc.

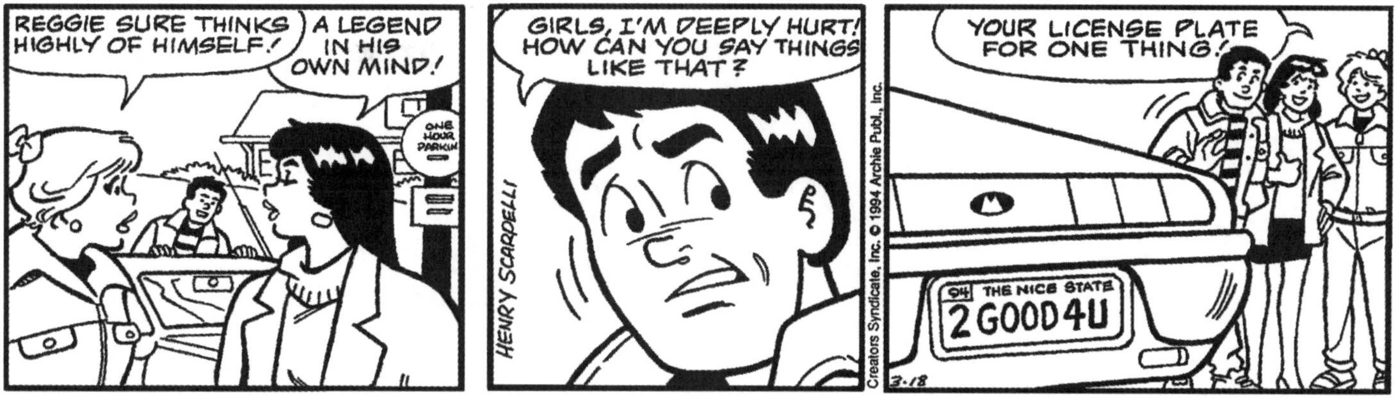
REGGIE SURE THINKS HIGHLY OF HIMSELF!
A LEGEND IN HIS OWN MIND!
ONE HOUR PARKIN
HENRY SCARPELLI
GIRLS, I'M DEEPLY HURT! HOW CAN YOU SAY THINGS LIKE THAT?
Creators Syndicate, Inc. © 1994 Archie Publ., Inc.
YOUR LICENSE PLATE FOR ONE THING!
94 THE NICE STATE
2 GOOD 4U
3-18

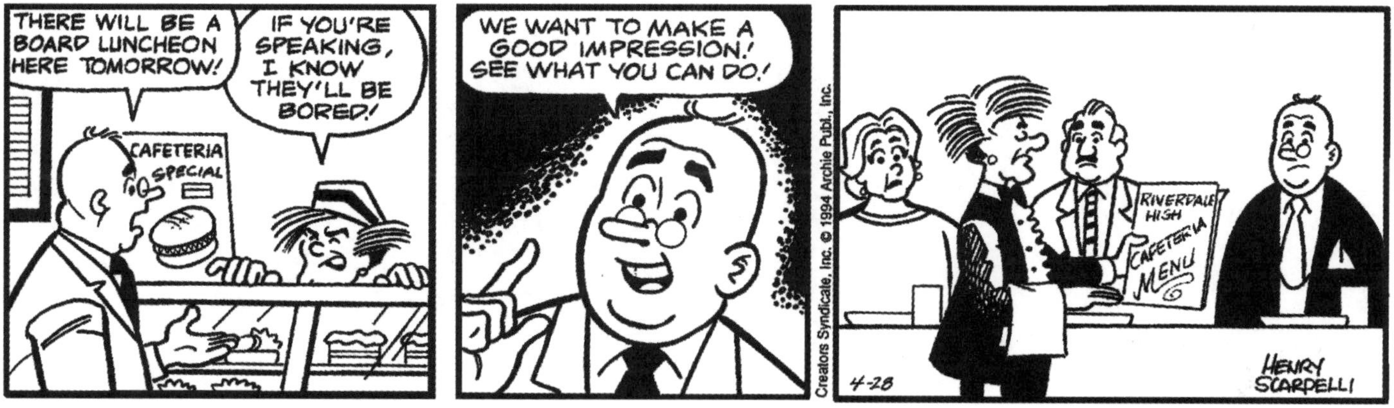
THERE WILL BE A BOARD LUNCHEON HERE TOMORROW!
IF YOU'RE SPEAKING, I KNOW THEY'LL BE BORED!
CAFETERIA SPECIAL
WE WANT TO MAKE A GOOD IMPRESSION! SEE WHAT YOU CAN DO!
Creators Syndicate, Inc. © 1994 Archie Publ., Inc.
RIVERDALE HIGH CAFETERIA MENU
4-28
HENRY SCARPELLI

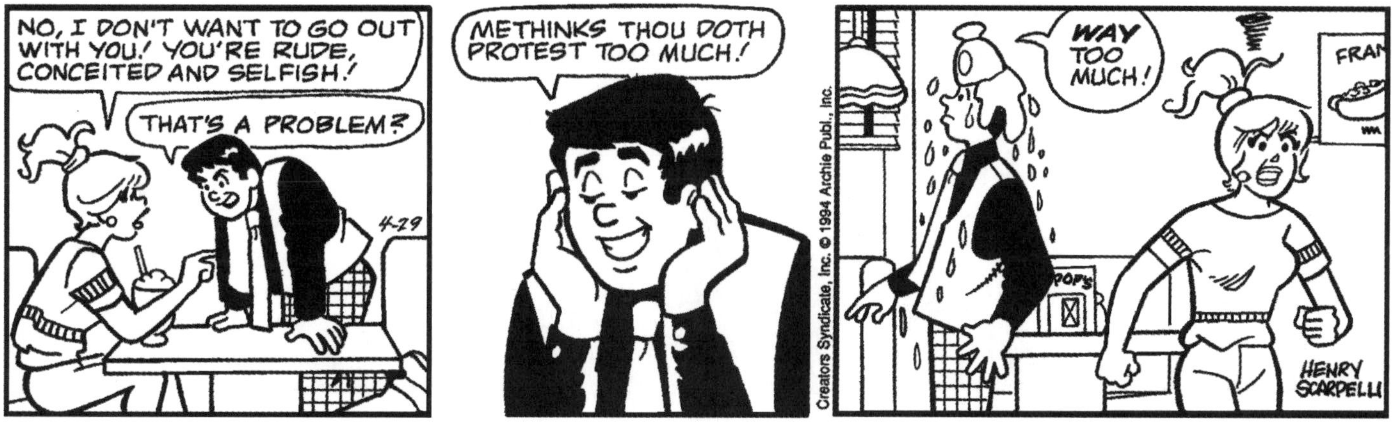
NO, I DON'T WANT TO GO OUT WITH YOU! YOU'RE RUDE, CONCEITED AND SELFISH!
THAT'S A PROBLEM?
4-29
METHINKS THOU DOTH PROTEST TOO MUCH!
Creators Syndicate, Inc. © 1994 Archie Publ., Inc.
WAY TOO MUCH!
POP'S
HENRY SCARPELLI

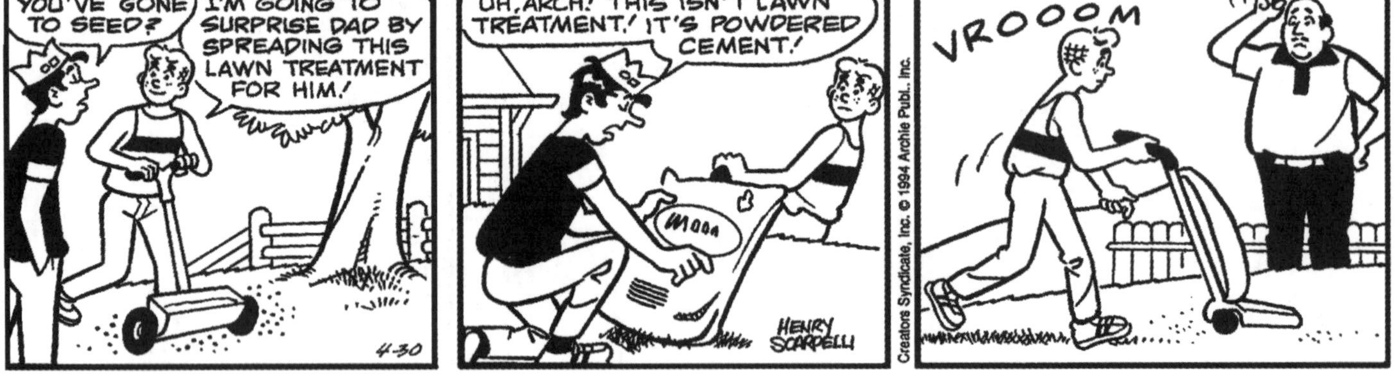
YOU'VE GONE TO SEED?
I'M GOING TO SURPRISE DAD BY SPREADING THIS LAWN TREATMENT FOR HIM!
4-30
UH, ARCH! THIS ISN'T LAWN TREATMENT! IT'S POWDERED CEMENT!
HENRY SCARPELLI
VROOOM

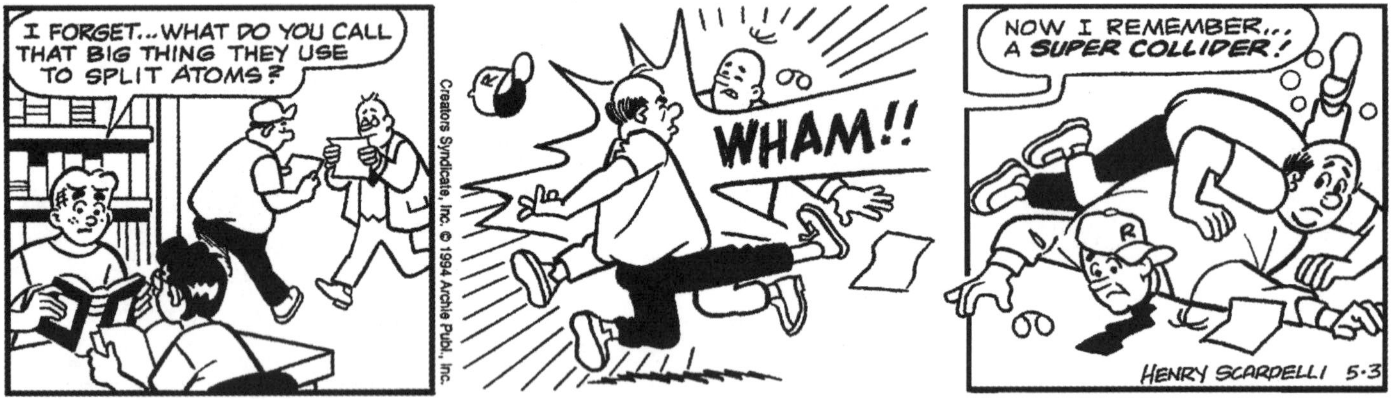
I FORGET... WHAT DO YOU CALL THAT BIG THING THEY USE TO SPLIT ATOMS?
WHAM!!
NOW I REMEMBER... A ***SUPER COLLIDER***!
HENRY SCARPELLI 5·3

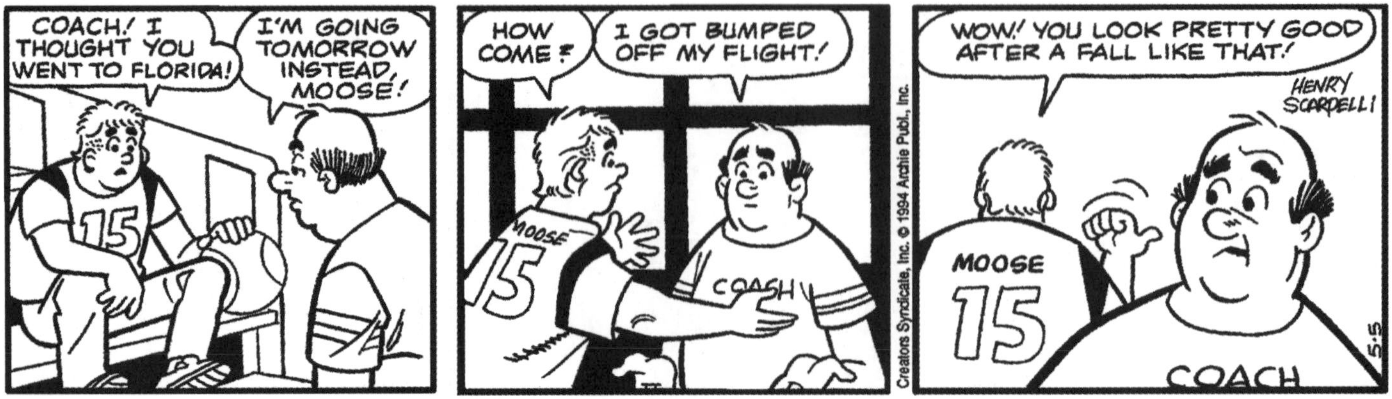
COACH! I THOUGHT YOU WENT TO FLORIDA!
I'M GOING TOMORROW INSTEAD, MOOSE!
HOW COME?
I GOT BUMPED OFF MY FLIGHT!
MOOSE 15
COACH
WOW! YOU LOOK PRETTY GOOD AFTER A FALL LIKE THAT!
HENRY SCARPELLI
MOOSE 15
COACH
5-5

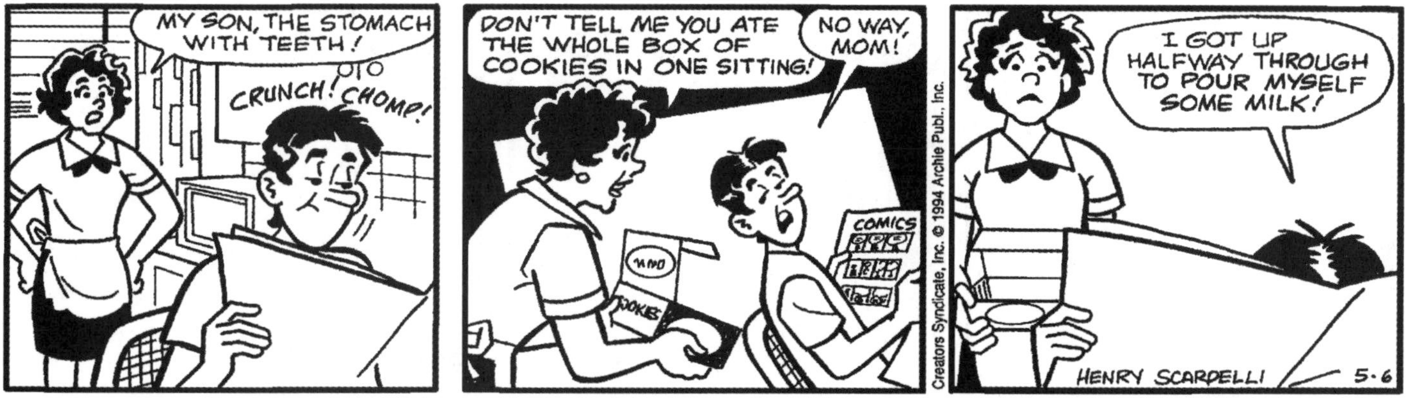
MY SON, THE STOMACH WITH TEETH!
CRUNCH! CHOMP!
DON'T TELL ME YOU ATE THE WHOLE BOX OF COOKIES IN ONE SITTING!
NO WAY, MOM!
COMICS
COOKIES
Creators Syndicate, Inc. © 1994 Archie Publ., Inc.
I GOT UP HALFWAY THROUGH TO POUR MYSELF SOME MILK!
HENRY SCARPELLI
5-6

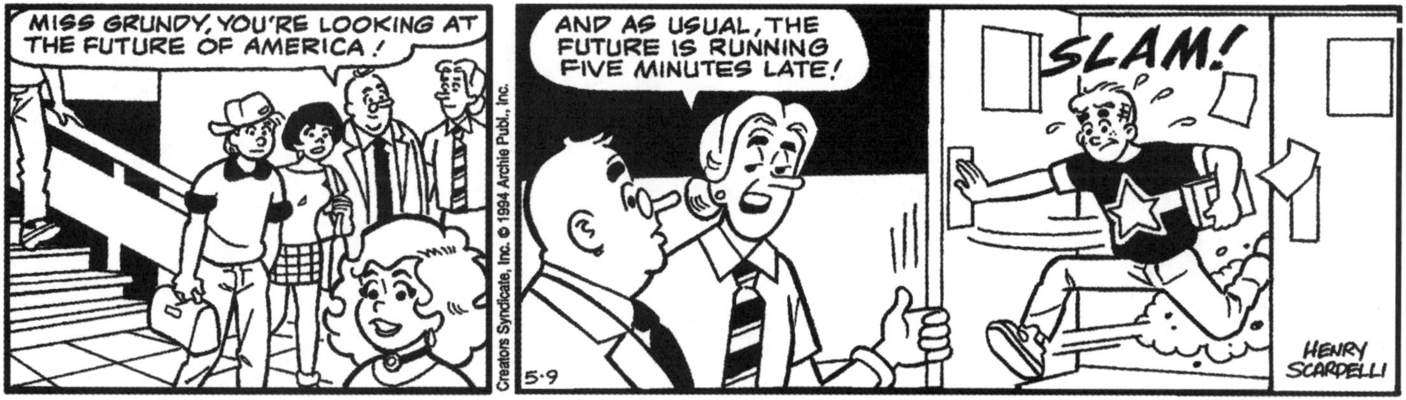
MISS GRUNDY, YOU'RE LOOKING AT THE FUTURE OF AMERICA!
Creators Syndicate, Inc. © 1994 Archie Publ., Inc.
AND AS USUAL, THE FUTURE IS RUNNING FIVE MINUTES LATE!
5-9
SLAM!
HENRY SCARPELLI

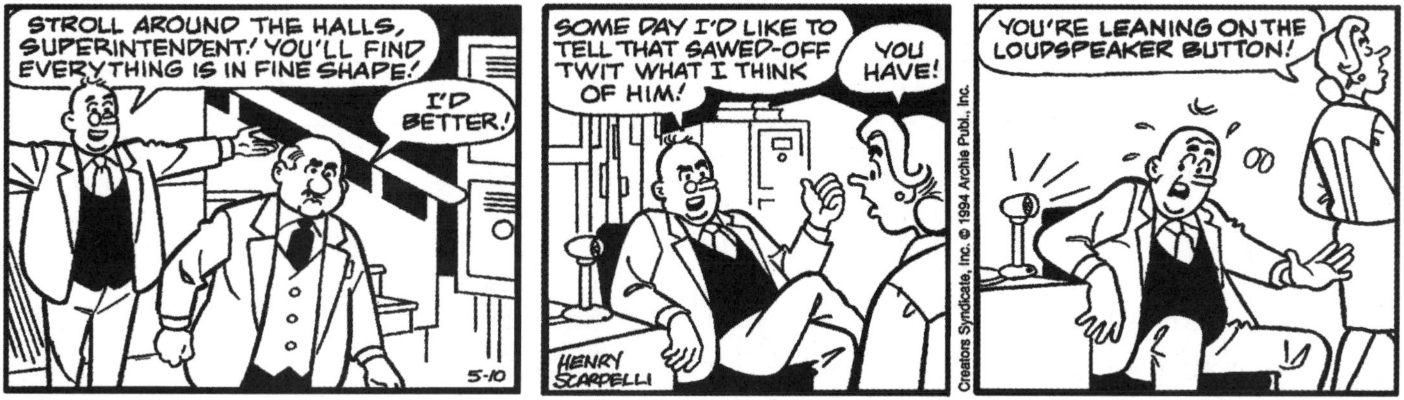
STROLL AROUND THE HALLS, SUPERINTENDENT! YOU'LL FIND EVERYTHING IS IN FINE SHAPE!
I'D BETTER!
5-10
SOME DAY I'D LIKE TO TELL THAT SAWED-OFF TWIT WHAT I THINK OF HIM!
YOU HAVE!
HENRY SCARPELLI
Creators Syndicate, Inc. © 1994 Archie Publ., Inc.
YOU'RE LEANING ON THE LOUDSPEAKER BUTTON!

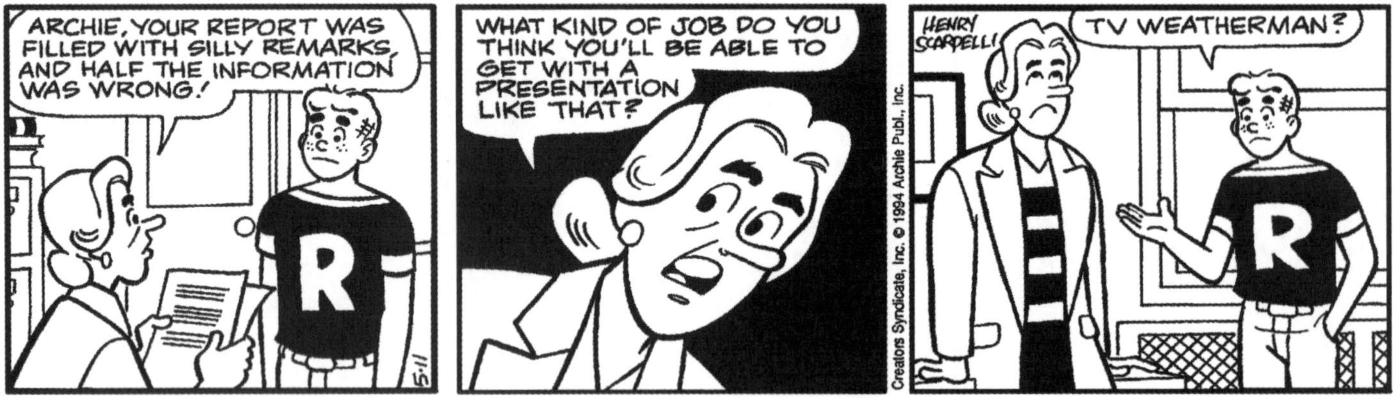
ARCHIE, YOUR REPORT WAS FILLED WITH SILLY REMARKS, AND HALF THE INFORMATION WAS WRONG!
5-11
WHAT KIND OF JOB DO YOU THINK YOU'LL BE ABLE TO GET WITH A PRESENTATION LIKE THAT?
HENRY SCARPELLI
TV WEATHERMAN?
Creators Syndicate, Inc. © 1994 Archie Publ., Inc.

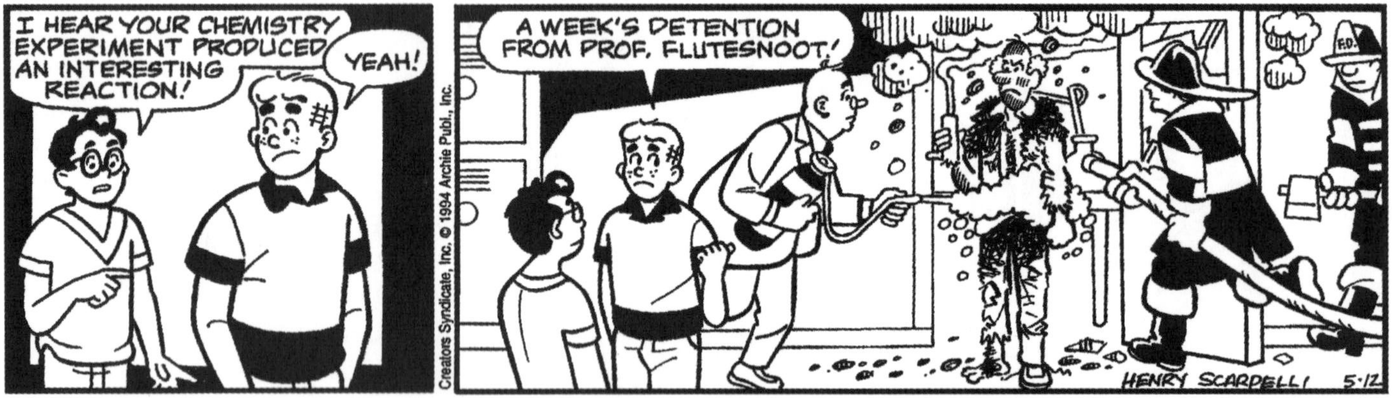
I HEAR YOUR CHEMISTRY EXPERIMENT PRODUCED AN INTERESTING REACTION!
YEAH!
Creators Syndicate, Inc. © 1994 Archie Publ., Inc.
A WEEK'S DETENTION FROM PROF. FLUTESNOOT!
F.D.
HENRY SCARPELLI
5-12

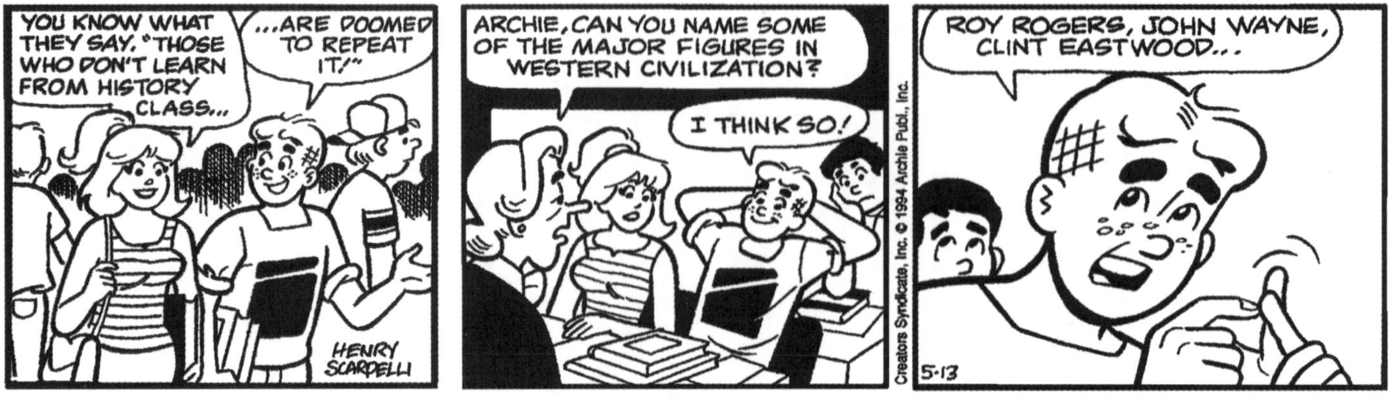
YOU KNOW WHAT THEY SAY. "THOSE WHO DON'T LEARN FROM HISTORY CLASS...
...ARE DOOMED TO REPEAT IT!"
HENRY SCARPELLI
ARCHIE, CAN YOU NAME SOME OF THE MAJOR FIGURES IN WESTERN CIVILIZATION?
I THINK SO!
Creators Syndicate, Inc. © 1994 Archie Publ., Inc.
5-13
ROY ROGERS, JOHN WAYNE, CLINT EASTWOOD...

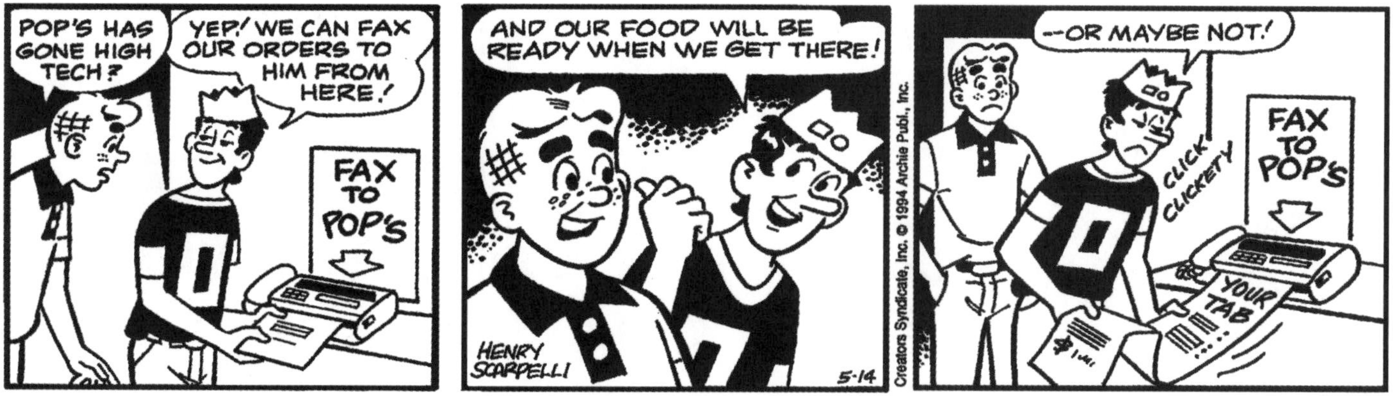
POP'S HAS GONE HIGH TECH?
YEP! WE CAN FAX OUR ORDERS TO HIM FROM HERE!
FAX TO POP'S
AND OUR FOOD WILL BE READY WHEN WE GET THERE!
HENRY SCARPELLI
5·14
Creators Syndicate, Inc. © 1994 Archie Publ., Inc.
--OR MAYBE NOT!
FAX TO POP'S
CLICK CLICKETY
YOUR TAB

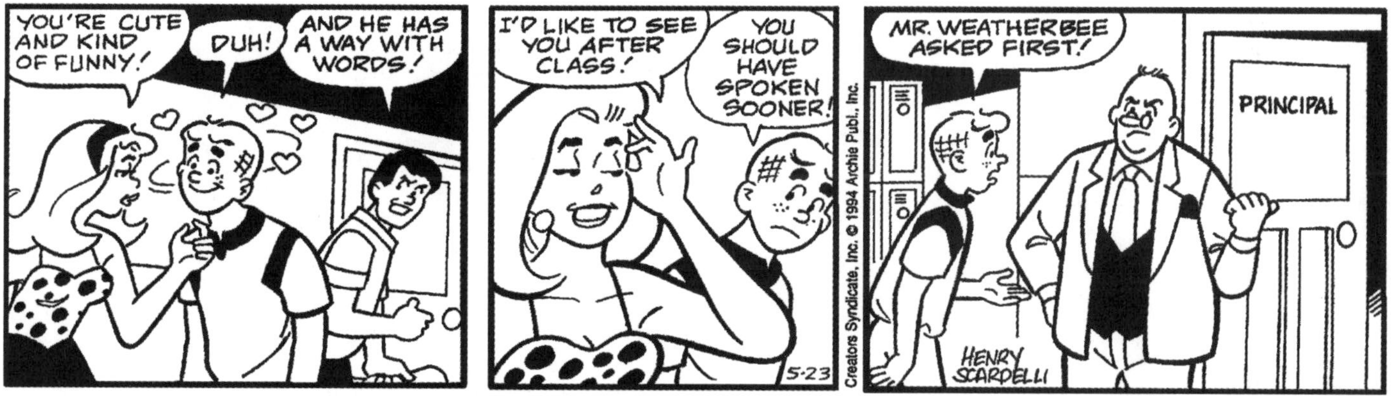
YOU'RE CUTE AND KIND OF FUNNY!
DUH!
AND HE HAS A WAY WITH WORDS!
I'D LIKE TO SEE YOU AFTER CLASS!
YOU SHOULD HAVE SPOKEN SOONER!
5·23
Creators Syndicate, Inc. © 1994 Archie Publ., Inc.
MR. WEATHERBEE ASKED FIRST!
PRINCIPAL
HENRY SCARPELLI

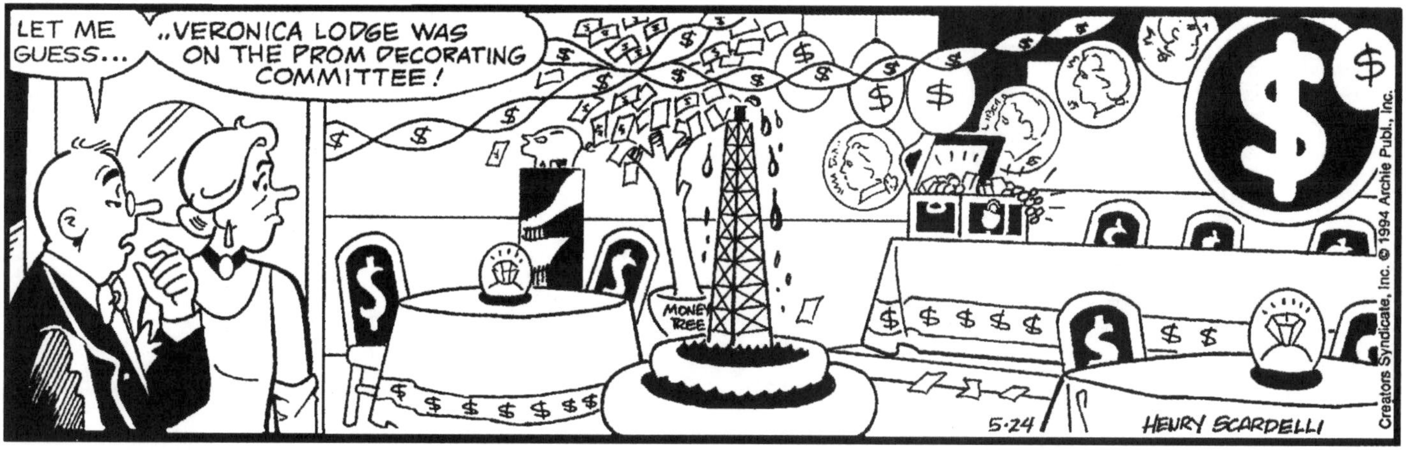
LET ME GUESS...
..VERONICA LODGE WAS ON THE PROM DECORATING COMMITTEE!
MONEY TREE
5·24
HENRY SCARPELLI
Creators Syndicate, Inc. © 1994 Archie Publ., Inc.

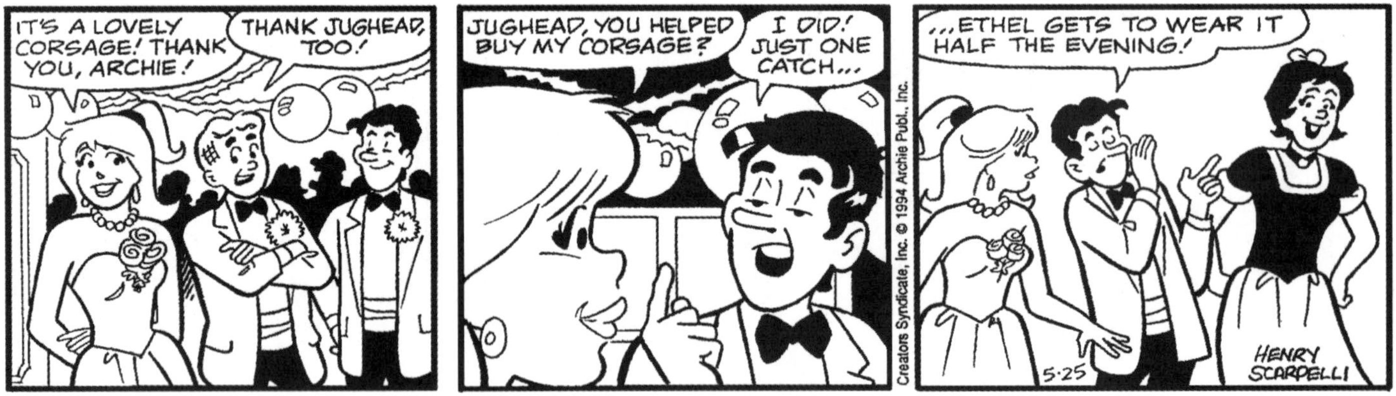
IT'S A LOVELY CORSAGE! THANK YOU, ARCHIE!
THANK JUGHEAD, TOO!
JUGHEAD, YOU HELPED BUY MY CORSAGE?
I DID! JUST ONE CATCH...
...ETHEL GETS TO WEAR IT HALF THE EVENING!
Creators Syndicate, Inc. © 1994 Archie Publ., Inc.
5·25
HENRY SCARPELLI

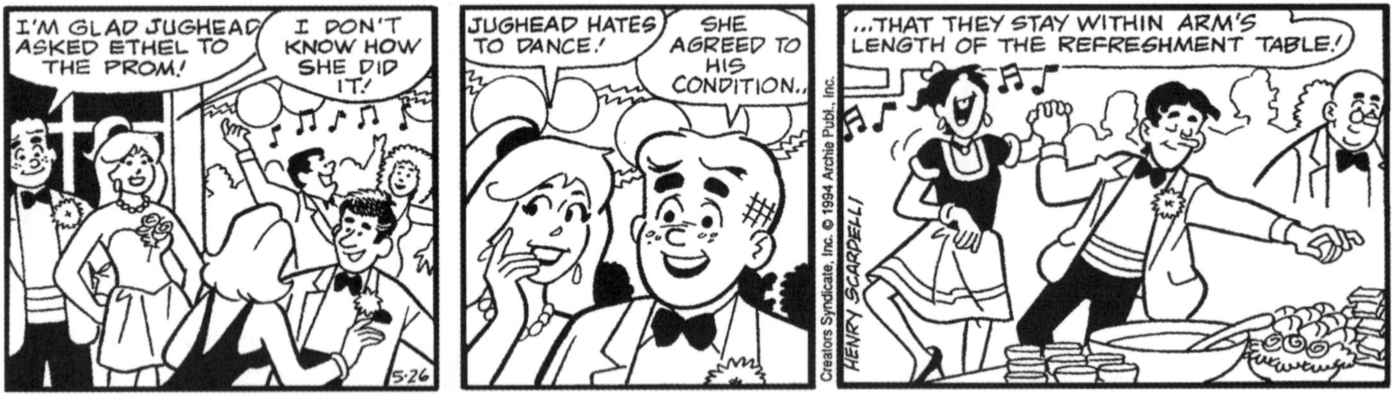
I'M GLAD JUGHEAD ASKED ETHEL TO THE PROM!
I DON'T KNOW HOW SHE DID IT!
5·26
JUGHEAD HATES TO DANCE!
SHE AGREED TO HIS CONDITION...
Creators Syndicate, Inc. © 1994 Archie Publ., Inc.
HENRY SCARPELLI
...THAT THEY STAY WITHIN ARM'S LENGTH OF THE REFRESHMENT TABLE!

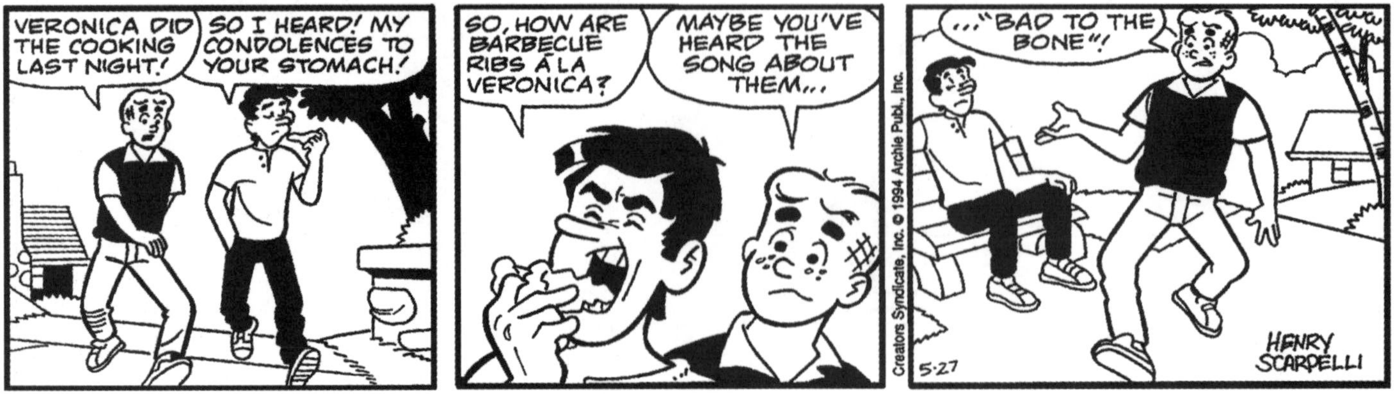
VERONICA DID THE COOKING LAST NIGHT!
SO I HEARD! MY CONDOLENCES TO YOUR STOMACH!
SO, HOW ARE BARBECUE RIBS Á LA VERONICA?
MAYBE YOU'VE HEARD THE SONG ABOUT THEM...
Creators Syndicate, Inc. © 1994 Archie Publ., Inc.
..."BAD TO THE BONE"!
5·27
HENRY SCARPELLI

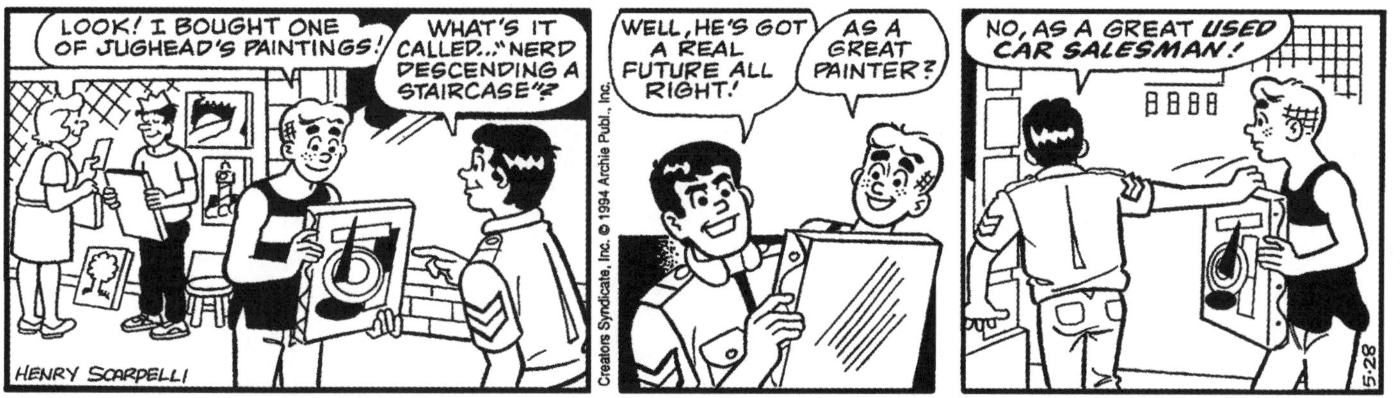
LOOK! I BOUGHT ONE OF JUGHEAD'S PAINTINGS!
WHAT'S IT CALLED..."NERD DESCENDING A STAIRCASE"?
HENRY SCARPELLI
Creators Syndicate, Inc. © 1994 Archie Publ., Inc.
WELL, HE'S GOT A REAL FUTURE ALL RIGHT!
AS A GREAT PAINTER?
NO, AS A GREAT USED CAR SALESMAN!
5-28

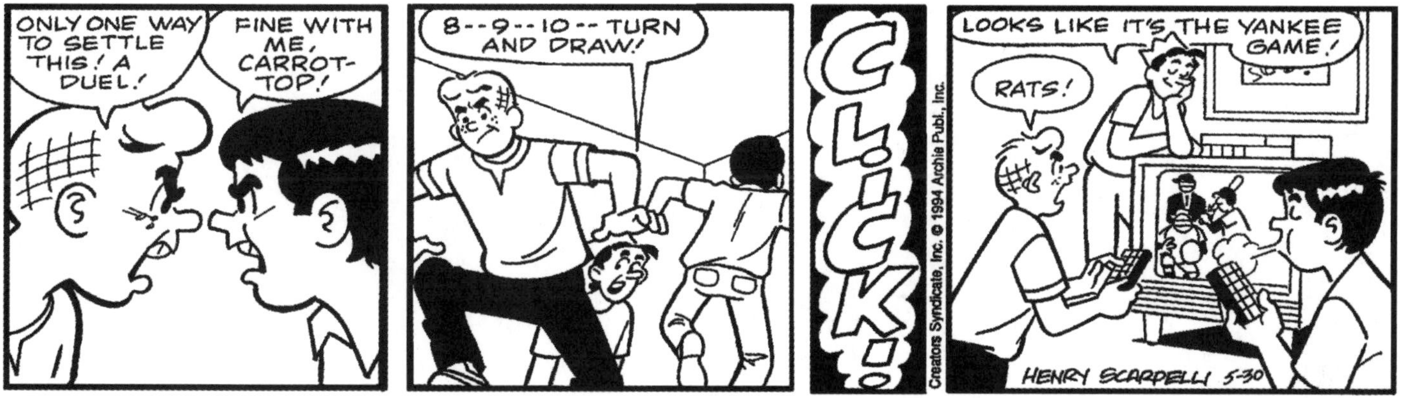
ONLY ONE WAY TO SETTLE THIS! A DUEL!
FINE WITH ME, CARROT-TOP!
8--9--10-- TURN AND DRAW!
CLICK!
Creators Syndicate, Inc. © 1994 Archie Publ., Inc.
LOOKS LIKE IT'S THE YANKEE GAME!
RATS!
HENRY SCARPELLI 5-30

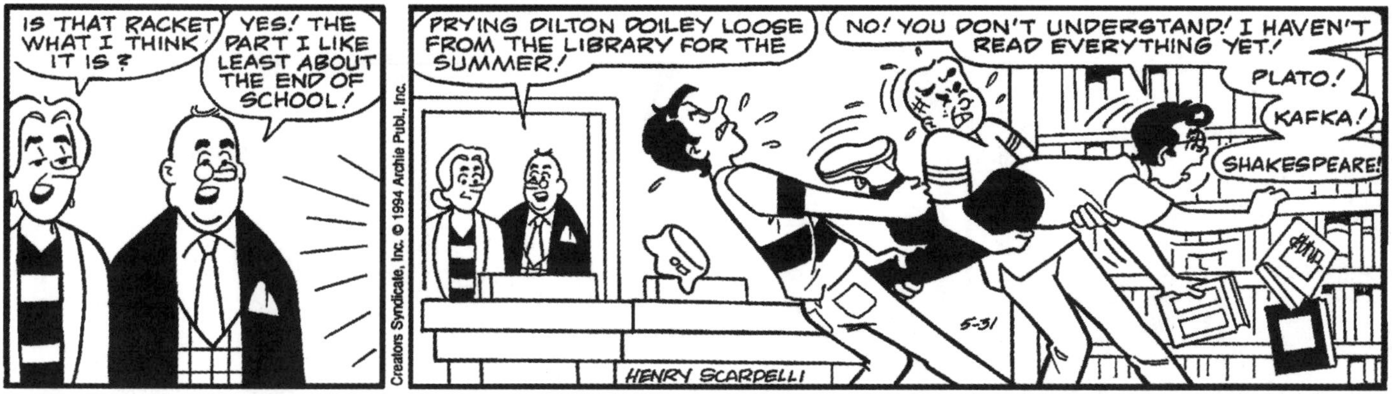
IS THAT RACKET WHAT I THINK IT IS?
YES! THE PART I LIKE LEAST ABOUT THE END OF SCHOOL!
Creators Syndicate, Inc. © 1994 Archie Publ., Inc.
PRYING DILTON DOILEY LOOSE FROM THE LIBRARY FOR THE SUMMER!
NO! YOU DON'T UNDERSTAND! I HAVEN'T READ EVERYTHING YET!
PLATO!
KAFKA!
SHAKESPEARE!
5-31
HENRY SCARPELLI

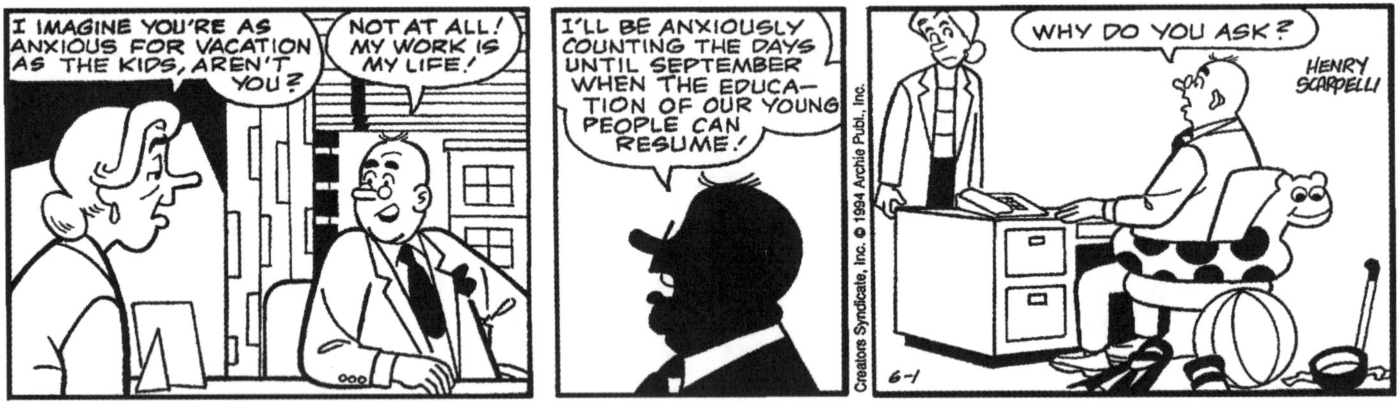
I IMAGINE YOU'RE AS ANXIOUS FOR VACATION AS THE KIDS, AREN'T YOU?
NOT AT ALL! MY WORK IS MY LIFE!
I'LL BE ANXIOUSLY COUNTING THE DAYS UNTIL SEPTEMBER WHEN THE EDUCATION OF OUR YOUNG PEOPLE CAN RESUME!
Creators Syndicate, Inc. © 1994 Archie Publ., Inc.
WHY DO YOU ASK?
HENRY SCARPELLI
6-1

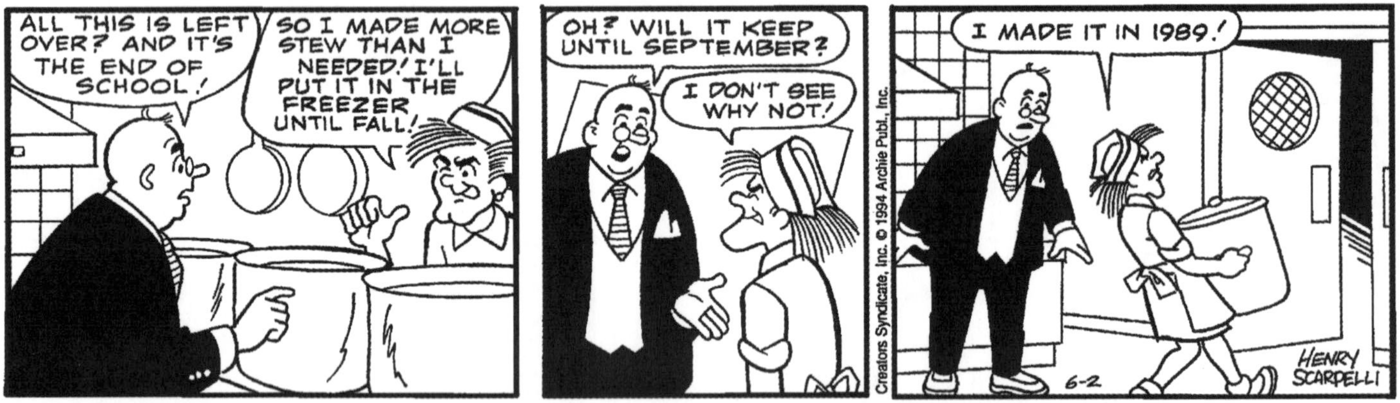
ALL THIS IS LEFT OVER? AND IT'S THE END OF SCHOOL!
SO I MADE MORE STEW THAN I NEEDED! I'LL PUT IT IN THE FREEZER UNTIL FALL!
OH? WILL IT KEEP UNTIL SEPTEMBER?
I DON'T SEE WHY NOT!
Creators Syndicate, Inc. © 1994 Archie Publ., Inc.
I MADE IT IN 1989!
6-2
HENRY SCARPELLI

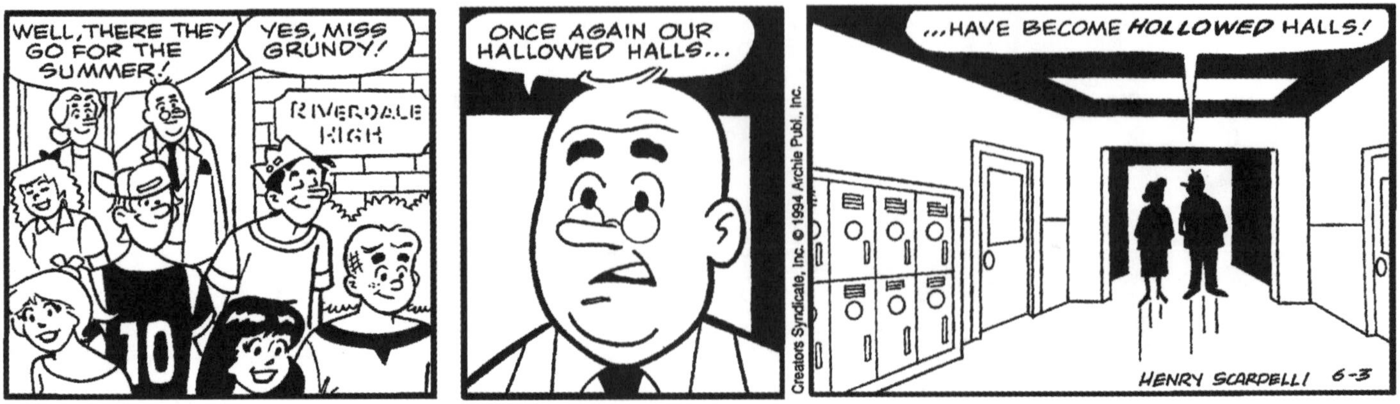
WELL, THERE THEY GO FOR THE SUMMER!
YES, MISS GRUNDY!
RIVERDALE HIGH
10
ONCE AGAIN OUR HALLOWED HALLS...
Creators Syndicate, Inc. © 1994 Archie Publ., Inc.
...HAVE BECOME ***HOLLOWED*** HALLS!
HENRY SCARPELLI 6-3

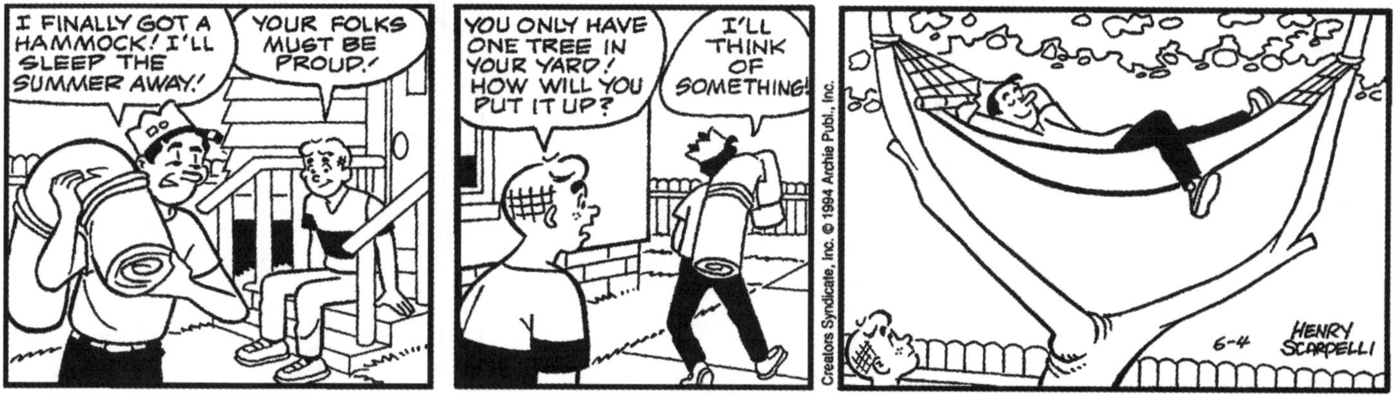
I FINALLY GOT A HAMMOCK! I'LL SLEEP THE SUMMER AWAY!
YOUR FOLKS MUST BE PROUD!
YOU ONLY HAVE ONE TREE IN YOUR YARD! HOW WILL YOU PUT IT UP?
I'LL THINK OF SOMETHING!
Creators Syndicate, Inc. © 1994 Archie Publ., Inc.
6-4
HENRY SCARPELLI

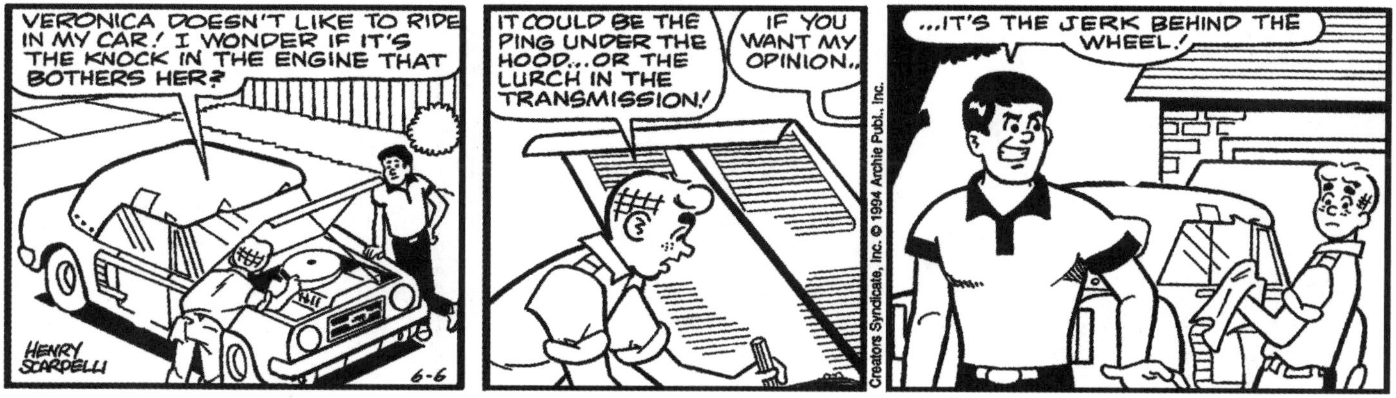
VERONICA DOESN'T LIKE TO RIDE IN MY CAR! I WONDER IF IT'S THE KNOCK IN THE ENGINE THAT BOTHERS HER?
HENRY SCARPELLI
6-6
IT COULD BE THE PING UNDER THE HOOD... OR THE LURCH IN THE TRANSMISSION!
IF YOU WANT MY OPINION..
Creators Syndicate, Inc. © 1994 Archie Publ., Inc.
...IT'S THE JERK BEHIND THE WHEEL!

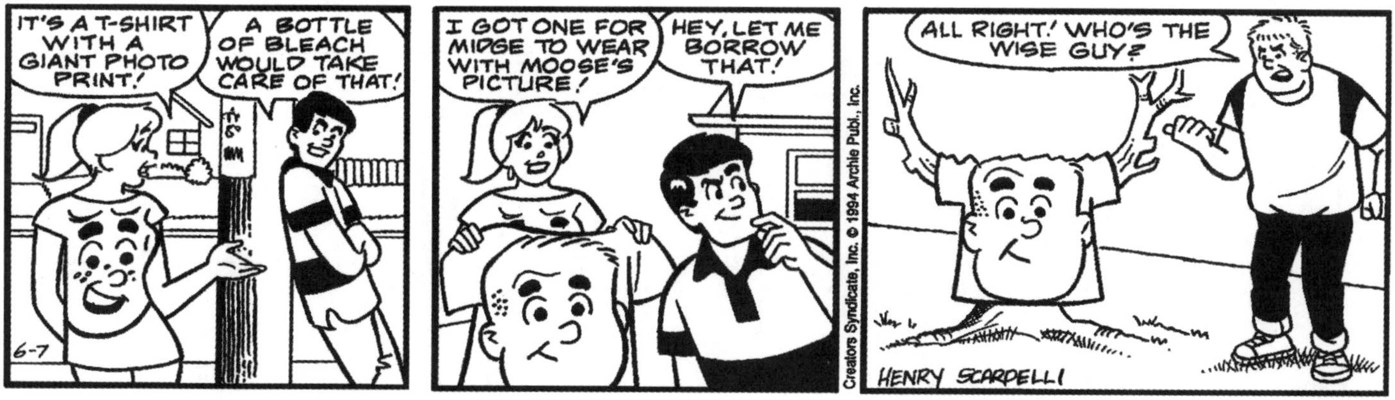
IT'S A T-SHIRT WITH A GIANT PHOTO PRINT!
A BOTTLE OF BLEACH WOULD TAKE CARE OF THAT!
6-7
I GOT ONE FOR MIDGE TO WEAR WITH MOOSE'S PICTURE!
HEY, LET ME BORROW THAT!
Creators Syndicate, Inc. © 1994 Archie Publ., Inc.
ALL RIGHT! WHO'S THE WISE GUY?
HENRY SCARPELLI

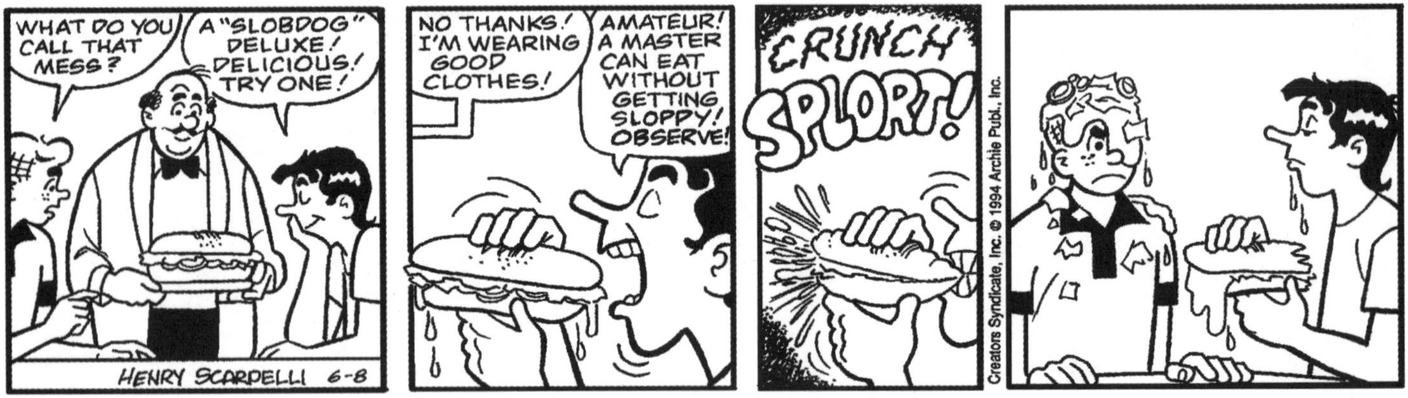
WHAT DO YOU CALL THAT MESS?
A "SLOBDOG" DELUXE! DELICIOUS! TRY ONE!
HENRY SCARPELLI 6-8
NO THANKS! I'M WEARING GOOD CLOTHES!
AMATEUR! A MASTER CAN EAT WITHOUT GETTING SLOPPY! OBSERVE!
CRUNCH
SPLORT!
Creators Syndicate, Inc. © 1994 Archie Publ., Inc.

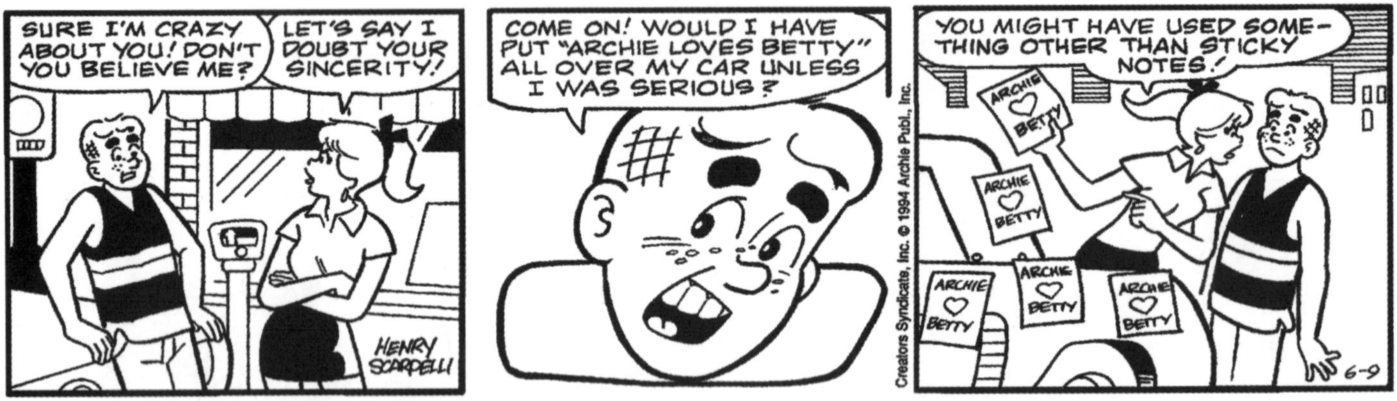
SURE I'M CRAZY ABOUT YOU! DON'T YOU BELIEVE ME?
LET'S SAY I DOUBT YOUR SINCERITY!
HENRY SCARPELLI
COME ON! WOULD I HAVE PUT "ARCHIE LOVES BETTY" ALL OVER MY CAR UNLESS I WAS SERIOUS?
Creators Syndicate, Inc. © 1994 Archie Publ., Inc.
YOU MIGHT HAVE USED SOMETHING OTHER THAN STICKY NOTES!
ARCHIE ♡ BETTY
6-9

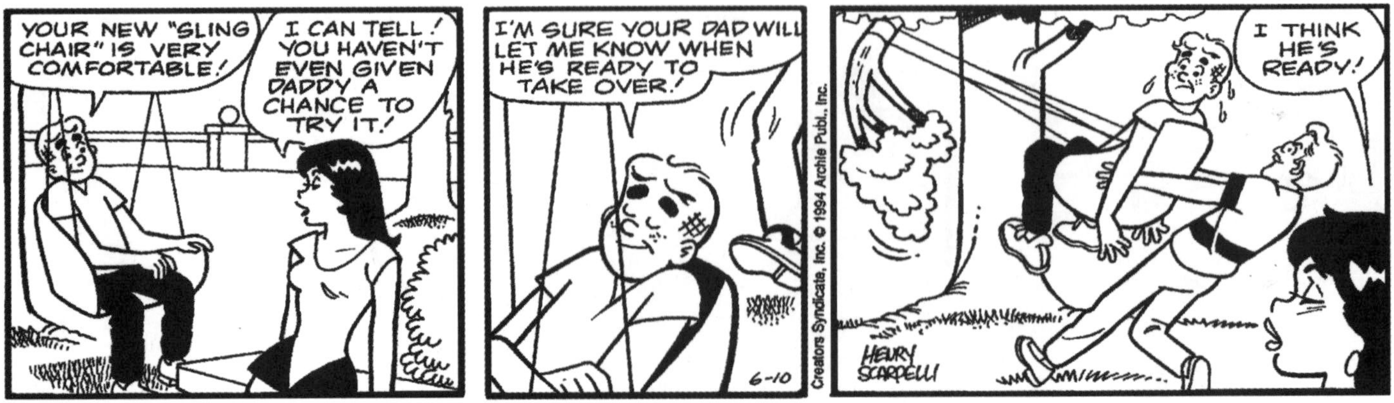
YOUR NEW "SLING CHAIR" IS VERY COMFORTABLE!
I CAN TELL! YOU HAVEN'T EVEN GIVEN DADDY A CHANCE TO TRY IT!
I'M SURE YOUR DAD WILL LET ME KNOW WHEN HE'S READY TO TAKE OVER!
6-10
Creators Syndicate, Inc. © 1994 Archie Publ., Inc.
I THINK HE'S READY!
HENRY SCARPELLI

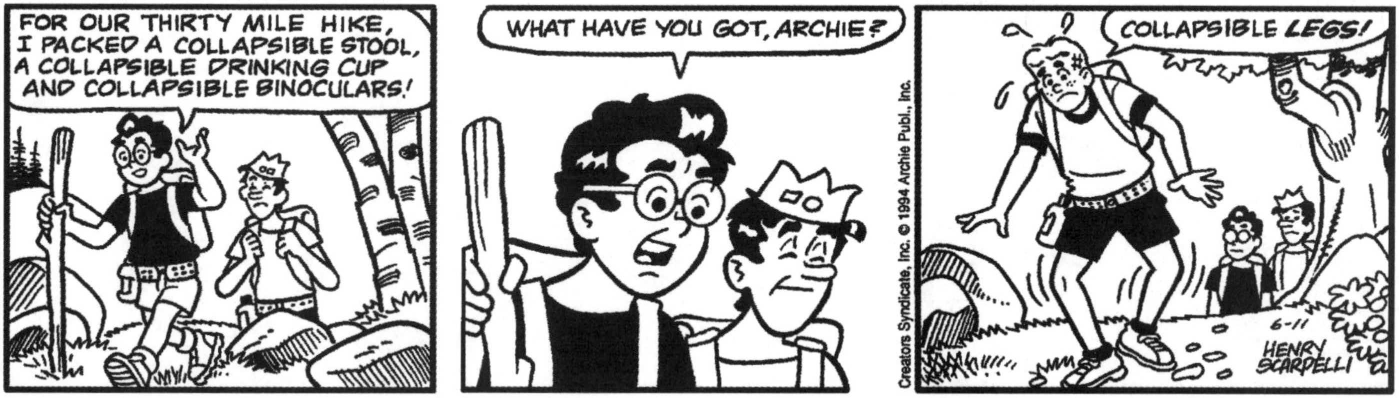
FOR OUR THIRTY MILE HIKE, I PACKED A COLLAPSIBLE STOOL, A COLLAPSIBLE DRINKING CUP AND COLLAPSIBLE BINOCULARS!
WHAT HAVE YOU GOT, ARCHIE?
Creators Syndicate, Inc. © 1994 Archie Publ., Inc.
COLLAPSIBLE LEGS!
6-11
HENRY SCARPELLI

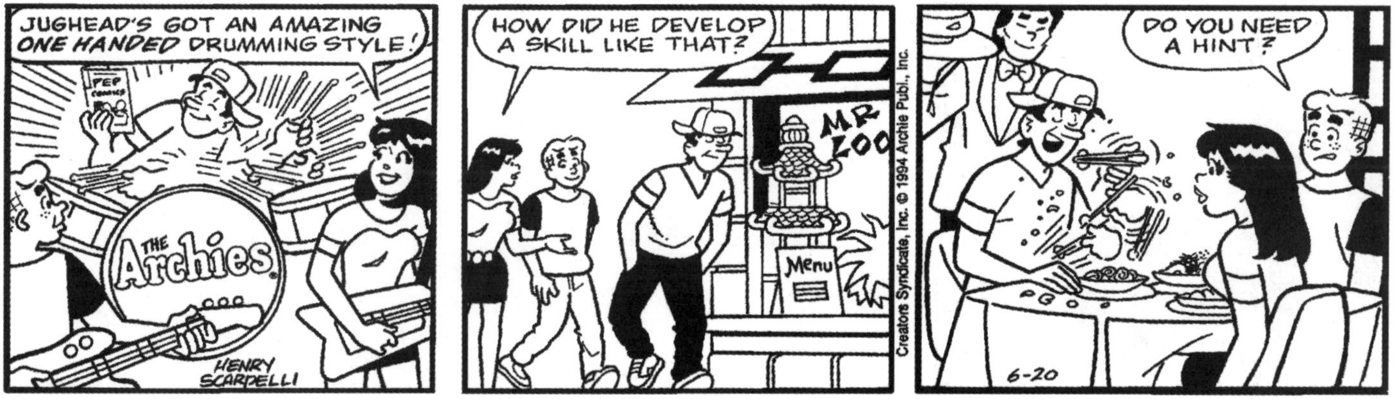
JUGHEAD'S GOT AN AMAZING ONE HANDED DRUMMING STYLE!
PEP COMICS
THE Archies
HENRY SCARPELLI
HOW DID HE DEVELOP A SKILL LIKE THAT?
MR ZOO
Menu
Creators Syndicate, Inc. © 1994 Archie Publ., Inc.
DO YOU NEED A HINT?
6-20

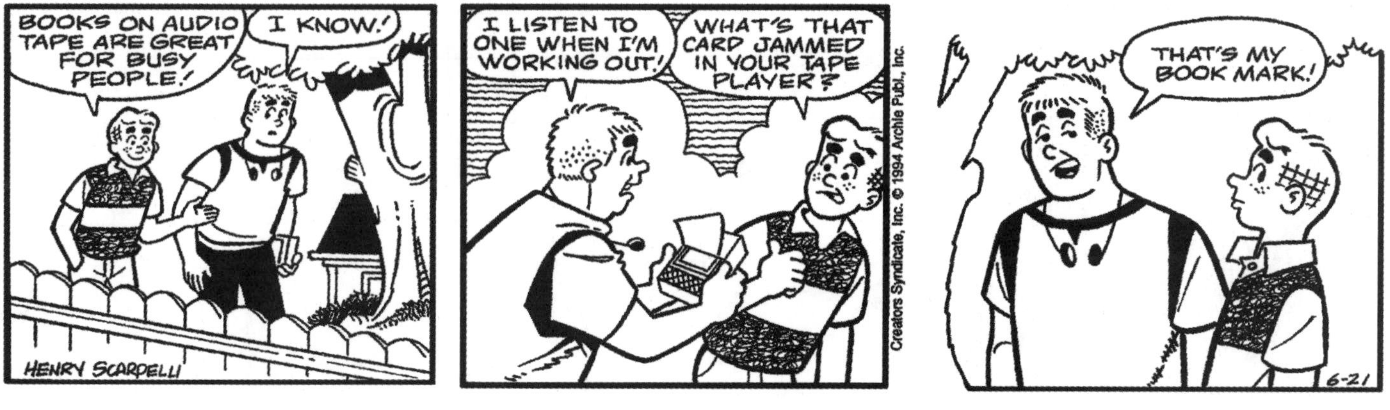
BOOKS ON AUDIO TAPE ARE GREAT FOR BUSY PEOPLE!
I KNOW!
HENRY SCARPELLI
I LISTEN TO ONE WHEN I'M WORKING OUT!
WHAT'S THAT CARD JAMMED IN YOUR TAPE PLAYER?
Creators Syndicate, Inc. © 1994 Archie Publ., Inc.
THAT'S MY BOOK MARK!
6-21

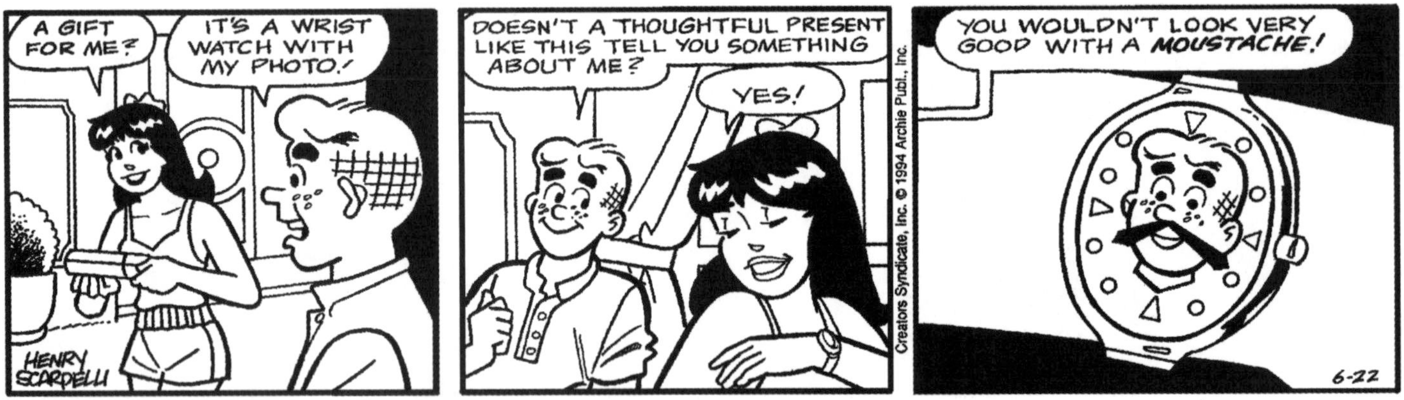
A GIFT FOR ME?
IT'S A WRIST WATCH WITH MY PHOTO!
HENRY SCARPELLI
DOESN'T A THOUGHTFUL PRESENT LIKE THIS TELL YOU SOMETHING ABOUT ME?
YES!
Creators Syndicate, Inc. © 1994 Archie Publ., Inc.
YOU WOULDN'T LOOK VERY GOOD WITH A **MOUSTACHE**!
6-22

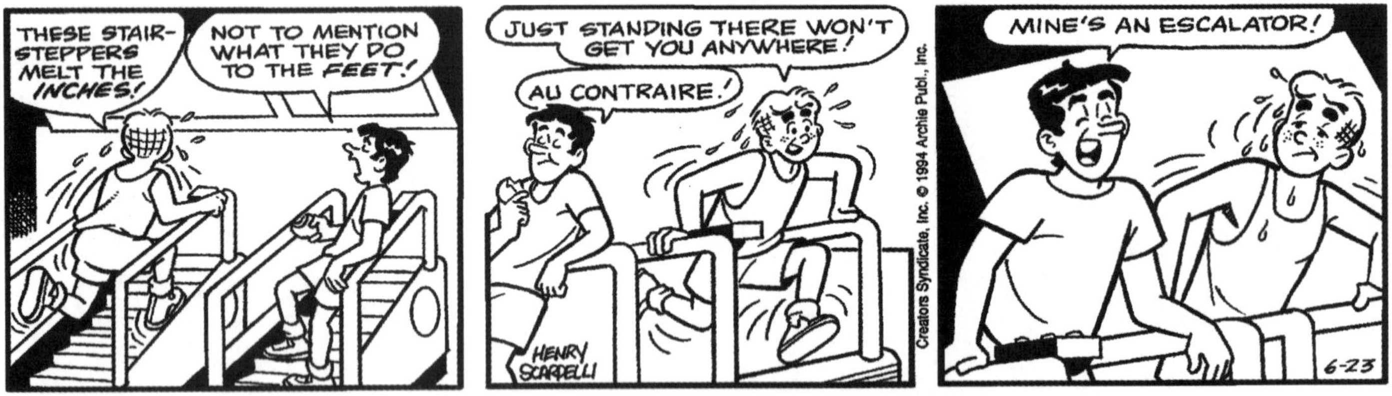
THESE STAIR-STEPPERS MELT THE *INCHES*!
NOT TO MENTION WHAT THEY DO TO THE *FEET*!
JUST STANDING THERE WON'T GET YOU ANYWHERE!
AU CONTRAIRE!
HENRY SCARPELLI
Creators Syndicate, Inc. © 1994 Archie Publ., Inc.
MINE'S AN ESCALATOR!
6-23

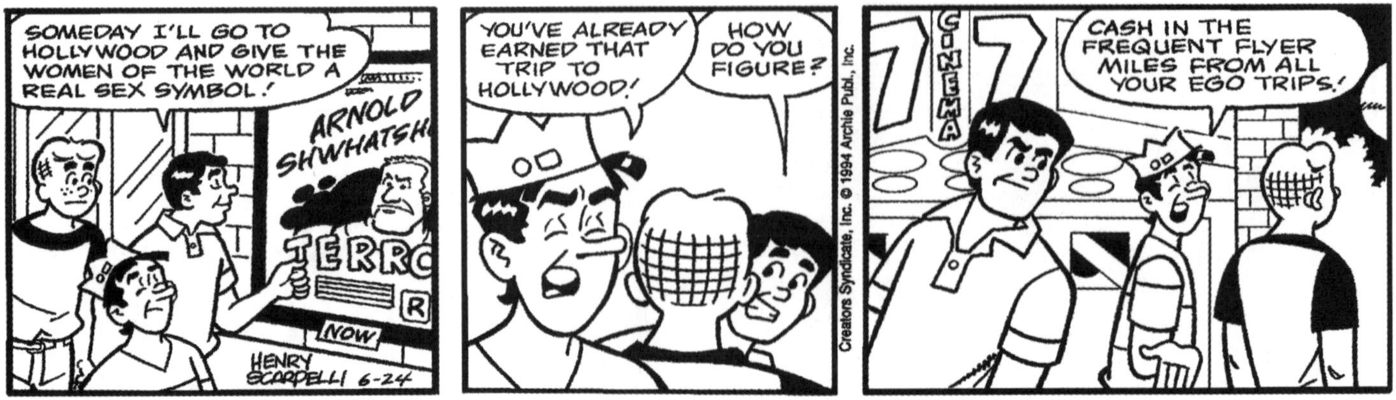
SOMEDAY I'LL GO TO HOLLYWOOD AND GIVE THE WOMEN OF THE WORLD A REAL SEX SYMBOL!
ARNOLD SHWHATSH
TERRO
R
NOW
HENRY SCARPELLI 6-24
YOU'VE ALREADY EARNED THAT TRIP TO HOLLYWOOD!
HOW DO YOU FIGURE?
Creators Syndicate, Inc. © 1994 Archie Publ., Inc.
CINEMA 7
CASH IN THE FREQUENT FLYER MILES FROM ALL YOUR EGO TRIPS!

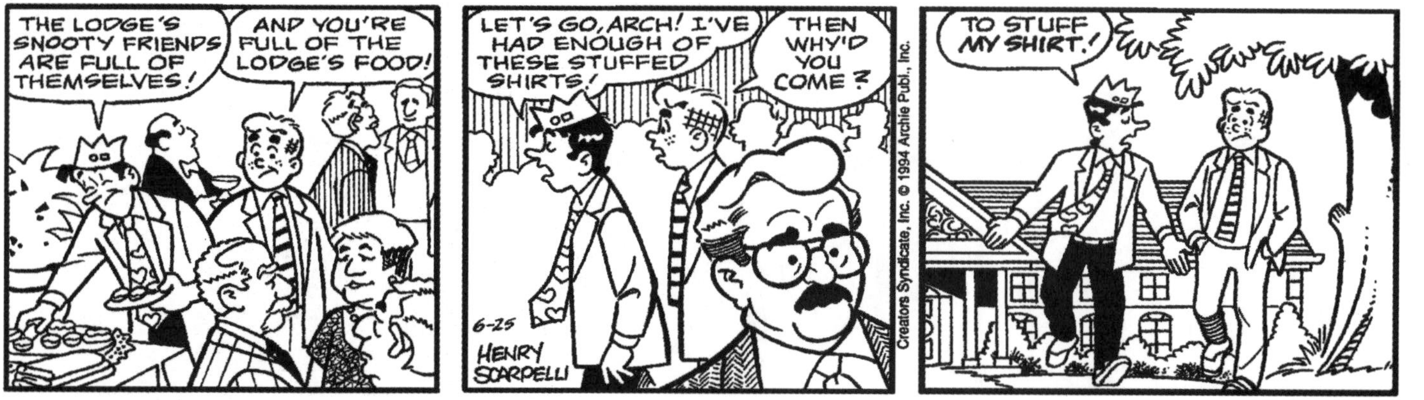
THE LODGE'S SNOOTY FRIENDS ARE FULL OF THEMSELVES!
AND YOU'RE FULL OF THE LODGE'S FOOD!
LET'S GO, ARCH! I'VE HAD ENOUGH OF THESE STUFFED SHIRTS!
THEN WHY'D YOU COME?
6-25
HENRY SCARPELLI
Creators Syndicate, Inc. © 1994 Archie Publ., Inc.
TO STUFF MY SHIRT!

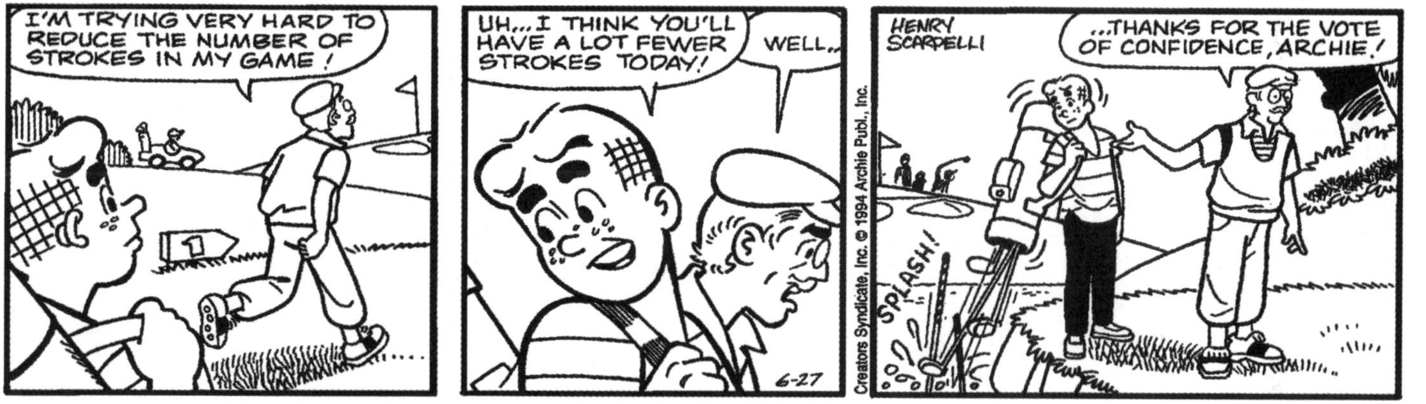
I'M TRYING VERY HARD TO REDUCE THE NUMBER OF STROKES IN MY GAME!
UH...I THINK YOU'LL HAVE A LOT FEWER STROKES TODAY!
WELL...
6-27
Creators Syndicate, Inc. © 1994 Archie Publ., Inc.
HENRY SCARPELLI
...THANKS FOR THE VOTE OF CONFIDENCE, ARCHIE!
SPLASH!

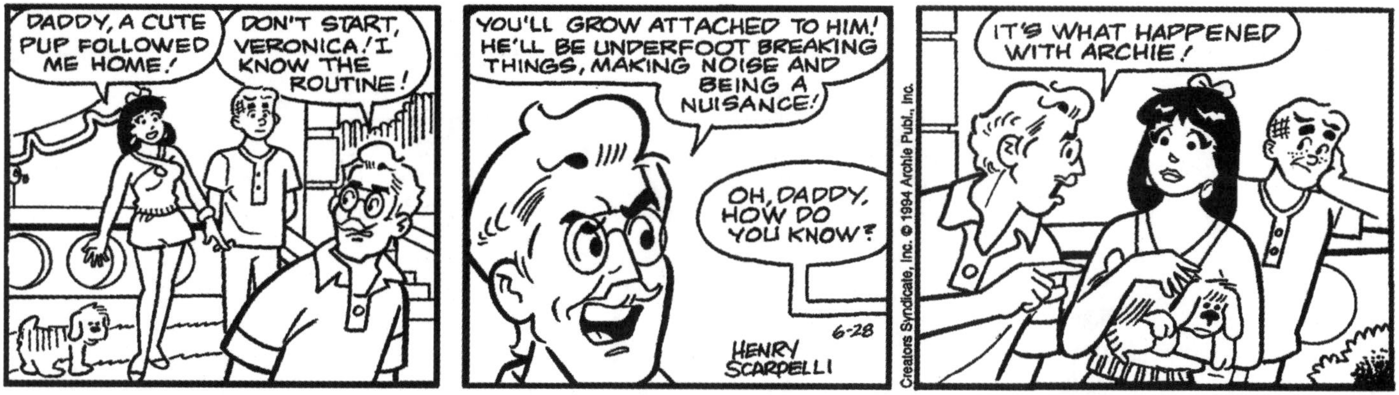
DADDY, A CUTE PUP FOLLOWED ME HOME!
DON'T START, VERONICA! I KNOW THE ROUTINE!
YOU'LL GROW ATTACHED TO HIM! HE'LL BE UNDERFOOT BREAKING THINGS, MAKING NOISE AND BEING A NUISANCE!
OH, DADDY, HOW DO YOU KNOW?
6-28
HENRY SCARPELLI
Creators Syndicate, Inc. © 1994 Archie Publ., Inc.
IT'S WHAT HAPPENED WITH ARCHIE!

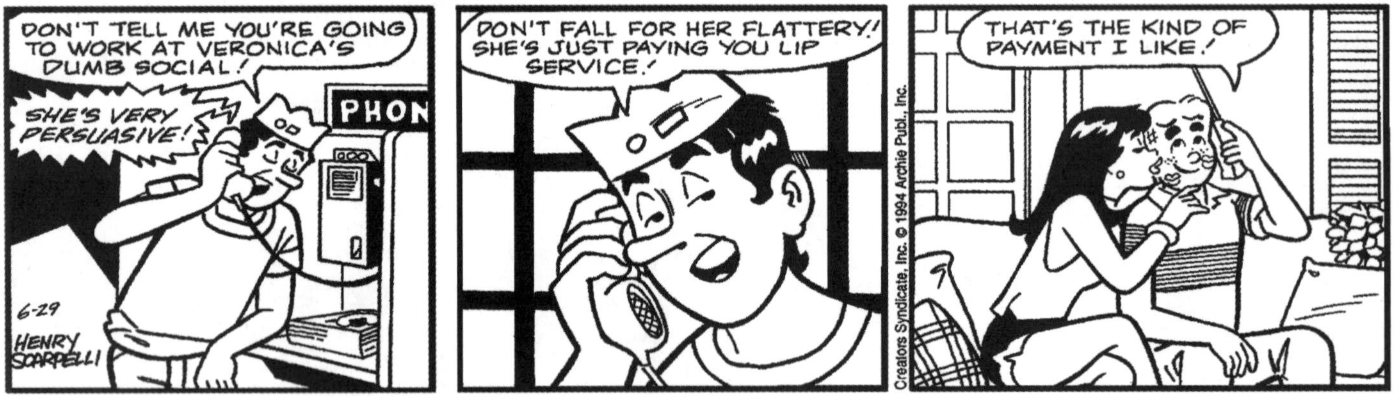
DON'T TELL ME YOU'RE GOING TO WORK AT VERONICA'S DUMB SOCIAL!
SHE'S VERY PERSUASIVE!
PHON
6-29
HENRY SCARPELLI
DON'T FALL FOR HER FLATTERY! SHE'S JUST PAYING YOU LIP SERVICE!
THAT'S THE KIND OF PAYMENT I LIKE!
Creators Syndicate, Inc. © 1994 Archie Publ., Inc.

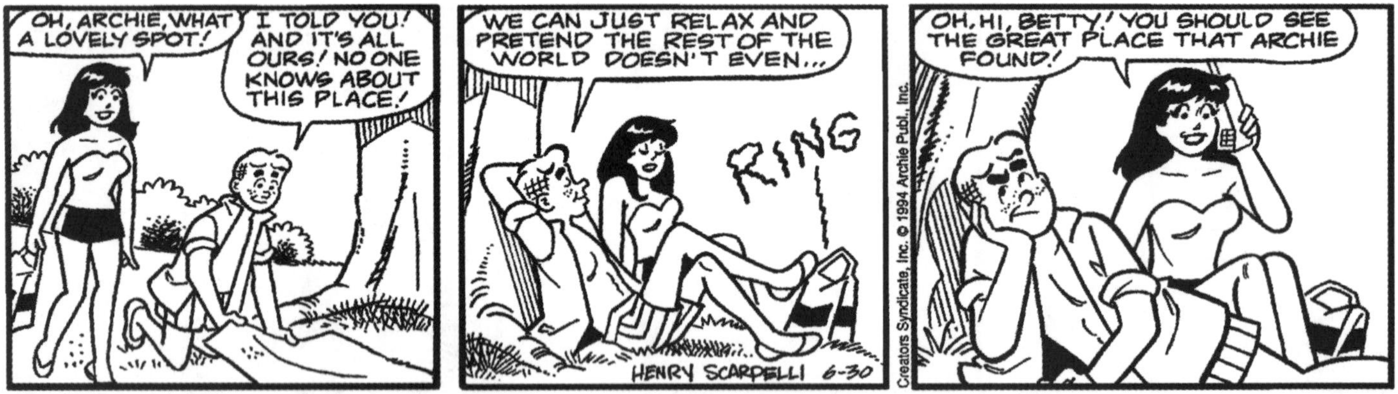
OH, ARCHIE, WHAT A LOVELY SPOT!
I TOLD YOU! AND IT'S ALL OURS! NO ONE KNOWS ABOUT THIS PLACE!
WE CAN JUST RELAX AND PRETEND THE REST OF THE WORLD DOESN'T EVEN...
RING
HENRY SCARPELLI 6-30
OH, HI, BETTY! YOU SHOULD SEE THE GREAT PLACE THAT ARCHIE FOUND!
Creators Syndicate, Inc. © 1994 Archie Publ., Inc.

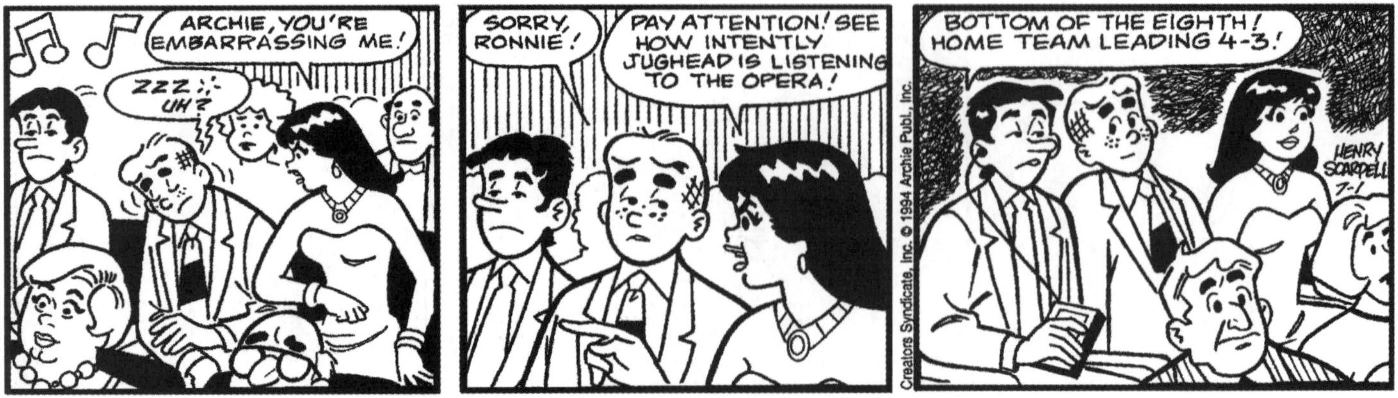
ARCHIE, YOU'RE EMBARRASSING ME!
ZZZ... UH?
SORRY, RONNIE!
PAY ATTENTION! SEE HOW INTENTLY JUGHEAD IS LISTENING TO THE OPERA!
BOTTOM OF THE EIGHTH! HOME TEAM LEADING 4-3!
HENRY SCARPELLI 7-1
Creators Syndicate, Inc. © 1994 Archie Publ., Inc.

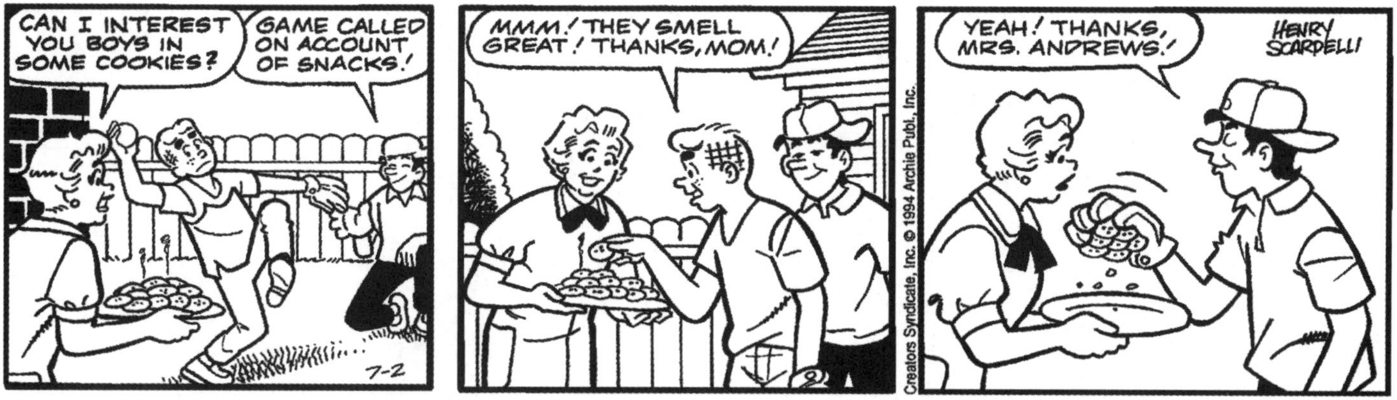
CAN I INTEREST YOU BOYS IN SOME COOKIES?
GAME CALLED ON ACCOUNT OF SNACKS!
7-2
MMM! THEY SMELL GREAT! THANKS, MOM!
Creators Syndicate, Inc. © 1994 Archie Publ., Inc.
YEAH! THANKS, MRS. ANDREWS!
HENRY SCARPELLI

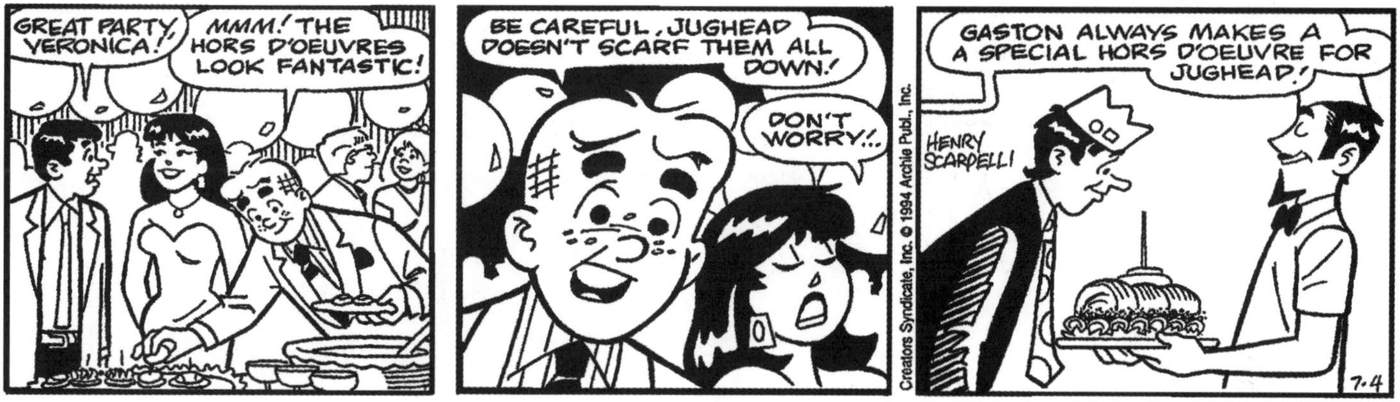
GREAT PARTY, VERONICA!
MMM! THE HORS D'OEUVRES LOOK FANTASTIC!
BE CAREFUL, JUGHEAD DOESN'T SCARF THEM ALL DOWN!
DON'T WORRY!..
Creators Syndicate, Inc. © 1994 Archie Publ., Inc.
GASTON ALWAYS MAKES A A SPECIAL HORS D'OEUVRE FOR JUGHEAD!
HENRY SCARPELLI
7-4

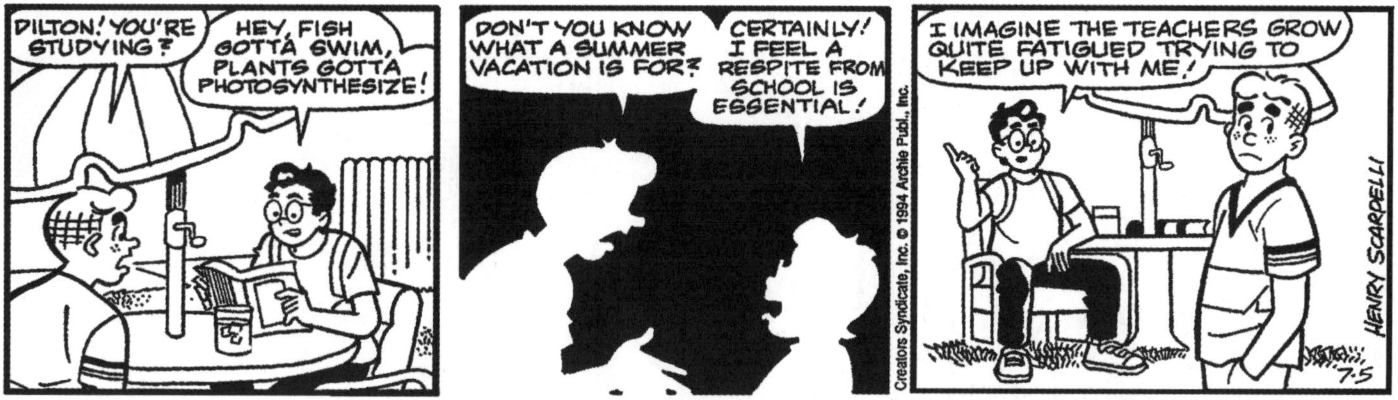
DILTON! YOU'RE STUDYING?
HEY, FISH GOTTA SWIM, PLANTS GOTTA PHOTOSYNTHESIZE!
DON'T YOU KNOW WHAT A SUMMER VACATION IS FOR?
CERTAINLY! I FEEL A RESPITE FROM SCHOOL IS ESSENTIAL!
Creators Syndicate, Inc. © 1994 Archie Publ., Inc.
I IMAGINE THE TEACHERS GROW QUITE FATIGUED TRYING TO KEEP UP WITH ME!
HENRY SCARPELLI
7-5

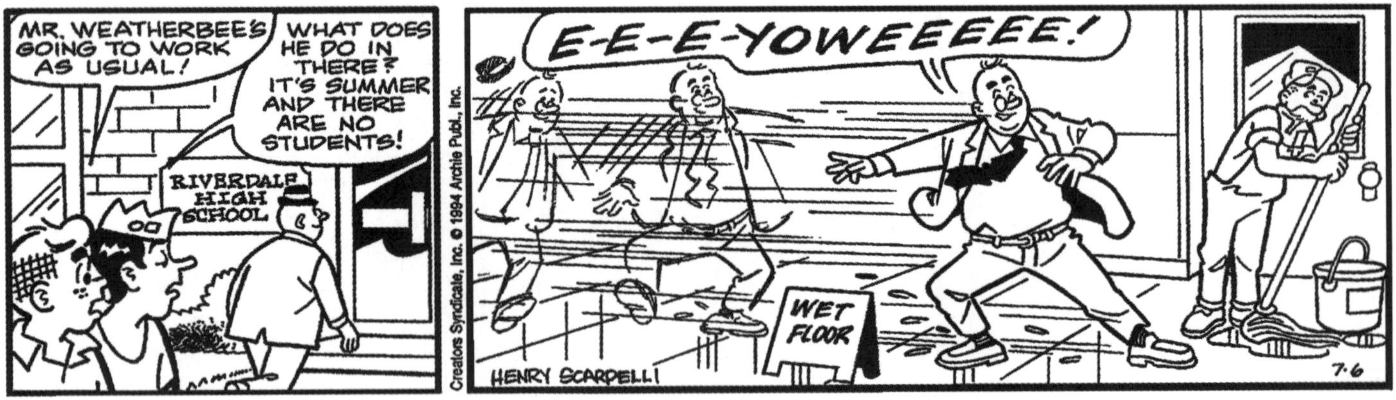
MR. WEATHERBEE'S GOING TO WORK AS USUAL!
WHAT DOES HE DO IN THERE? IT'S SUMMER AND THERE ARE NO STUDENTS!
RIVERDALE HIGH SCHOOL
Creators Syndicate, Inc. © 1994 Archie Publ., Inc.
E-E-E-YOWEEEEEE!
WET FLOOR
HENRY SCARPELLI
7·6

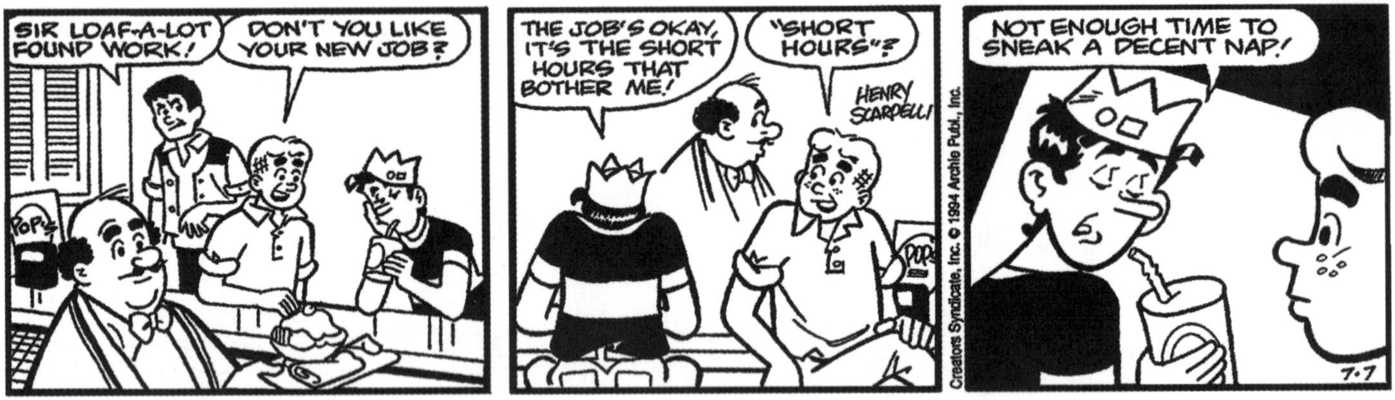
SIR LOAF-A-LOT FOUND WORK!
DON'T YOU LIKE YOUR NEW JOB?
POP'S
THE JOB'S OKAY, IT'S THE SHORT HOURS THAT BOTHER ME!
"SHORT HOURS"?
HENRY SCARPELLI
Creators Syndicate, Inc. © 1994 Archie Publ., Inc.
NOT ENOUGH TIME TO SNEAK A DECENT NAP!
7·7

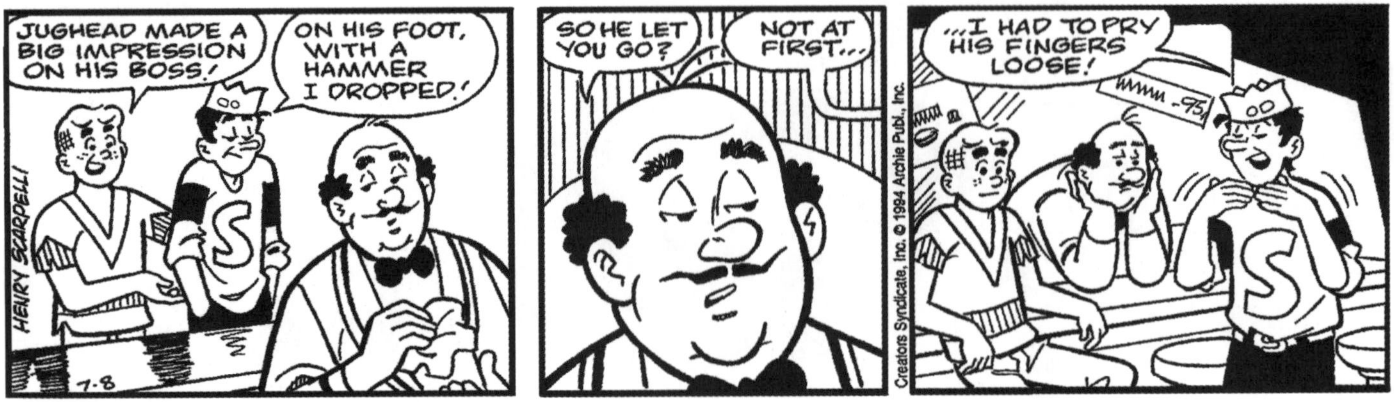
JUGHEAD MADE A BIG IMPRESSION ON HIS BOSS!
ON HIS FOOT, WITH A HAMMER I DROPPED!
HENRY SCARPELLI
7-8
SO HE LET YOU GO?
NOT AT FIRST...
Creators Syndicate, Inc. © 1994 Archie Publ., Inc.
...I HAD TO PRY HIS FINGERS LOOSE!

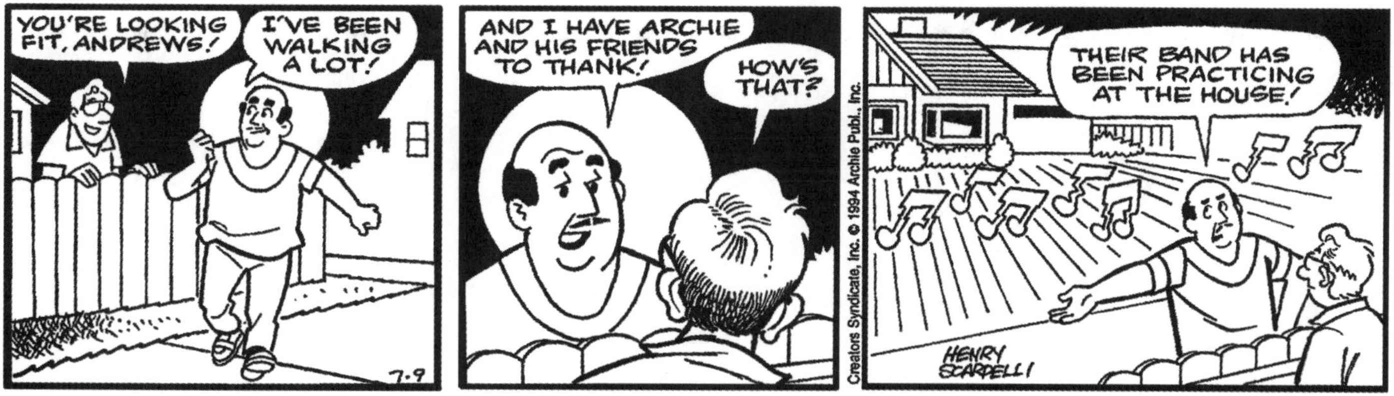
YOU'RE LOOKING FIT, ANDREWS!
I'VE BEEN WALKING A LOT!
7-9
AND I HAVE ARCHIE AND HIS FRIENDS TO THANK!
HOW'S THAT?
Creators Syndicate, Inc. © 1994 Archie Publ., Inc.
THEIR BAND HAS BEEN PRACTICING AT THE HOUSE!
HENRY SCARPELLI

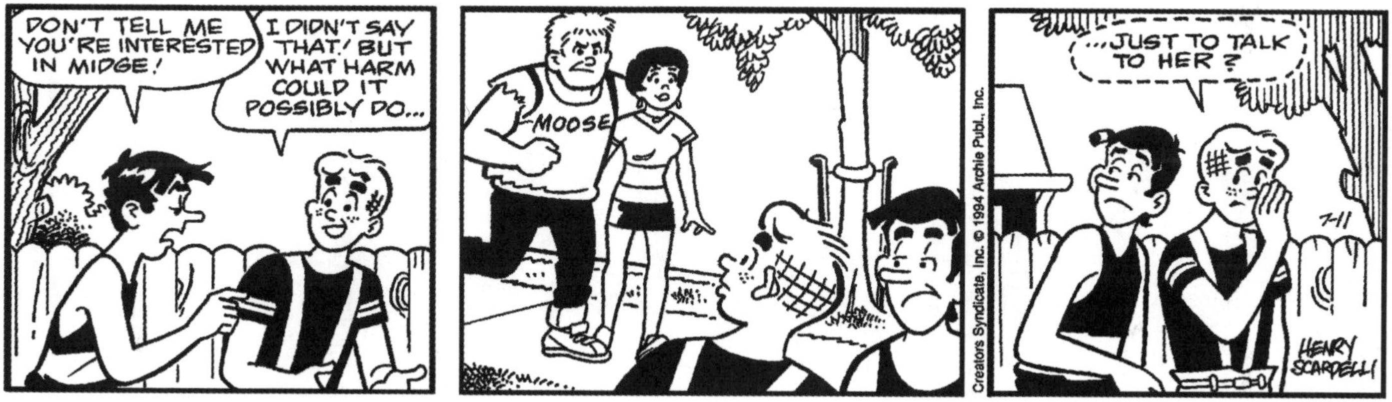
DON'T TELL ME YOU'RE INTERESTED IN MIDGE!
I DIDN'T SAY THAT! BUT WHAT HARM COULD IT POSSIBLY DO...
MOOSE
Creators Syndicate, Inc. © 1994 Archie Publ., Inc.
...JUST TO TALK TO HER?
7-11
HENRY SCARPELLI

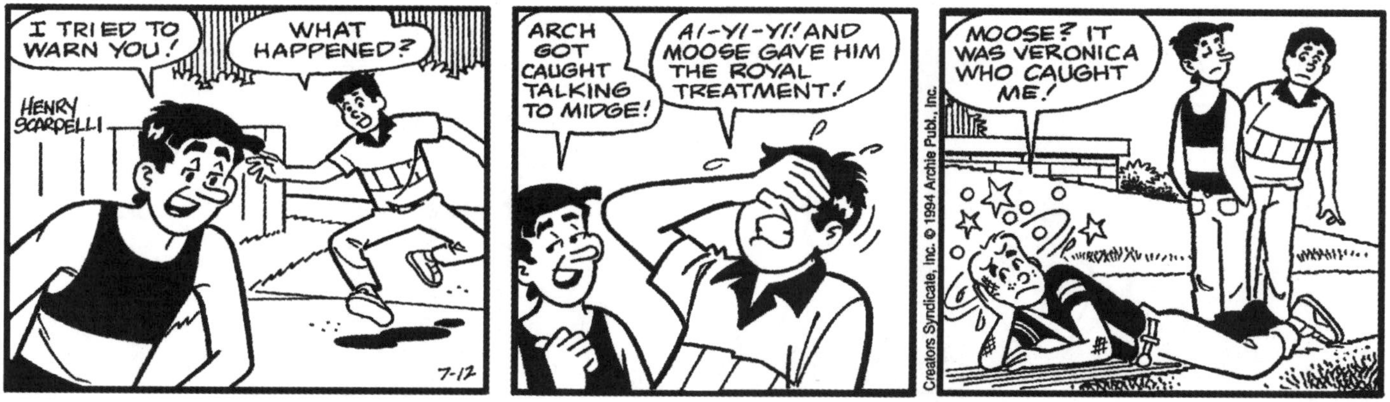
I TRIED TO WARN YOU!
WHAT HAPPENED?
HENRY SCARPELLI
7-12
ARCH GOT CAUGHT TALKING TO MIDGE!
AI-YI-YI! AND MOOSE GAVE HIM THE ROYAL TREATMENT!
Creators Syndicate, Inc. © 1994 Archie Publ., Inc.
MOOSE? IT WAS VERONICA WHO CAUGHT ME!

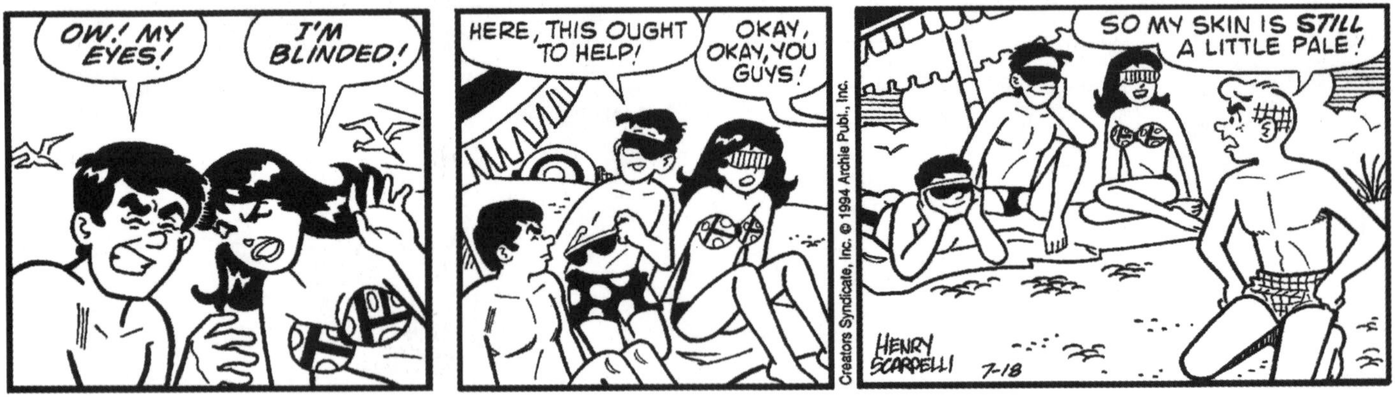
OW! MY EYES!
I'M BLINDED!
HERE, THIS OUGHT TO HELP!
OKAY, OKAY, YOU GUYS!
Creators Syndicate, Inc. © 1994 Archie Publ., Inc.
SO MY SKIN IS STILL A LITTLE PALE!
HENRY SCARPELLI
7-18

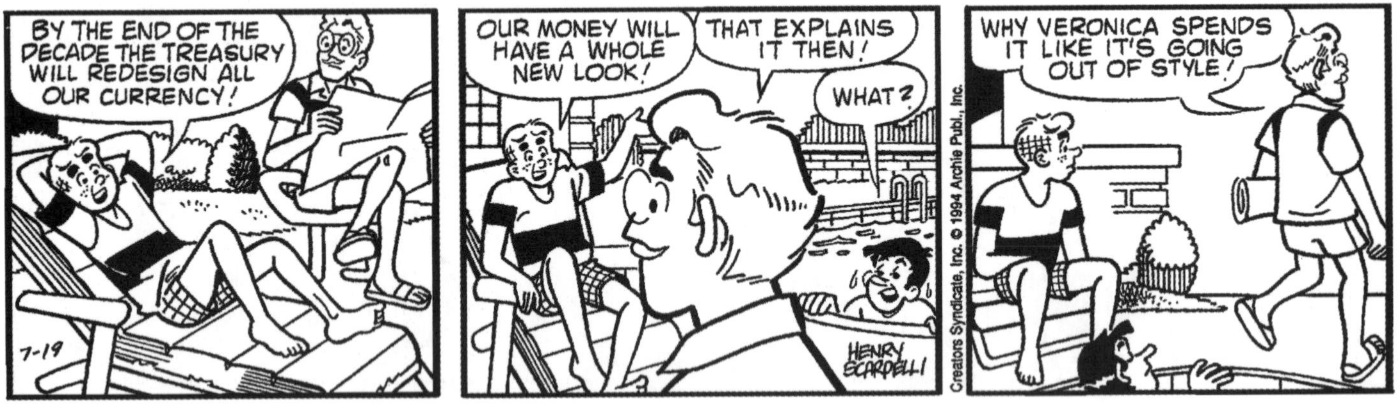
BY THE END OF THE DECADE THE TREASURY WILL REDESIGN ALL OUR CURRENCY!
7-19
OUR MONEY WILL HAVE A WHOLE NEW LOOK!
THAT EXPLAINS IT THEN!
WHAT?
HENRY SCARPELLI
Creators Syndicate, Inc. © 1994 Archie Publ., Inc.
WHY VERONICA SPENDS IT LIKE IT'S GOING OUT OF STYLE!

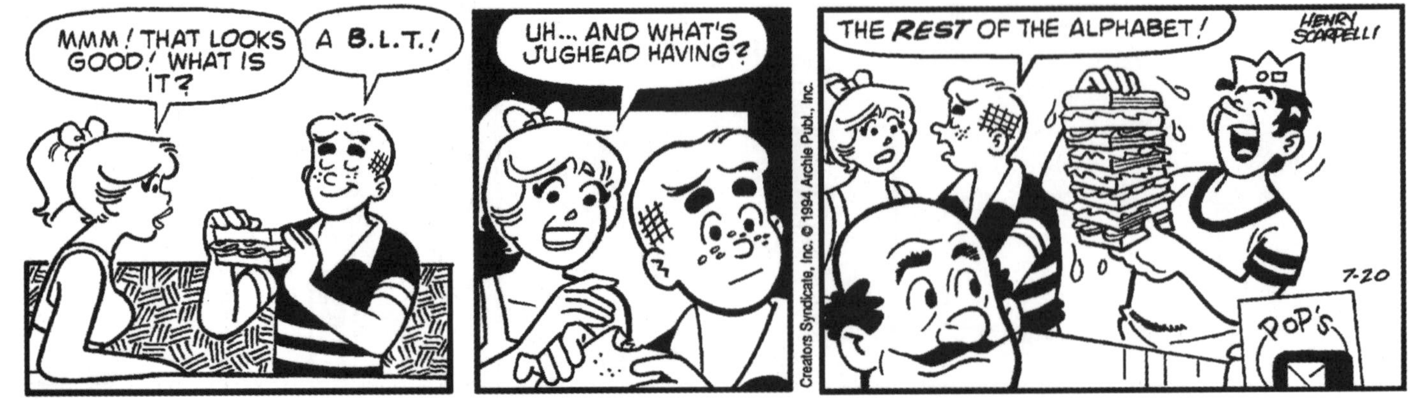
MMM! THAT LOOKS GOOD! WHAT IS IT?
A B.L.T.!
UH... AND WHAT'S JUGHEAD HAVING?
Creators Syndicate, Inc. © 1994 Archie Publ., Inc.
THE REST OF THE ALPHABET!
HENRY SCARPELLI
7-20
POP'S

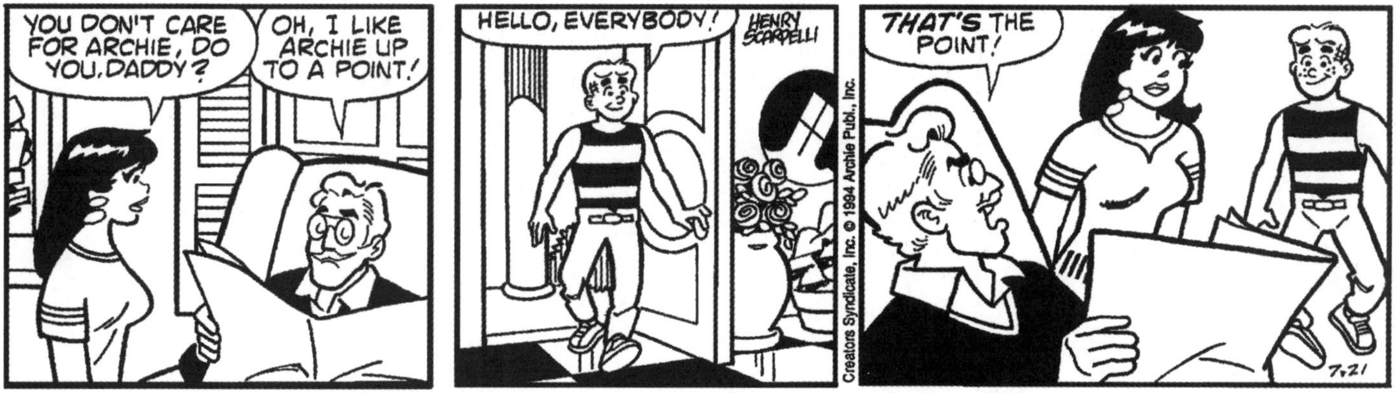
YOU DON'T CARE FOR ARCHIE, DO YOU, DADDY?
OH, I LIKE ARCHIE UP TO A POINT!
HELLO, EVERYBODY!
HENRY SCARPELLI
Creators Syndicate, Inc. © 1994 Archie Publ., Inc.
THAT'S THE POINT!
7-21

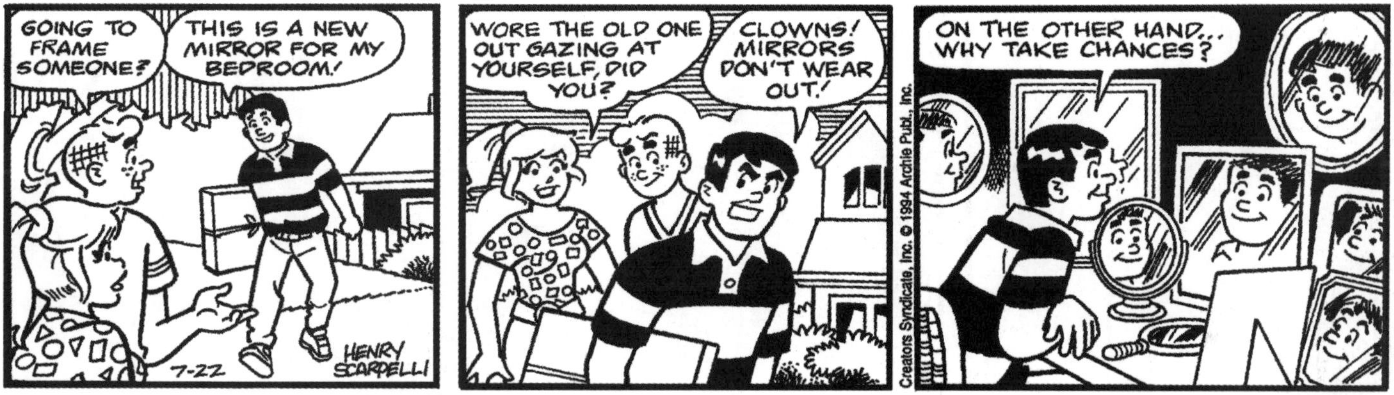
GOING TO FRAME SOMEONE?
THIS IS A NEW MIRROR FOR MY BEDROOM!
7-22
HENRY SCARPELLI
WORE THE OLD ONE OUT GAZING AT YOURSELF, DID YOU?
CLOWNS! MIRRORS DON'T WEAR OUT!
Creators Syndicate, Inc. © 1994 Archie Publ., Inc.
ON THE OTHER HAND... WHY TAKE CHANCES?

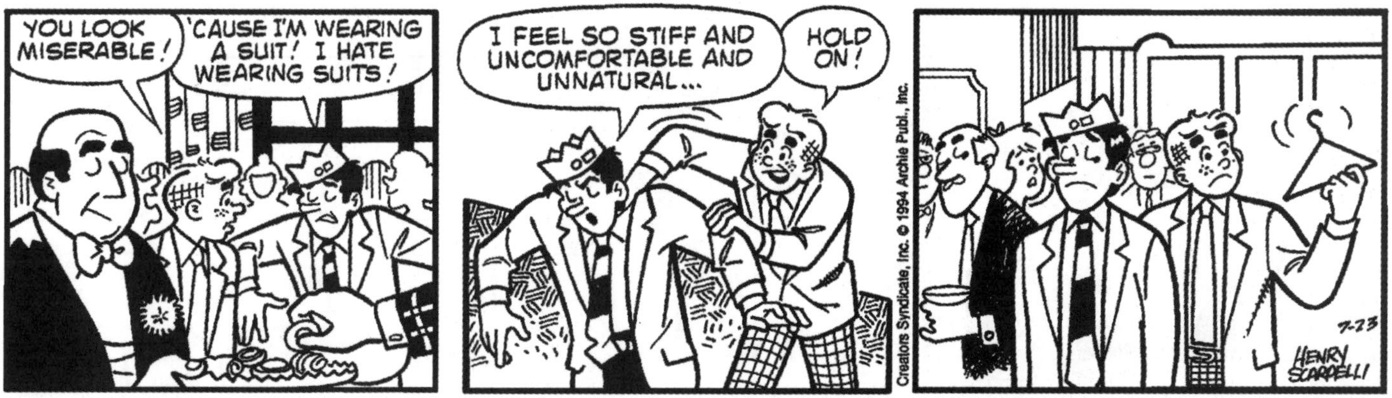
YOU LOOK MISERABLE!
'CAUSE I'M WEARING A SUIT! I HATE WEARING SUITS!
I FEEL SO STIFF AND UNCOMFORTABLE AND UNNATURAL...
HOLD ON!
Creators Syndicate, Inc. © 1994 Archie Publ., Inc.
7-23
HENRY SCARPELLI

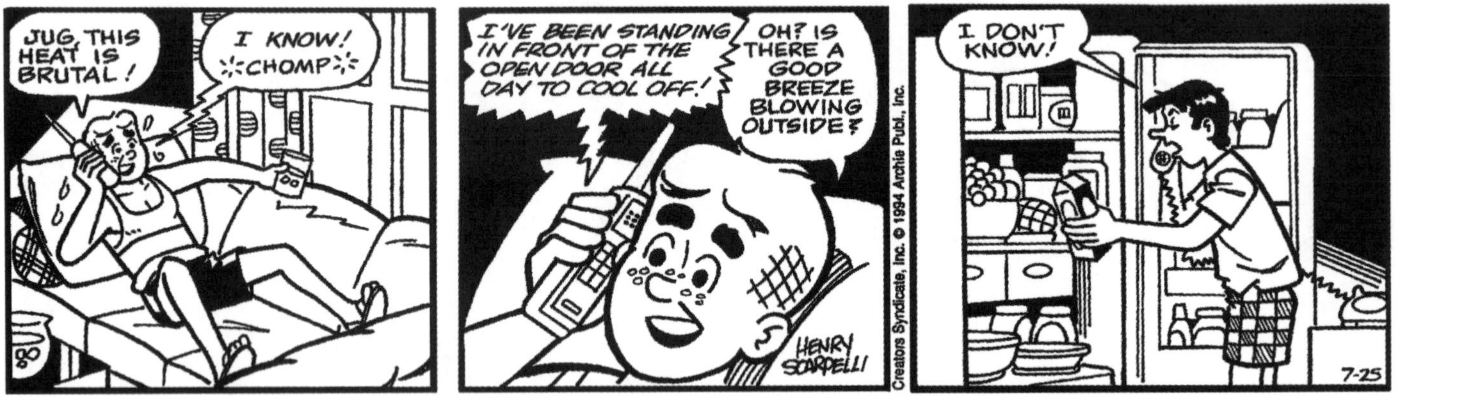
JUG, THIS HEAT IS BRUTAL!
I KNOW! CHOMP
I'VE BEEN STANDING IN FRONT OF THE OPEN DOOR ALL DAY TO COOL OFF!
OH? IS THERE A GOOD BREEZE BLOWING OUTSIDE?
HENRY SCARPELLI
Creators Syndicate, Inc. © 1994 Archie Publ., Inc.
I DON'T KNOW!
7-25

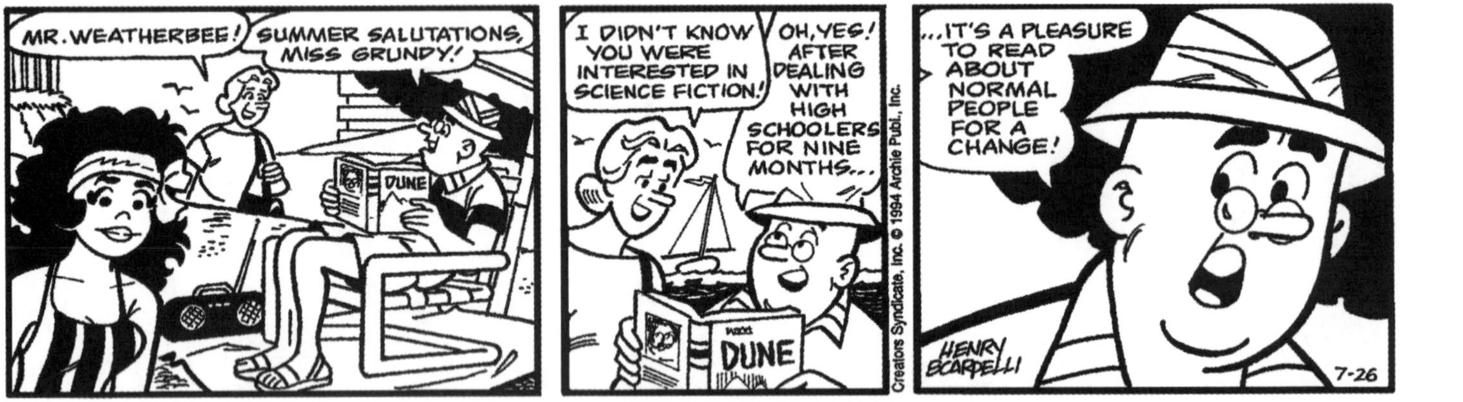
MR. WEATHERBEE!
SUMMER SALUTATIONS, MISS GRUNDY!
DUNE
I DIDN'T KNOW YOU WERE INTERESTED IN SCIENCE FICTION!
OH, YES! AFTER DEALING WITH HIGH SCHOOLERS FOR NINE MONTHS...
DUNE
Creators Syndicate, Inc. © 1994 Archie Publ., Inc.
...IT'S A PLEASURE TO READ ABOUT NORMAL PEOPLE FOR A CHANGE!
HENRY SCARPELLI
7-26

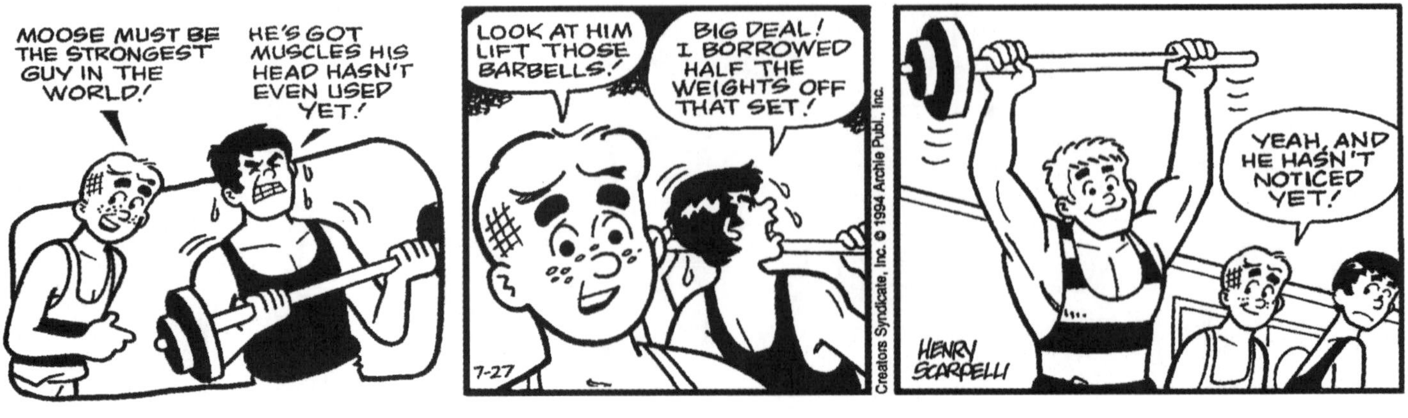
MOOSE MUST BE THE STRONGEST GUY IN THE WORLD!
HE'S GOT MUSCLES HIS HEAD HASN'T EVEN USED YET!
LOOK AT HIM LIFT THOSE BARBELLS!
BIG DEAL! I BORROWED HALF THE WEIGHTS OFF THAT SET!
7-27
Creators Syndicate, Inc. © 1994 Archie Publ., Inc.
YEAH, AND HE HASN'T NOTICED YET!
HENRY SCARPELLI

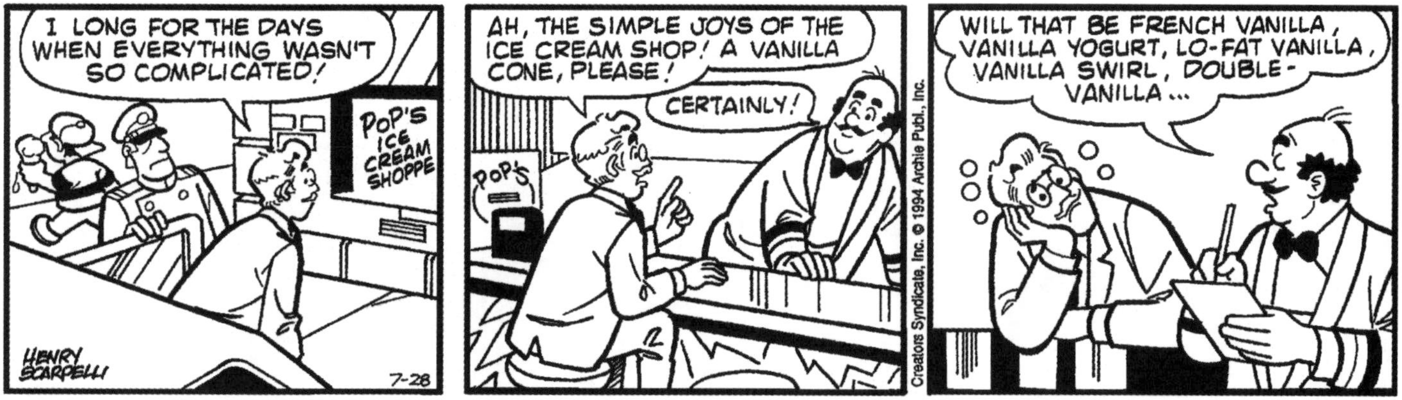
I LONG FOR THE DAYS WHEN EVERYTHING WASN'T SO COMPLICATED!
POP'S ICE CREAM SHOPPE
HENRY SCARPELLI
7-28
AH, THE SIMPLE JOYS OF THE ICE CREAM SHOP! A VANILLA CONE, PLEASE!
CERTAINLY!
POP'S
Creators Syndicate, Inc. © 1994 Archie Publ., Inc.
WILL THAT BE FRENCH VANILLA, VANILLA YOGURT, LO-FAT VANILLA, VANILLA SWIRL, DOUBLE-VANILLA...

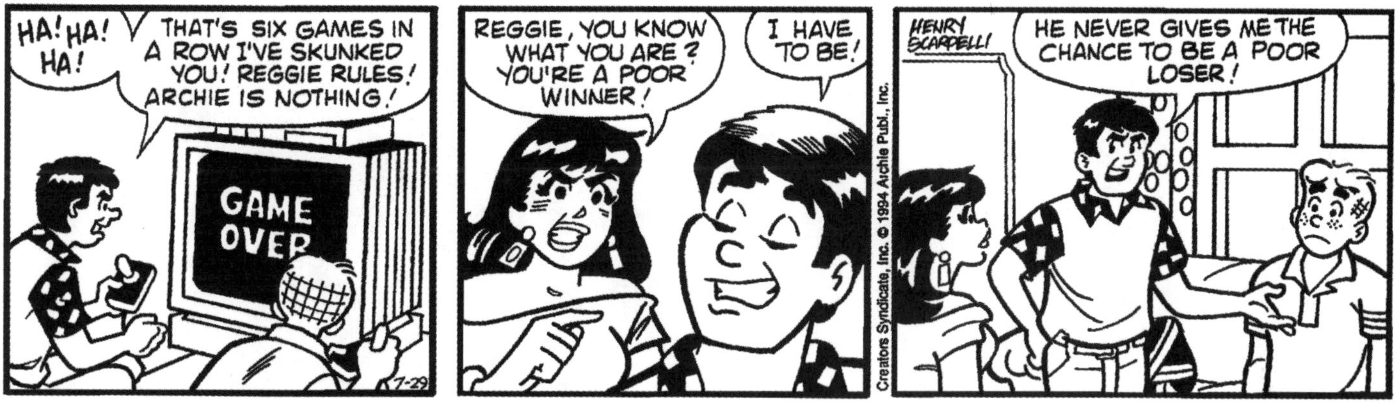
HA! HA! HA!
THAT'S SIX GAMES IN A ROW I'VE SKUNKED YOU! REGGIE RULES! ARCHIE IS NOTHING!
GAME OVER
7-29
REGGIE, YOU KNOW WHAT YOU ARE? YOU'RE A POOR WINNER!
I HAVE TO BE!
Creators Syndicate, Inc. © 1994 Archie Publ., Inc.
HENRY SCARPELLI
HE NEVER GIVES ME THE CHANCE TO BE A POOR LOSER!

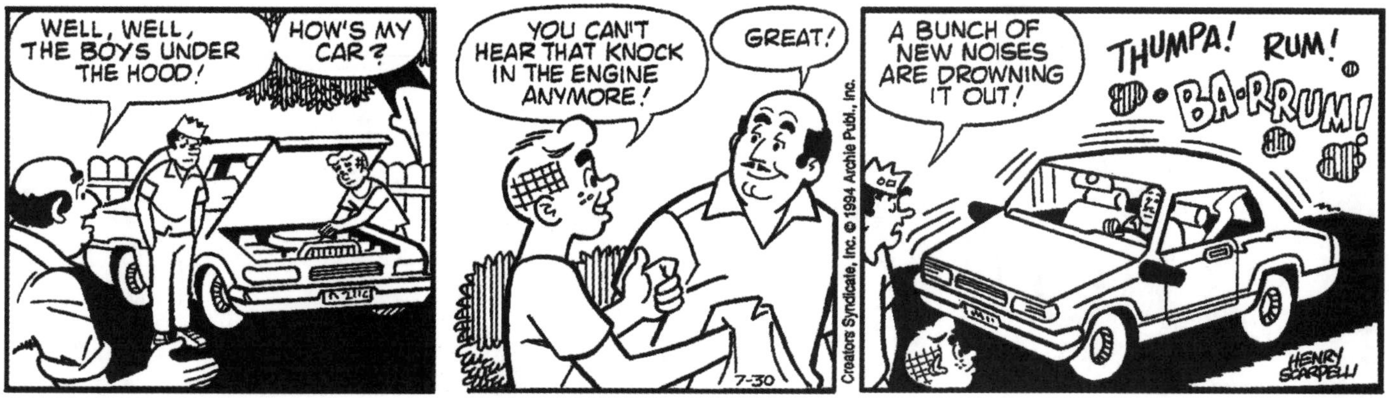
WELL, WELL, THE BOYS UNDER THE HOOD!
HOW'S MY CAR?
YOU CAN'T HEAR THAT KNOCK IN THE ENGINE ANYMORE!
GREAT!
7-30
Creators Syndicate, Inc. © 1994 Archie Publ., Inc.
A BUNCH OF NEW NOISES ARE DROWNING IT OUT!
THUMPA! RUM!
BA-RRUM!
HENRY SCARPELLI

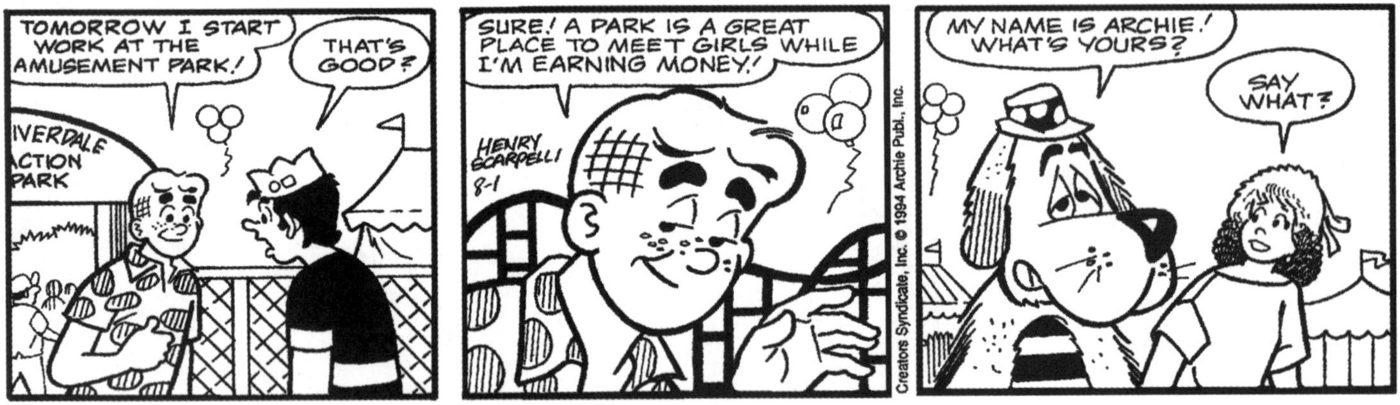
TOMORROW I START WORK AT THE AMUSEMENT PARK!
THAT'S GOOD?
IVERDALE ACTION PARK
SURE! A PARK IS A GREAT PLACE TO MEET GIRLS WHILE I'M EARNING MONEY!
HENRY SCARPELLI 8-1
Creators Syndicate, Inc. © 1994 Archie Publ., Inc.
MY NAME IS ARCHIE! WHAT'S YOURS?
SAY WHAT?

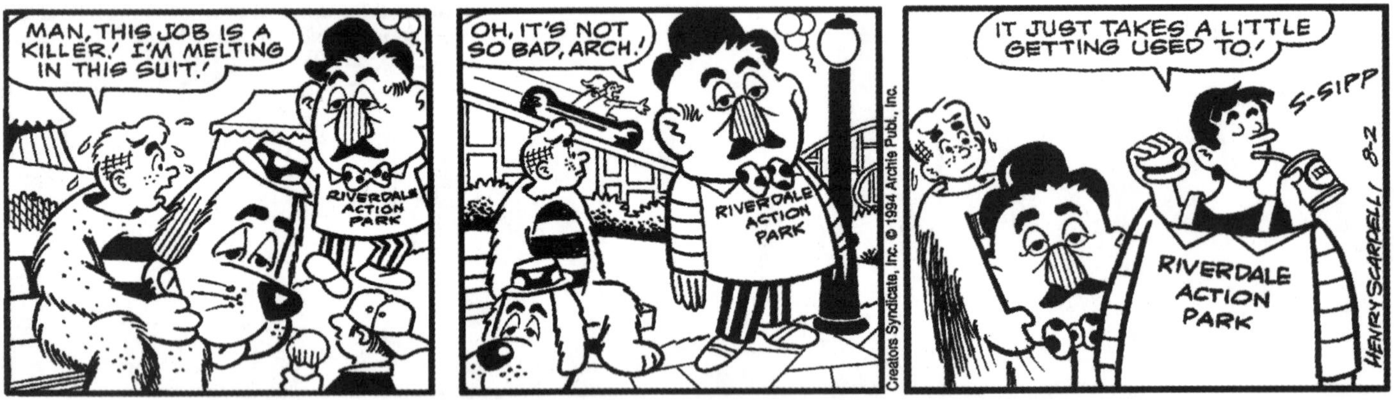
MAN, THIS JOB IS A KILLER! I'M MELTING IN THIS SUIT!
RIVERDALE ACTION PARK
OH, IT'S NOT SO BAD, ARCH!
RIVERDALE ACTION PARK
Creators Syndicate, Inc. © 1994 Archie Publ., Inc.
IT JUST TAKES A LITTLE GETTING USED TO!
S-SIPP
RIVERDALE ACTION PARK
HENRY SCARPELLI 8-2

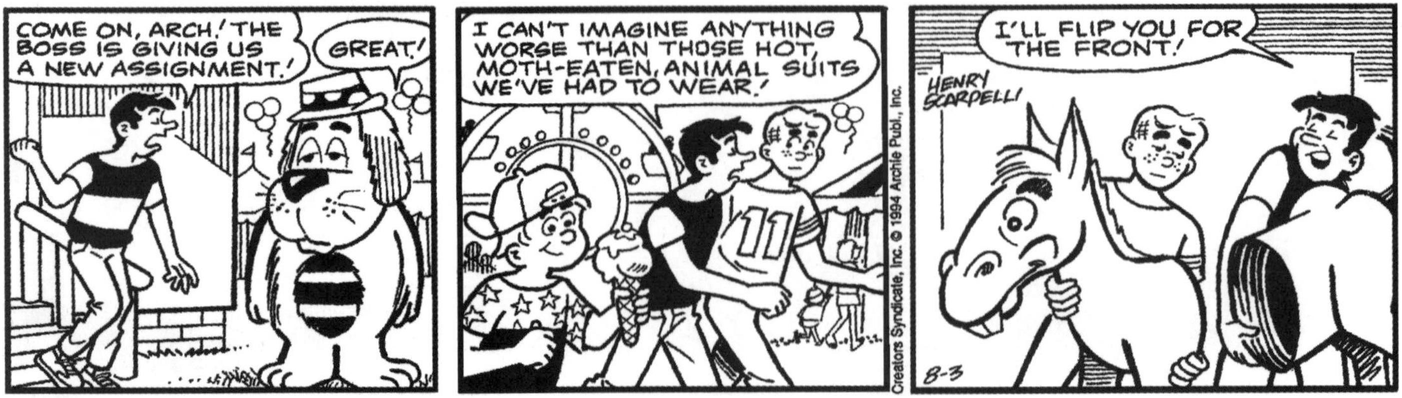
COME ON, ARCH! THE BOSS IS GIVING US A NEW ASSIGNMENT!
GREAT!
I CAN'T IMAGINE ANYTHING WORSE THAN THOSE HOT, MOTH-EATEN, ANIMAL SUITS WE'VE HAD TO WEAR!
11
Creators Syndicate, Inc. © 1994 Archie Publ., Inc.
I'LL FLIP YOU FOR THE FRONT!
HENRY SCARPELLI
8-3

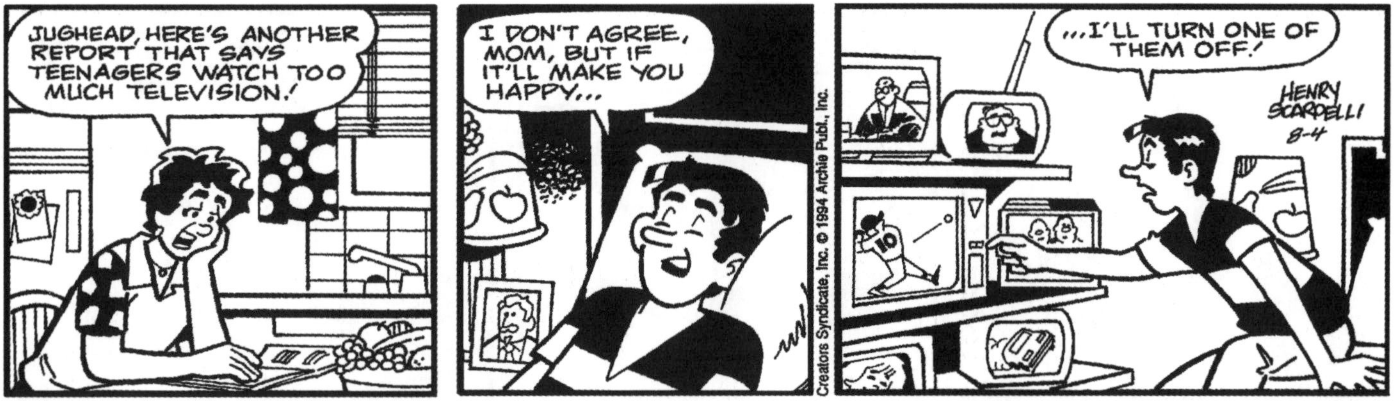
JUGHEAD, HERE'S ANOTHER REPORT THAT SAYS TEENAGERS WATCH TOO MUCH TELEVISION!
I DON'T AGREE, MOM, BUT IF IT'LL MAKE YOU HAPPY...
...I'LL TURN ONE OF THEM OFF!
HENRY SCARPELLI 8-4
Creators Syndicate, Inc. © 1994 Archie Publ., Inc.

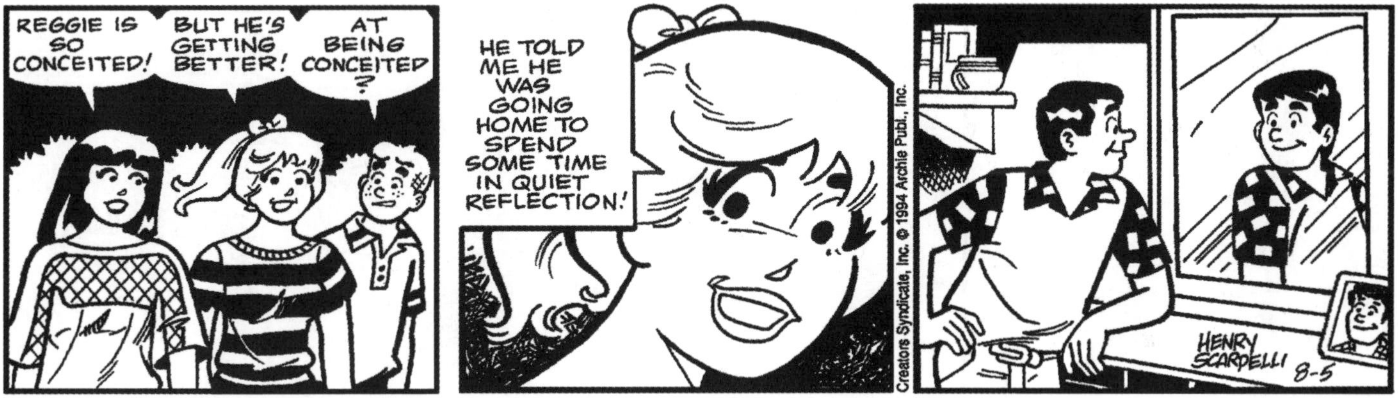
REGGIE IS SO CONCEITED!
BUT HE'S GETTING BETTER!
AT BEING CONCEITED?
HE TOLD ME HE WAS GOING HOME TO SPEND SOME TIME IN QUIET REFLECTION!
HENRY SCARPELLI 8-5
Creators Syndicate, Inc. © 1994 Archie Publ., Inc.

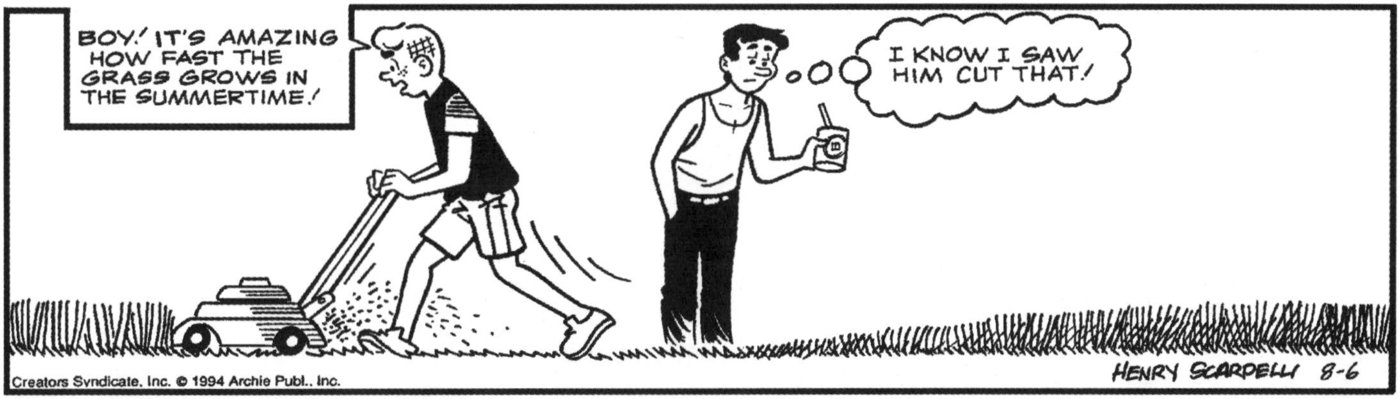
BOY! IT'S AMAZING HOW FAST THE GRASS GROWS IN THE SUMMERTIME!
I KNOW I SAW HIM CUT THAT!
Creators Syndicate, Inc. © 1994 Archie Publ., Inc.
HENRY SCARPELLI 8-6

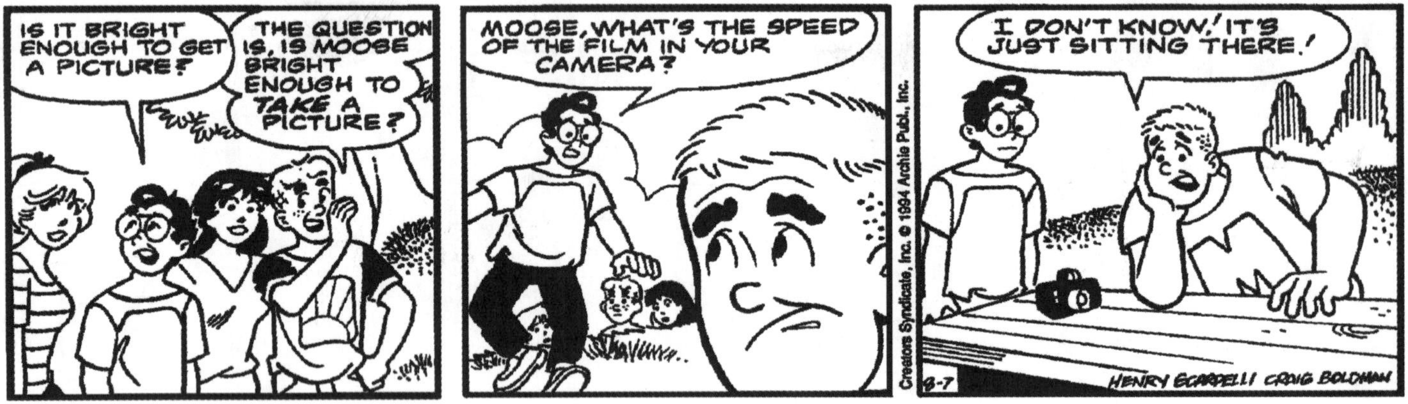
IS IT BRIGHT ENOUGH TO GET A PICTURE?
THE QUESTION IS, IS MOOSE BRIGHT ENOUGH TO TAKE A PICTURE?
MOOSE, WHAT'S THE SPEED OF THE FILM IN YOUR CAMERA?
I DON'T KNOW! IT'S JUST SITTING THERE!
Creators Syndicate, Inc. © 1994 Archie Publ., Inc.
8-7
HENRY SCARPELLI CRAIG BOLDMAN

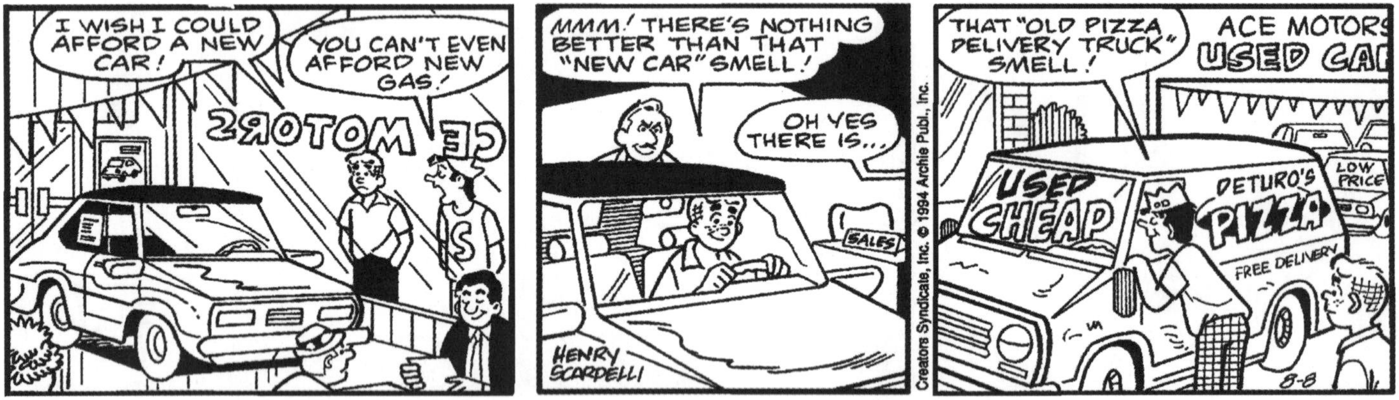
I WISH I COULD AFFORD A NEW CAR!
YOU CAN'T EVEN AFFORD NEW GAS!
MMM! THERE'S NOTHING BETTER THAN THAT "NEW CAR" SMELL!
OH YES THERE IS...
SALES
HENRY SCARPELLI
THAT "OLD PIZZA DELIVERY TRUCK" SMELL!
ACE MOTORS
USED CA
LOW PRICE
USED CHEAP
DETURO'S PIZZA
FREE DELIVERY
8-8
Creators Syndicate, Inc. © 1994 Archie Publ., Inc.

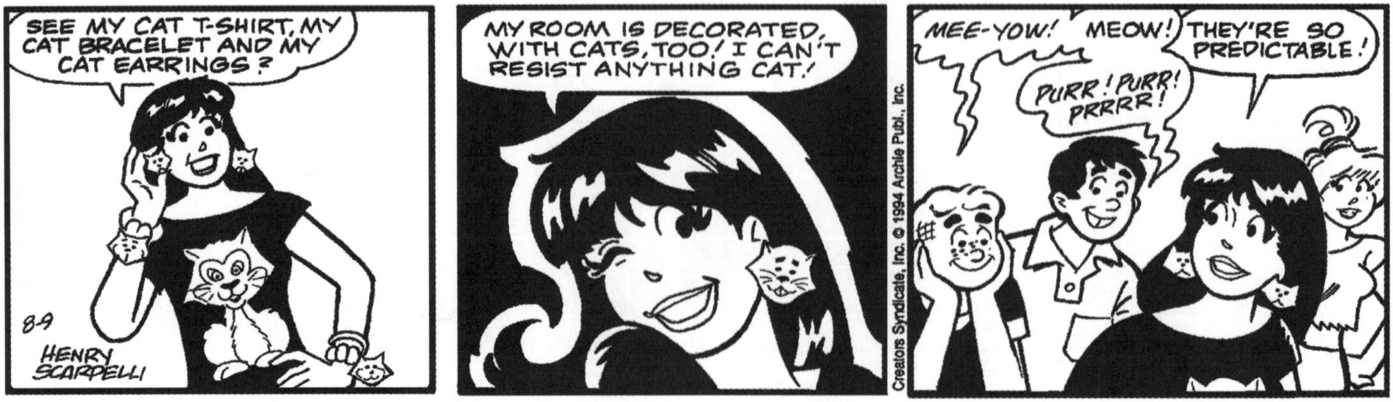
SEE MY CAT T-SHIRT, MY CAT BRACELET AND MY CAT EARRINGS?
8-9
HENRY SCARPELLI
MY ROOM IS DECORATED WITH CATS, TOO! I CAN'T RESIST ANYTHING CAT!
MEE-YOW!
MEOW!
PURR! PURR! PRRRR!
THEY'RE SO PREDICTABLE!
Creators Syndicate, Inc. © 1994 Archie Publ., Inc.

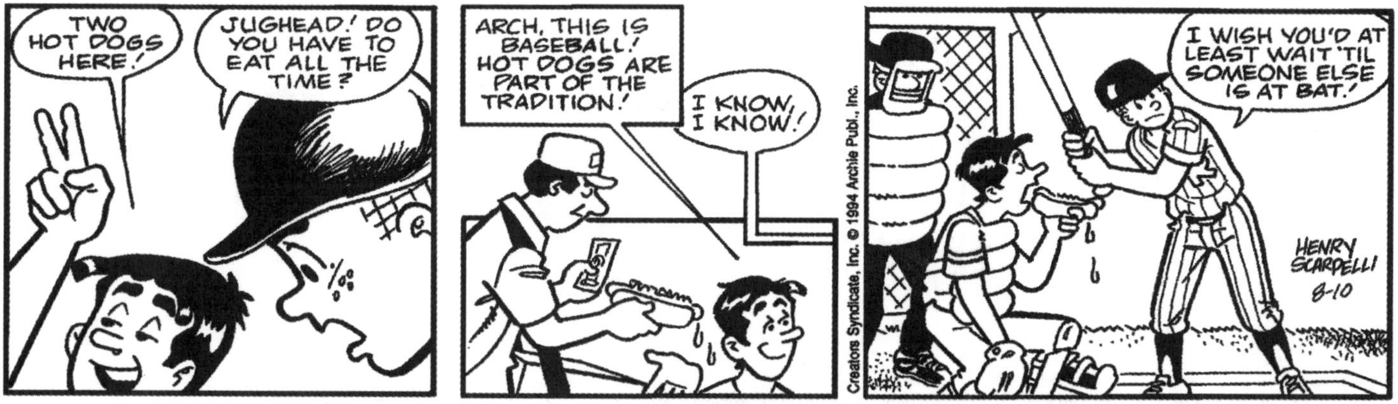
TWO HOT DOGS HERE!
JUGHEAD! DO YOU HAVE TO EAT ALL THE TIME?
ARCH, THIS IS BASEBALL! HOT DOGS ARE PART OF THE TRADITION!
I KNOW, I KNOW!
Creators Syndicate, Inc. © 1994 Archie Publ., Inc.
I WISH YOU'D AT LEAST WAIT 'TIL SOMEONE ELSE IS AT BAT!
HENRY SCARPELLI
8-10

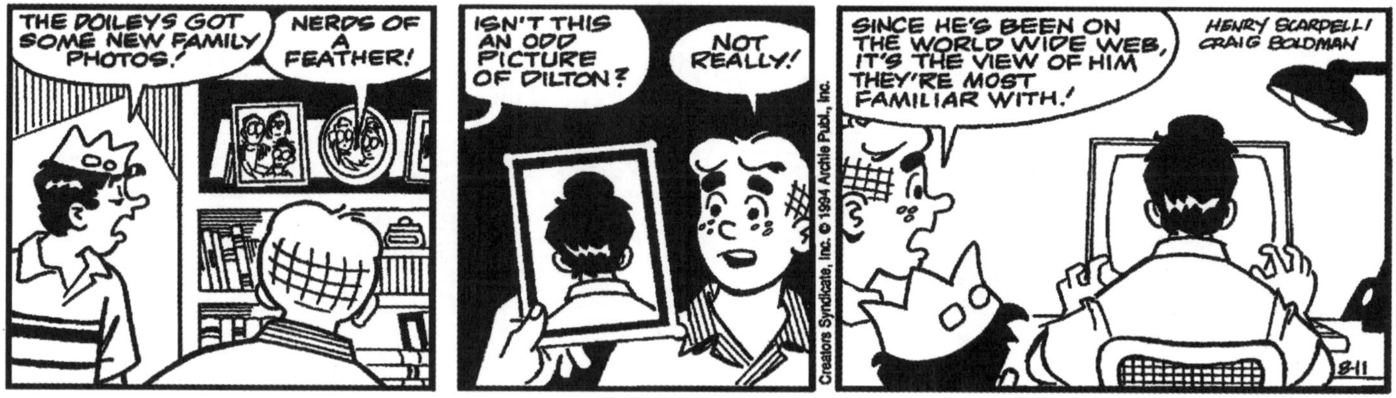
THE DOILEYS GOT SOME NEW FAMILY PHOTOS!
NERDS OF A FEATHER!
ISN'T THIS AN ODD PICTURE OF DILTON?
NOT REALLY!
Creators Syndicate, Inc. © 1994 Archie Publ., Inc.
SINCE HE'S BEEN ON THE WORLD WIDE WEB, IT'S THE VIEW OF HIM THEY'RE MOST FAMILIAR WITH!
HENRY SCARPELLI / CRAIG BOLDMAN
8-11

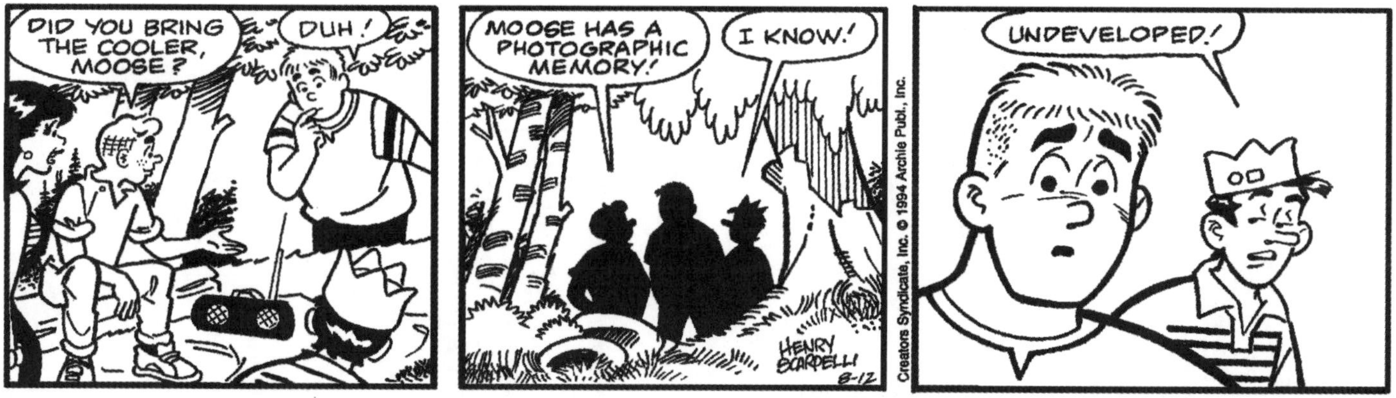
DID YOU BRING THE COOLER, MOOSE?
DUH!
MOOSE HAS A PHOTOGRAPHIC MEMORY!
I KNOW!
HENRY SCARPELLI
8-12
Creators Syndicate, Inc. © 1994 Archie Publ., Inc.
UNDEVELOPED!

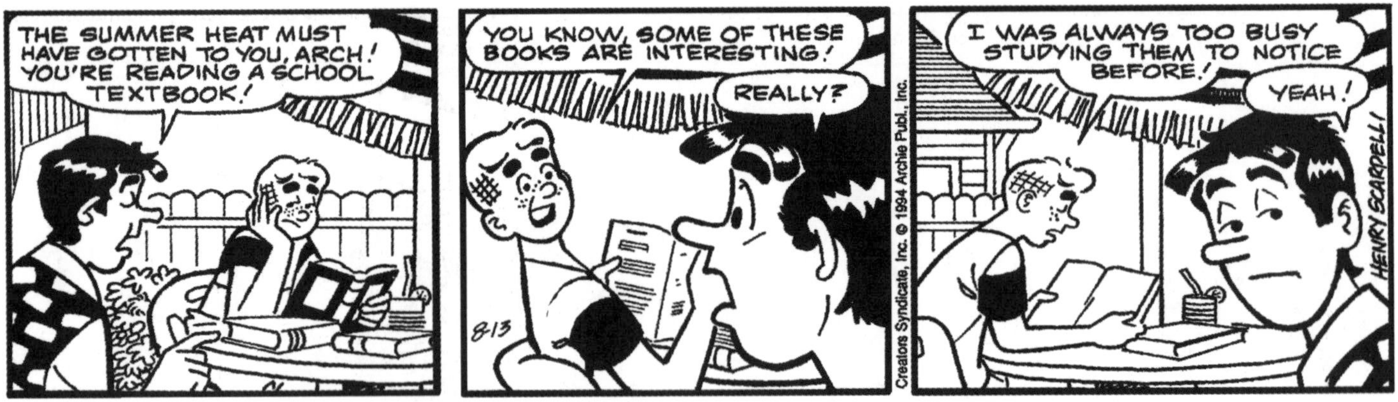
THE SUMMER HEAT MUST HAVE GOTTEN TO YOU, ARCH! YOU'RE READING A SCHOOL TEXTBOOK!
YOU KNOW, SOME OF THESE BOOKS ARE INTERESTING!
REALLY?
8-13
Creators Syndicate, Inc. © 1994 Archie Publ., Inc.
I WAS ALWAYS TOO BUSY STUDYING THEM TO NOTICE BEFORE!
YEAH!
HENRY SCARPELLI!

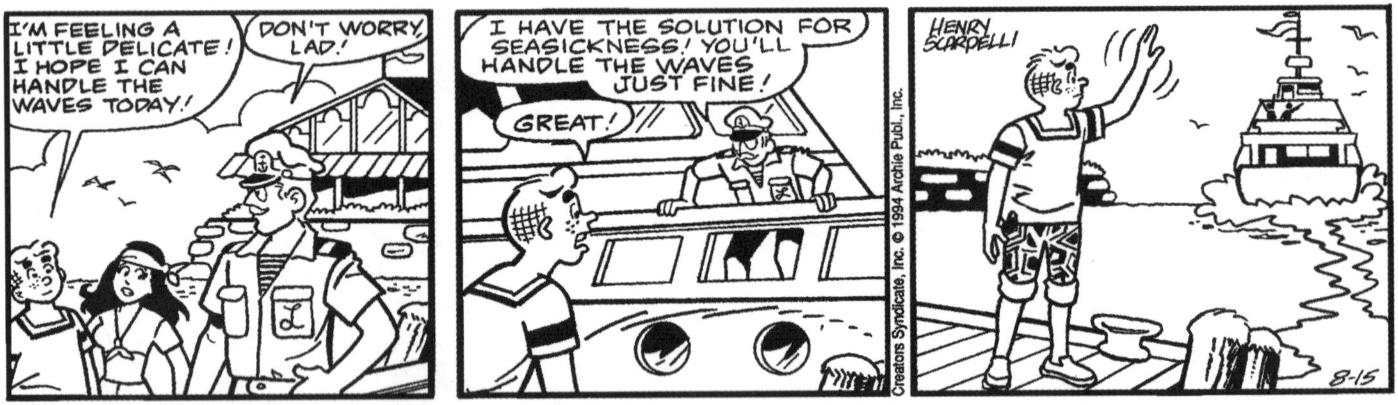
I'M FEELING A LITTLE DELICATE! I HOPE I CAN HANDLE THE WAVES TODAY!
DON'T WORRY, LAD!
I HAVE THE SOLUTION FOR SEASICKNESS! YOU'LL HANDLE THE WAVES JUST FINE!
GREAT!
Creators Syndicate, Inc. © 1994 Archie Publ., Inc.
HENRY SCARPELLI!
8-15

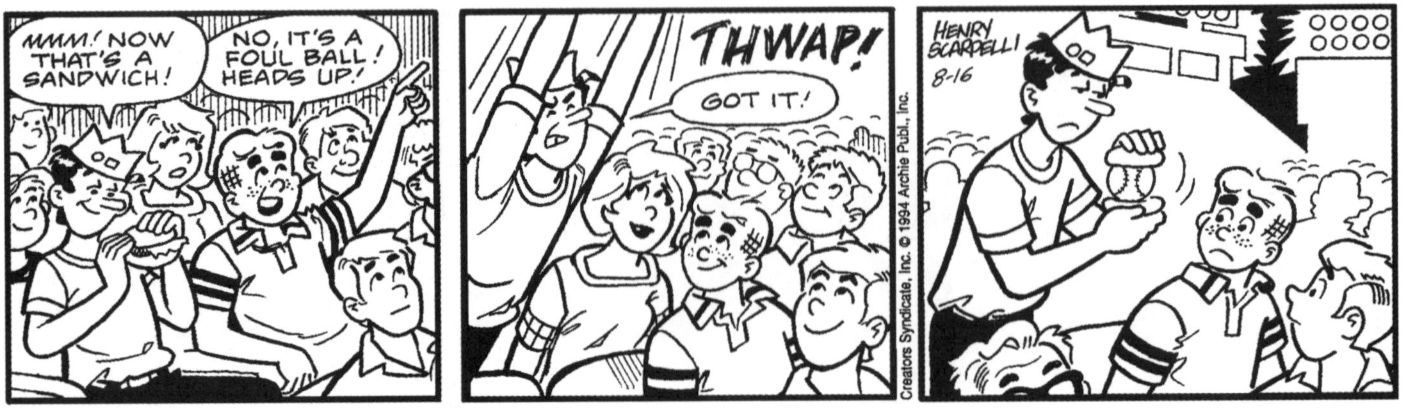
MMM! NOW THAT'S A SANDWICH!
NO, IT'S A FOUL BALL! HEADS UP!
THWAP!
GOT IT!
Creators Syndicate, Inc. © 1994 Archie Publ., Inc.
HENRY SCARPELLI!
8-16

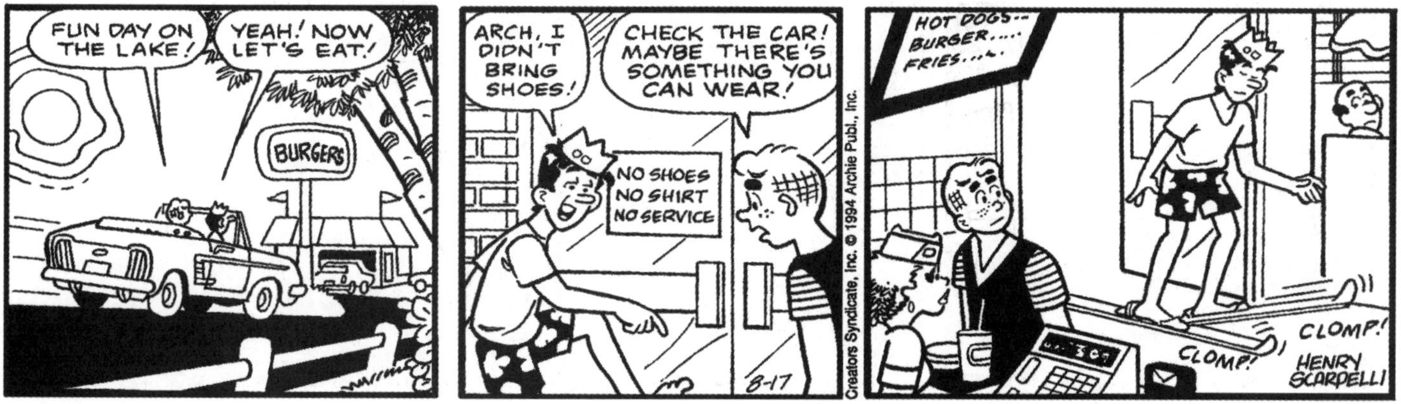
FUN DAY ON THE LAKE!
YEAH! NOW LET'S EAT!
BURGERS
ARCH, I DIDN'T BRING SHOES!
CHECK THE CAR! MAYBE THERE'S SOMETHING YOU CAN WEAR!
NO SHOES NO SHIRT NO SERVICE
8-17
Creators Syndicate, Inc. © 1994 Archie Publ., Inc.
HOT DOGS... BURGER..... FRIES.....
CLOMP!
CLOMP!
HENRY SCARPELLI

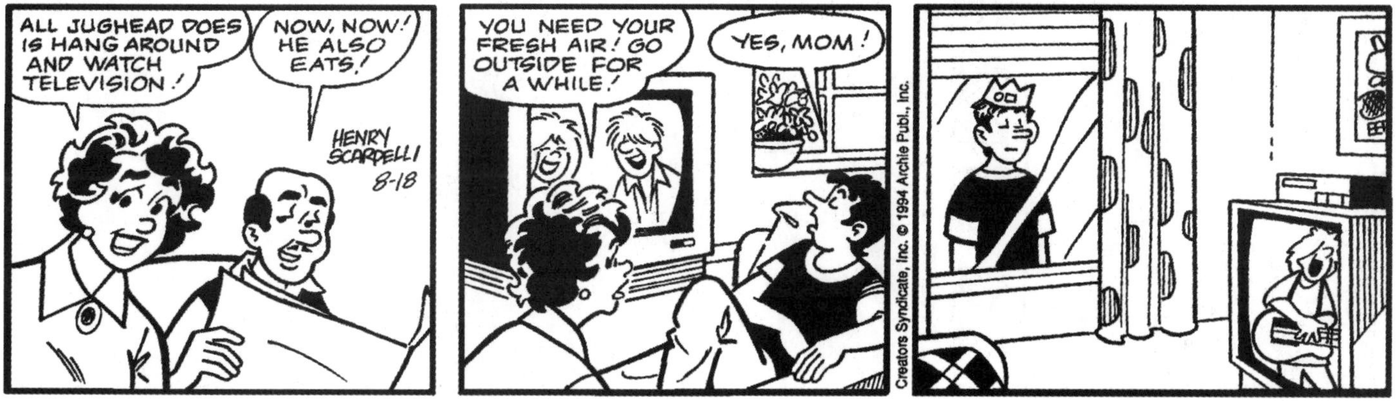
ALL JUGHEAD DOES IS HANG AROUND AND WATCH TELEVISION!
NOW, NOW! HE ALSO EATS!
HENRY SCARPELLI
8-18
YOU NEED YOUR FRESH AIR! GO OUTSIDE FOR A WHILE!
YES, MOM!
Creators Syndicate, Inc. © 1994 Archie Publ., Inc.

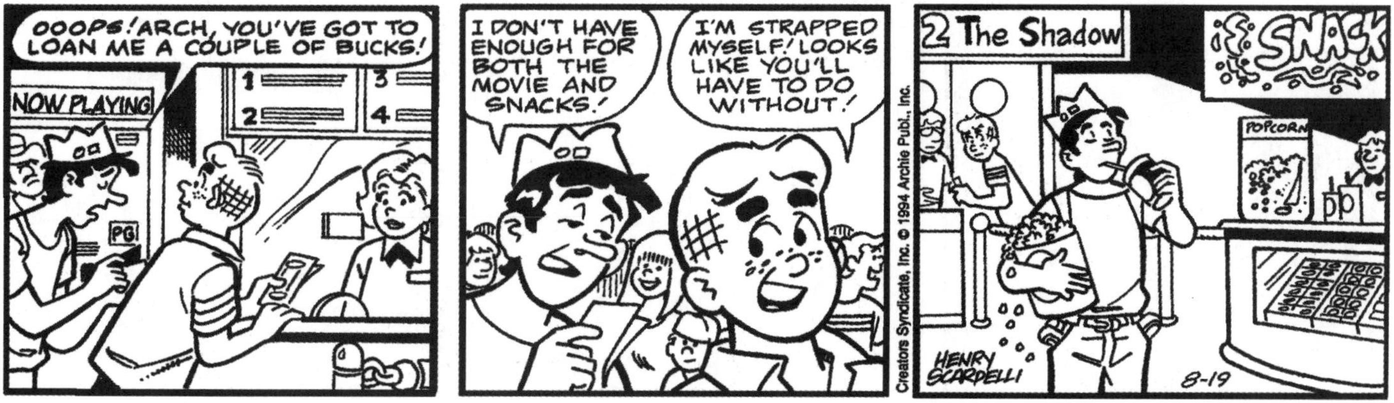
OOOPS! ARCH, YOU'VE GOT TO LOAN ME A COUPLE OF BUCKS!
NOW PLAYING
PG
I DON'T HAVE ENOUGH FOR BOTH THE MOVIE AND SNACKS!
I'M STRAPPED MYSELF! LOOKS LIKE YOU'LL HAVE TO DO WITHOUT!
Creators Syndicate, Inc. © 1994 Archie Publ., Inc.
2 The Shadow
SNACK
POPCORN
HENRY SCARPELLI
8-19

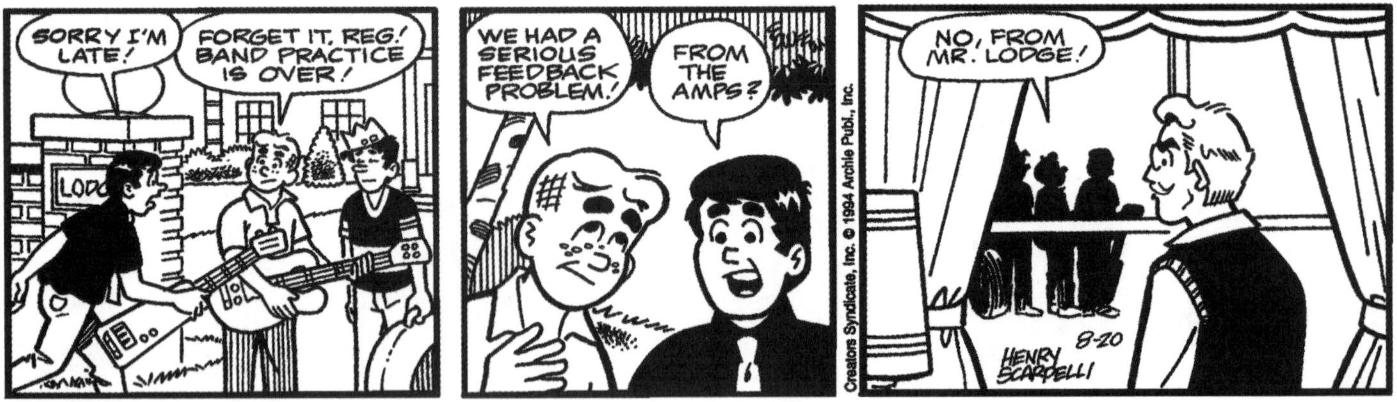
SORRY I'M LATE!
FORGET IT, REG! BAND PRACTICE IS OVER!
WE HAD A SERIOUS FEEDBACK PROBLEM!
FROM THE AMPS?
NO, FROM MR. LODGE!
Creators Syndicate, Inc. © 1994 Archie Publ., Inc.
HENRY SCARPELLI
8-20

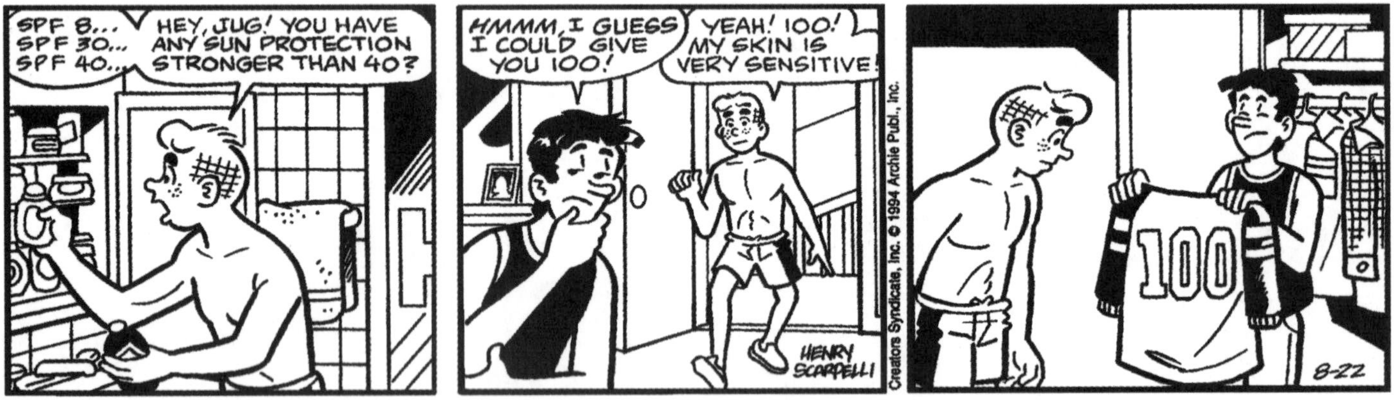
SPF 8... SPF 30... SPF 40...
HEY, JUG! YOU HAVE ANY SUN PROTECTION STRONGER THAN 40?
HMMM, I GUESS I COULD GIVE YOU 100!
YEAH! 100! MY SKIN IS VERY SENSITIVE!
HENRY SCARPELLI
Creators Syndicate, Inc. © 1994 Archie Publ., Inc.
100
8-22

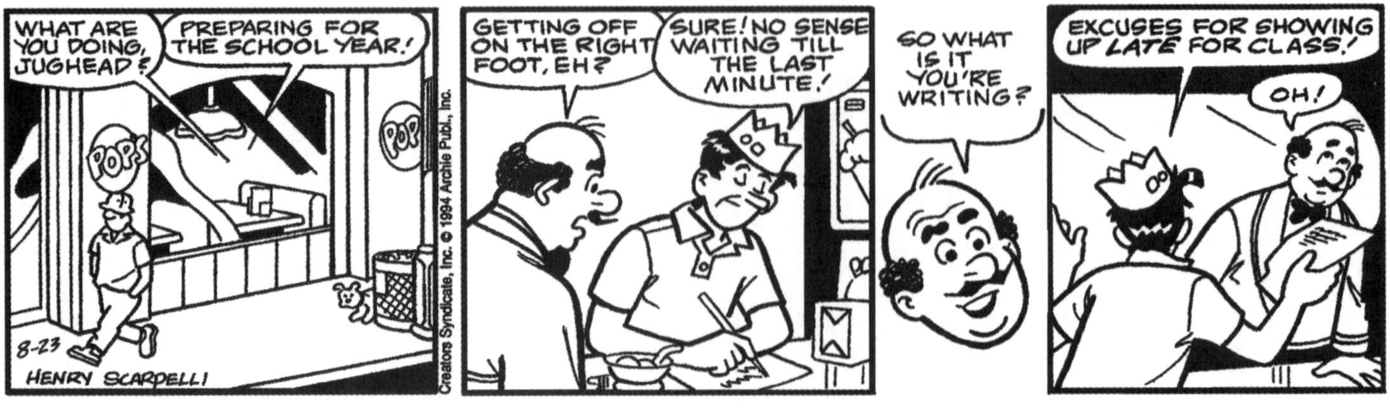
WHAT ARE YOU DOING, JUGHEAD?
PREPARING FOR THE SCHOOL YEAR!
POP'S
8-23
HENRY SCARPELLI
Creators Syndicate, Inc. © 1994 Archie Publ., Inc.
GETTING OFF ON THE RIGHT FOOT, EH?
SURE! NO SENSE WAITING TILL THE LAST MINUTE!
SO WHAT IS IT YOU'RE WRITING?
EXCUSES FOR SHOWING UP *LATE* FOR CLASS!
OH!

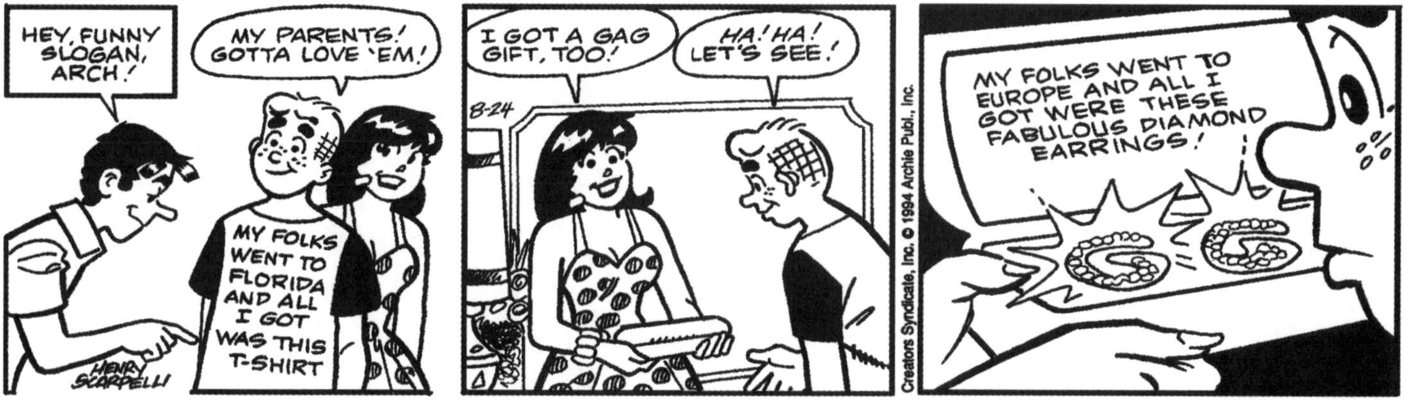
HEY, FUNNY SLOGAN, ARCH!
MY PARENTS! GOTTA LOVE 'EM!
MY FOLKS WENT TO FLORIDA AND ALL I GOT WAS THIS T-SHIRT
HENRY SCARPELLI
I GOT A GAG GIFT, TOO!
HA! HA! LET'S SEE!
8-24
MY FOLKS WENT TO EUROPE AND ALL I GOT WERE THESE FABULOUS DIAMOND EARRINGS!
Creators Syndicate, Inc. © 1994 Archie Publ., Inc.

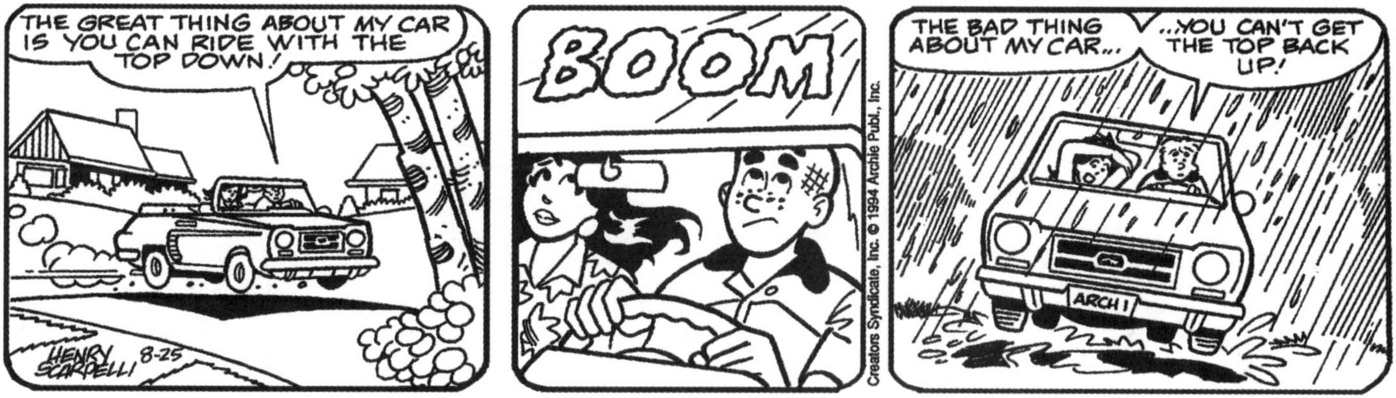
THE GREAT THING ABOUT MY CAR IS YOU CAN RIDE WITH THE TOP DOWN!
HENRY SCARPELLI 8-25
BOOM
Creators Syndicate, Inc. © 1994 Archie Publ., Inc.
THE BAD THING ABOUT MY CAR...
...YOU CAN'T GET THE TOP BACK UP!
ARCH 1

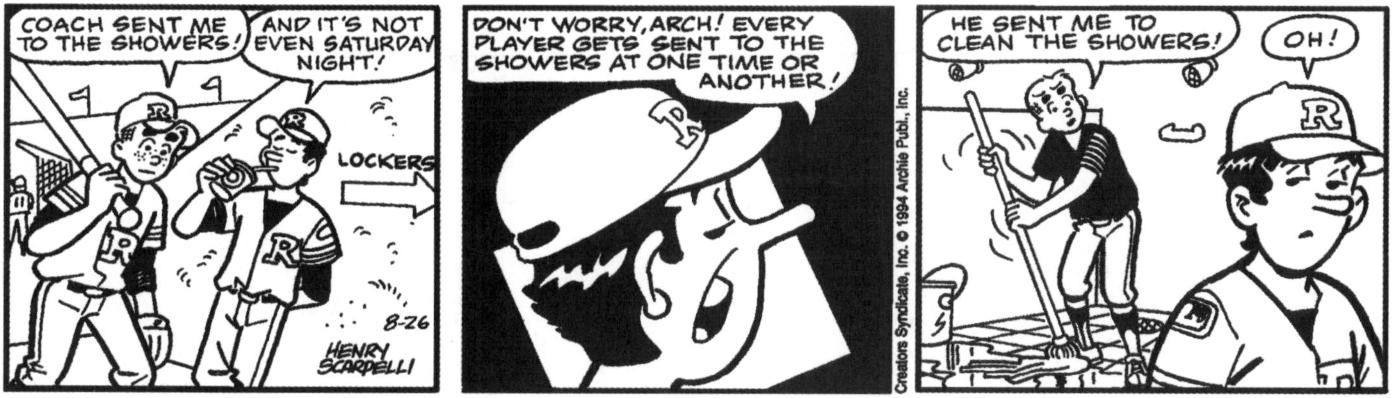
COACH SENT ME TO THE SHOWERS!
AND IT'S NOT EVEN SATURDAY NIGHT!
LOCKERS
8-26
HENRY SCARPELLI
DON'T WORRY, ARCH! EVERY PLAYER GETS SENT TO THE SHOWERS AT ONE TIME OR ANOTHER!
HE SENT ME TO CLEAN THE SHOWERS!
OH!
Creators Syndicate, Inc. © 1994 Archie Publ., Inc.

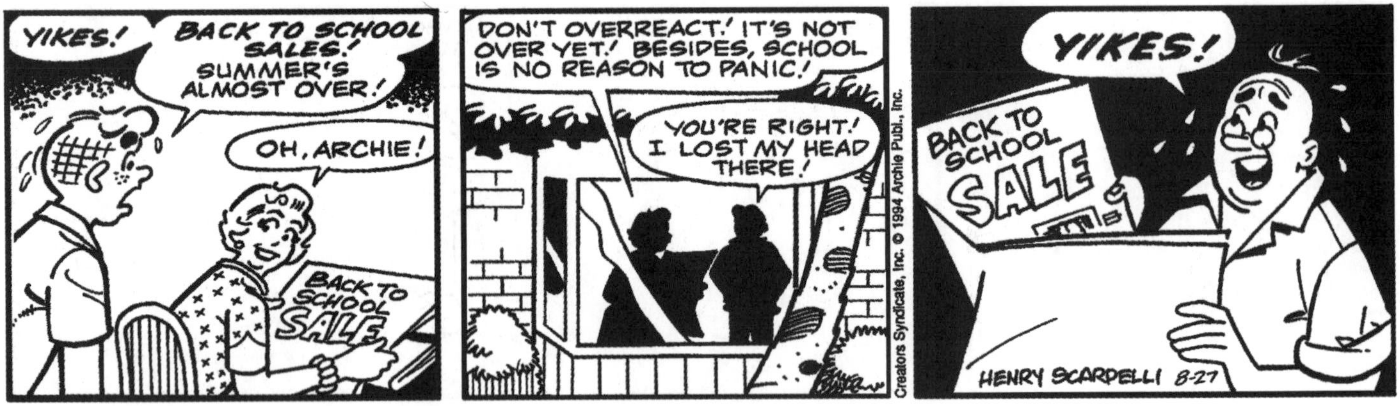
YIKES!
BACK TO SCHOOL SALES! SUMMER'S ALMOST OVER!
OH, ARCHIE!
BACK TO SCHOOL SALE
DON'T OVERREACT! IT'S NOT OVER YET! BESIDES, SCHOOL IS NO REASON TO PANIC!
YOU'RE RIGHT! I LOST MY HEAD THERE!
Creators Syndicate, Inc. © 1994 Archie Publ., Inc.
YIKES!
BACK TO SCHOOL SALE
HENRY SCARPELLI 8-27

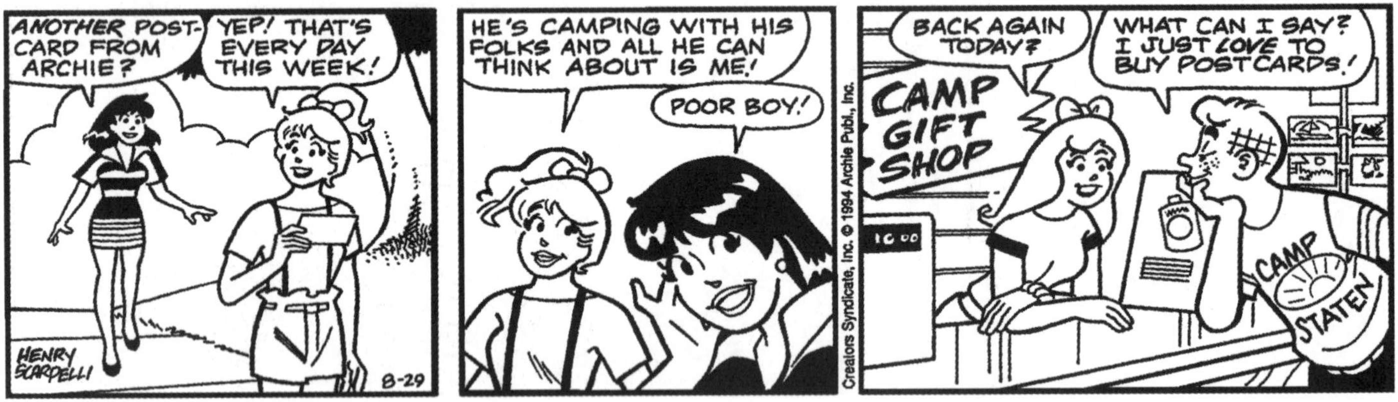
ANOTHER POST-CARD FROM ARCHIE?
YEP! THAT'S EVERY DAY THIS WEEK!
HENRY SCARPELLI
8-29
HE'S CAMPING WITH HIS FOLKS AND ALL HE CAN THINK ABOUT IS ME!
POOR BOY!
Creators Syndicate, Inc. © 1994 Archie Publ., Inc.
BACK AGAIN TODAY?
WHAT CAN I SAY? I JUST LOVE TO BUY POSTCARDS!
CAMP GIFT SHOP
CAMP STATEN

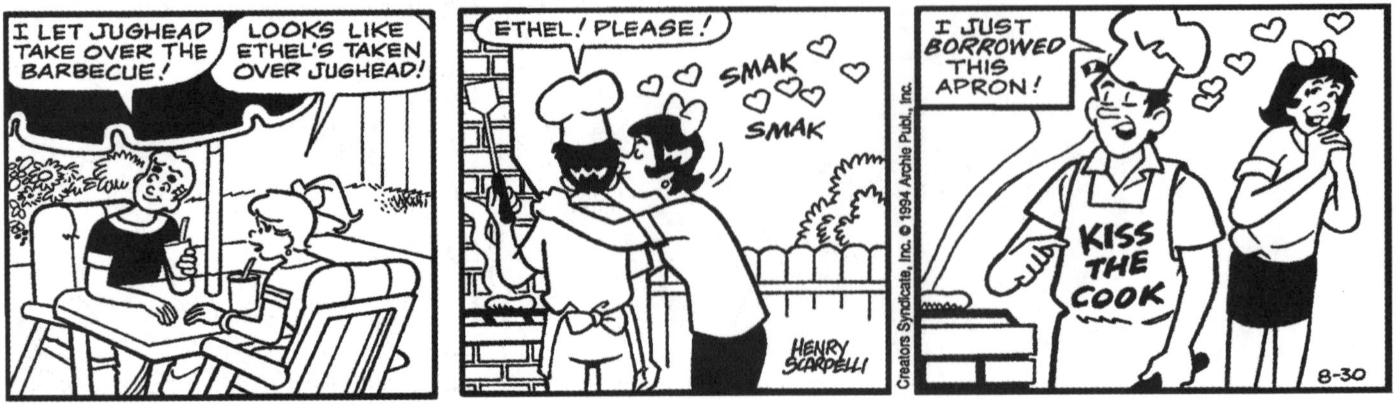
I LET JUGHEAD TAKE OVER THE BARBECUE!
LOOKS LIKE ETHEL'S TAKEN OVER JUGHEAD!
ETHEL! PLEASE!
SMAK
SMAK
HENRY SCARPELLI
Creators Syndicate, Inc. © 1994 Archie Publ., Inc.
I JUST BORROWED THIS APRON!
KISS THE COOK
8-30

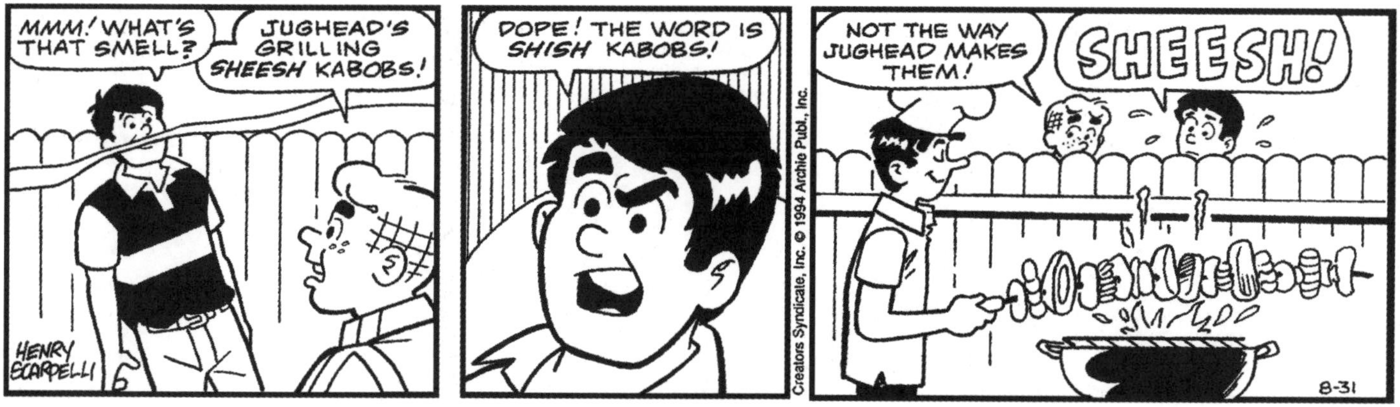
MMM! WHAT'S THAT SMELL?
JUGHEAD'S GRILLING SHEESH KABOBS!
HENRY SCARPELLI
DOPE! THE WORD IS SHISH KABOBS!
NOT THE WAY JUGHEAD MAKES THEM!
SHEESH!
8-31
Creators Syndicate, Inc. © 1994 Archie Publ., Inc.

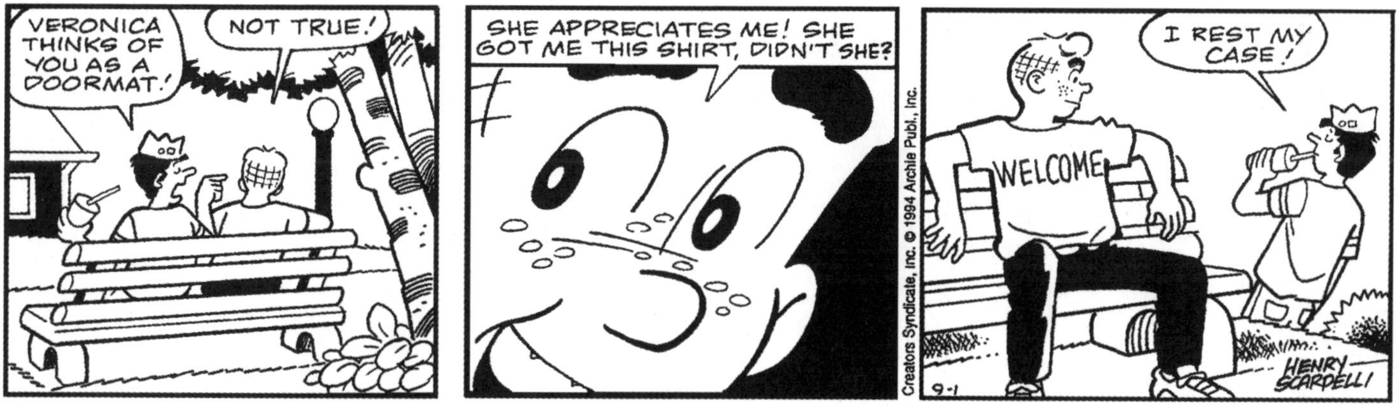
VERONICA THINKS OF YOU AS A DOORMAT!
NOT TRUE!
SHE APPRECIATES ME! SHE GOT ME THIS SHIRT, DIDN'T SHE?
I REST MY CASE!
WELCOME
9-1
HENRY SCARPELLI
Creators Syndicate, Inc. © 1994 Archie Publ., Inc.

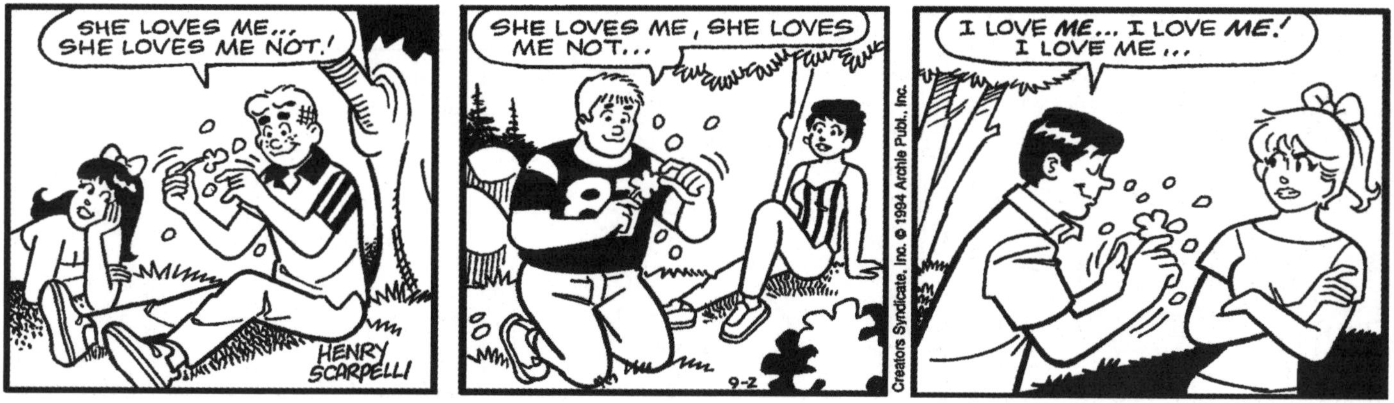
SHE LOVES ME... SHE LOVES ME NOT!
HENRY SCARPELLI
SHE LOVES ME, SHE LOVES ME NOT...
9-2
I LOVE ME... I LOVE ME! I LOVE ME...
Creators Syndicate, Inc. © 1994 Archie Publ., Inc.

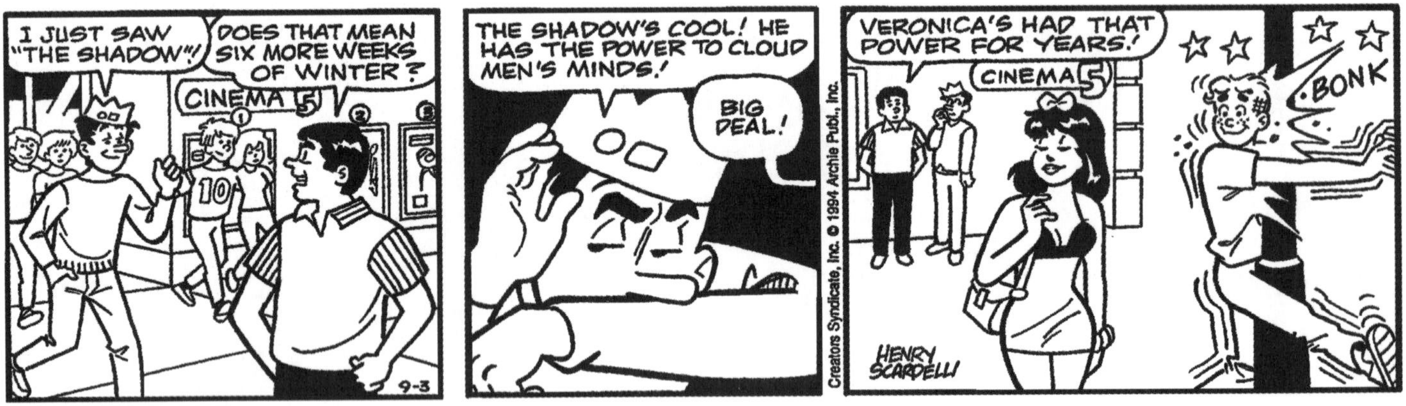
I JUST SAW "THE SHADOW"!
DOES THAT MEAN SIX MORE WEEKS OF WINTER?
CINEMA 5
9-3
THE SHADOW'S COOL! HE HAS THE POWER TO CLOUD MEN'S MINDS!
BIG DEAL!
Creators Syndicate, Inc. © 1994 Archie Publ., Inc.
VERONICA'S HAD THAT POWER FOR YEARS!
CINEMA 5
BONK
HENRY SCARPELLI

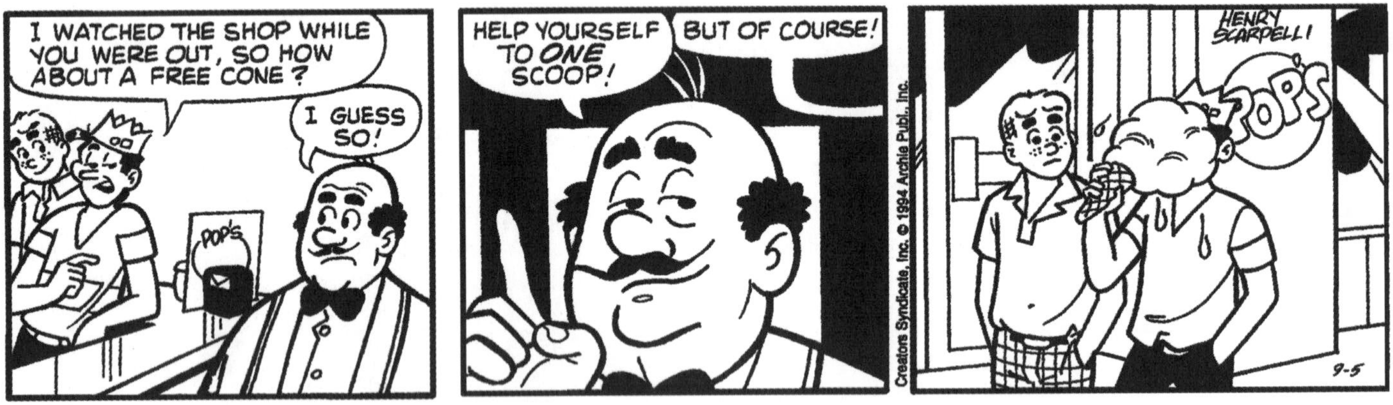
I WATCHED THE SHOP WHILE YOU WERE OUT, SO HOW ABOUT A FREE CONE?
I GUESS SO!
POP'S
HELP YOURSELF TO ONE SCOOP!
BUT OF COURSE!
Creators Syndicate, Inc. © 1994 Archie Publ., Inc.
HENRY SCARPELLI
POP'S
9-5

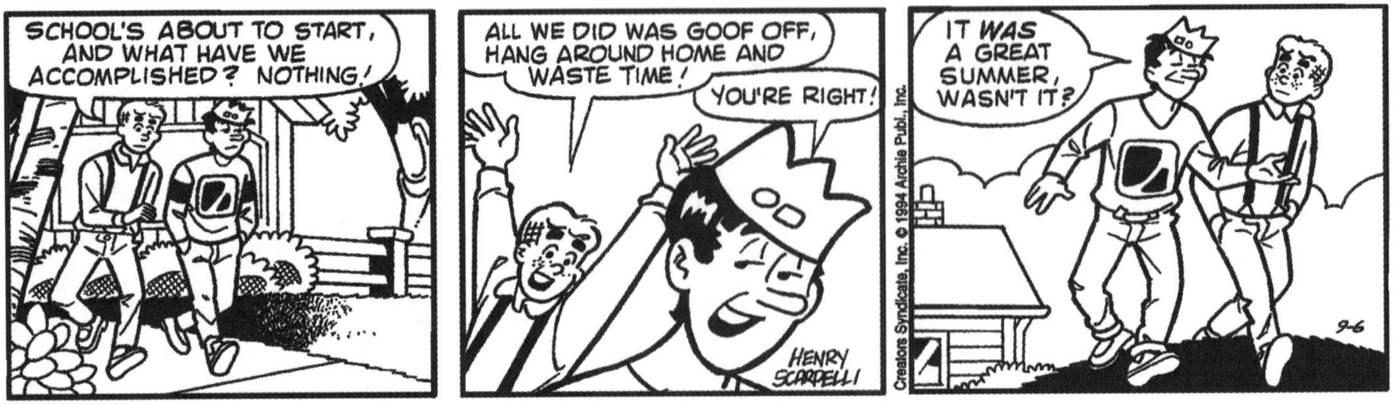
SCHOOL'S ABOUT TO START, AND WHAT HAVE WE ACCOMPLISHED? NOTHING!
ALL WE DID WAS GOOF OFF, HANG AROUND HOME AND WASTE TIME!
YOU'RE RIGHT!
HENRY SCARPELLI
Creators Syndicate, Inc. © 1994 Archie Publ., Inc.
IT WAS A GREAT SUMMER, WASN'T IT?
9-6

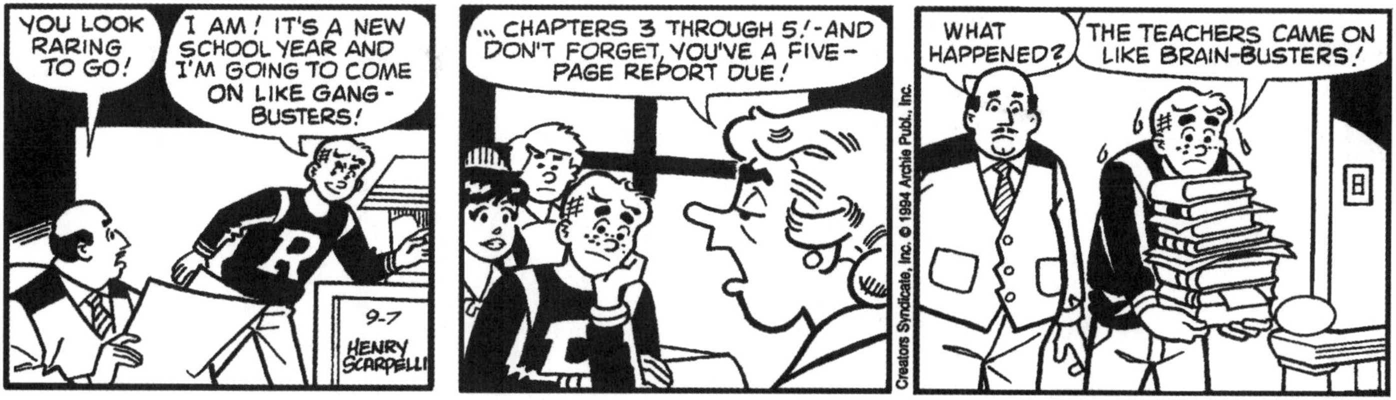
YOU LOOK RARING TO GO!
I AM! IT'S A NEW SCHOOL YEAR AND I'M GOING TO COME ON LIKE GANG-BUSTERS!
9-7
HENRY SCARPELLI
...CHAPTERS 3 THROUGH 5!-AND DON'T FORGET, YOU'VE A FIVE-PAGE REPORT DUE!
Creators Syndicate, Inc. © 1994 Archie Publ., Inc.
WHAT HAPPENED?
THE TEACHERS CAME ON LIKE BRAIN-BUSTERS!

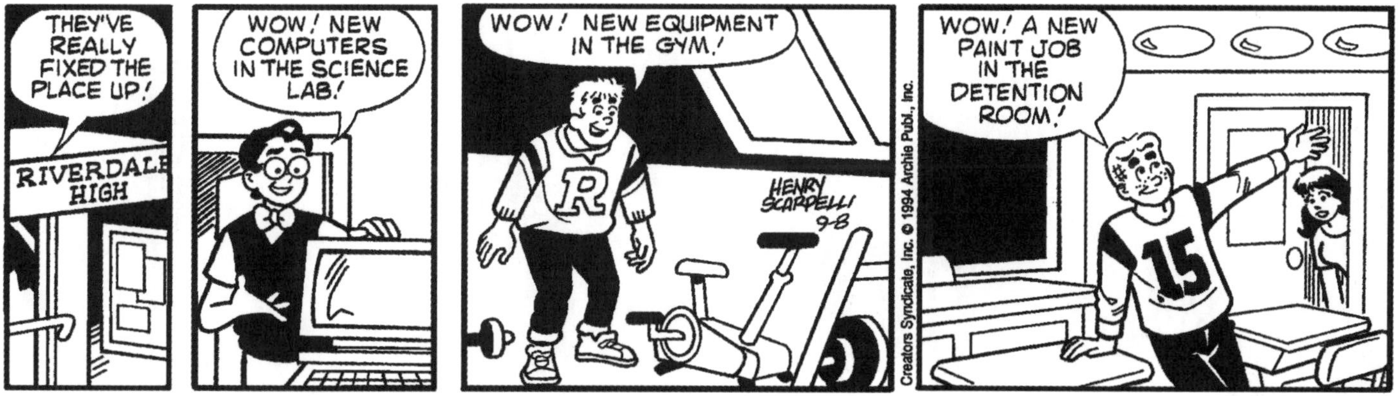
THEY'VE REALLY FIXED THE PLACE UP!
RIVERDALE HIGH
WOW! NEW COMPUTERS IN THE SCIENCE LAB!
WOW! NEW EQUIPMENT IN THE GYM!
HENRY SCARPELLI
9-8
Creators Syndicate, Inc. © 1994 Archie Publ., Inc.
WOW! A NEW PAINT JOB IN THE DETENTION ROOM!
15

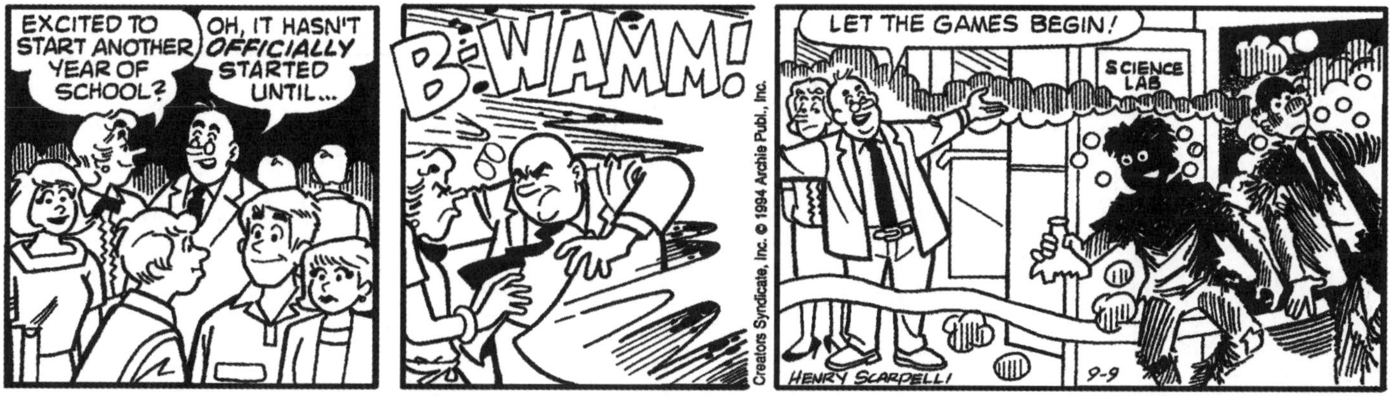
EXCITED TO START ANOTHER YEAR OF SCHOOL?
OH, IT HASN'T *OFFICIALLY* STARTED UNTIL...
B-WAMM!
Creators Syndicate, Inc. © 1994 Archie Publ., Inc.
LET THE GAMES BEGIN!
SCIENCE LAB
HENRY SCARPELLI
9-9

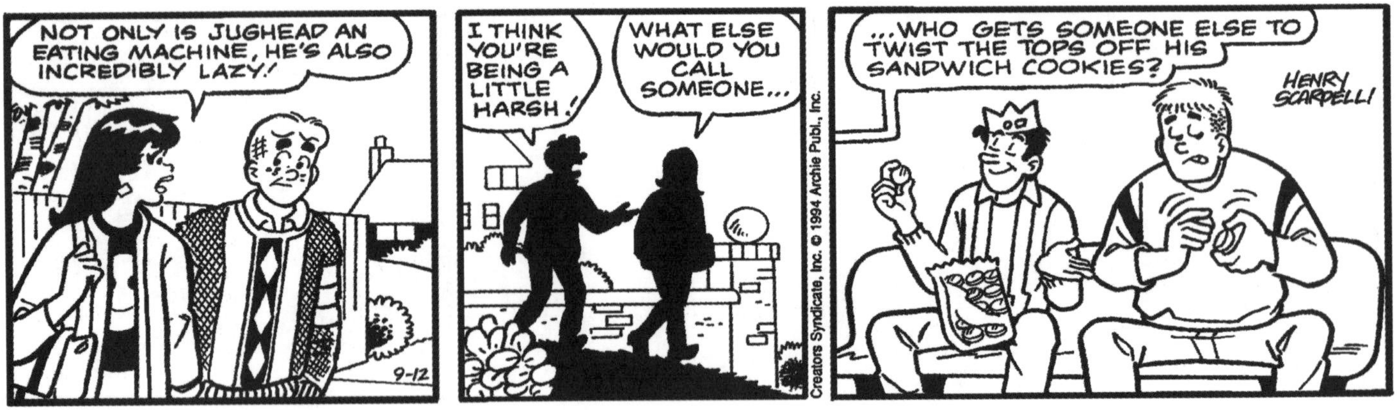
NOT ONLY IS JUGHEAD AN EATING MACHINE, HE'S ALSO INCREDIBLY LAZY!
9-12
I THINK YOU'RE BEING A LITTLE HARSH!
WHAT ELSE WOULD YOU CALL SOMEONE...
Creators Syndicate, Inc. © 1994 Archie Publ., Inc.
...WHO GETS SOMEONE ELSE TO TWIST THE TOPS OFF HIS SANDWICH COOKIES?
HENRY SCARPELLI

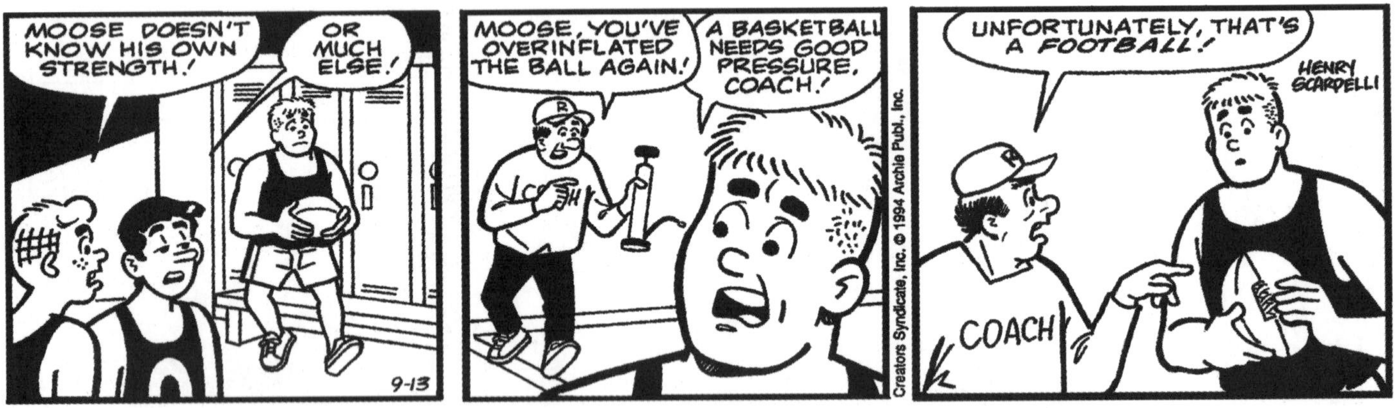
MOOSE DOESN'T KNOW HIS OWN STRENGTH!
OR MUCH ELSE!
9-13
MOOSE, YOU'VE OVERINFLATED THE BALL AGAIN!
A BASKETBALL NEEDS GOOD PRESSURE, COACH!
Creators Syndicate, Inc. © 1994 Archie Publ., Inc.
UNFORTUNATELY, THAT'S A *FOOTBALL*!
HENRY SCARPELLI
COACH

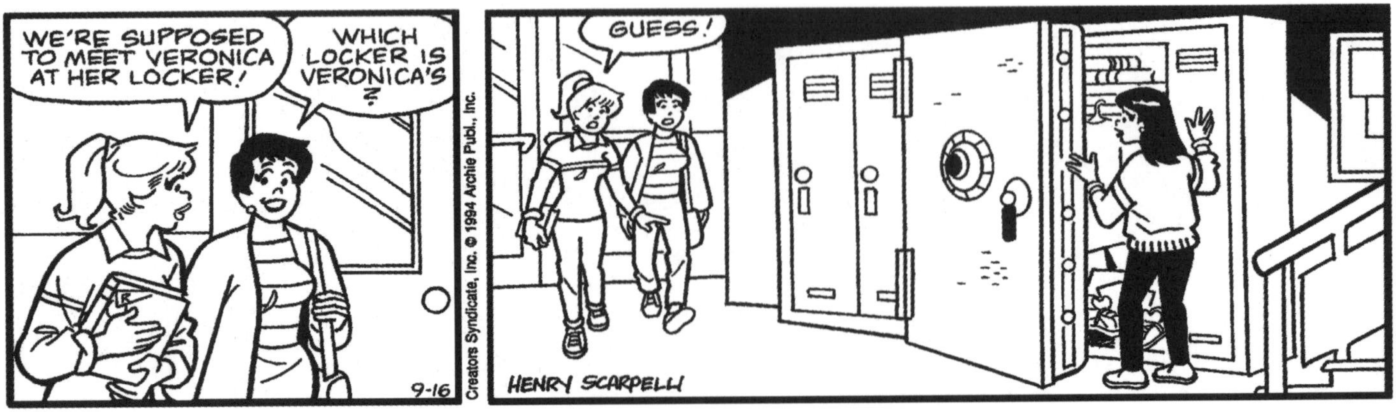
WE'RE SUPPOSED TO MEET VERONICA AT HER LOCKER!
WHICH LOCKER IS VERONICA'S?
9-16
Creators Syndicate, Inc. © 1994 Archie Publ., Inc.
GUESS!
HENRY SCARPELLI

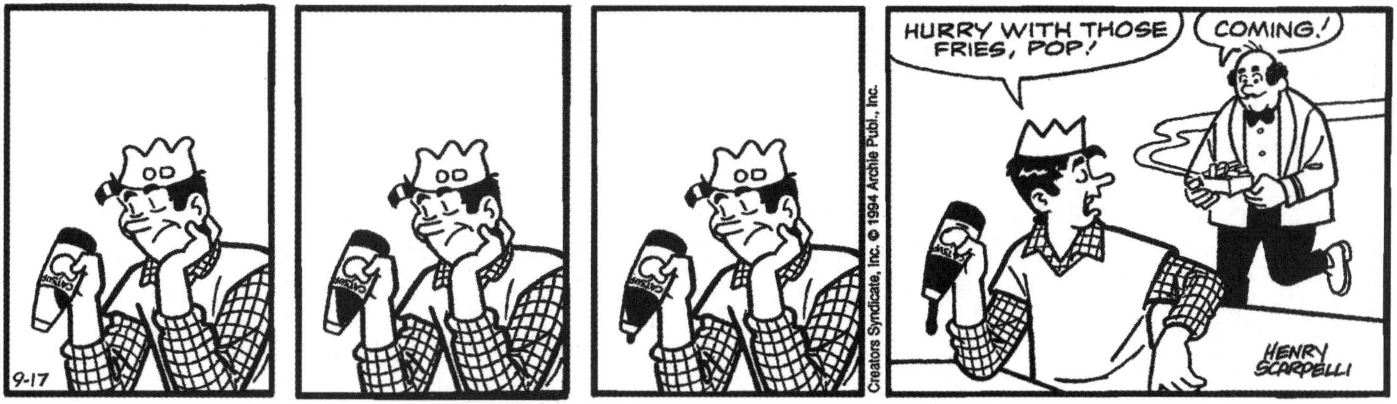
9-17
Creators Syndicate, Inc. © 1994 Archie Publ., Inc.
HURRY WITH THOSE FRIES, POP!
COMING!
HENRY SCARPELLI

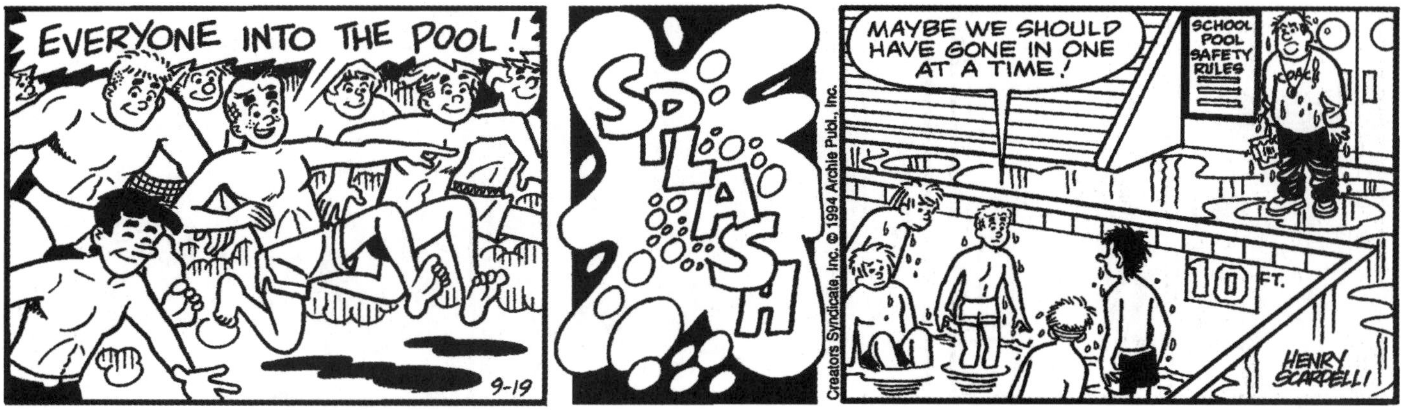
EVERYONE INTO THE POOL!
9-19
SPLASH
Creators Syndicate, Inc. © 1994 Archie Publ., Inc.
MAYBE WE SHOULD HAVE GONE IN ONE AT A TIME!
SCHOOL POOL SAFETY RULES
COACH
10 FT.
HENRY SCARPELLI

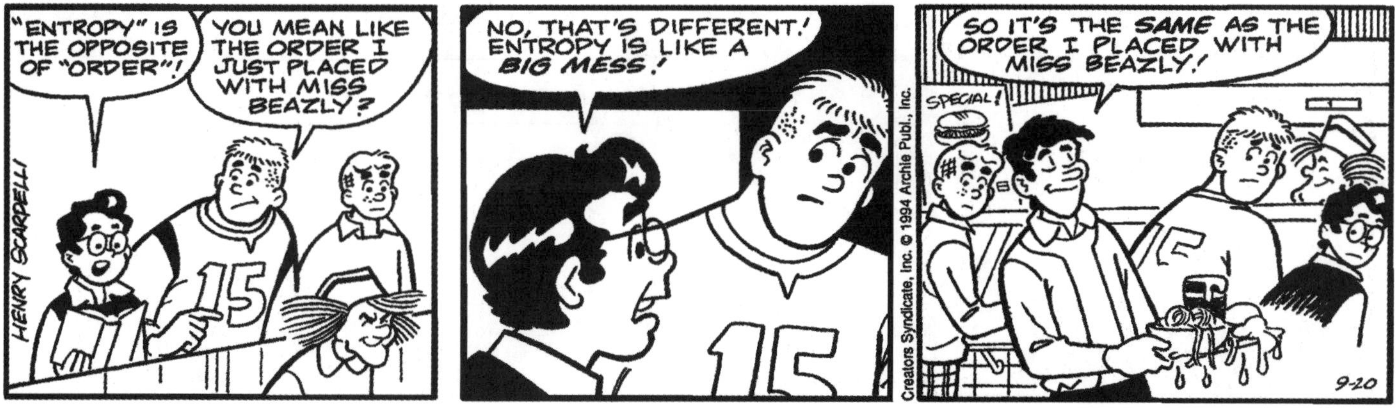
"ENTROPY" IS THE OPPOSITE OF "ORDER"!
YOU MEAN LIKE THE ORDER I JUST PLACED WITH MISS BEAZLY?
HENRY SCARPELLI
15
NO, THAT'S DIFFERENT! ENTROPY IS LIKE A *BIG MESS*!
15
Creators Syndicate, Inc. © 1994 Archie Publ., Inc.
SO IT'S THE *SAME* AS THE ORDER I PLACED WITH MISS BEAZLY!
SPECIAL!
9-20

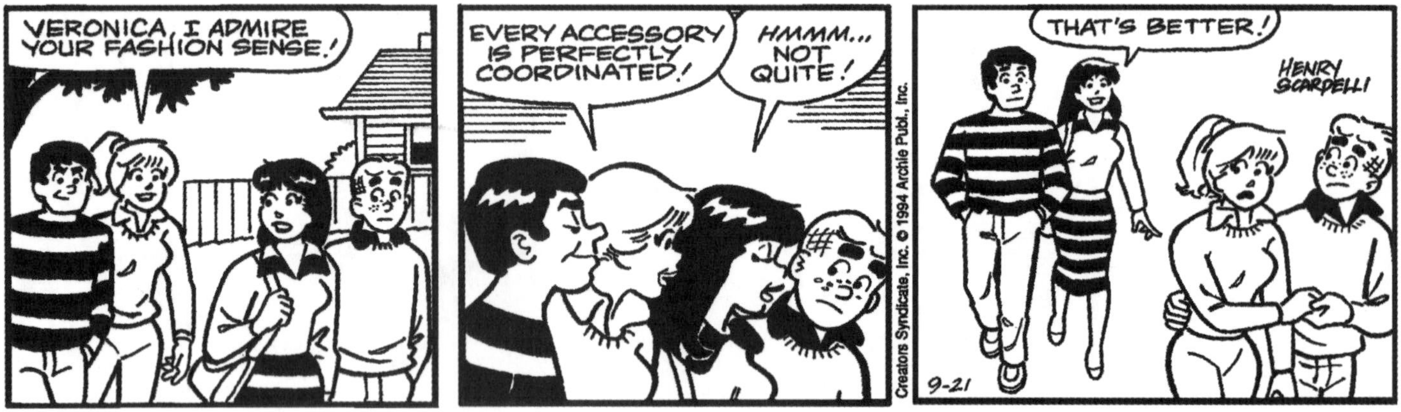
VERONICA, I ADMIRE YOUR FASHION SENSE!
EVERY ACCESSORY IS PERFECTLY COORDINATED!
HMMM... NOT QUITE!
Creators Syndicate, Inc. © 1994 Archie Publ., Inc.
9-21
THAT'S BETTER!
HENRY SCARPELLI

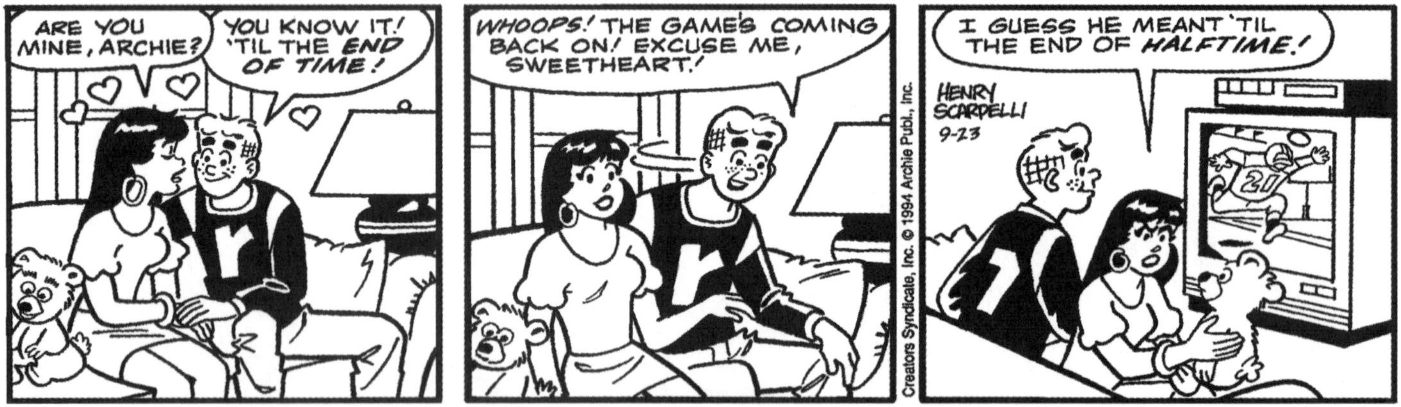
ARE YOU MINE, ARCHIE?
YOU KNOW IT! 'TIL THE END OF TIME!
WHOOPS! THE GAME'S COMING BACK ON! EXCUSE ME, SWEETHEART!
Creators Syndicate, Inc. © 1994 Archie Publ., Inc.
HENRY SCARPELLI
9-23
I GUESS HE MEANT 'TIL THE END OF HALFTIME!

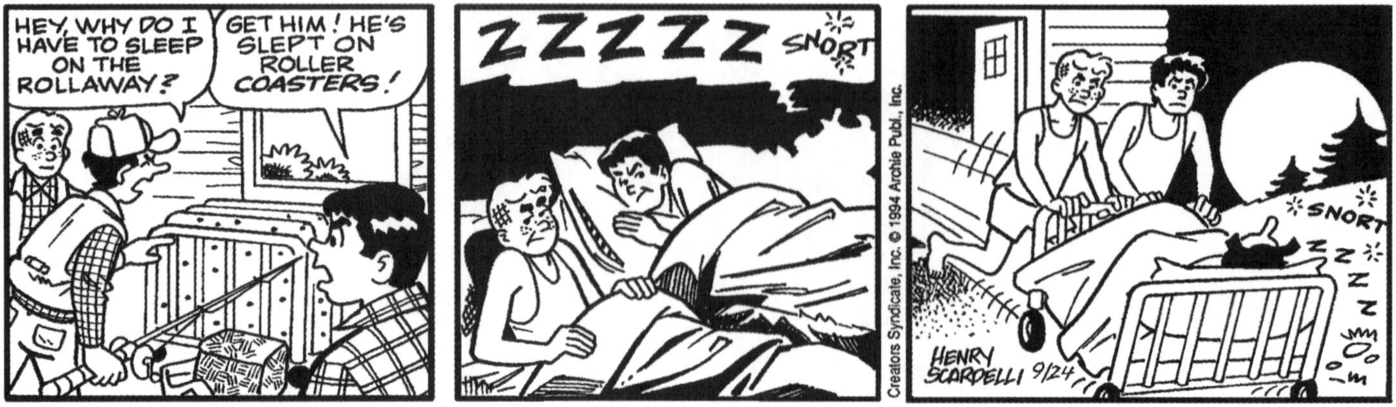
HEY, WHY DO I HAVE TO SLEEP ON THE ROLLAWAY?
GET HIM! HE'S SLEPT ON ROLLER COASTERS!
ZZZZZZ
SNORT
Creators Syndicate, Inc. © 1994 Archie Publ., Inc.
SNORT
Z Z Z Z
HENRY SCARPELLI 9/24

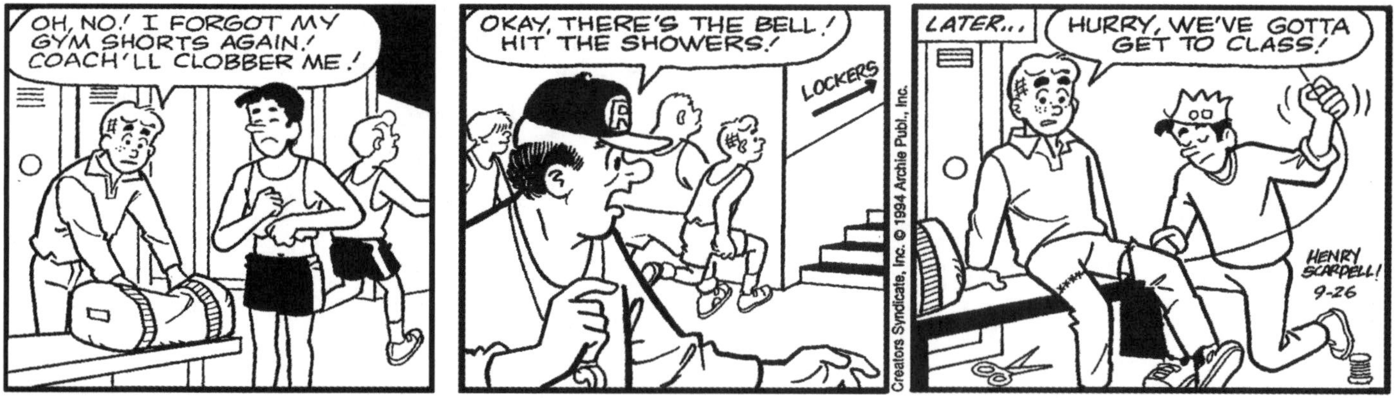
OH, NO! I FORGOT MY GYM SHORTS AGAIN! COACH'LL CLOBBER ME!
OKAY, THERE'S THE BELL! HIT THE SHOWERS!
LOCKERS
LATER...
HURRY, WE'VE GOTTA GET TO CLASS!
HENRY SCARPELLI! 9-26
Creators Syndicate, Inc. © 1994 Archie Publ., Inc.

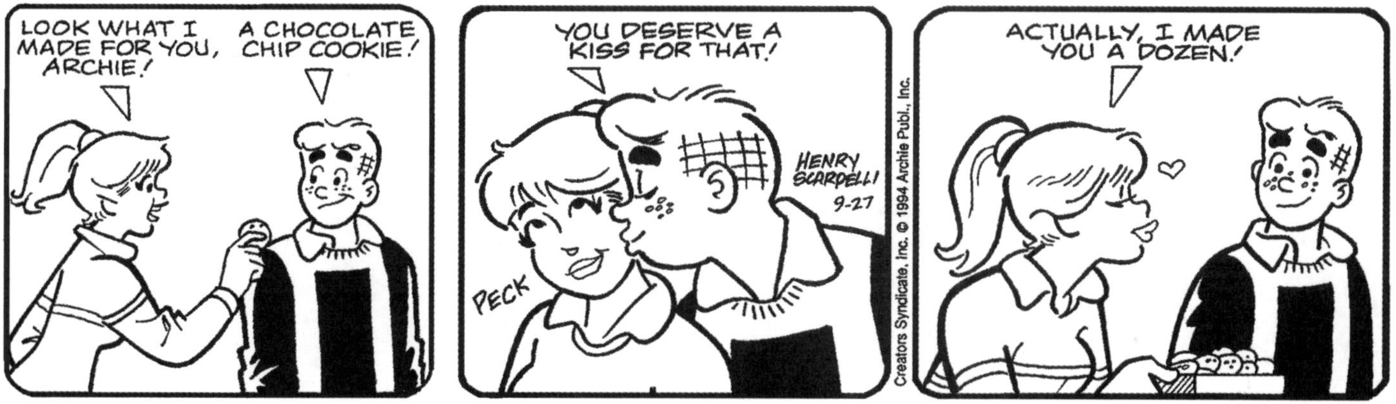
LOOK WHAT I MADE FOR YOU, ARCHIE!
A CHOCOLATE CHIP COOKIE!
YOU DESERVE A KISS FOR THAT!
PECK
HENRY SCARPELLI 9-27
ACTUALLY, I MADE YOU A DOZEN!
Creators Syndicate, Inc. © 1994 Archie Publ., Inc.

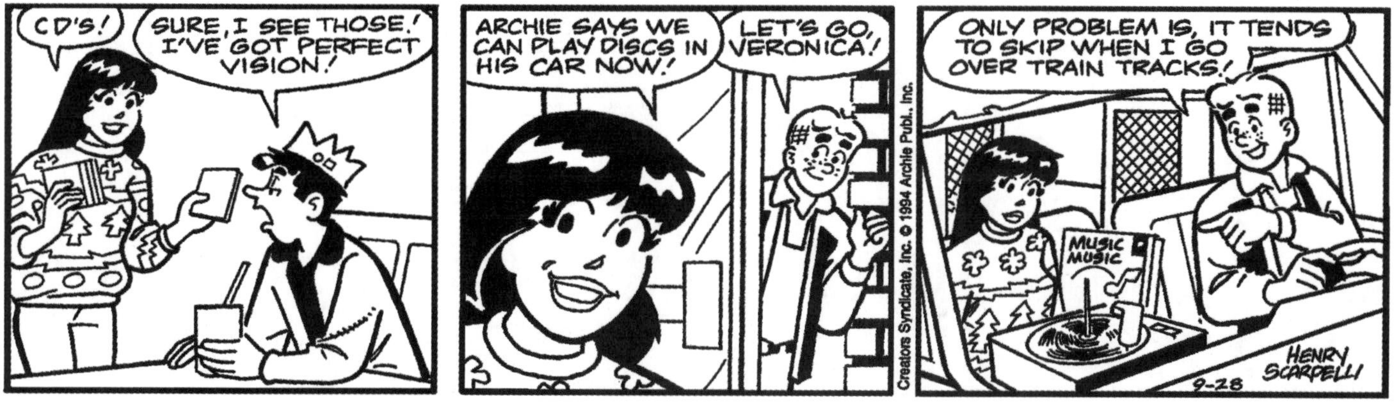
CD'S!
SURE, I SEE THOSE! I'VE GOT PERFECT VISION!
ARCHIE SAYS WE CAN PLAY DISCS IN HIS CAR NOW!
LET'S GO, VERONICA!
ONLY PROBLEM IS, IT TENDS TO SKIP WHEN I GO OVER TRAIN TRACKS!
MUSIC MUSIC
HENRY SCARPELLI 9-28
Creators Syndicate, Inc. © 1994 Archie Publ., Inc.

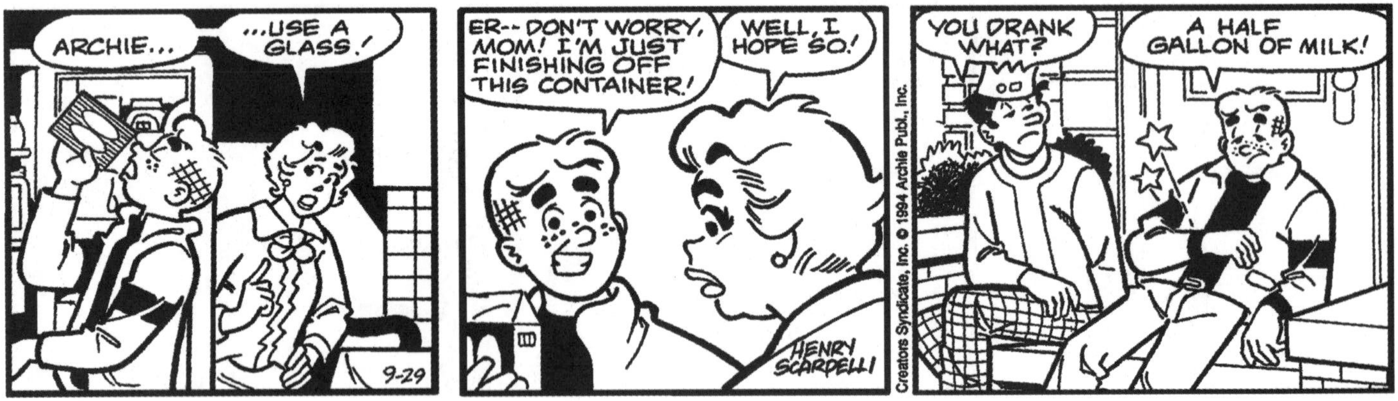
ARCHIE...
...USE A GLASS!
9-29
ER-- DON'T WORRY, MOM! I'M JUST FINISHING OFF THIS CONTAINER!
WELL, I HOPE SO!
HENRY SCARPELLI
YOU DRANK WHAT?
A HALF GALLON OF MILK!
Creators Syndicate, Inc. © 1994 Archie Publ., Inc.

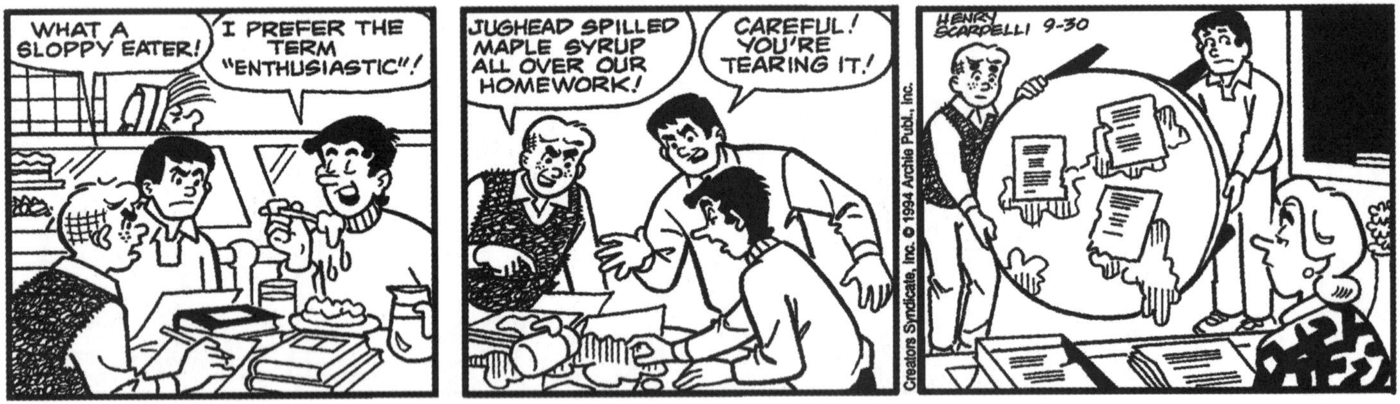
WHAT A SLOPPY EATER!
I PREFER THE TERM "ENTHUSIASTIC"!
JUGHEAD SPILLED MAPLE SYRUP ALL OVER OUR HOMEWORK!
CAREFUL! YOU'RE TEARING IT!
HENRY SCARPELLI 9-30
Creators Syndicate, Inc. © 1994 Archie Publ., Inc.

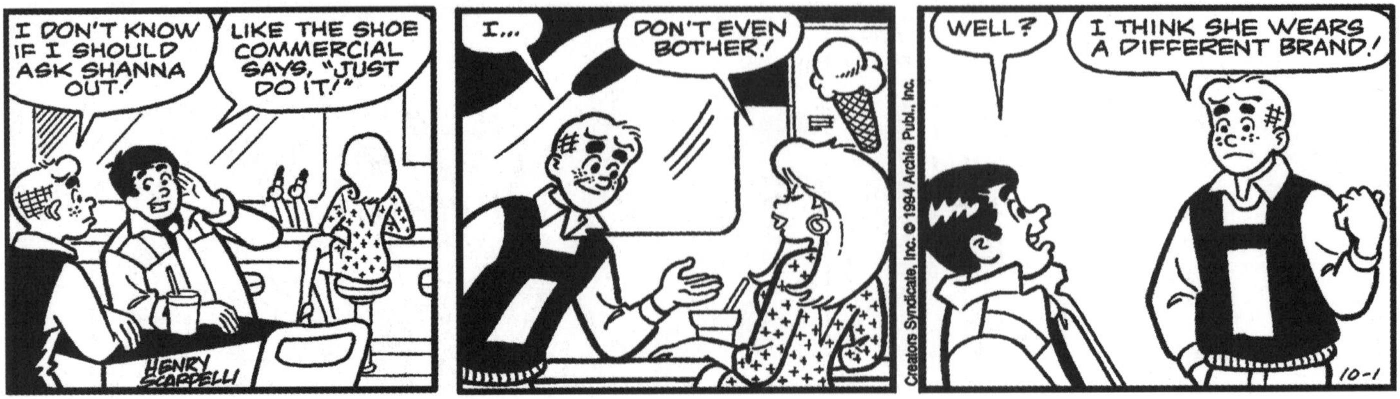
I DON'T KNOW IF I SHOULD ASK SHANNA OUT!
LIKE THE SHOE COMMERCIAL SAYS, "JUST DO IT!"
HENRY SCARPELLI
I...
DON'T EVEN BOTHER!
WELL?
I THINK SHE WEARS A DIFFERENT BRAND!
10-1
Creators Syndicate, Inc. © 1994 Archie Publ., Inc.

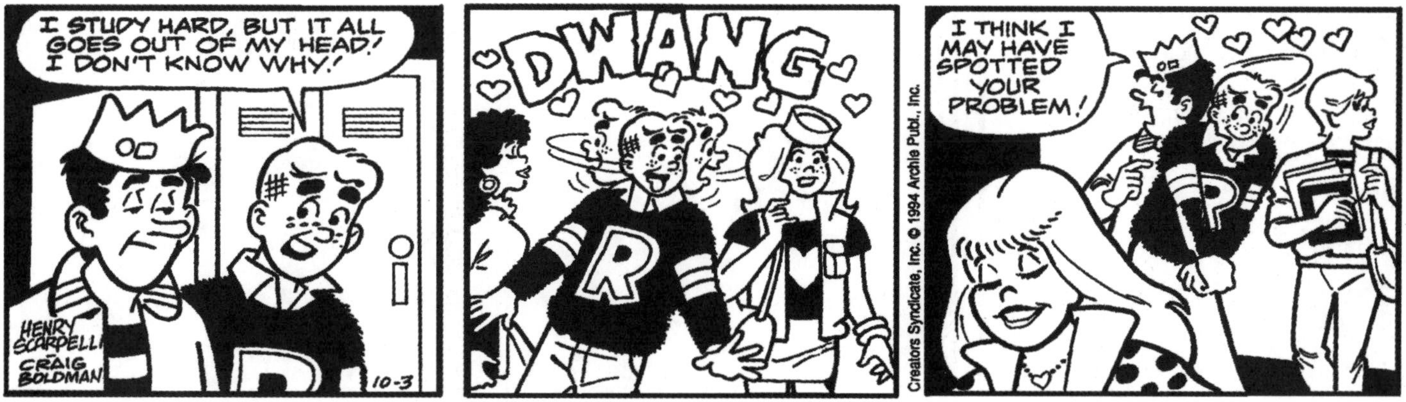
I STUDY HARD, BUT IT ALL GOES OUT OF MY HEAD! I DON'T KNOW WHY!
HENRY SCARPELLI
CRAIG BOLDMAN
10-3
DWANG
Creators Syndicate, Inc. © 1994 Archie Publ., Inc.
I THINK I MAY HAVE SPOTTED YOUR PROBLEM!

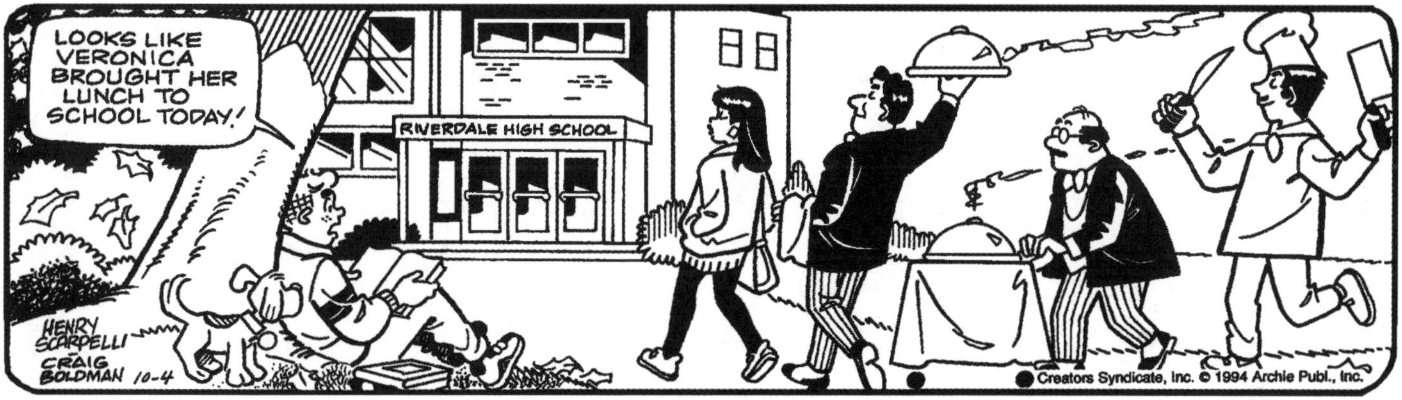
LOOKS LIKE VERONICA BROUGHT HER LUNCH TO SCHOOL TODAY!
RIVERDALE HIGH SCHOOL
HENRY SCARPELLI
CRAIG BOLDMAN
10-4
Creators Syndicate, Inc. © 1994 Archie Publ., Inc.

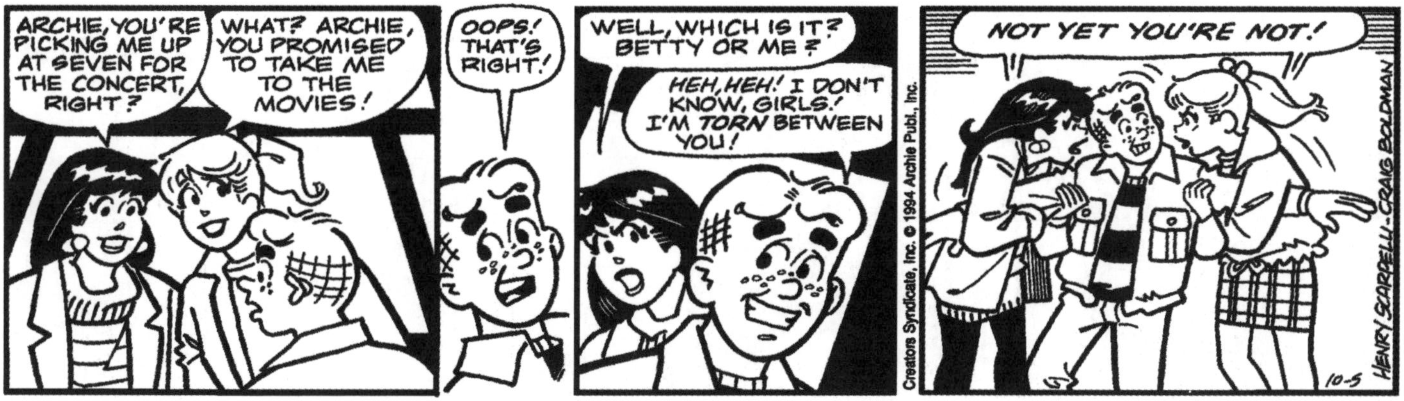
ARCHIE, YOU'RE PICKING ME UP AT SEVEN FOR THE CONCERT, RIGHT?
WHAT? ARCHIE, YOU PROMISED TO TAKE ME TO THE MOVIES!
OOPS! THAT'S RIGHT!
WELL, WHICH IS IT? BETTY OR ME?
HEH, HEH! I DON'T KNOW, GIRLS! I'M TORN BETWEEN YOU!
Creators Syndicate, Inc. © 1994 Archie Publ., Inc.
NOT YET YOU'RE NOT!
HENRY SCARPELLI · CRAIG BOLDMAN
10-5

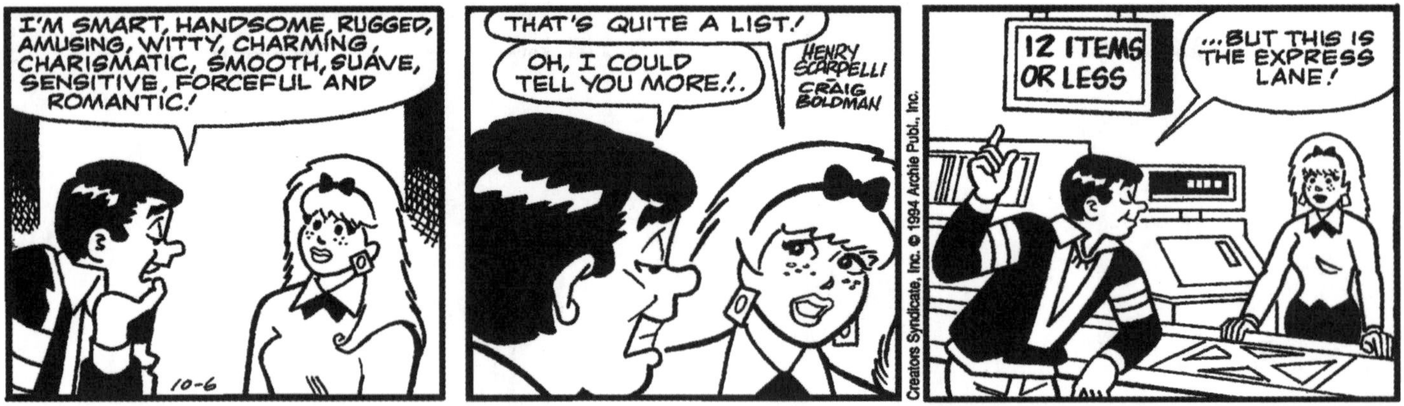
I'M SMART, HANDSOME, RUGGED, AMUSING, WITTY, CHARMING, CHARISMATIC, SMOOTH, SUAVE, SENSITIVE, FORCEFUL AND ROMANTIC!
10-6
THAT'S QUITE A LIST!
OH, I COULD TELL YOU MORE!..
HENRY SCARPELLI
CRAIG BOLDMAN
Creators Syndicate, Inc. © 1994 Archie Publ., Inc.
12 ITEMS OR LESS
...BUT THIS IS THE EXPRESS LANE!

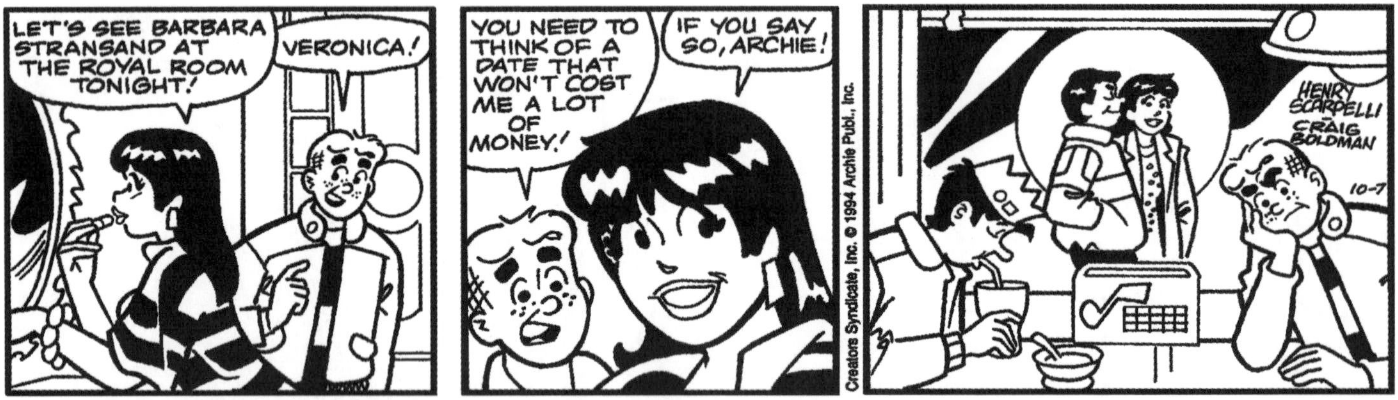
LET'S SEE BARBARA STRANSAND AT THE ROYAL ROOM TONIGHT!
VERONICA!
YOU NEED TO THINK OF A DATE THAT WON'T COST ME A LOT OF MONEY!
IF YOU SAY SO, ARCHIE!
Creators Syndicate, Inc. © 1994 Archie Publ., Inc.
HENRY SCARPELLI
CRAIG BOLDMAN
10-7

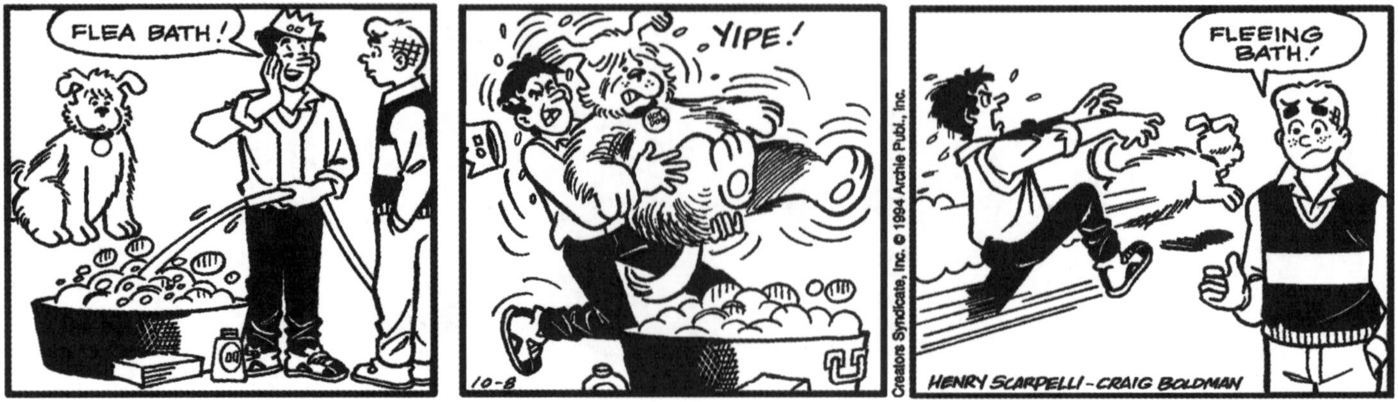
FLEA BATH!
YIPE!
10-8
Creators Syndicate, Inc. © 1994 Archie Publ., Inc.
FLEEING BATH!
HENRY SCARPELLI - CRAIG BOLDMAN

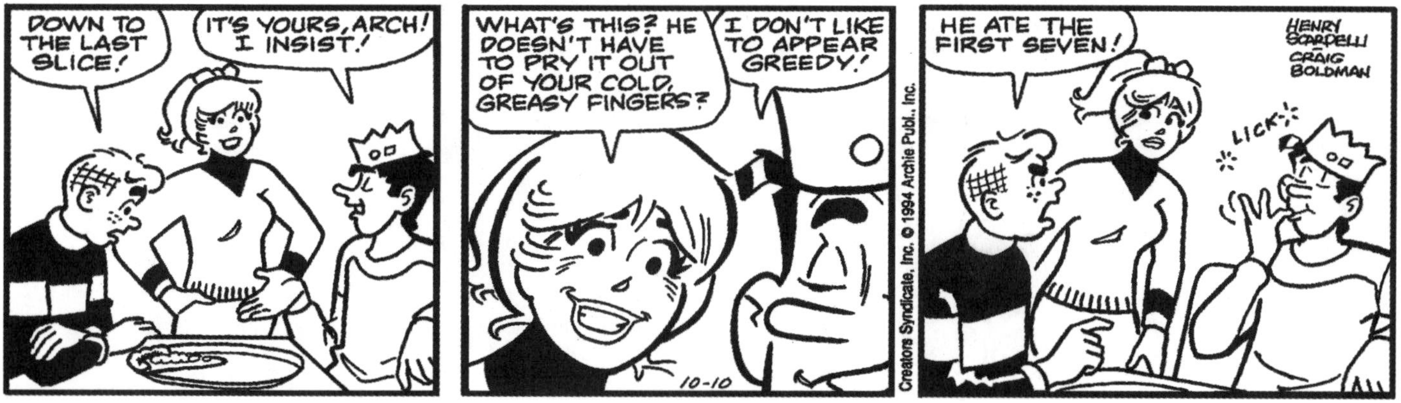
DOWN TO THE LAST SLICE!
IT'S YOURS, ARCH! I INSIST!
WHAT'S THIS? HE DOESN'T HAVE TO PRY IT OUT OF YOUR COLD, GREASY FINGERS?
I DON'T LIKE TO APPEAR GREEDY!
10-10
Creators Syndicate, Inc. © 1994 Archie Publ., Inc.
HE ATE THE FIRST SEVEN!
HENRY SCARPELLI
CRAIG BOLDMAN
LICK

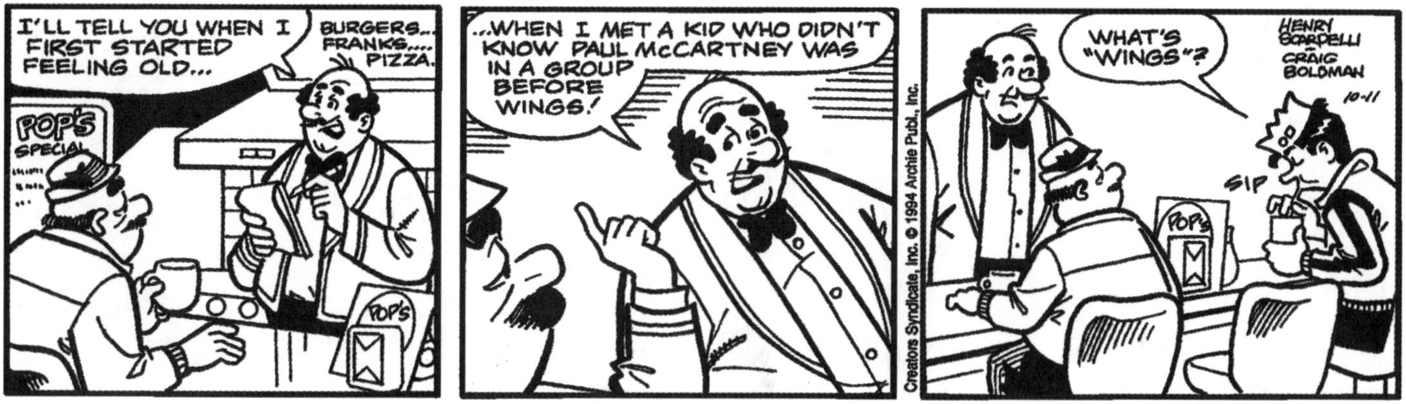
I'LL TELL YOU WHEN I FIRST STARTED FEELING OLD...
BURGERS... FRANKS.... PIZZA.
POP'S SPECIAL
POP'S
...WHEN I MET A KID WHO DIDN'T KNOW PAUL McCARTNEY WAS IN A GROUP BEFORE WINGS!
Creators Syndicate, Inc. © 1994 Archie Publ., Inc.
WHAT'S "WINGS"?
HENRY SCARPELLI
CRAIG BOLDMAN
10-11
SIP
POP'S

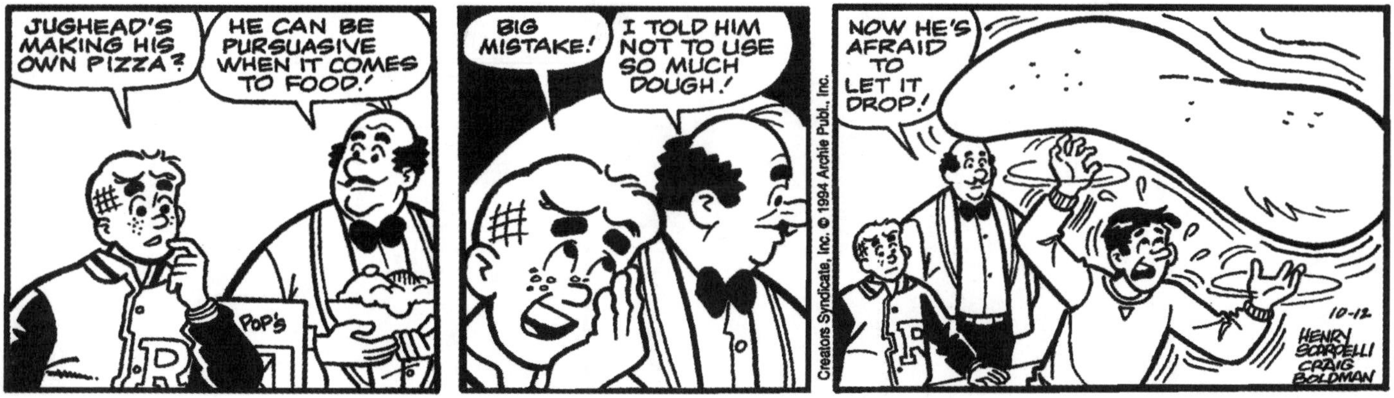
JUGHEAD'S MAKING HIS OWN PIZZA?
HE CAN BE PURSUASIVE WHEN IT COMES TO FOOD!
POP'S
BIG MISTAKE!
I TOLD HIM NOT TO USE SO MUCH DOUGH!
Creators Syndicate, Inc. © 1994 Archie Publ., Inc.
NOW HE'S AFRAID TO LET IT DROP!
10-12
HENRY SCARPELLI
CRAIG BOLDMAN

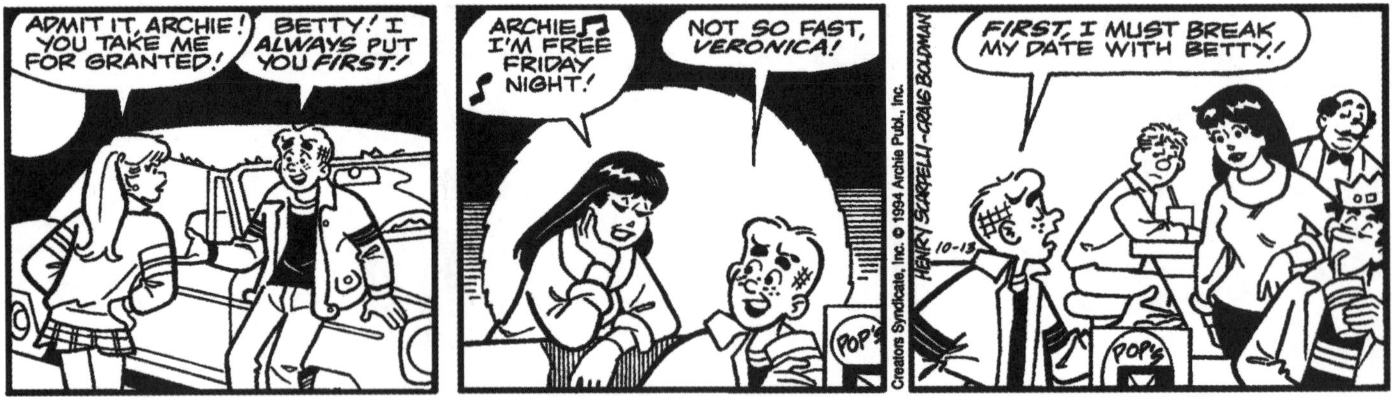
ADMIT IT, ARCHIE! YOU TAKE ME FOR GRANTED!
BETTY! I ALWAYS PUT YOU FIRST!
ARCHIE♫ I'M FREE FRIDAY NIGHT!
NOT SO FAST, VERONICA!
Creators Syndicate, Inc. © 1994 Archie Publ., Inc.
HENRY SCARPELLI–CRAIG BOLDMAN
10-13
FIRST, I MUST BREAK MY DATE WITH BETTY!
POP'S

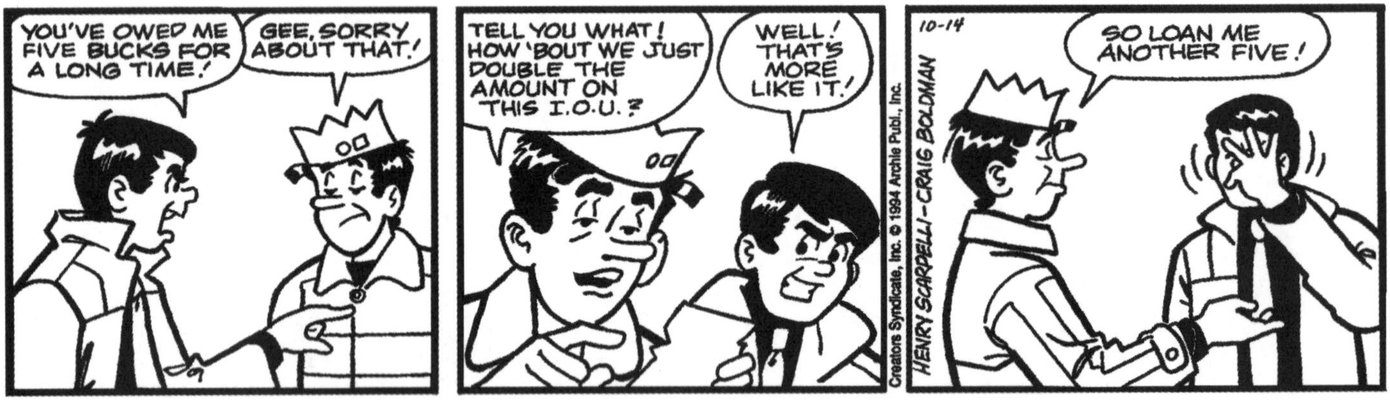
YOU'VE OWED ME FIVE BUCKS FOR A LONG TIME!
GEE, SORRY ABOUT THAT!
TELL YOU WHAT! HOW 'BOUT WE JUST DOUBLE THE AMOUNT ON THIS I.O.U.?
WELL! THAT'S MORE LIKE IT!
Creators Syndicate, Inc. © 1994 Archie Publ., Inc.
HENRY SCARPELLI–CRAIG BOLDMAN
10-14
SO LOAN ME ANOTHER FIVE!

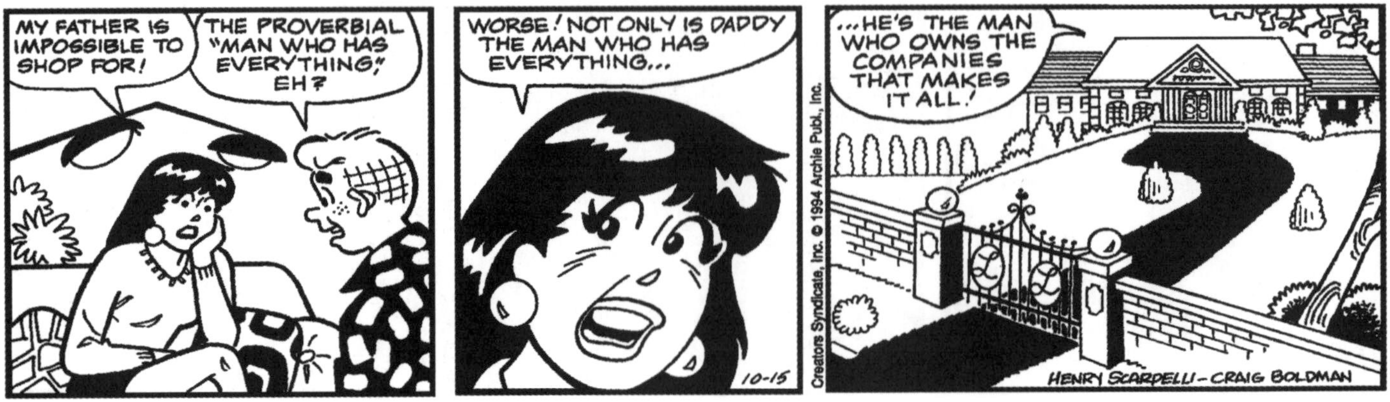
MY FATHER IS IMPOSSIBLE TO SHOP FOR!
THE PROVERBIAL "MAN WHO HAS EVERYTHING," EH?
WORSE! NOT ONLY IS DADDY THE MAN WHO HAS EVERYTHING...
10-15
Creators Syndicate, Inc. © 1994 Archie Publ., Inc.
...HE'S THE MAN WHO OWNS THE COMPANIES THAT MAKES IT ALL!
HENRY SCARPELLI–CRAIG BOLDMAN

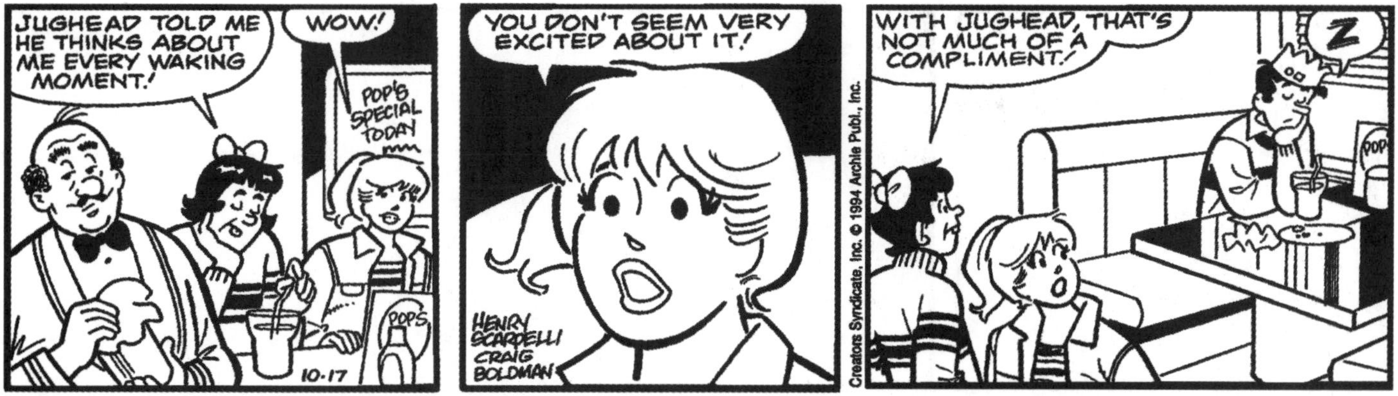
JUGHEAD TOLD ME HE THINKS ABOUT ME EVERY WAKING MOMENT!
WOW!
POP'S SPECIAL TODAY
POP'S
10-17
YOU DON'T SEEM VERY EXCITED ABOUT IT!
HENRY SCARPELLI CRAIG BOLDMAN
Creators Syndicate, Inc. © 1994 Archie Publ., Inc.
WITH JUGHEAD, THAT'S NOT MUCH OF A COMPLIMENT!
Z
POP

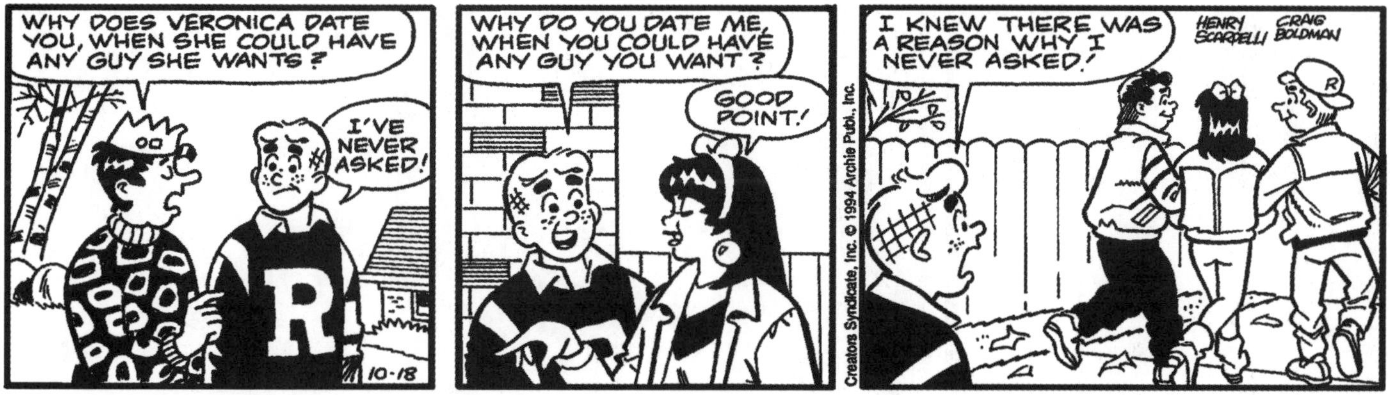
WHY DOES VERONICA DATE YOU, WHEN SHE COULD HAVE ANY GUY SHE WANTS?
I'VE NEVER ASKED!
R
10-18
WHY DO YOU DATE ME, WHEN YOU COULD HAVE ANY GUY YOU WANT?
GOOD POINT!
Creators Syndicate, Inc. © 1994 Archie Publ., Inc.
I KNEW THERE WAS A REASON WHY I NEVER ASKED!
HENRY SCARPELLI CRAIG BOLDMAN
R

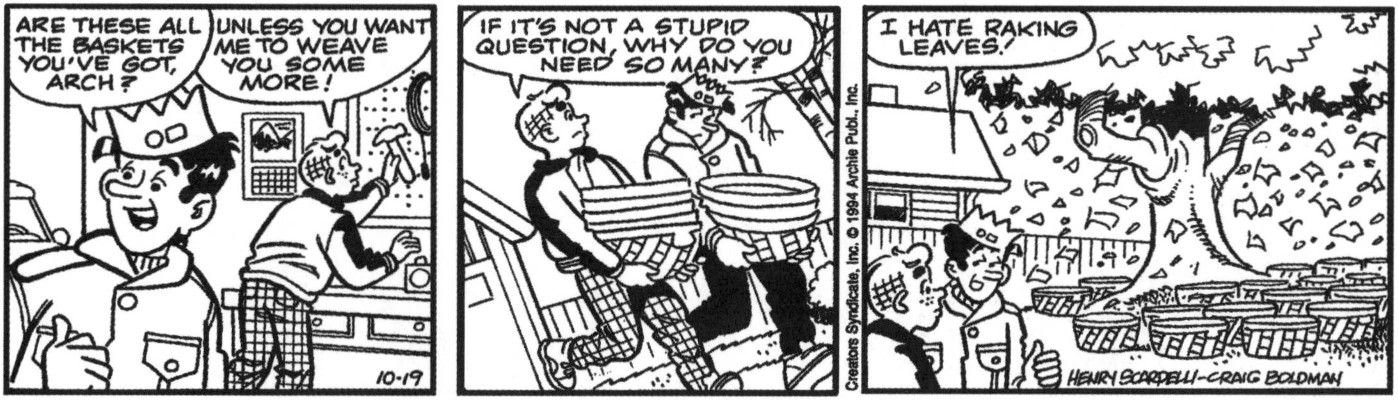
ARE THESE ALL THE BASKETS YOU'VE GOT, ARCH?
UNLESS YOU WANT ME TO WEAVE YOU SOME MORE!
10-19
IF IT'S NOT A STUPID QUESTION, WHY DO YOU NEED SO MANY?
Creators Syndicate, Inc. © 1994 Archie Publ., Inc.
I HATE RAKING LEAVES!
HENRY SCARPELLI-CRAIG BOLDMAN

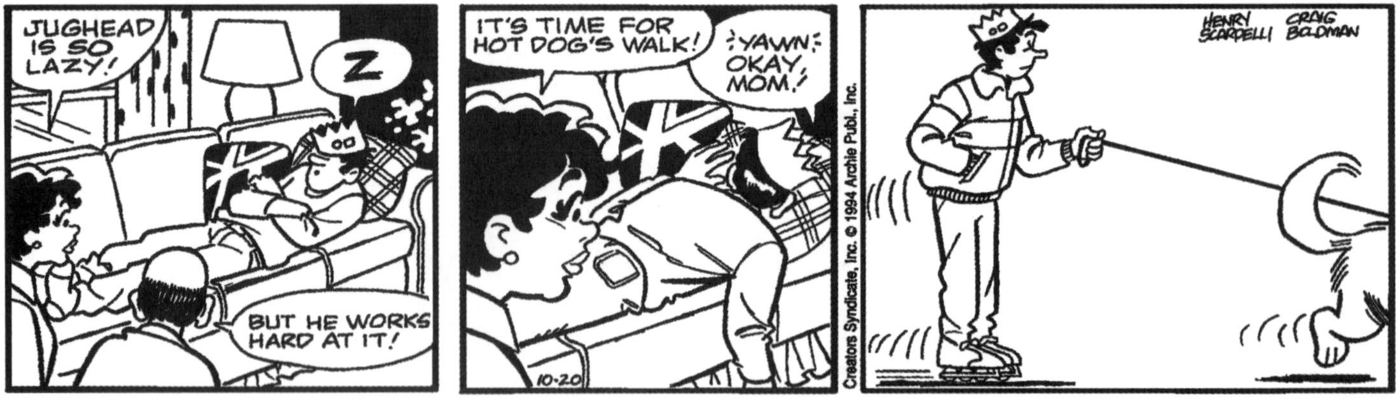
JUGHEAD IS SO LAZY!
Z
BUT HE WORKS HARD AT IT!
IT'S TIME FOR HOT DOG'S WALK!
:YAWN: OKAY, MOM!
10-20
Creators Syndicate, Inc. © 1994 Archie Publ., Inc.
HENRY SCARPELLI CRAIG BOLDMAN

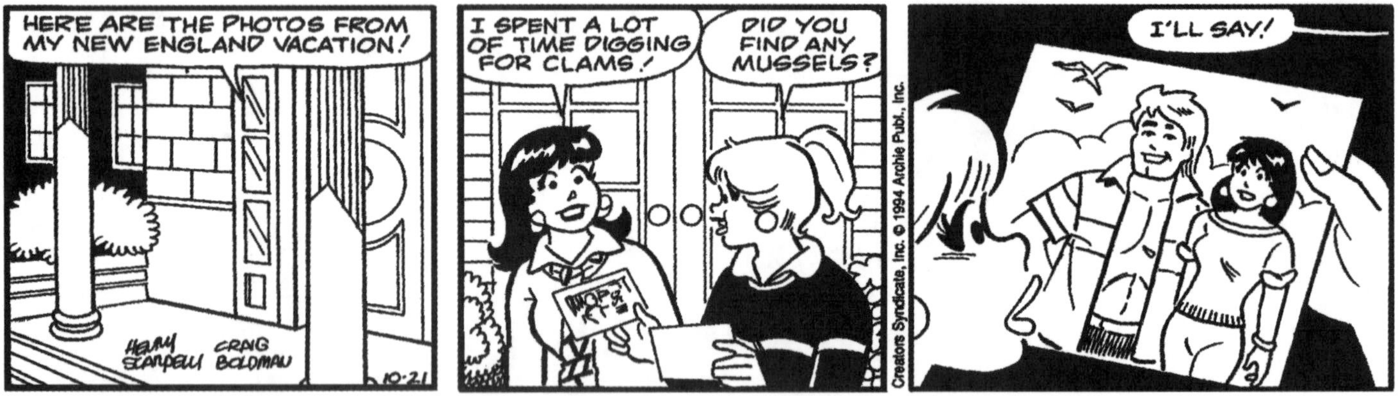
HERE ARE THE PHOTOS FROM MY NEW ENGLAND VACATION!
HENRY SCARPELLI CRAIG BOLDMAN
10-21
I SPENT A LOT OF TIME DIGGING FOR CLAMS!
DID YOU FIND ANY MUSSELS?
Creators Syndicate, Inc. © 1994 Archie Publ., Inc.
I'LL SAY!

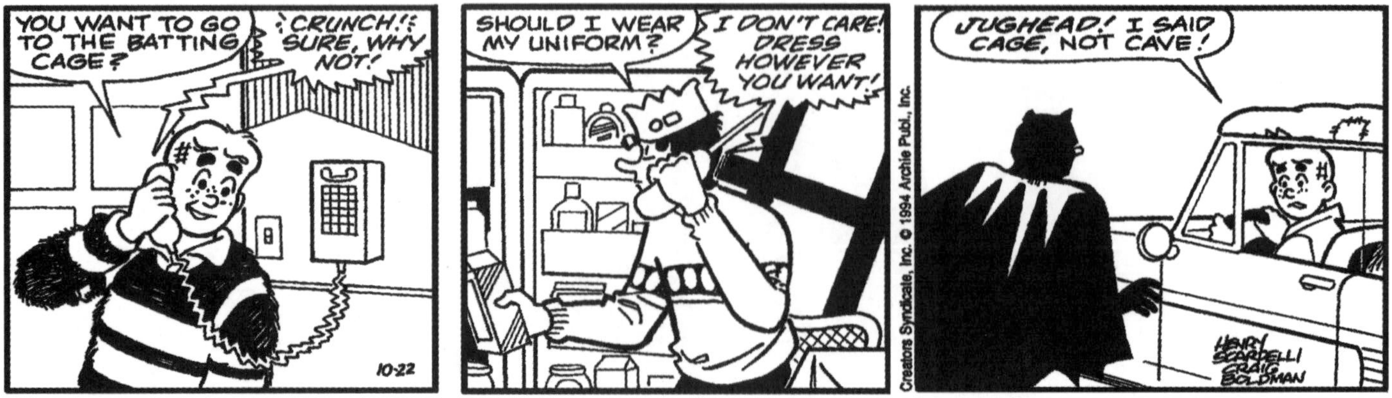
YOU WANT TO GO TO THE BATTING CAGE?
:CRUNCH!: SURE, WHY NOT!
10-22
SHOULD I WEAR MY UNIFORM?
I DON'T CARE! DRESS HOWEVER YOU WANT!
Creators Syndicate, Inc. © 1994 Archie Publ., Inc.
JUGHEAD! I SAID CAGE, NOT CAVE!
HENRY SCARPELLI CRAIG BOLDMAN

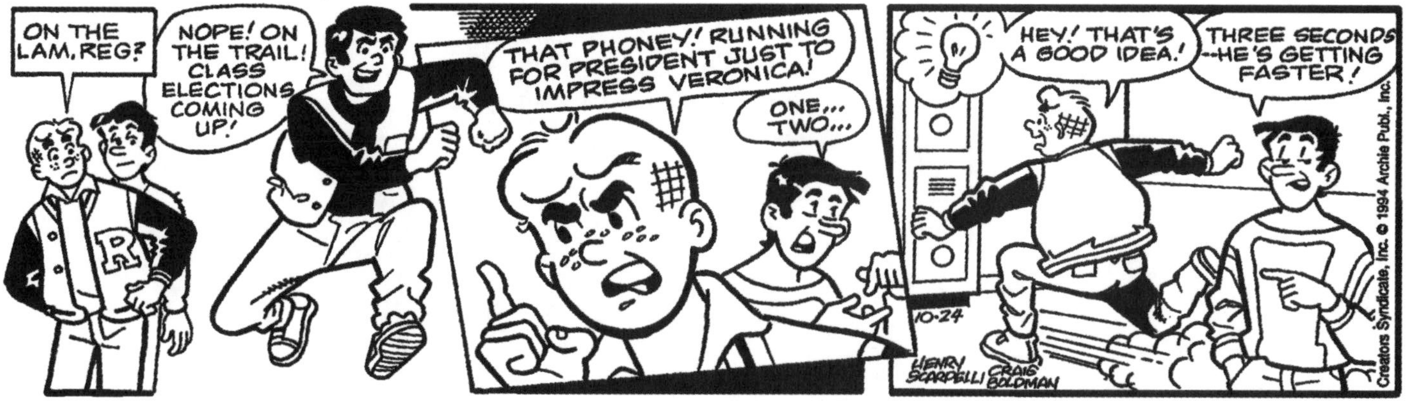
ON THE LAM, REG?
NOPE! ON THE TRAIL! CLASS ELECTIONS COMING UP!
THAT PHONEY! RUNNING FOR PRESIDENT JUST TO IMPRESS VERONICA!
ONE... TWO...
HEY! THAT'S A GOOD IDEA!
THREE SECONDS --HE'S GETTING FASTER!
10-24
HENRY SCARPELLI CRAIG BOLDMAN
Creators Syndicate, Inc. © 1994 Archie Publ., Inc.

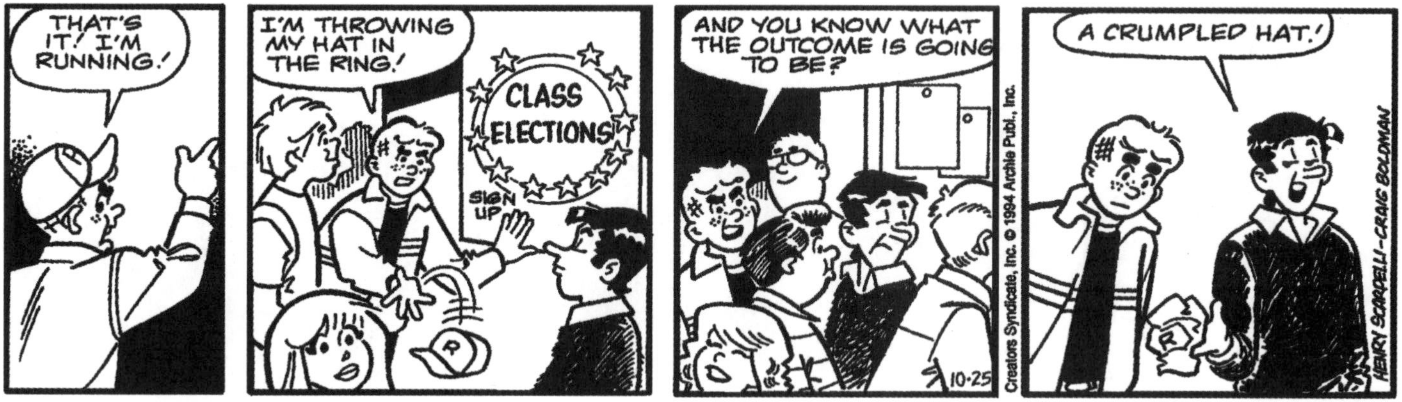
THAT'S IT! I'M RUNNING!
I'M THROWING MY HAT IN THE RING!
CLASS ELECTIONS
SIGN UP
AND YOU KNOW WHAT THE OUTCOME IS GOING TO BE?
10-25
Creators Syndicate, Inc. © 1994 Archie Publ., Inc.
A CRUMPLED HAT!
HENRY SCARPELLI-CRAIG BOLDMAN

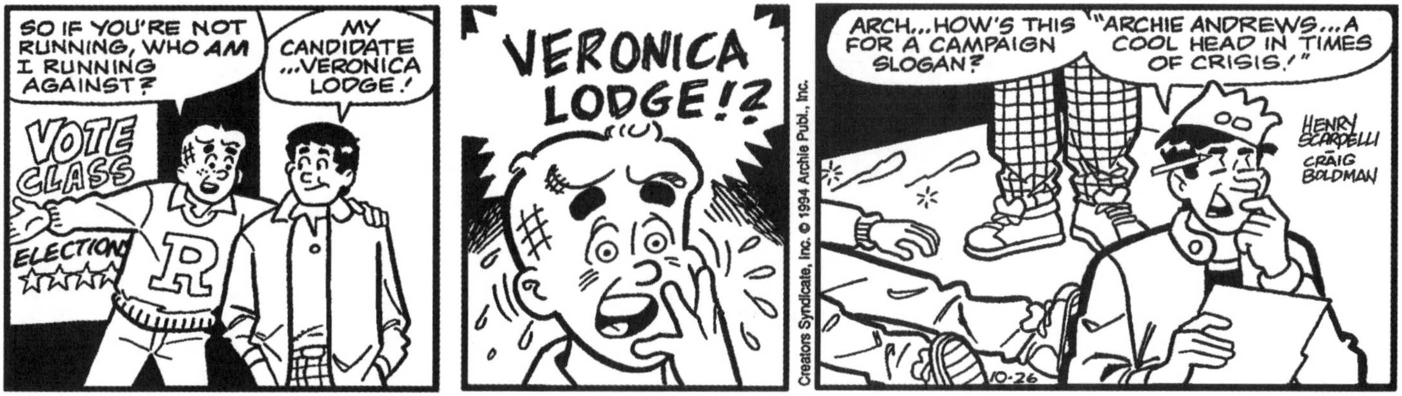
SO IF YOU'RE NOT RUNNING, WHO AM I RUNNING AGAINST?
MY CANDIDATE ...VERONICA LODGE!
VOTE CLASS ELECTION
VERONICA LODGE!?
Creators Syndicate, Inc. © 1994 Archie Publ., Inc.
ARCH... HOW'S THIS FOR A CAMPAIGN SLOGAN?
"ARCHIE ANDREWS... A COOL HEAD IN TIMES OF CRISIS!"
HENRY SCARPELLI - CRAIG BOLDMAN
10-26

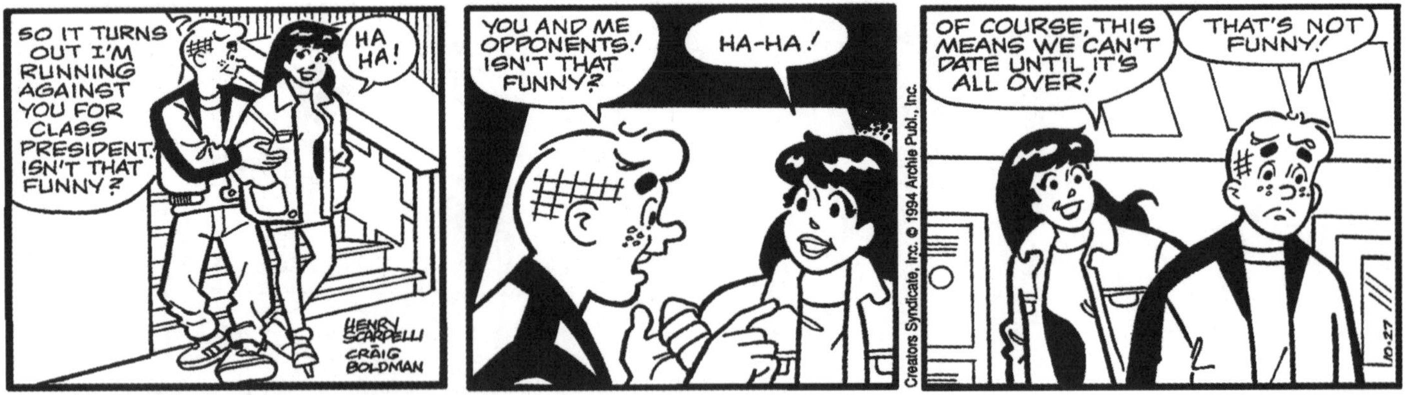
SO IT TURNS OUT I'M RUNNING AGAINST YOU FOR CLASS PRESIDENT! ISN'T THAT FUNNY?
HA HA!
HENRY SCARPELLI
CRAIG BOLDMAN
YOU AND ME OPPONENTS! ISN'T THAT FUNNY?
HA-HA!
Creators Syndicate, Inc. © 1994 Archie Publ., Inc.
OF COURSE, THIS MEANS WE CAN'T DATE UNTIL IT'S ALL OVER!
THAT'S NOT FUNNY!
10-27

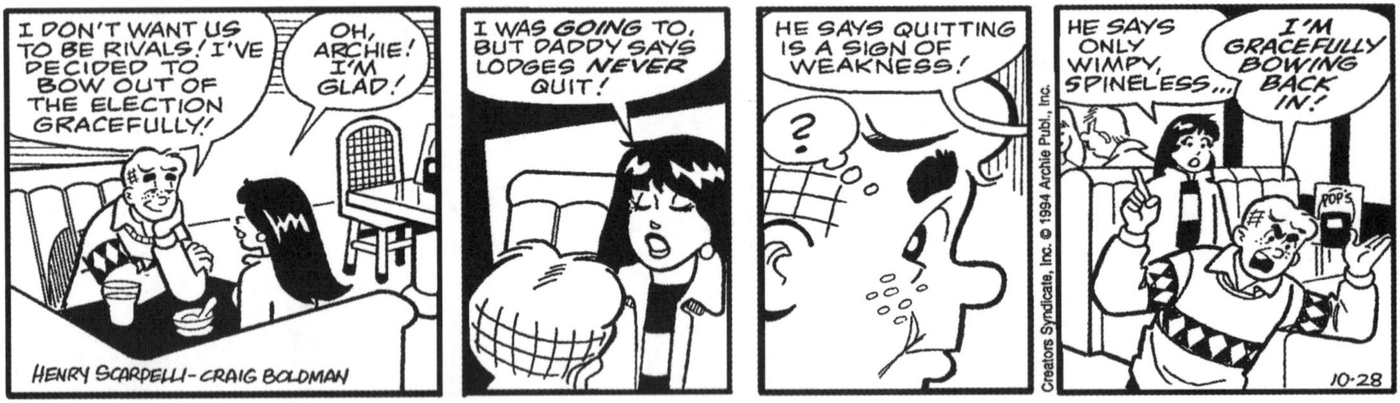
I DON'T WANT US TO BE RIVALS! I'VE DECIDED TO BOW OUT OF THE ELECTION GRACEFULLY!
OH, ARCHIE! I'M GLAD!
HENRY SCARPELLI-CRAIG BOLDMAN
I WAS GOING TO, BUT DADDY SAYS LODGES NEVER QUIT!
HE SAYS QUITTING IS A SIGN OF WEAKNESS!
?
Creators Syndicate, Inc. © 1994 Archie Publ., Inc.
HE SAYS ONLY WIMPY, SPINELESS...
I'M GRACEFULLY BOWING BACK IN!
POP'S
10-28

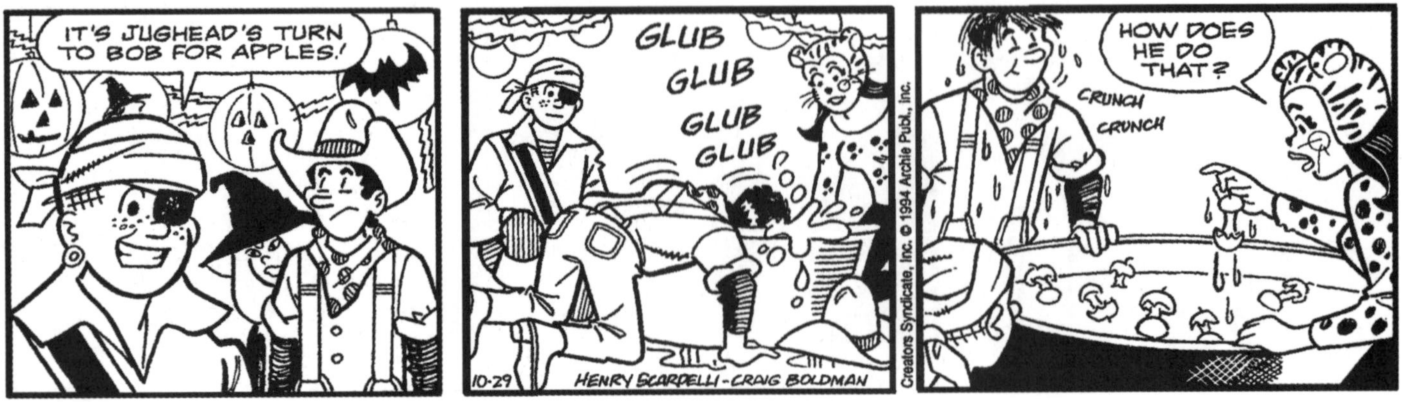
IT'S JUGHEAD'S TURN TO BOB FOR APPLES!
GLUB
GLUB
GLUB
GLUB
10-29
HENRY SCARPELLI-CRAIG BOLDMAN
Creators Syndicate, Inc. © 1994 Archie Publ., Inc.
HOW DOES HE DO THAT?
CRUNCH
CRUNCH

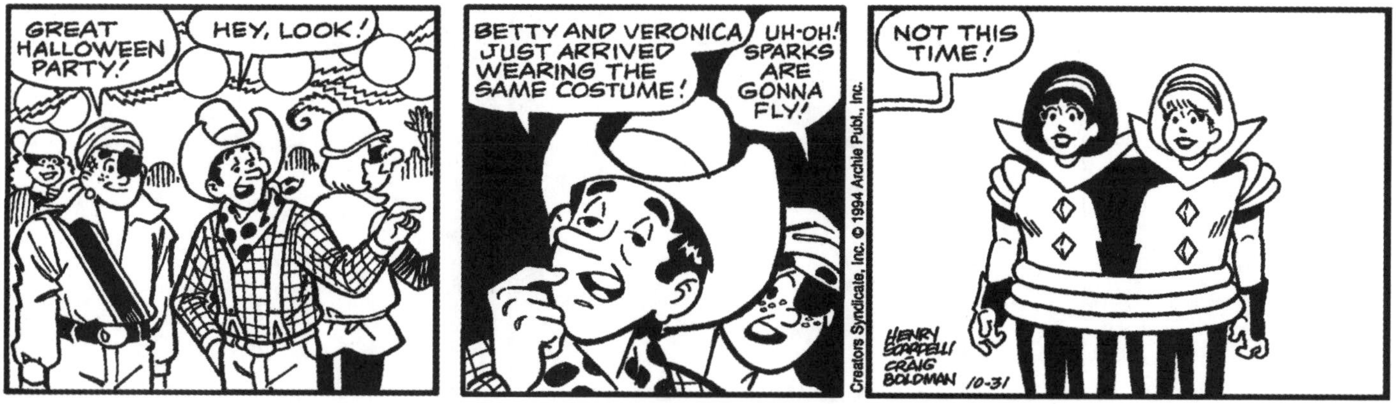
GREAT HALLOWEEN PARTY!
HEY, LOOK!
BETTY AND VERONICA JUST ARRIVED WEARING THE SAME COSTUME!
UH-OH! SPARKS ARE GONNA FLY!
Creators Syndicate, Inc. © 1994 Archie Publ., Inc.
NOT THIS TIME!
HENRY SCARPELLI
CRAIG BOLDMAN 10-31

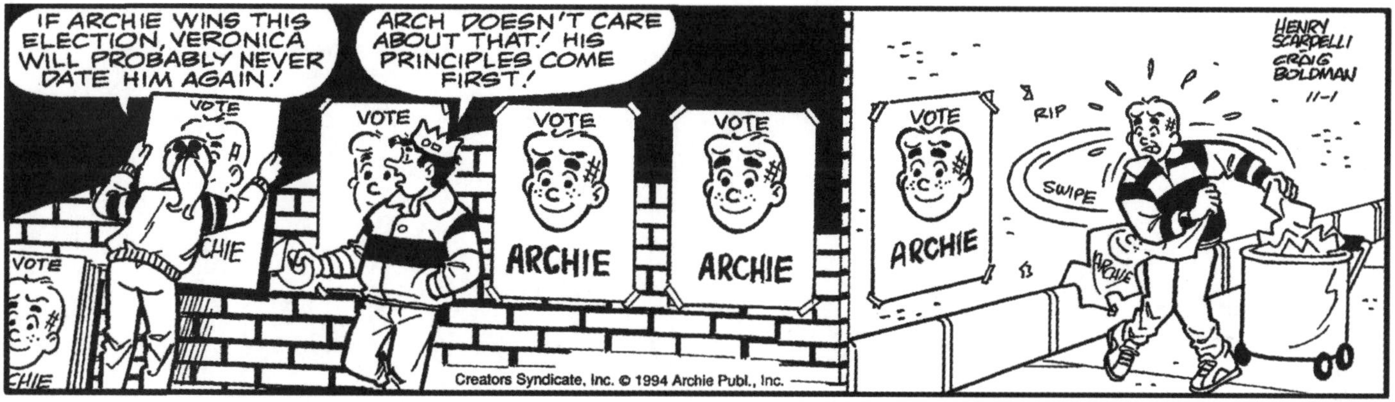
IF ARCHIE WINS THIS ELECTION, VERONICA WILL PROBABLY NEVER DATE HIM AGAIN!
ARCH DOESN'T CARE ABOUT THAT! HIS PRINCIPLES COME FIRST!
VOTE
ARCHIE
VOTE
ARCHIE
Creators Syndicate, Inc. © 1994 Archie Publ., Inc.
HENRY SCARPELLI
CRAIG BOLDMAN 11-1
VOTE
ARCHIE
RIP
SWIPE

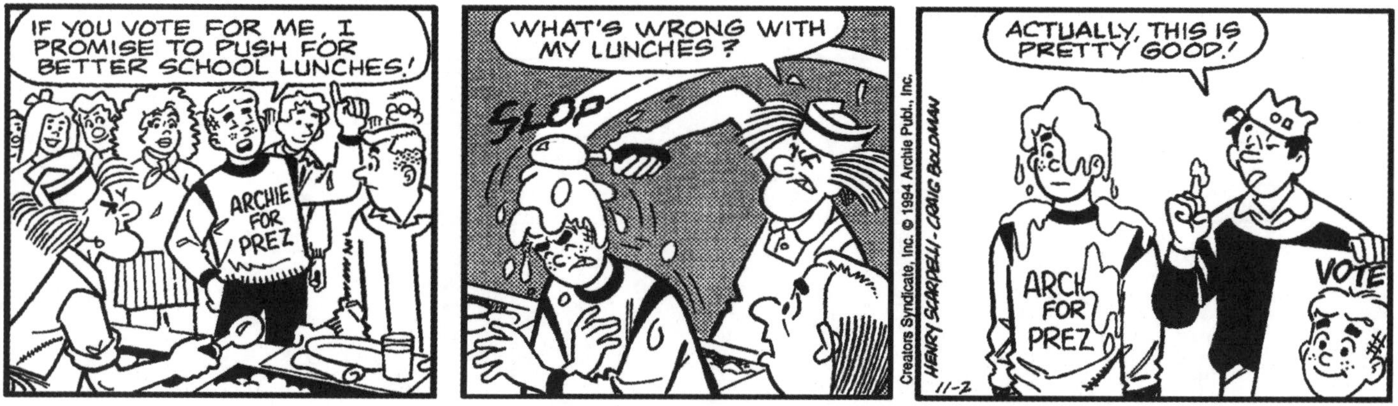
IF YOU VOTE FOR ME, I PROMISE TO PUSH FOR BETTER SCHOOL LUNCHES!
ARCHIE FOR PREZ
WHAT'S WRONG WITH MY LUNCHES?
SLOP
Creators Syndicate, Inc. © 1994 Archie Publ., Inc.
HENRY SCARPELLI - CRAIG BOLDMAN 11-2
ACTUALLY, THIS IS PRETTY GOOD!
ARCH FOR PREZ
VOTE

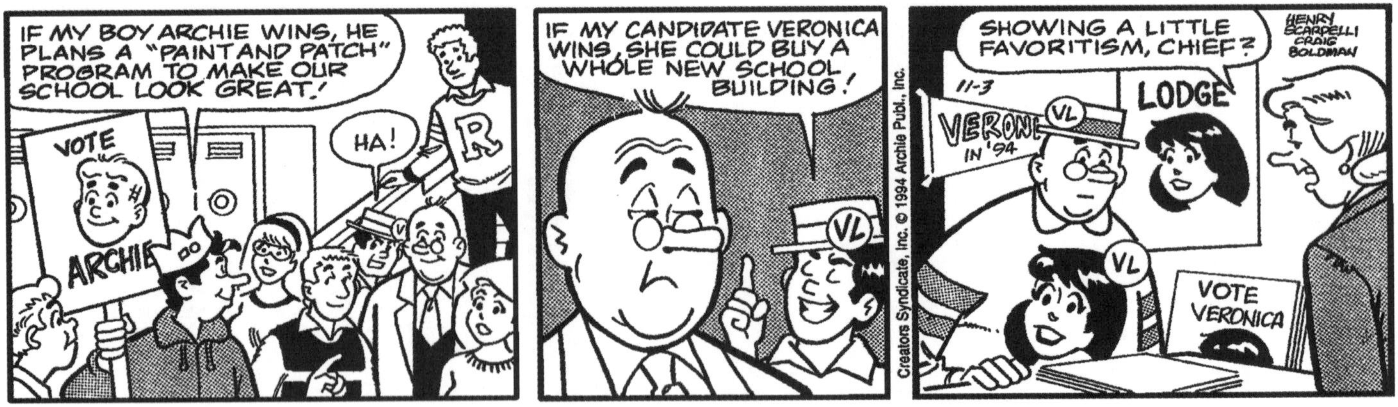
IF MY BOY ARCHIE WINS, HE PLANS A "PAINT AND PATCH" PROGRAM TO MAKE OUR SCHOOL LOOK GREAT!
HA!
VOTE ARCHIE
R
IF MY CANDIDATE VERONICA WINS, SHE COULD BUY A WHOLE NEW SCHOOL BUILDING!
VL
Creators Syndicate, Inc. © 1994 Archie Publ., Inc.
SHOWING A LITTLE FAVORITISM, CHIEF?
HENRY SCARPELLI CRAIG BOLDMAN
11-3
LODGE
IN '94
VL
VOTE VERONICA

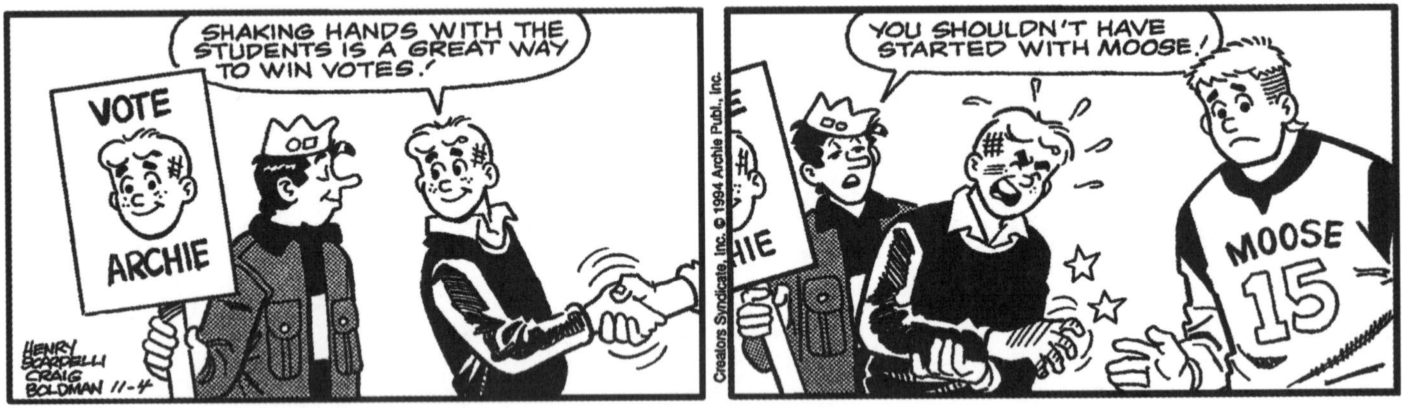
SHAKING HANDS WITH THE STUDENTS IS A GREAT WAY TO WIN VOTES!
VOTE ARCHIE
HENRY SCARPELLI CRAIG BOLDMAN 11-4
Creators Syndicate, Inc. © 1994 Archie Publ., Inc.
YOU SHOULDN'T HAVE STARTED WITH MOOSE!
MOOSE 15

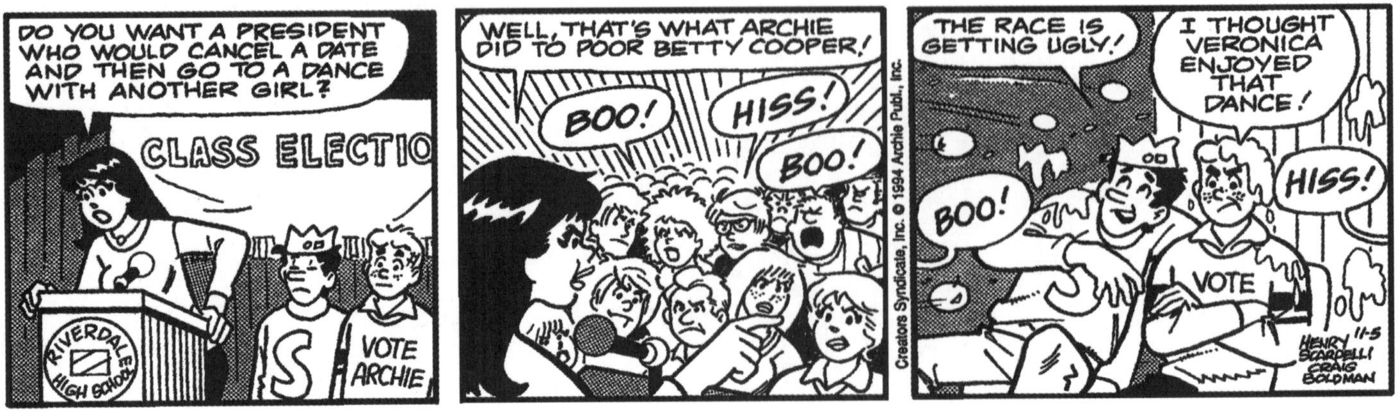
DO YOU WANT A PRESIDENT WHO WOULD CANCEL A DATE AND THEN GO TO A DANCE WITH ANOTHER GIRL?
CLASS ELECTIO
RIVERDALE HIGH SCHOOL
S
VOTE ARCHIE
WELL, THAT'S WHAT ARCHIE DID TO POOR BETTY COOPER!
BOO!
HISS!
BOO!
Creators Syndicate, Inc. © 1994 Archie Publ., Inc.
THE RACE IS GETTING UGLY!
I THOUGHT VERONICA ENJOYED THAT DANCE!
BOO!
HISS!
VOTE
HENRY SCARPELLI CRAIG BOLDMAN 11-5

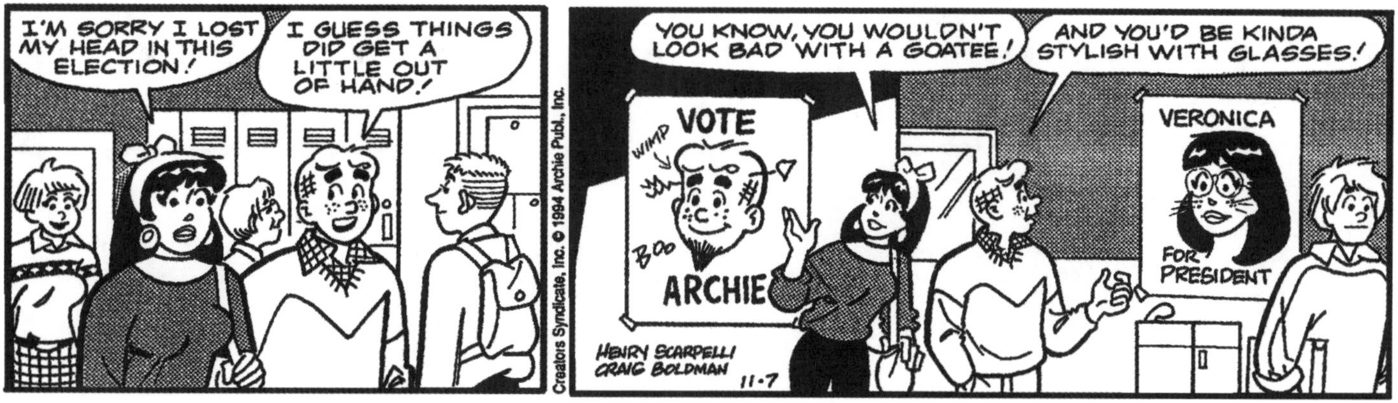
I'M SORRY I LOST MY HEAD IN THIS ELECTION!
I GUESS THINGS DID GET A LITTLE OUT OF HAND!
YOU KNOW, YOU WOULDN'T LOOK BAD WITH A GOATEE!
AND YOU'D BE KINDA STYLISH WITH GLASSES!
VOTE
WIMP
BOO
ARCHIE
VERONICA
FOR PRESIDENT
HENRY SCARPELLI
CRAIG BOLDMAN
11-7
Creators Syndicate, Inc. © 1994 Archie Publ., Inc.

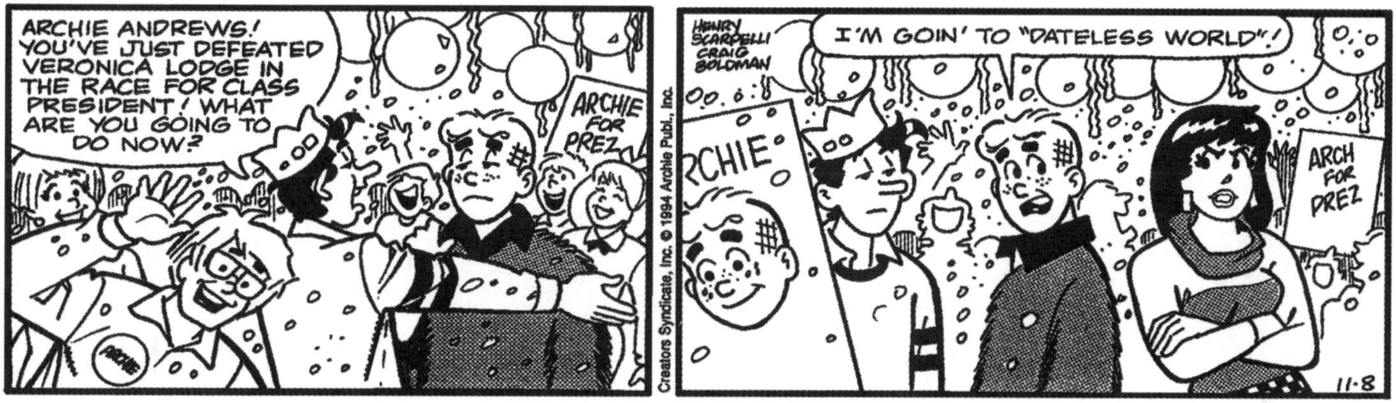
ARCHIE ANDREWS! YOU'VE JUST DEFEATED VERONICA LODGE IN THE RACE FOR CLASS PRESIDENT! WHAT ARE YOU GOING TO DO NOW?
ARCHIE FOR PREZ
ARCHIE
Creators Syndicate, Inc. © 1994 Archie Publ., Inc.
HENRY SCARPELLI
CRAIG BOLDMAN
I'M GOIN' TO "DATELESS WORLD"!
RCHIE
ARCH FOR PREZ
11-8

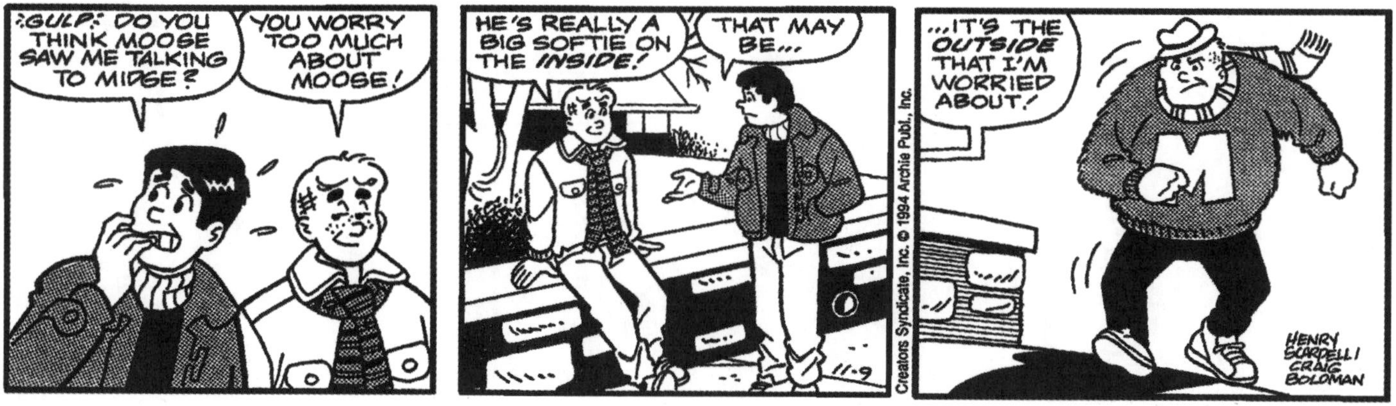
GULP DO YOU THINK MOOSE SAW ME TALKING TO MIDGE?
YOU WORRY TOO MUCH ABOUT MOOSE!
HE'S REALLY A BIG SOFTIE ON THE INSIDE!
THAT MAY BE...
11-9
Creators Syndicate, Inc. © 1994 Archie Publ., Inc.
...IT'S THE OUTSIDE THAT I'M WORRIED ABOUT!
M
HENRY SCARPELLI
CRAIG BOLDMAN

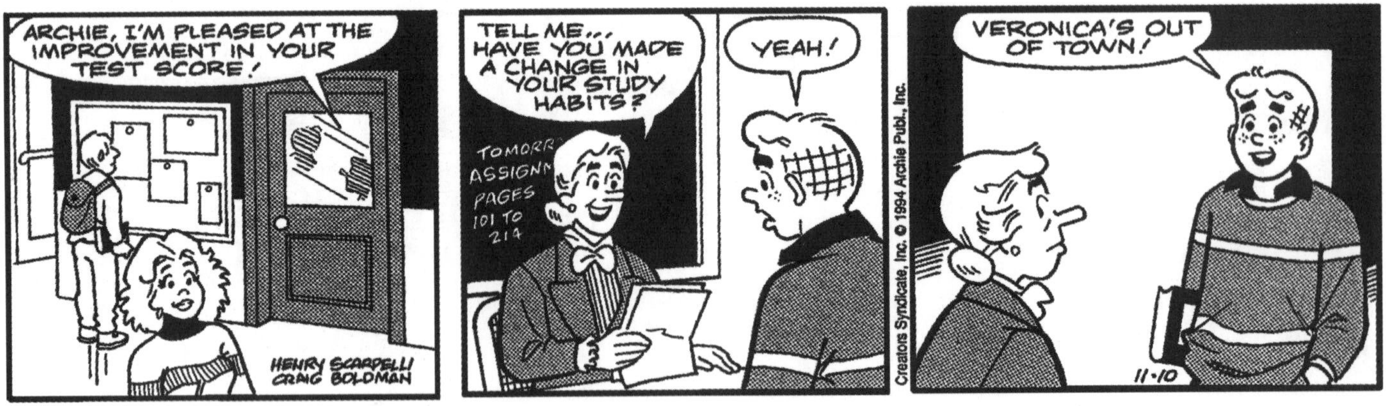
ARCHIE, I'M PLEASED AT THE IMPROVEMENT IN YOUR TEST SCORE!
HENRY SCARPELLI
CRAIG BOLDMAN
TELL ME... HAVE YOU MADE A CHANGE IN YOUR STUDY HABITS?
TOMORR
ASSIGNM
PAGES
101 TO
214
YEAH!
Creators Syndicate, Inc. © 1994 Archie Publ., Inc.
VERONICA'S OUT OF TOWN!
11-10

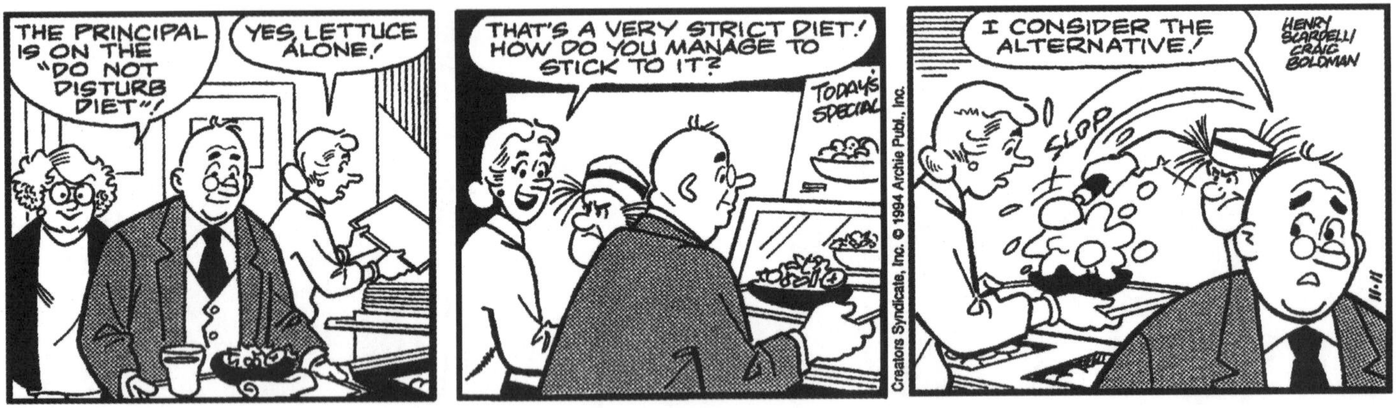
THE PRINCIPAL IS ON THE "DO NOT DISTURB DIET"!
YES, LETTUCE ALONE!
THAT'S A VERY STRICT DIET! HOW DO YOU MANAGE TO STICK TO IT?
TODAY'S SPECIAL
Creators Syndicate, Inc. © 1994 Archie Publ., Inc.
I CONSIDER THE ALTERNATIVE!
HENRY SCARPELLI
CRAIG BOLDMAN
SLOP
11-11

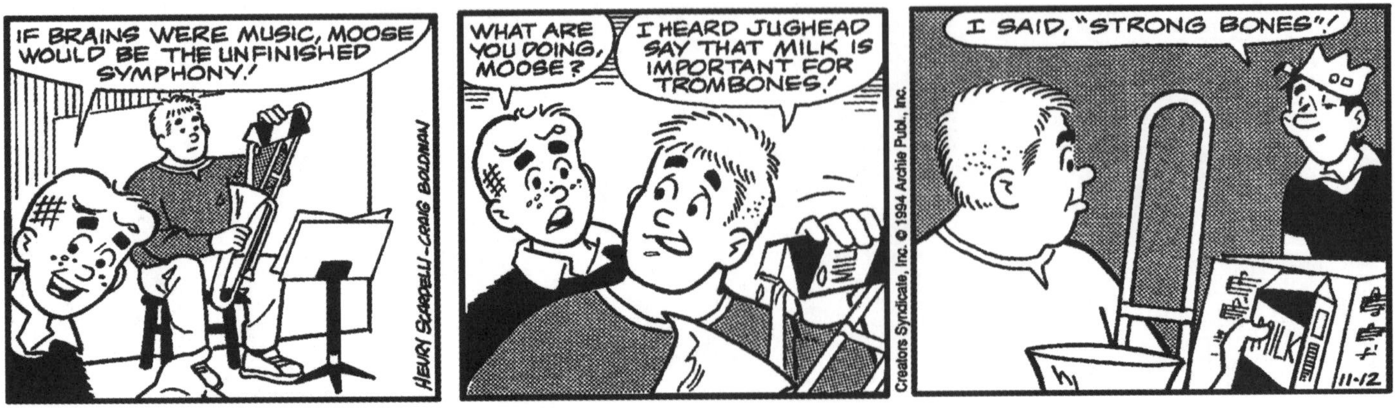
IF BRAINS WERE MUSIC, MOOSE WOULD BE THE UNFINISHED SYMPHONY!
HENRY SCARPELLI-CRAIG BOLDMAN
WHAT ARE YOU DOING, MOOSE?
I HEARD JUGHEAD SAY THAT MILK IS IMPORTANT FOR TROMBONES!
Creators Syndicate, Inc. © 1994 Archie Publ., Inc.
I SAID, "STRONG BONES"!
MILK
11-12

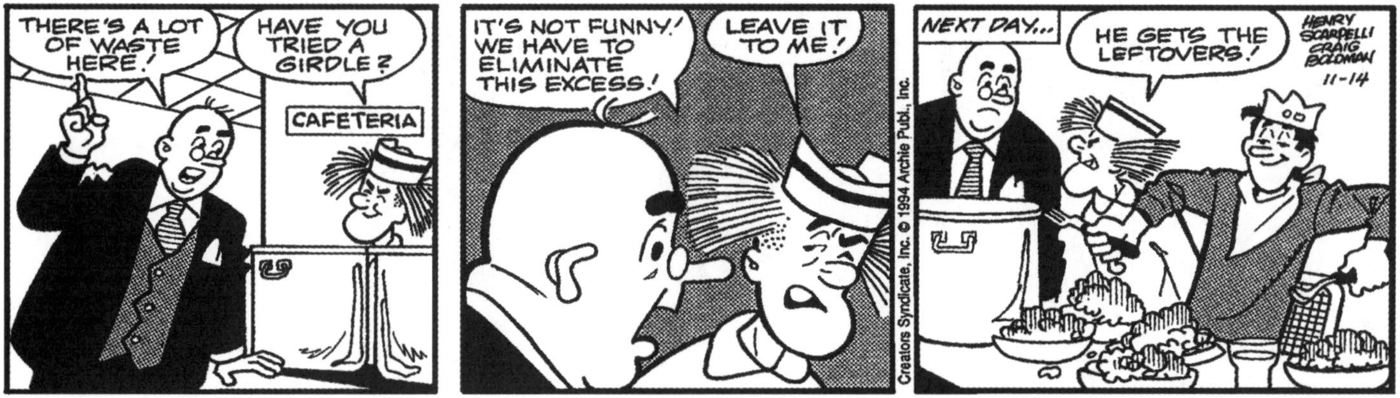
THERE'S A LOT OF WASTE HERE!
HAVE YOU TRIED A GIRDLE?
CAFETERIA
IT'S NOT FUNNY! WE HAVE TO ELIMINATE THIS EXCESS!
LEAVE IT TO ME!
Creators Syndicate, Inc. © 1994 Archie Publ., Inc.
NEXT DAY...
HE GETS THE LEFTOVERS!
HENRY SCARPELLI CRAIG BOLDMAN
11-14

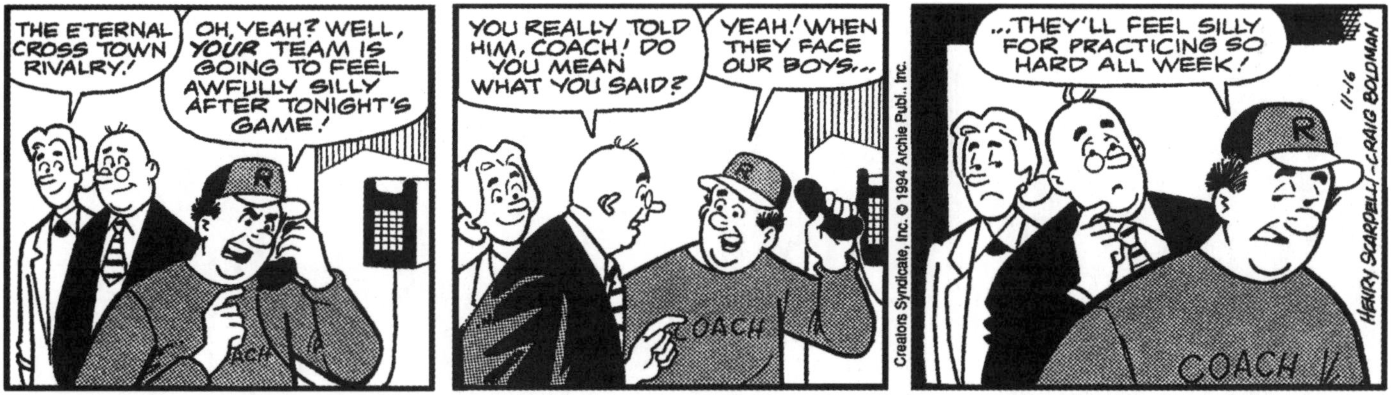
THE ETERNAL CROSS TOWN RIVALRY!
OH, YEAH? WELL, YOUR TEAM IS GOING TO FEEL AWFULLY SILLY AFTER TONIGHT'S GAME!
YOU REALLY TOLD HIM, COACH! DO YOU MEAN WHAT YOU SAID?
YEAH! WHEN THEY FACE OUR BOYS...
COACH
Creators Syndicate, Inc. © 1994 Archie Publ., Inc.
...THEY'LL FEEL SILLY FOR PRACTICING SO HARD ALL WEEK!
11-16
HENRY SCARPELLI - CRAIG BOLDMAN
COACH

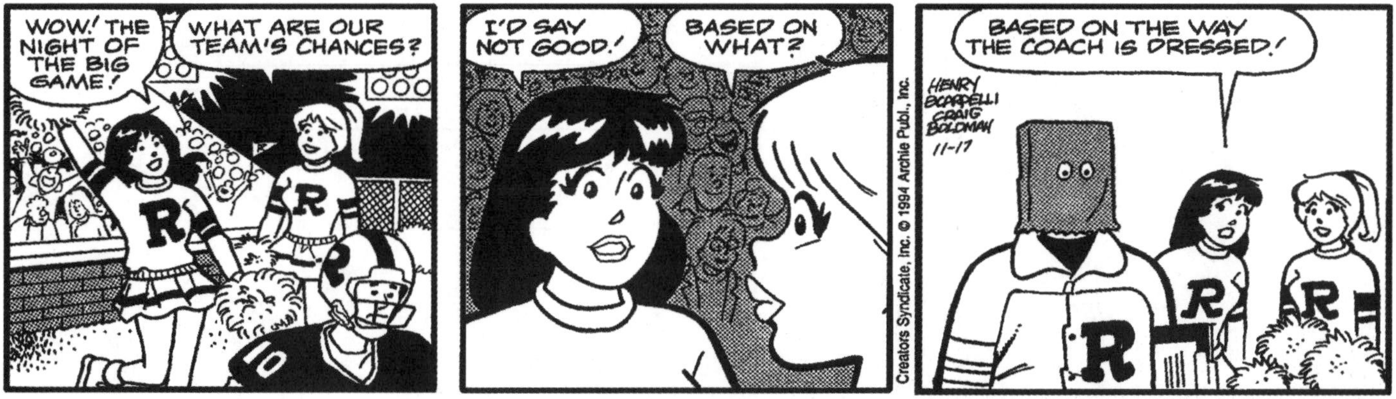
WOW! THE NIGHT OF THE BIG GAME!
WHAT ARE OUR TEAM'S CHANCES?
I'D SAY NOT GOOD!
BASED ON WHAT?
Creators Syndicate, Inc. © 1994 Archie Publ., Inc.
HENRY SCARPELLI CRAIG BOLDMAN
11-17
BASED ON THE WAY THE COACH IS DRESSED!

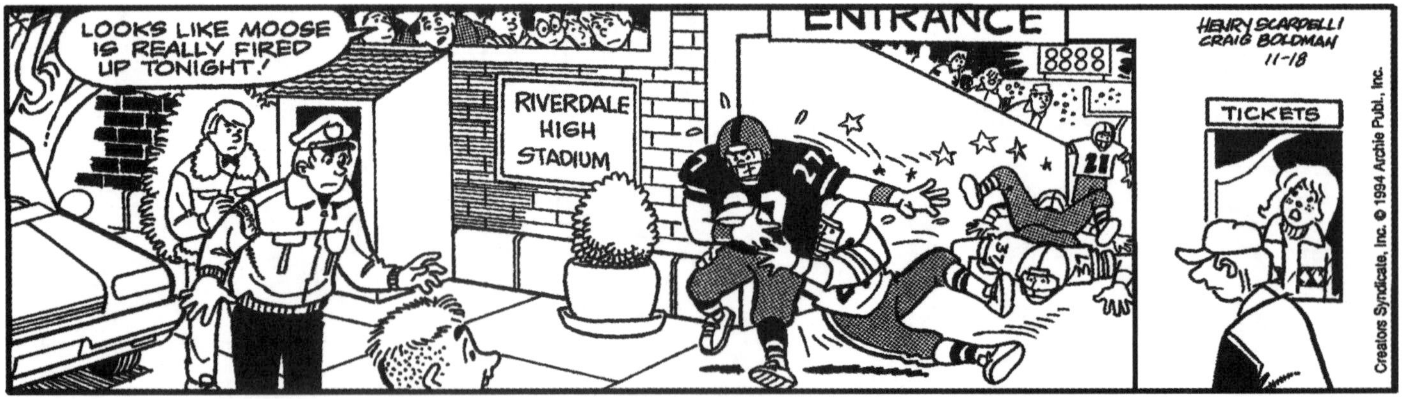
LOOKS LIKE MOOSE IS REALLY FIRED UP TONIGHT!
ENTRANCE
RIVERDALE HIGH STADIUM
TICKETS
HENRY SCARPELLI
CRAIG BOLDMAN
11-18
Creators Syndicate, Inc. © 1994 Archie Publ., Inc.

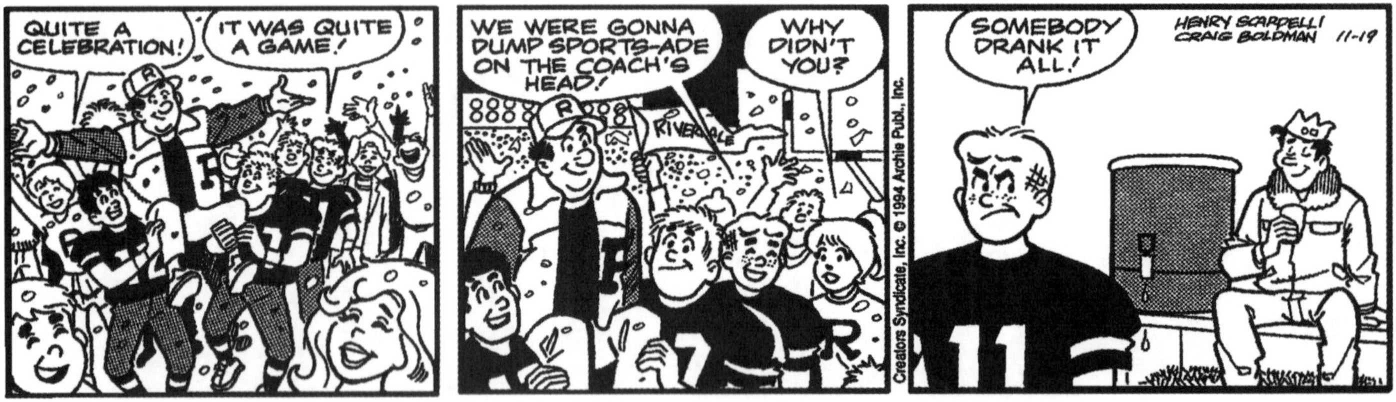
QUITE A CELEBRATION!
IT WAS QUITE A GAME!
WE WERE GONNA DUMP SPORTS-ADE ON THE COACH'S HEAD!
WHY DIDN'T YOU?
RIVERDALE
Creators Syndicate, Inc. © 1994 Archie Publ., Inc.
SOMEBODY DRANK IT ALL!
HENRY SCARPELLI
CRAIG BOLDMAN
11-19

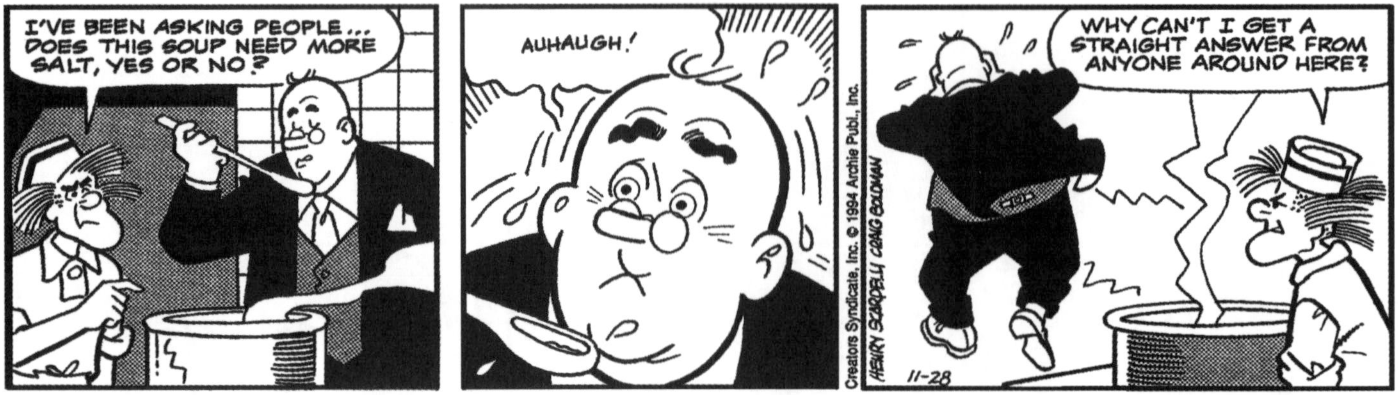
I'VE BEEN ASKING PEOPLE... DOES THIS SOUP NEED MORE SALT, YES OR NO?
AUHAUGH!
Creators Syndicate, Inc. © 1994 Archie Publ., Inc.
HENRY SCARPELLI CRAIG BOLDMAN
11-28
WHY CAN'T I GET A STRAIGHT ANSWER FROM ANYONE AROUND HERE?

DOCTOR SAYS DADDY NEEDS TO RELAX!

ENVIRONMENTAL SOUNDS! I'LL LOSE MYSELF IN THE OCEAN WAVES!

AH! I FEEL LIKE I'M DANGLING MY TOOTSIES IN THE WATER OFF THE BEACH AT CANCUN!

11-29

HENRY SCARPELLI CRAIG BOLDMAN

Creators Syndicate, Inc. © 1994 Archie Publ., Inc.

DOESN'T THAT MOUSTACHE HOLD A LOT OF SOUP?

YA, BUT WE SVENSONS ALWAYS WEAR DER LONG MOUSTACHE!

MOUSTACHE WAX WOULD KEEP IT OUT OF THE WAY!

DAT BE GOOD IDEA! I DO IT TOMORROW!

11-30

NOW I CAN'T SEE ANYTHING!

HENRY SCARPELLI CRAIG BOLDMAN

CAFETERIA TODAY'S MENU

Creators Syndicate, Inc. © 1994 Archie Publ., Inc.

Jughead®

I DON'T WANT TO SEE YOU EATING IN THE HALLS BETWEEN CLASSES ANYMORE!

YES'M!

CRUNCH CRUNCH CHOMP!

12-1

HENRY SCARPELLI CRAIG BOLDMAN

Creators Syndicate, Inc. © 1994 Archie Publ., Inc.

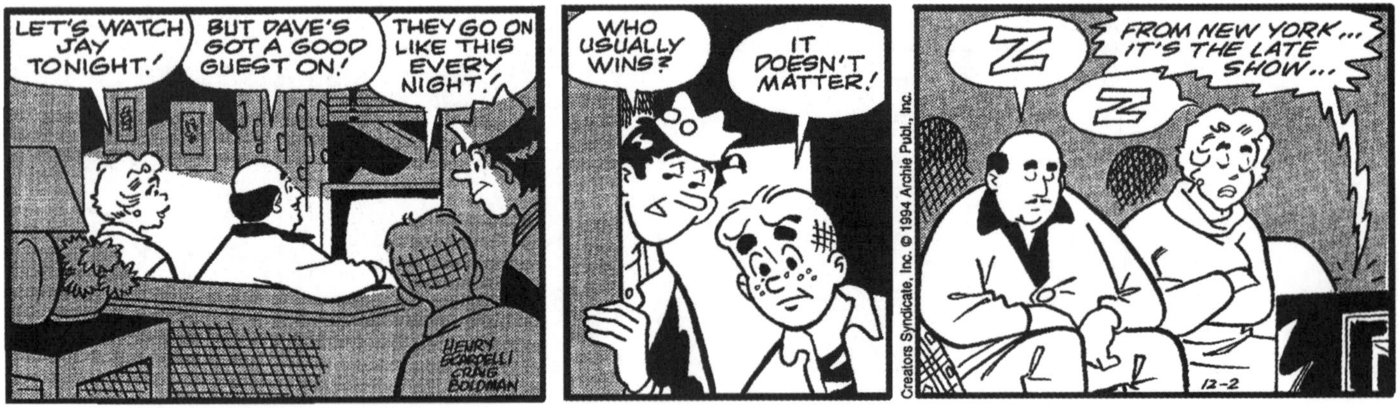
LET'S WATCH JAY TONIGHT.!
BUT DAVE'S GOT A GOOD GUEST ON!
THEY GO ON LIKE THIS EVERY NIGHT!
HENRY SCARPELLI CRAIG BOLDMAN
WHO USUALLY WINS?
IT DOESN'T MATTER!
Creators Syndicate, Inc. © 1994 Archie Publ., Inc.
Z
Z
FROM NEW YORK... IT'S THE LATE SHOW...
12-2

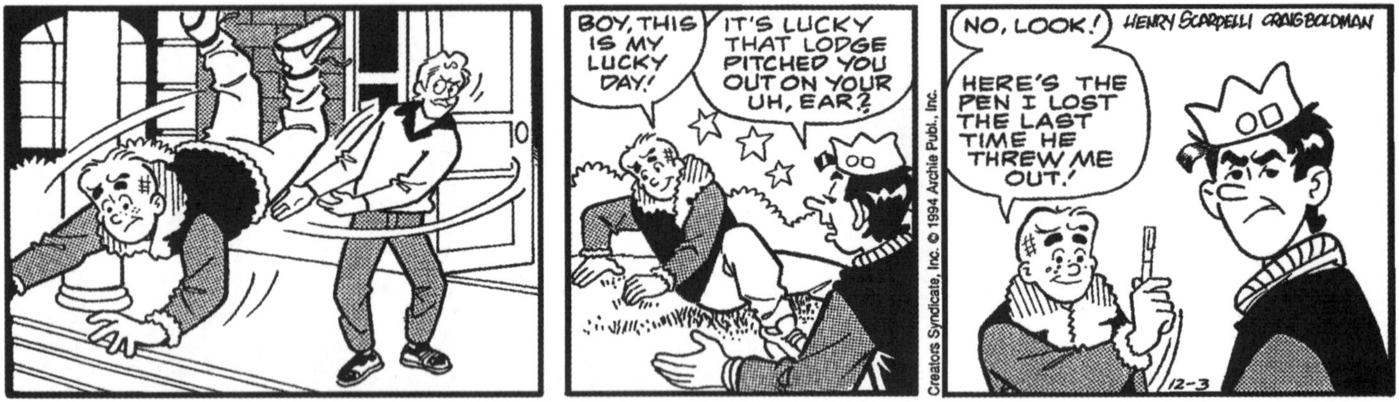
BOY, THIS IS MY LUCKY DAY!
IT'S LUCKY THAT LODGE PITCHED YOU OUT ON YOUR UH, EAR?
Creators Syndicate, Inc. © 1994 Archie Publ., Inc.
NO, LOOK!
HENRY SCARPELLI CRAIG BOLDMAN
HERE'S THE PEN I LOST THE LAST TIME HE THREW ME OUT!
12-3

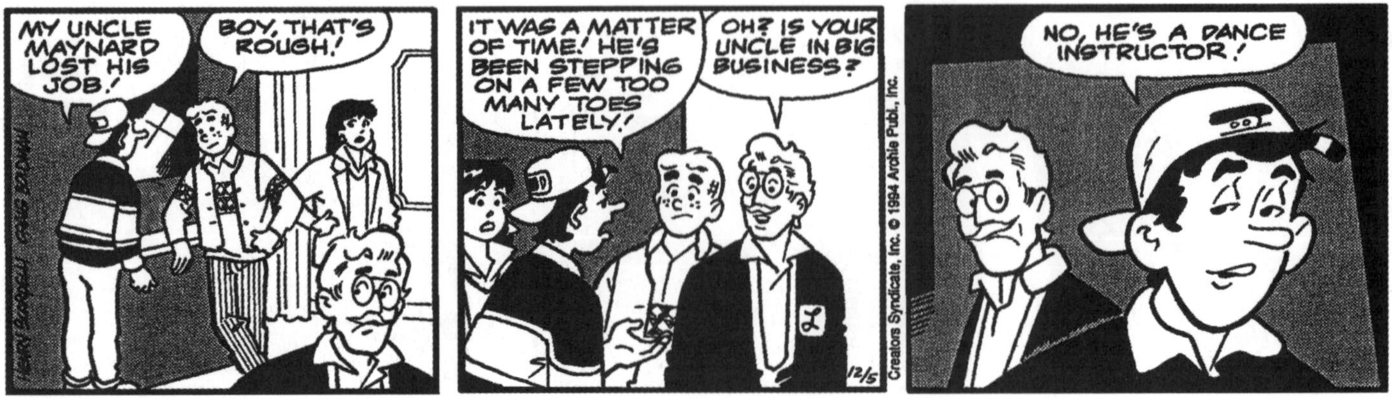
MY UNCLE MAYNARD LOST HIS JOB!
BOY, THAT'S ROUGH!
HENRY SCARPELLI CRAIG BOLDMAN
IT WAS A MATTER OF TIME! HE'S BEEN STEPPING ON A FEW TOO MANY TOES LATELY!
OH? IS YOUR UNCLE IN BIG BUSINESS?
12/5
Creators Syndicate, Inc. © 1994 Archie Publ., Inc.
NO, HE'S A DANCE INSTRUCTOR!

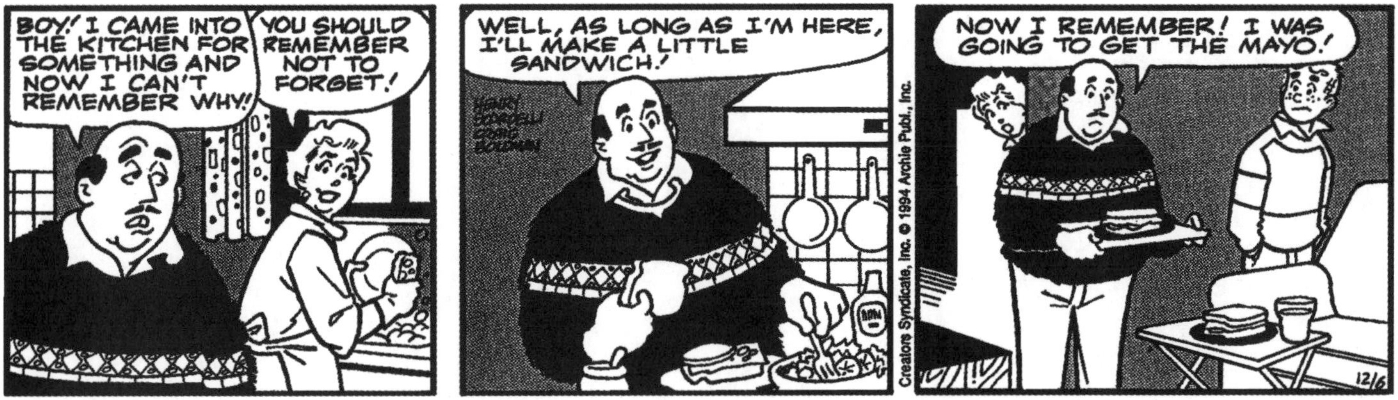
BOY! I CAME INTO THE KITCHEN FOR SOMETHING AND NOW I CAN'T REMEMBER WHY!
YOU SHOULD REMEMBER NOT TO FORGET!
WELL, AS LONG AS I'M HERE, I'LL MAKE A LITTLE SANDWICH!
NOW I REMEMBER! I WAS GOING TO GET THE MAYO!
Creators Syndicate, Inc. © 1994 Archie Publ., Inc.
12/6

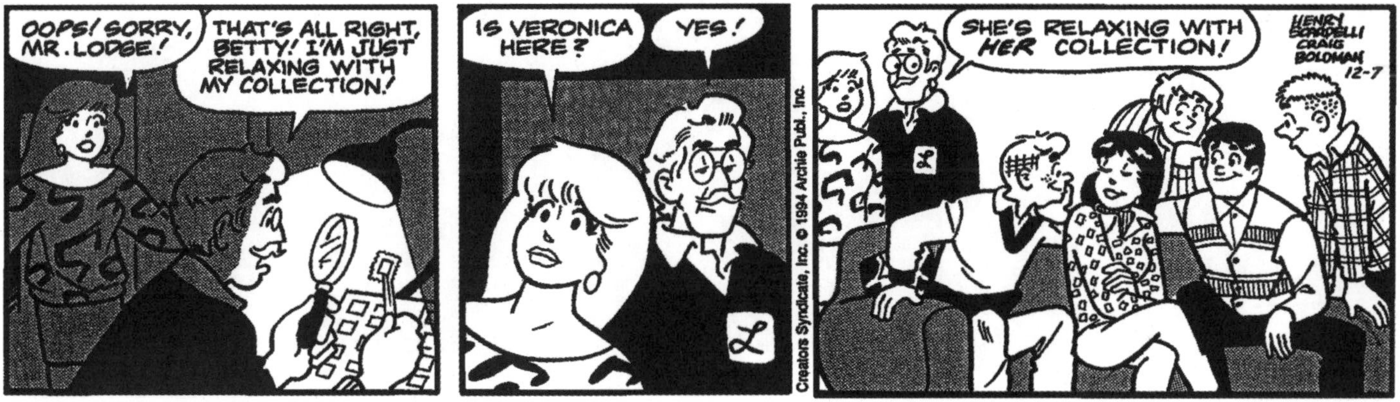
OOPS! SORRY, MR. LODGE!
THAT'S ALL RIGHT, BETTY! I'M JUST RELAXING WITH MY COLLECTION!
IS VERONICA HERE?
YES!
Creators Syndicate, Inc. © 1994 Archie Publ., Inc.
SHE'S RELAXING WITH HER COLLECTION!
HENRY SCARPELLI CRAIG BOLDMAN 12-7

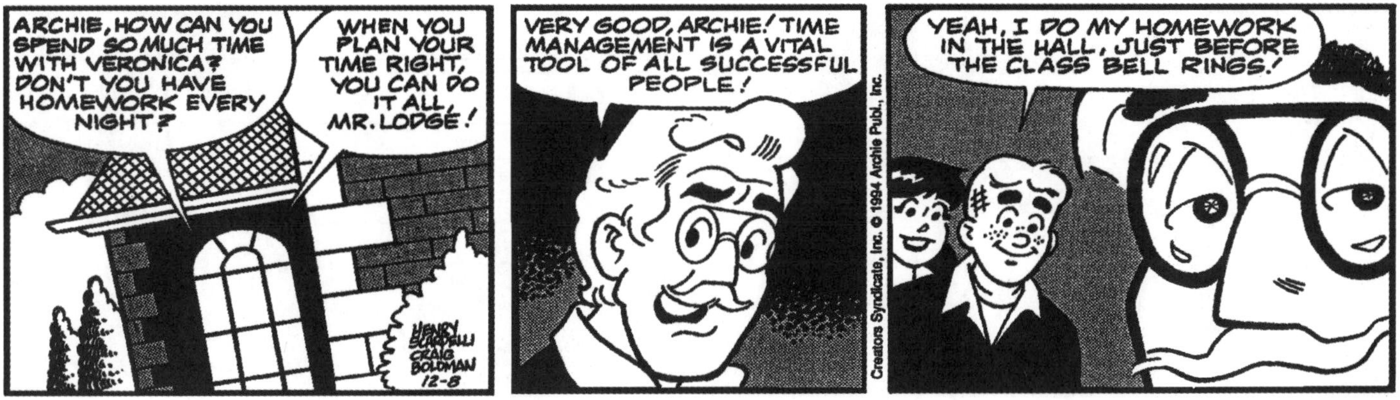
ARCHIE, HOW CAN YOU SPEND SO MUCH TIME WITH VERONICA? DON'T YOU HAVE HOMEWORK EVERY NIGHT?
WHEN YOU PLAN YOUR TIME RIGHT, YOU CAN DO IT ALL, MR. LODGE!
HENRY SCARPELLI CRAIG BOLDMAN 12-8
VERY GOOD, ARCHIE! TIME MANAGEMENT IS A VITAL TOOL OF ALL SUCCESSFUL PEOPLE!
Creators Syndicate, Inc. © 1994 Archie Publ., Inc.
YEAH, I DO MY HOMEWORK IN THE HALL, JUST BEFORE THE CLASS BELL RINGS!

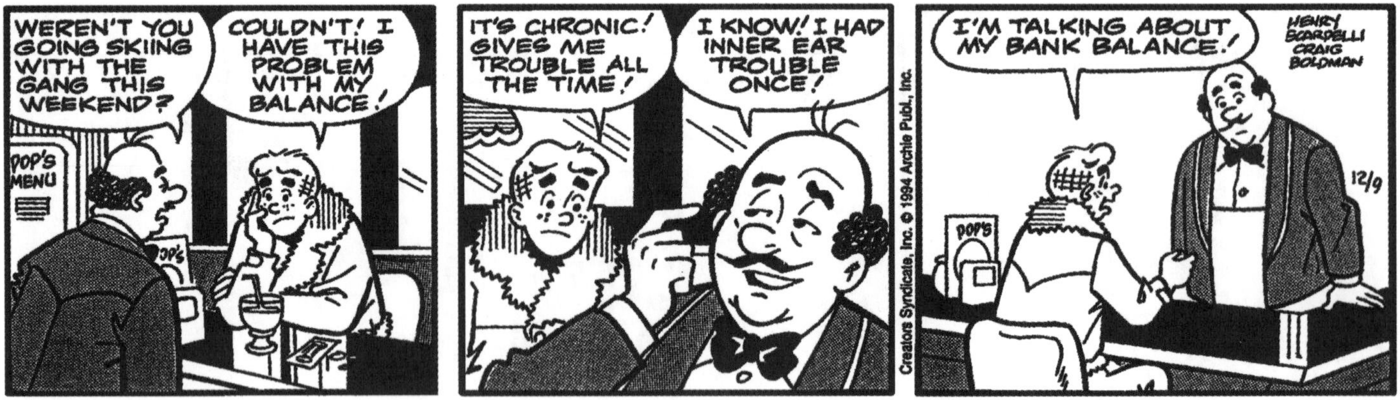
WEREN'T YOU GOING SKIING WITH THE GANG THIS WEEKEND?
COULDN'T! I HAVE THIS PROBLEM WITH MY BALANCE!
POP'S MENU
IT'S CHRONIC! GIVES ME TROUBLE ALL THE TIME!
I KNOW! I HAD INNER EAR TROUBLE ONCE!
Creators Syndicate, Inc. © 1994 Archie Publ., Inc.
I'M TALKING ABOUT MY BANK BALANCE!
HENRY SCARPELLI CRAIG BOLDMAN
12/9

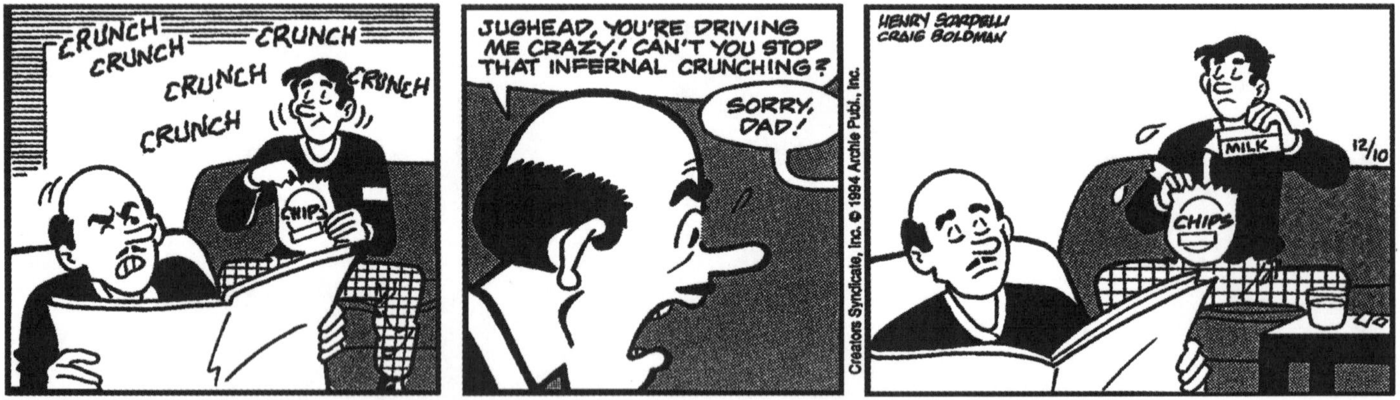
CRUNCH CRUNCH CRUNCH CRUNCH CRUNCH CRUNCH
CHIPS
JUGHEAD, YOU'RE DRIVING ME CRAZY! CAN'T YOU STOP THAT INFERNAL CRUNCHING?
SORRY, DAD!
Creators Syndicate, Inc. © 1994 Archie Publ., Inc.
HENRY SCARPELLI CRAIG BOLDMAN
MILK
CHIPS
12/10

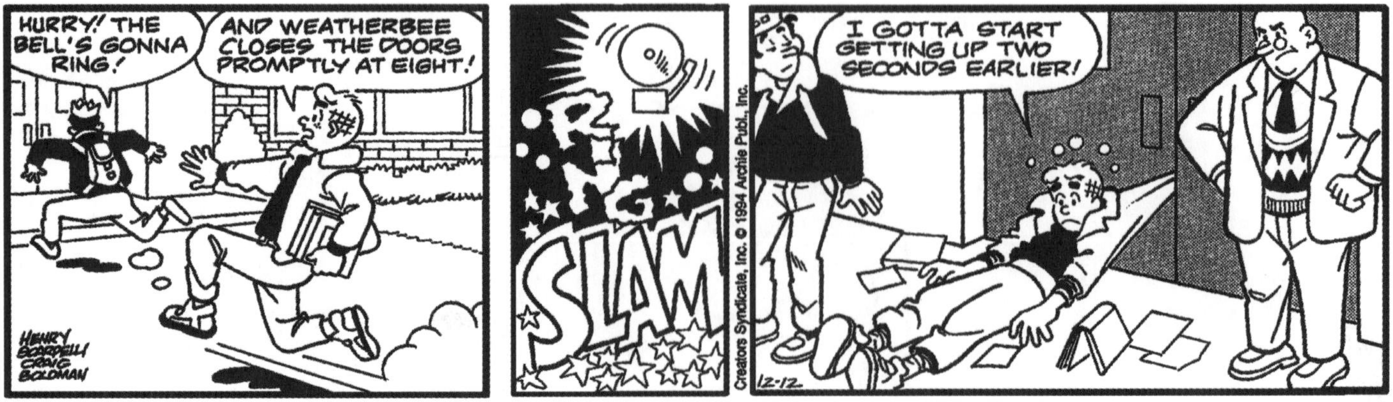
HURRY! THE BELL'S GONNA RING!
AND WEATHERBEE CLOSES THE DOORS PROMPTLY AT EIGHT!
HENRY SCARPELLI CRAIG BOLDMAN
RING
SLAM
Creators Syndicate, Inc. © 1994 Archie Publ., Inc.
12-12
I GOTTA START GETTING UP TWO SECONDS EARLIER!

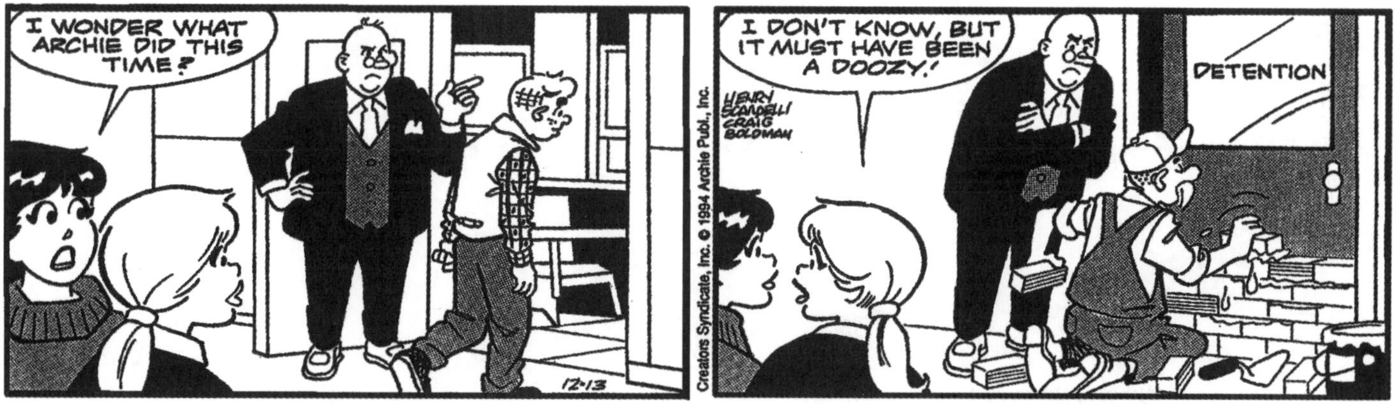
I WONDER WHAT ARCHIE DID THIS TIME?
12·13
Creators Syndicate, Inc. © 1994 Archie Publ., Inc.
I DON'T KNOW, BUT IT MUST HAVE BEEN A DOOZY!
HENRY SCARPELLI CRAIG BOLDMAN
DETENTION

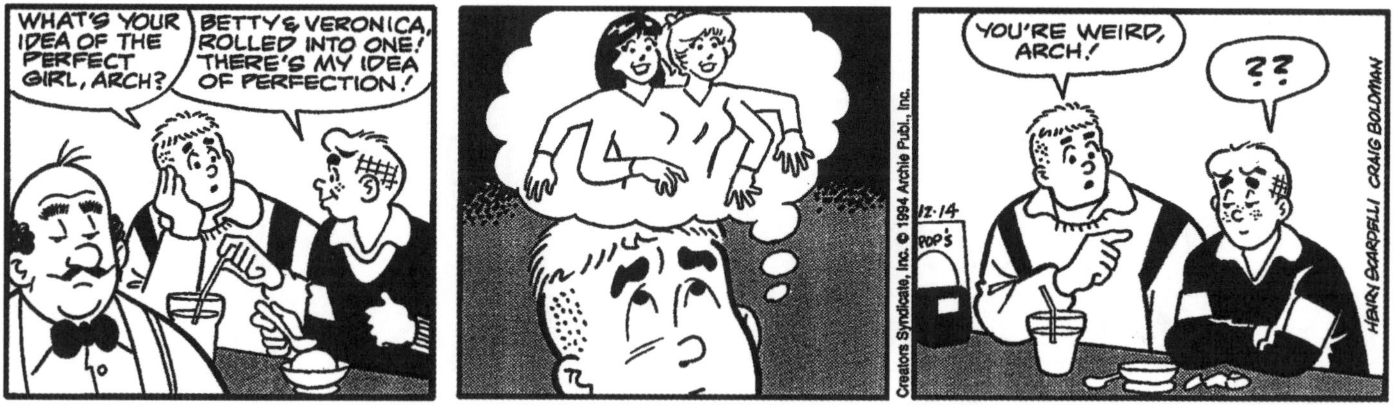
WHAT'S YOUR IDEA OF THE PERFECT GIRL, ARCH?
BETTY & VERONICA, ROLLED INTO ONE! THERE'S MY IDEA OF PERFECTION!
Creators Syndicate, Inc. © 1994 Archie Publ., Inc.
12·14
POP'S
YOU'RE WEIRD, ARCH!
??
HENRY SCARPELLI CRAIG BOLDMAN

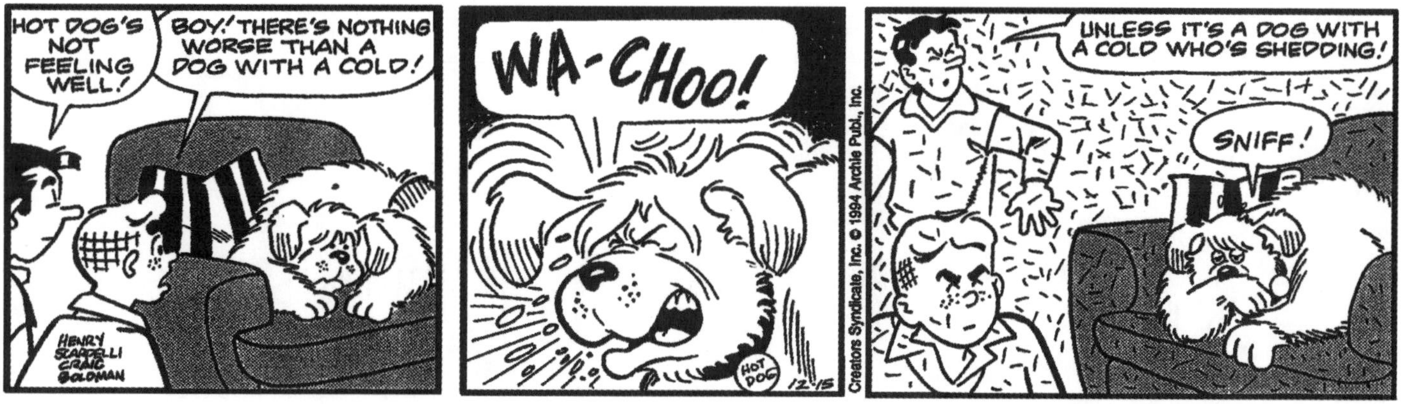
HOT DOG'S NOT FEELING WELL!
BOY! THERE'S NOTHING WORSE THAN A DOG WITH A COLD!
HENRY SCARPELLI CRAIG BOLDMAN
WA-CHOO!
HOT DOG
12·15
Creators Syndicate, Inc. © 1994 Archie Publ., Inc.
UNLESS IT'S A DOG WITH A COLD WHO'S SHEDDING!
SNIFF!

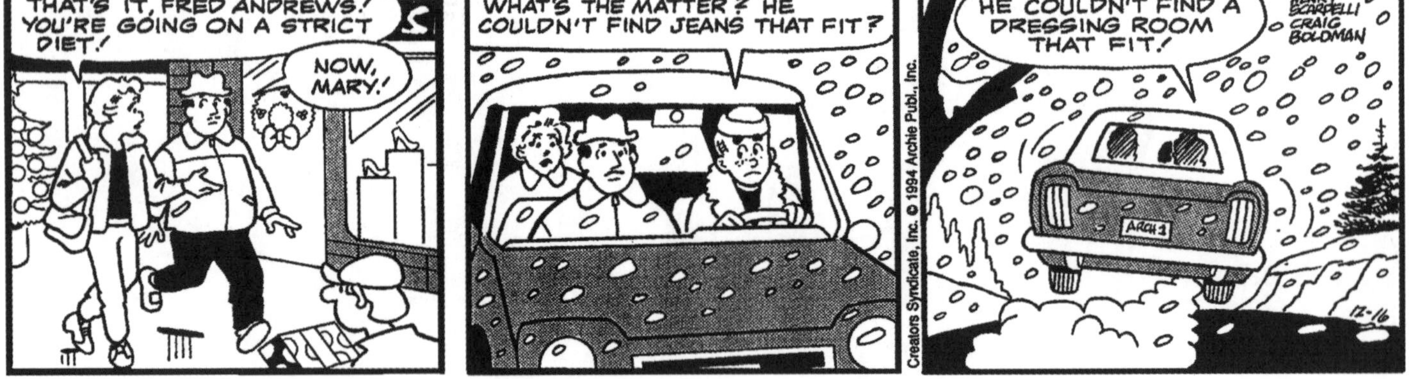
THAT'S IT, FRED ANDREWS! YOU'RE GOING ON A STRICT DIET!
NOW, MARY!
WHAT'S THE MATTER? HE COULDN'T FIND JEANS THAT FIT?
HE COULDN'T FIND A DRESSING ROOM THAT FIT!
HENRY SCARPELLI CRAIG BOLDMAN
ARCH 1
12-16
Creators Syndicate, Inc. © 1994 Archie Publ., Inc.

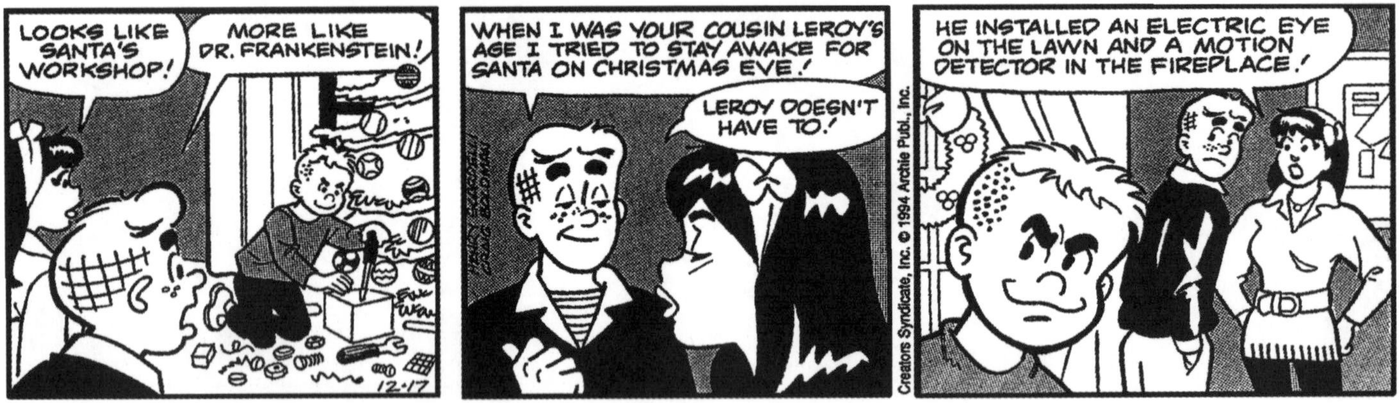
LOOKS LIKE SANTA'S WORKSHOP!
MORE LIKE DR. FRANKENSTEIN!
12-17
WHEN I WAS YOUR COUSIN LEROY'S AGE I TRIED TO STAY AWAKE FOR SANTA ON CHRISTMAS EVE!
LEROY DOESN'T HAVE TO!
HE INSTALLED AN ELECTRIC EYE ON THE LAWN AND A MOTION DETECTOR IN THE FIREPLACE!
Creators Syndicate, Inc. © 1994 Archie Publ., Inc.

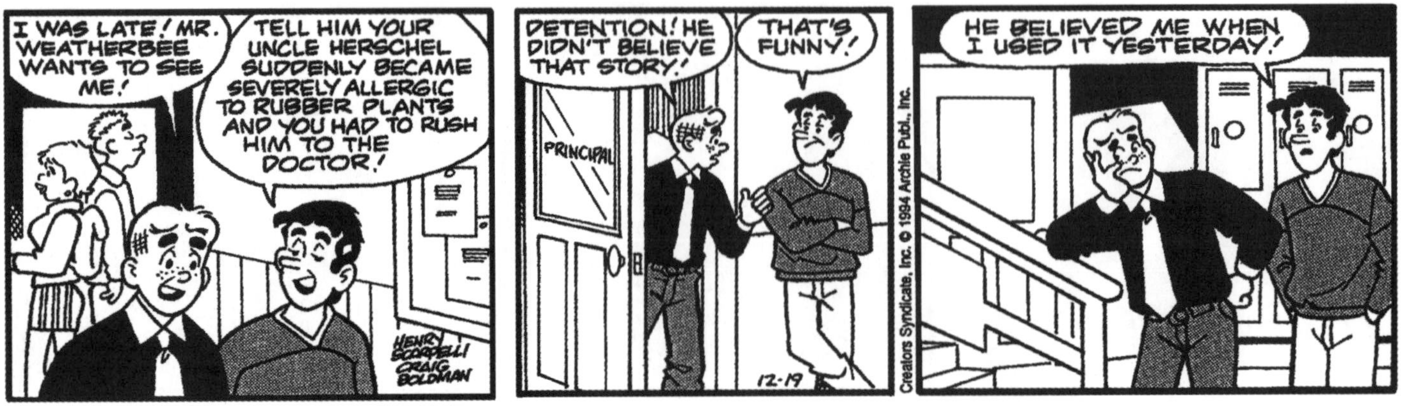
I WAS LATE! MR. WEATHERBEE WANTS TO SEE ME!
TELL HIM YOUR UNCLE HERSCHEL SUDDENLY BECAME SEVERELY ALLERGIC TO RUBBER PLANTS AND YOU HAD TO RUSH HIM TO THE DOCTOR!
HENRY SCARPELLI CRAIG BOLDMAN
DETENTION! HE DIDN'T BELIEVE THAT STORY!
THAT'S FUNNY!
PRINCIPAL
12-19
HE BELIEVED ME WHEN I USED IT YESTERDAY!
Creators Syndicate, Inc. © 1994 Archie Publ., Inc.

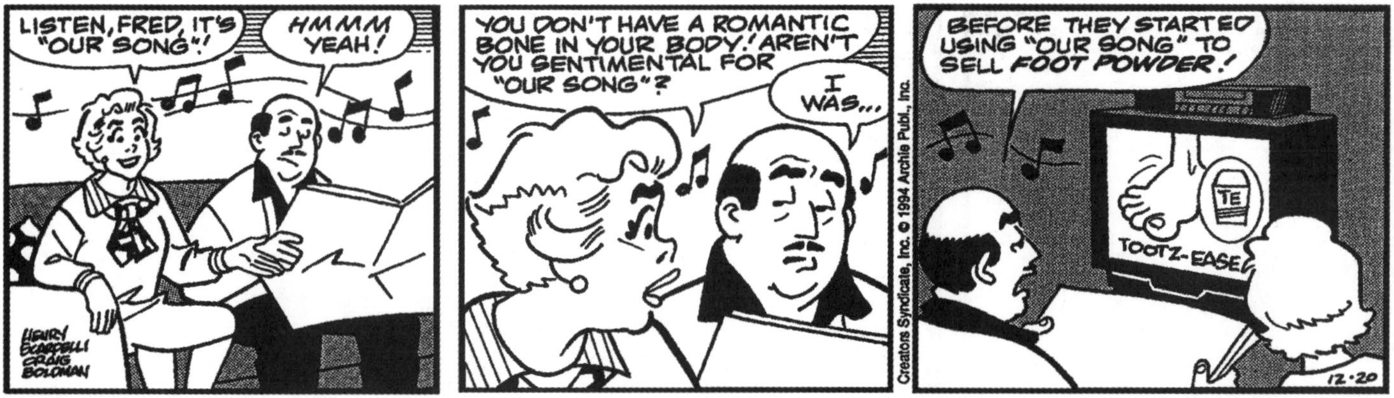
LISTEN, FRED, IT'S "OUR SONG"!
HMMM YEAH!
HENRY SCARPELLI CRAIG BOLDMAN
YOU DON'T HAVE A ROMANTIC BONE IN YOUR BODY! AREN'T YOU SENTIMENTAL FOR "OUR SONG"?
I WAS...
Creators Syndicate, Inc. © 1994 Archie Publ., Inc.
BEFORE THEY STARTED USING "OUR SONG" TO SELL FOOT POWDER!
TE
TOOTZ-EASE
12·20

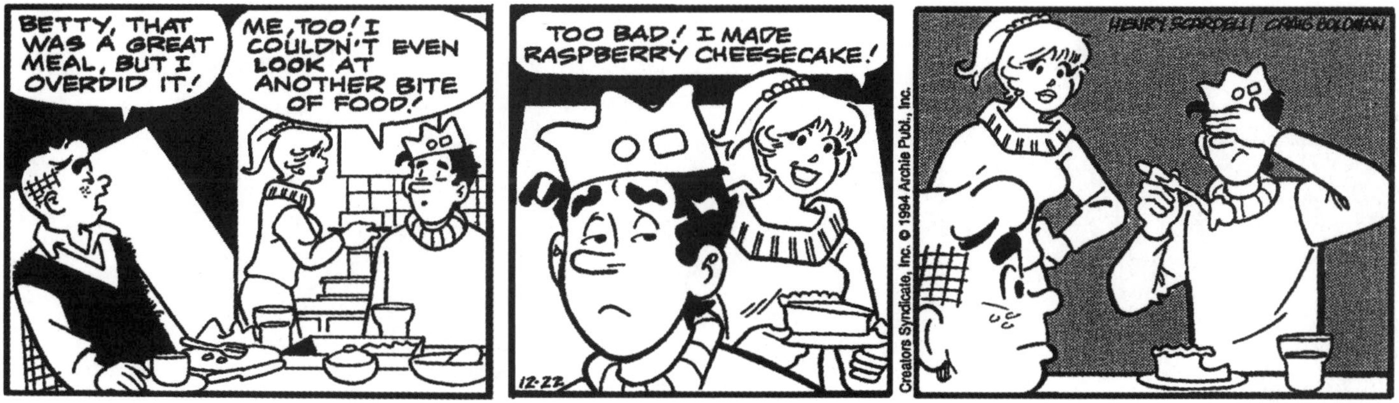
BETTY, THAT WAS A GREAT MEAL, BUT I OVERDID IT!
ME, TOO! I COULDN'T EVEN LOOK AT ANOTHER BITE OF FOOD!
TOO BAD! I MADE RASPBERRY CHEESECAKE!
12·22
Creators Syndicate, Inc. © 1994 Archie Publ., Inc.
HENRY SCARPELLI CRAIG BOLDMAN

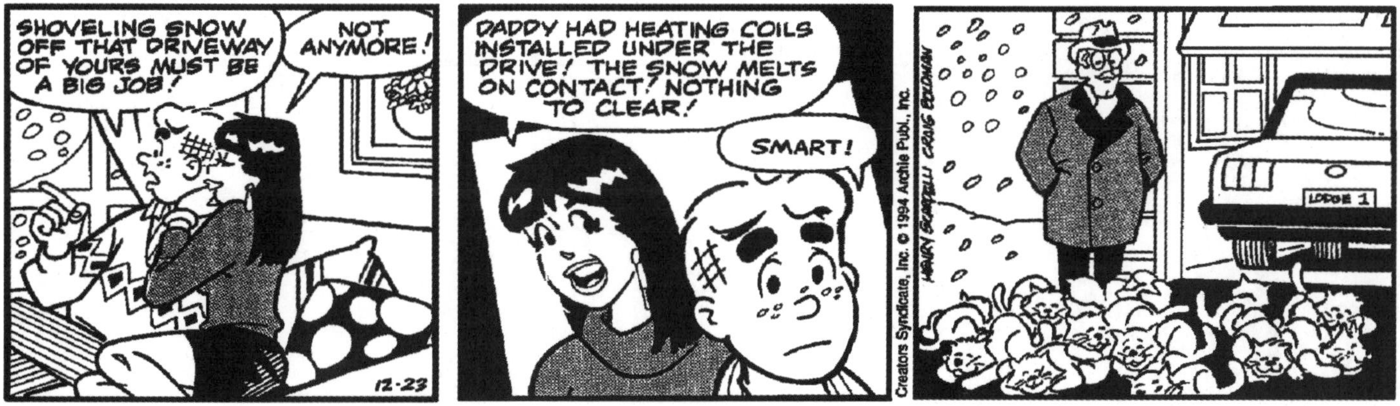
SHOVELING SNOW OFF THAT DRIVEWAY OF YOURS MUST BE A BIG JOB!
NOT ANYMORE!
12·23
DADDY HAD HEATING COILS INSTALLED UNDER THE DRIVE! THE SNOW MELTS ON CONTACT! NOTHING TO CLEAR!
SMART!
Creators Syndicate, Inc. © 1994 Archie Publ., Inc.
HENRY SCARPELLI CRAIG BOLDMAN
LODGE 1

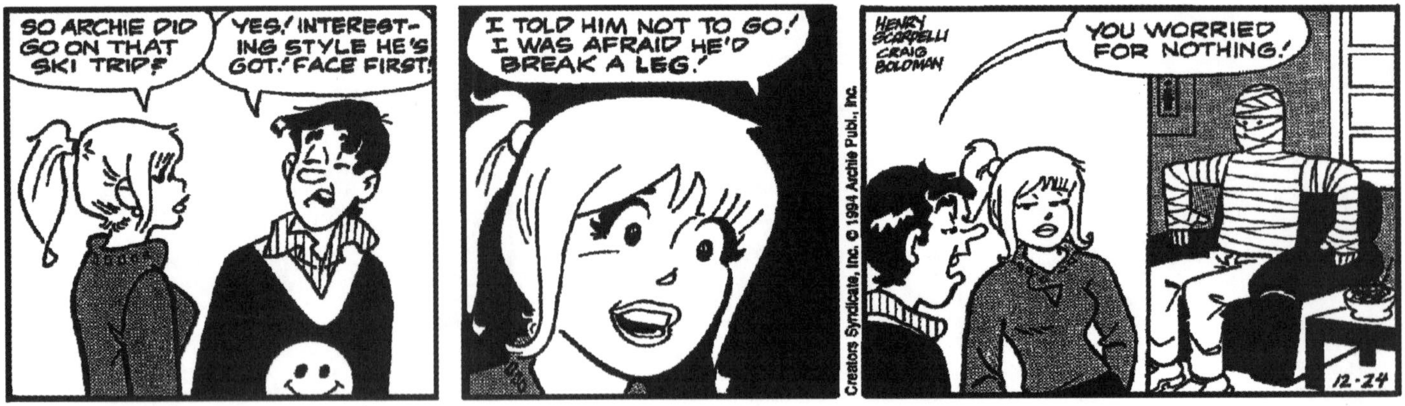
SO ARCHIE DID GO ON THAT SKI TRIP?
YES! INTERESTING STYLE HE'S GOT! FACE FIRST!
I TOLD HIM NOT TO GO! I WAS AFRAID HE'D BREAK A LEG!
Creators Syndicate, Inc. © 1994 Archie Publ., Inc.
HENRY SCARPELLI CRAIG BOLDMAN
YOU WORRIED FOR NOTHING!
12-24

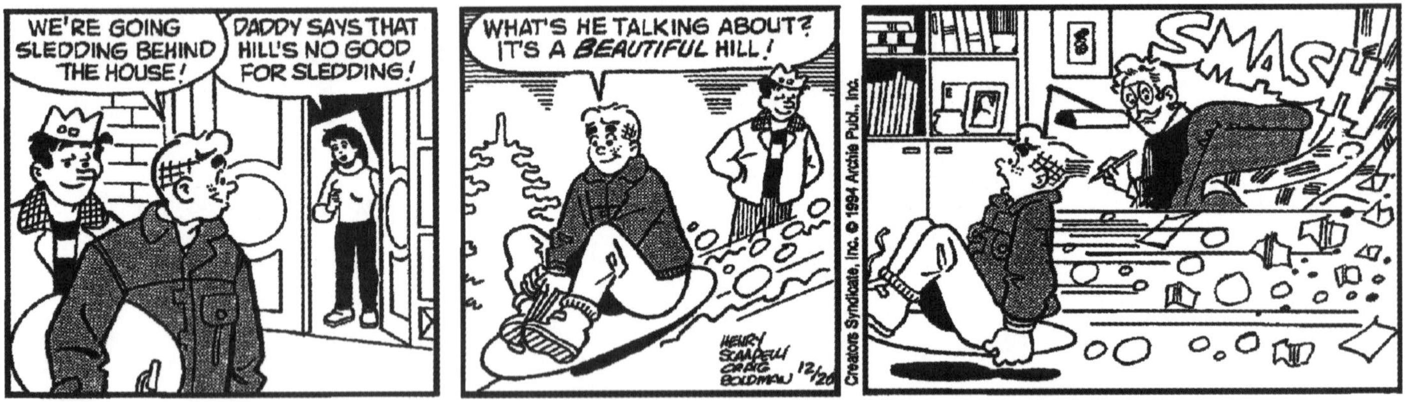
WE'RE GOING SLEDDING BEHIND THE HOUSE!
DADDY SAYS THAT HILL'S NO GOOD FOR SLEDDING!
WHAT'S HE TALKING ABOUT? IT'S A BEAUTIFUL HILL!
HENRY SCARPELLI CRAIG BOLDMAN 12/26
Creators Syndicate, Inc. © 1994 Archie Publ., Inc.
SMASH

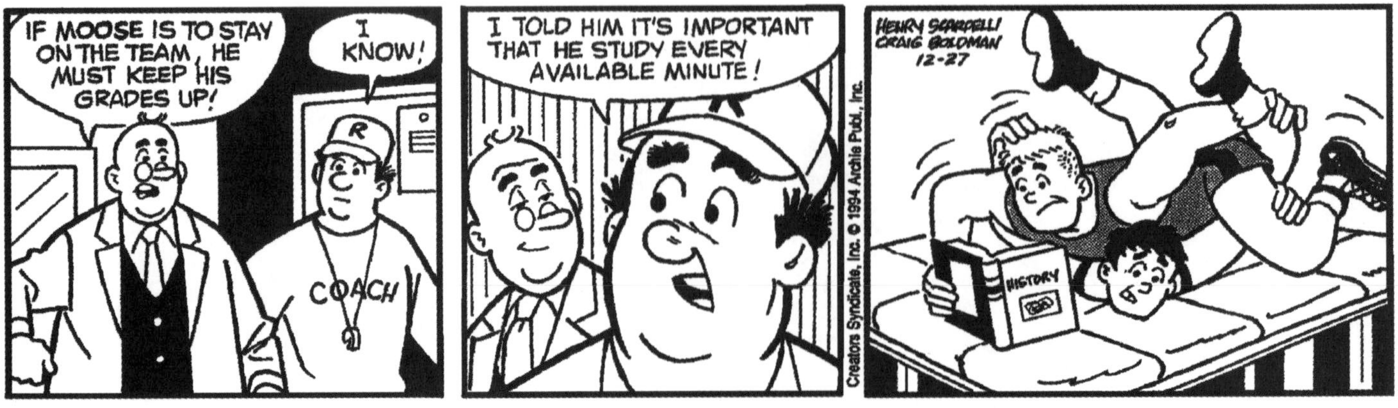
IF MOOSE IS TO STAY ON THE TEAM, HE MUST KEEP HIS GRADES UP!
I KNOW!
COACH
I TOLD HIM IT'S IMPORTANT THAT HE STUDY EVERY AVAILABLE MINUTE!
Creators Syndicate, Inc. © 1994 Archie Publ., Inc.
HENRY SCARPELLI CRAIG BOLDMAN 12-27
HISTORY

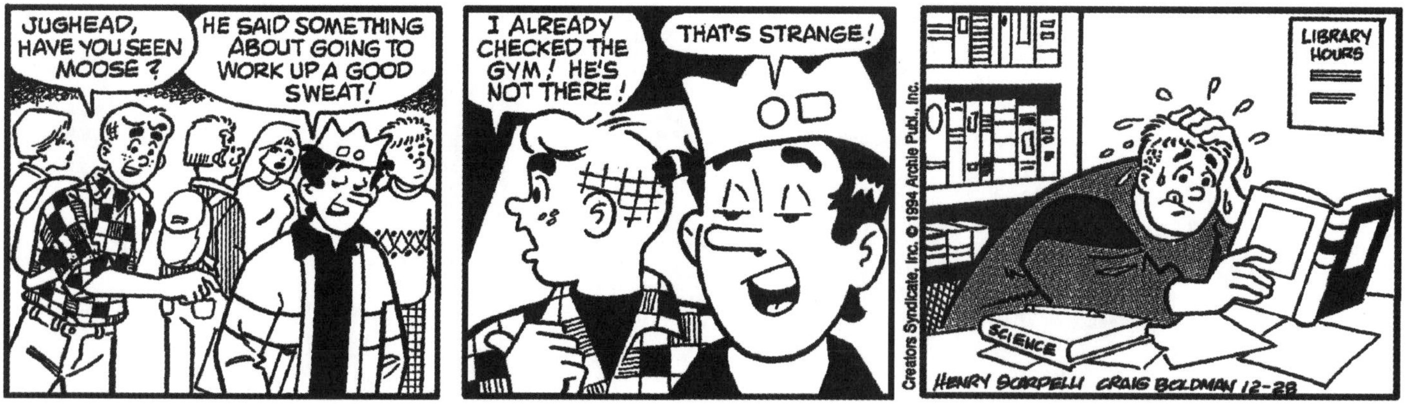
JUGHEAD, HAVE YOU SEEN MOOSE ?
HE SAID SOMETHING ABOUT GOING TO WORK UP A GOOD SWEAT!
I ALREADY CHECKED THE GYM! HE'S NOT THERE!
THAT'S STRANGE!
LIBRARY HOURS
SCIENCE
HENRY SCARPELLI CRAIG BOLDMAN 12-28
Creators Syndicate, Inc. © 1994 Archie Publ., Inc.

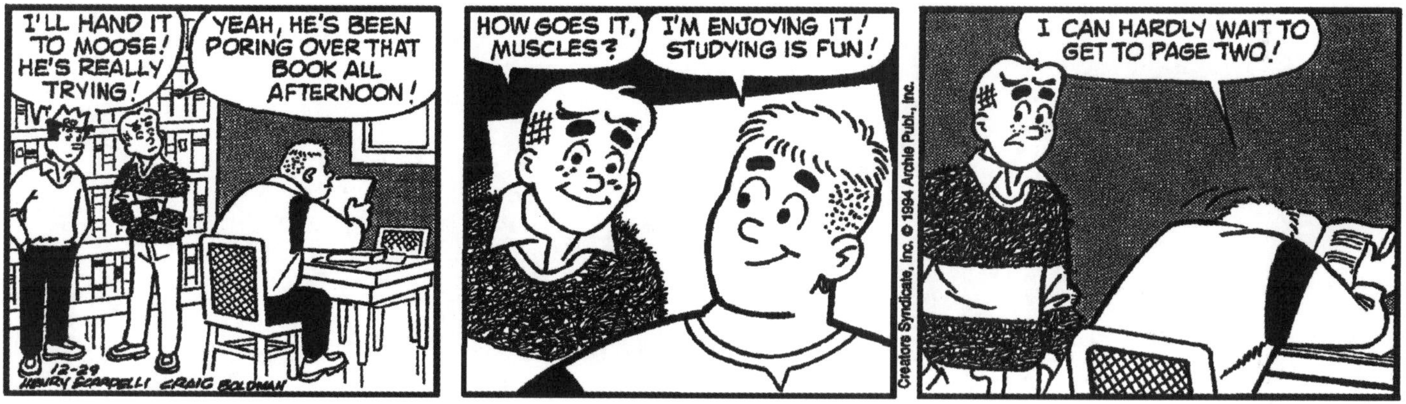
I'LL HAND IT TO MOOSE! HE'S REALLY TRYING!
YEAH, HE'S BEEN PORING OVER THAT BOOK ALL AFTERNOON!
12-29
HENRY SCARPELLI CRAIG BOLDMAN
HOW GOES IT, MUSCLES?
I'M ENJOYING IT! STUDYING IS FUN!
I CAN HARDLY WAIT TO GET TO PAGE TWO!
Creators Syndicate, Inc. © 1994 Archie Publ., Inc.

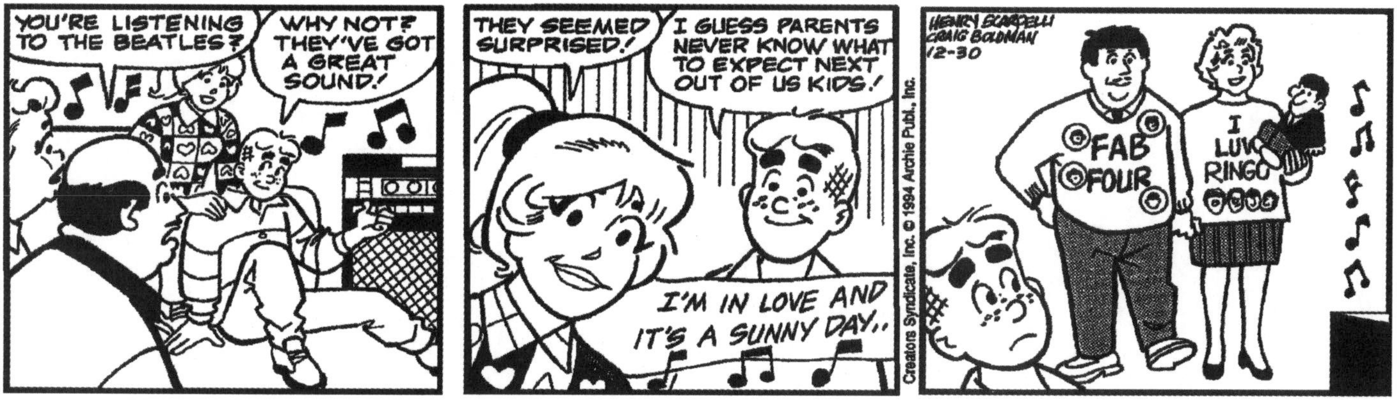
YOU'RE LISTENING TO THE BEATLES?
WHY NOT? THEY'VE GOT A GREAT SOUND!
THEY SEEMED SURPRISED!
I GUESS PARENTS NEVER KNOW WHAT TO EXPECT NEXT OUT OF US KIDS!
I'M IN LOVE AND IT'S A SUNNY DAY..
HENRY SCARPELLI CRAIG BOLDMAN 12-30
FAB FOUR
I LUV RINGO
Creators Syndicate, Inc. © 1994 Archie Publ., Inc.

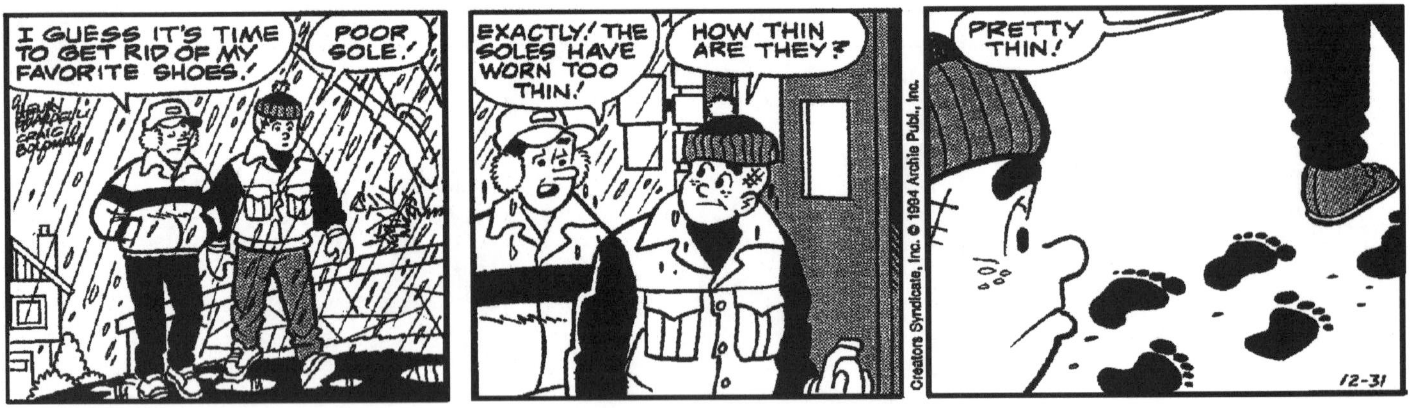
I GUESS IT'S TIME TO GET RID OF MY FAVORITE SHOES!
POOR SOLE!
EXACTLY! THE SOLES HAVE WORN TOO THIN!
HOW THIN ARE THEY?
PRETTY THIN!
Creators Syndicate, Inc. © 1994 Archie Publ., Inc.
12-31

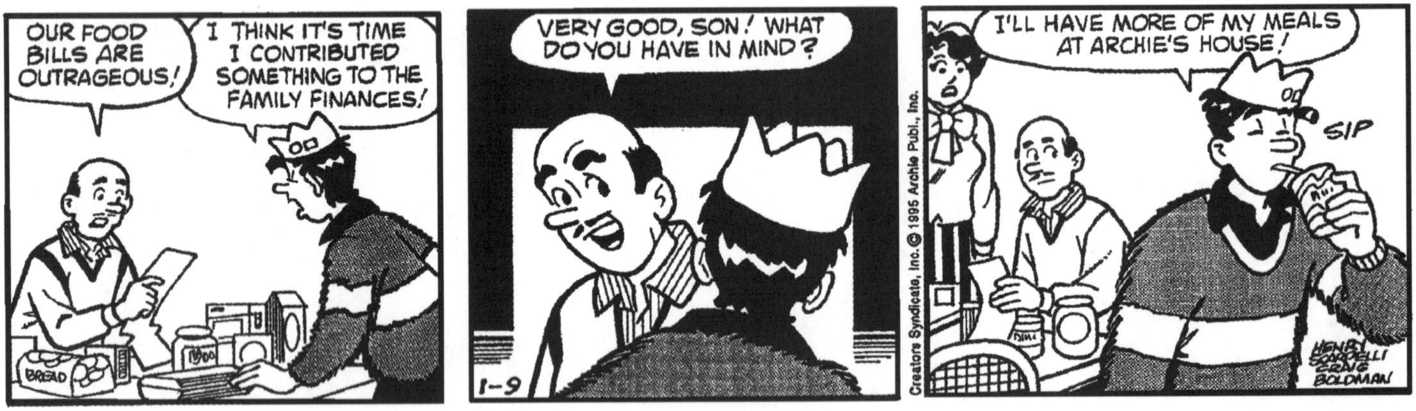
OUR FOOD BILLS ARE OUTRAGEOUS!
I THINK IT'S TIME I CONTRIBUTED SOMETHING TO THE FAMILY FINANCES!
BREAD
VERY GOOD, SON! WHAT DO YOU HAVE IN MIND?
1-9
I'LL HAVE MORE OF MY MEALS AT ARCHIE'S HOUSE!
SIP
HENRY SCARPELLI CRAIG BOLDMAN
Creators Syndicate, Inc. © 1995 Archie Publ., Inc.

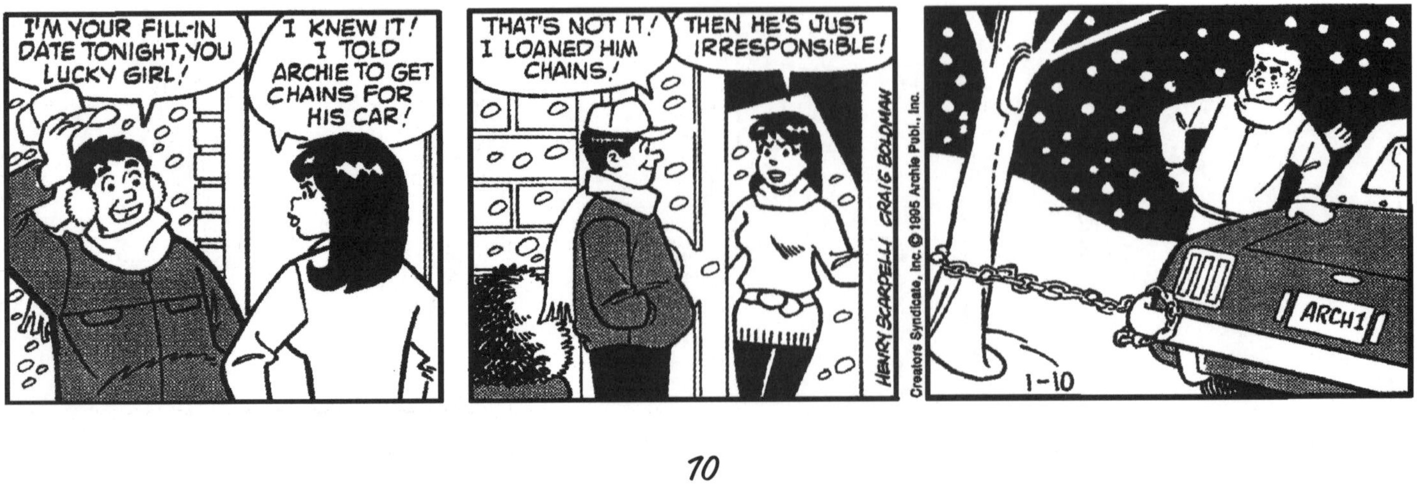
I'M YOUR FILL-IN DATE TONIGHT, YOU LUCKY GIRL!
I KNEW IT! I TOLD ARCHIE TO GET CHAINS FOR HIS CAR!
THAT'S NOT IT! I LOANED HIM CHAINS!
THEN HE'S JUST IRRESPONSIBLE!
HENRY SCARPELLI CRAIG BOLDMAN
Creators Syndicate, Inc. © 1995 Archie Publ., Inc.
ARCH1
1-10

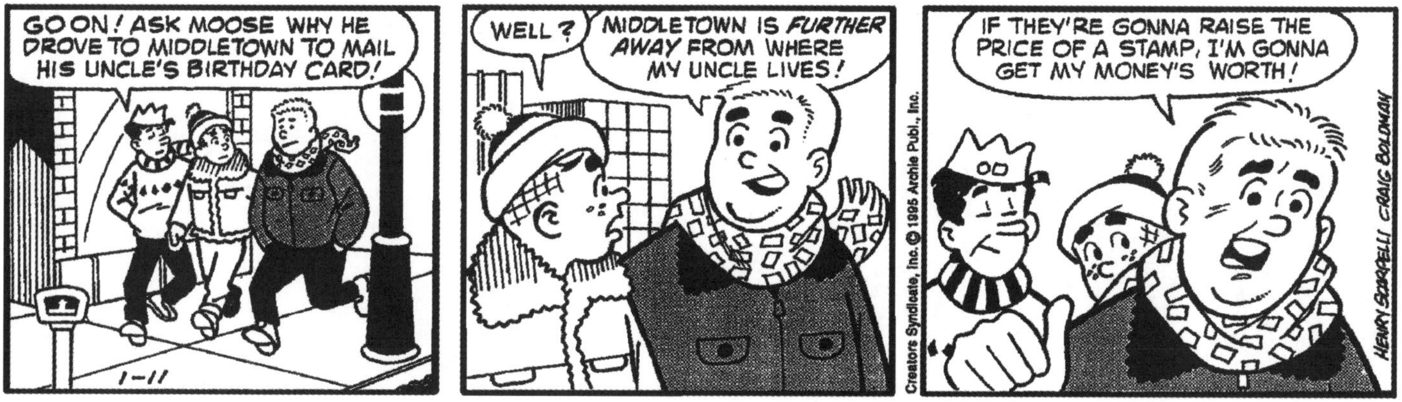
GO ON! ASK MOOSE WHY HE DROVE TO MIDDLETOWN TO MAIL HIS UNCLE'S BIRTHDAY CARD!
1-11
WELL?
MIDDLETOWN IS *FURTHER AWAY* FROM WHERE MY UNCLE LIVES!
IF THEY'RE GONNA RAISE THE PRICE OF A STAMP, I'M GONNA GET MY MONEY'S WORTH!
Creators Syndicate, Inc. © 1995 Archie Publ., Inc.
HENRY SCARPELLI CRAIG BOLDMAN

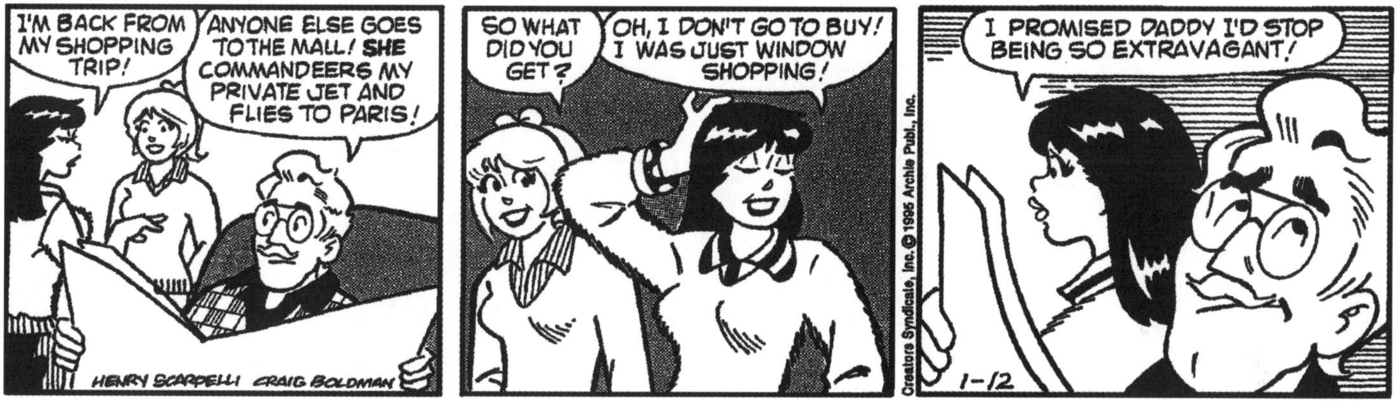
I'M BACK FROM MY SHOPPING TRIP!
ANYONE ELSE GOES TO THE MALL! **SHE** COMMANDEERS MY PRIVATE JET AND FLIES TO PARIS!
HENRY SCARPELLI CRAIG BOLDMAN
SO WHAT DID YOU GET?
OH, I DON'T GO TO BUY! I WAS JUST WINDOW SHOPPING!
Creators Syndicate, Inc. © 1995 Archie Publ., Inc.
I PROMISED DADDY I'D STOP BEING SO EXTRAVAGANT!
1-12

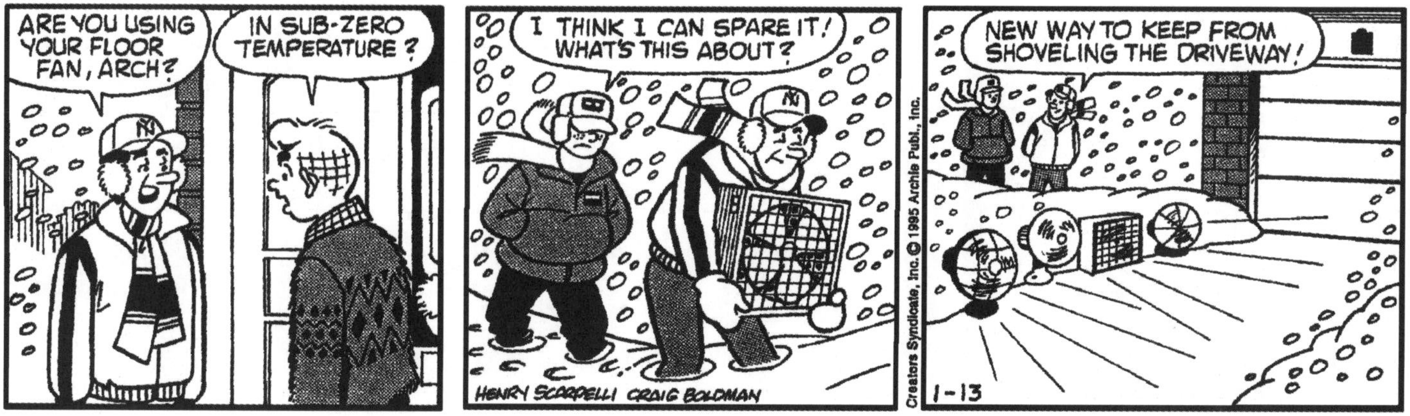
ARE YOU USING YOUR FLOOR FAN, ARCH?
IN SUB-ZERO TEMPERATURE?
I THINK I CAN SPARE IT! WHAT'S THIS ABOUT?
HENRY SCARPELLI CRAIG BOLDMAN
Creators Syndicate, Inc. © 1995 Archie Publ., Inc.
NEW WAY TO KEEP FROM SHOVELING THE DRIVEWAY!
1-13

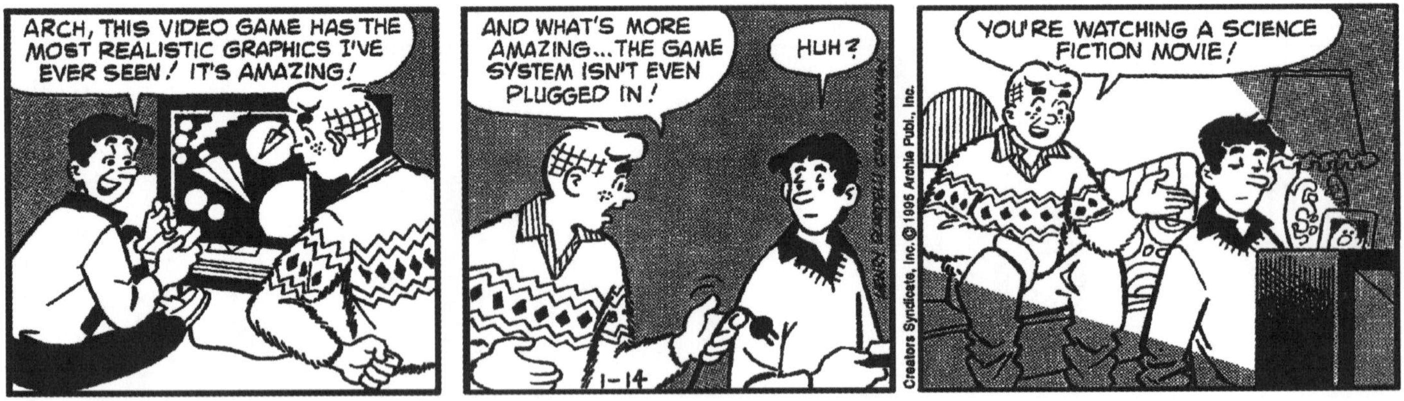
ARCH, THIS VIDEO GAME HAS THE MOST REALISTIC GRAPHICS I'VE EVER SEEN! IT'S AMAZING!
AND WHAT'S MORE AMAZING... THE GAME SYSTEM ISN'T EVEN PLUGGED IN!
HUH?
1-14
Creators Syndicate, Inc. © 1995 Archie Publ., Inc.
YOU'RE WATCHING A SCIENCE FICTION MOVIE!

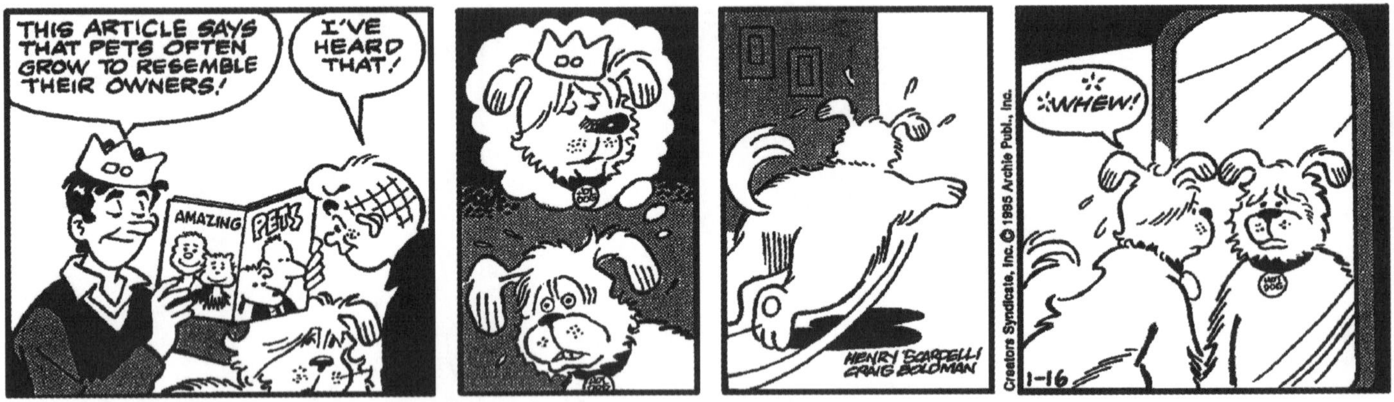
THIS ARTICLE SAYS THAT PETS OFTEN GROW TO RESEMBLE THEIR OWNERS!
I'VE HEARD THAT!
AMAZING PETS
HENRY SCARPELLI
CRAIG BOLDMAN
Creators Syndicate, Inc. © 1995 Archie Publ., Inc.
WHEW!
1-16

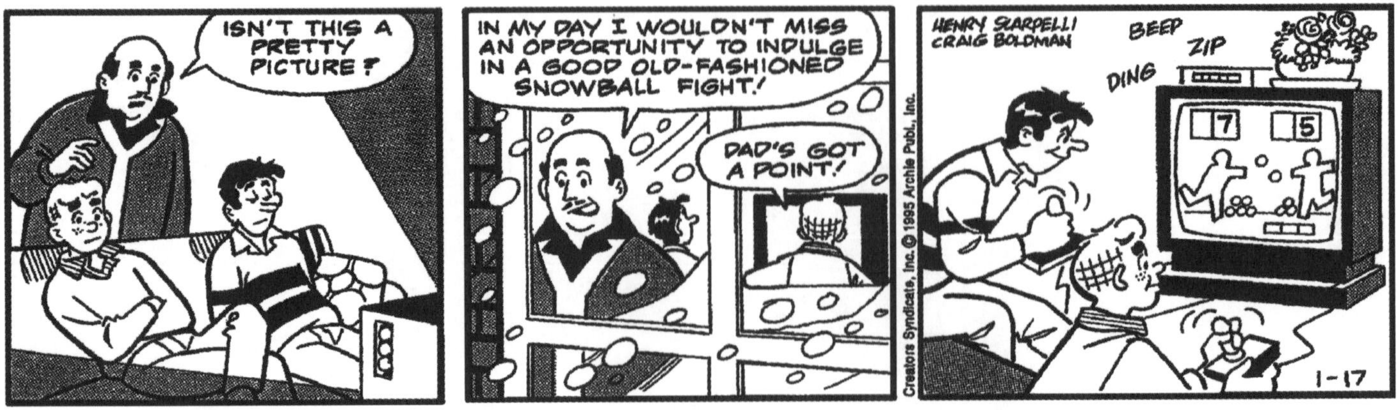
ISN'T THIS A PRETTY PICTURE?
IN MY DAY I WOULDN'T MISS AN OPPORTUNITY TO INDULGE IN A GOOD OLD-FASHIONED SNOWBALL FIGHT!
DAD'S GOT A POINT!
Creators Syndicate, Inc. © 1995 Archie Publ., Inc.
HENRY SCARPELLI
CRAIG BOLDMAN
BEEP
ZIP
DING
7
5
1-17

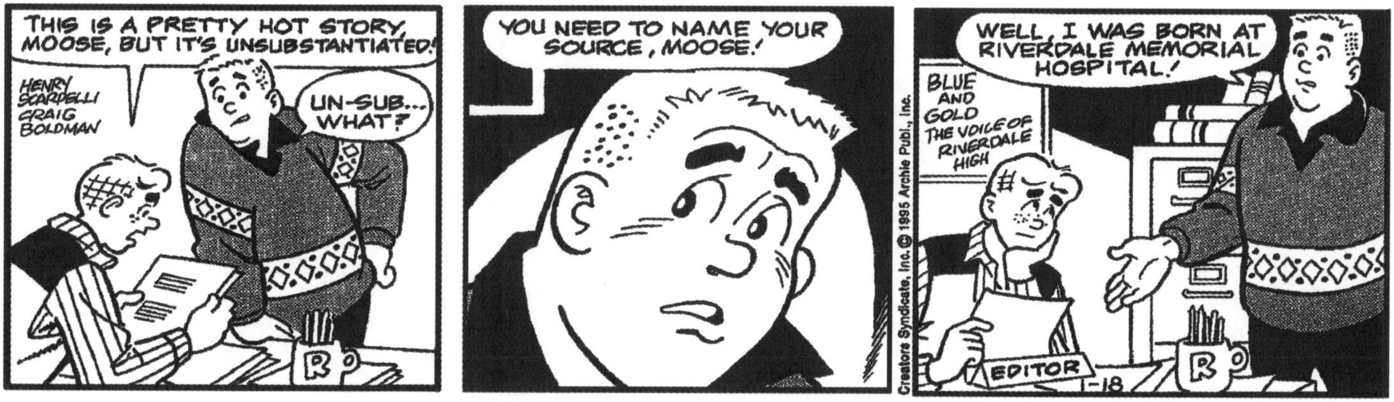
THIS IS A PRETTY HOT STORY, MOOSE, BUT IT'S UNSUBSTANTIATED!
HENRY SCARPELLI CRAIG BOLDMAN
UN-SUB... WHAT?
YOU NEED TO NAME YOUR SOURCE, MOOSE!
WELL, I WAS BORN AT RIVERDALE MEMORIAL HOSPITAL!
BLUE AND GOLD THE VOICE OF RIVERDALE HIGH
EDITOR
1-18
Creators Syndicate, Inc. © 1995 Archie Publ., Inc.

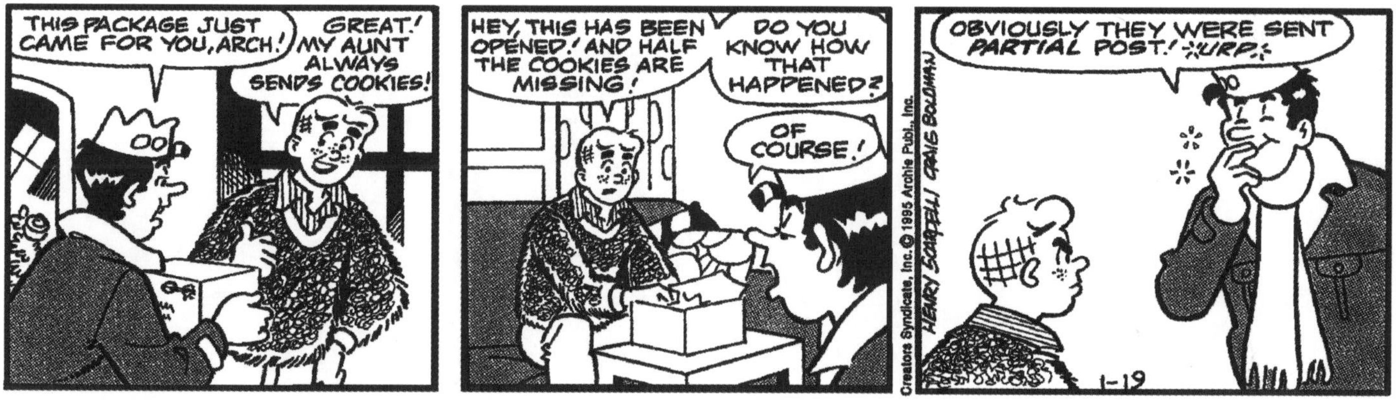
THIS PACKAGE JUST CAME FOR YOU, ARCH!
GREAT! MY AUNT ALWAYS SENDS COOKIES!
HEY, THIS HAS BEEN OPENED! AND HALF THE COOKIES ARE MISSING!
DO YOU KNOW HOW THAT HAPPENED?
OF COURSE!
OBVIOUSLY THEY WERE SENT *PARTIAL* POST! *URP*
HENRY SCARPELLI CRAIG BOLDMAN
1-19
Creators Syndicate, Inc. © 1995 Archie Publ., Inc.

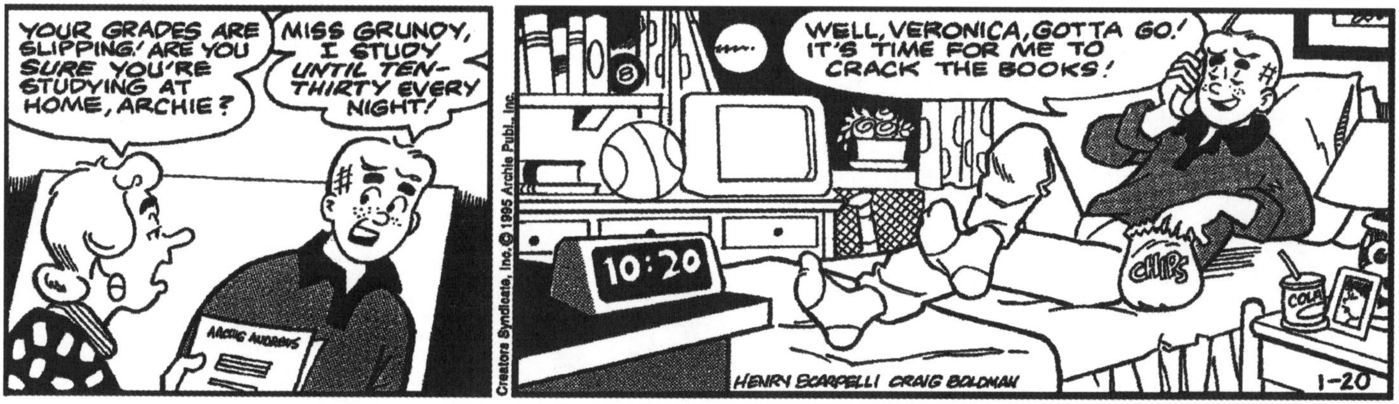
YOUR GRADES ARE SLIPPING! ARE YOU *SURE* YOU'RE STUDYING AT HOME, ARCHIE?
MISS GRUNDY, I STUDY *UNTIL TEN-THIRTY* EVERY NIGHT!
ARCHIE ANDREWS
WELL, VERONICA, GOTTA GO! IT'S TIME FOR ME TO CRACK THE BOOKS!
10:20
CHIPS
COLA
HENRY SCARPELLI CRAIG BOLDMAN
1-20
Creators Syndicate, Inc. © 1995 Archie Publ., Inc.

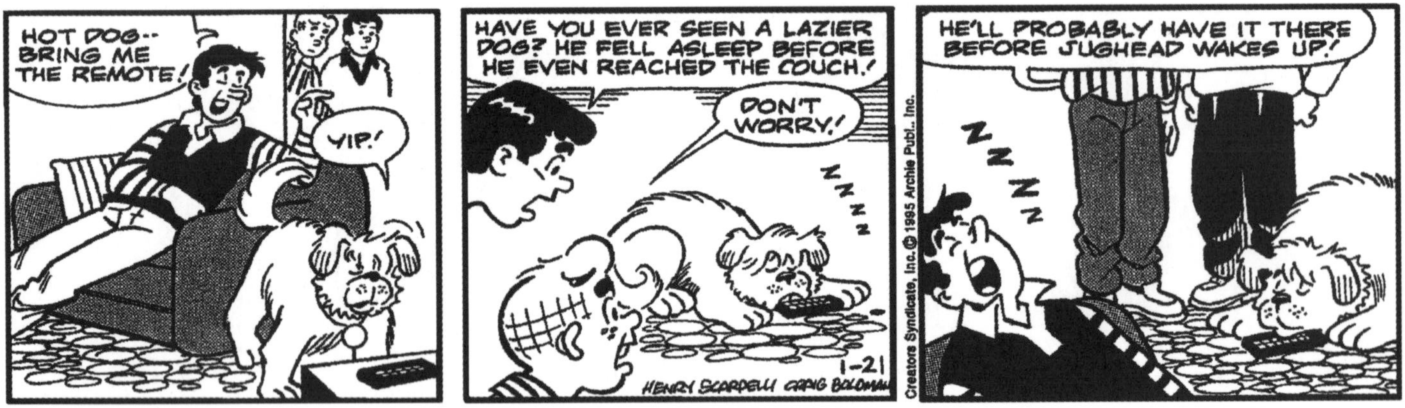
HOT DOG-- BRING ME THE REMOTE!
YIP!
HAVE YOU EVER SEEN A LAZIER DOG? HE FELL ASLEEP BEFORE HE EVEN REACHED THE COUCH!
DON'T WORRY!
Z Z Z Z
1-21
HENRY SCARPELLI CRAIG BOLDMAN
HE'LL PROBABLY HAVE IT THERE BEFORE JUGHEAD WAKES UP!
Z Z Z Z
Creators Syndicate, Inc. © 1995 Archie Publ., Inc.

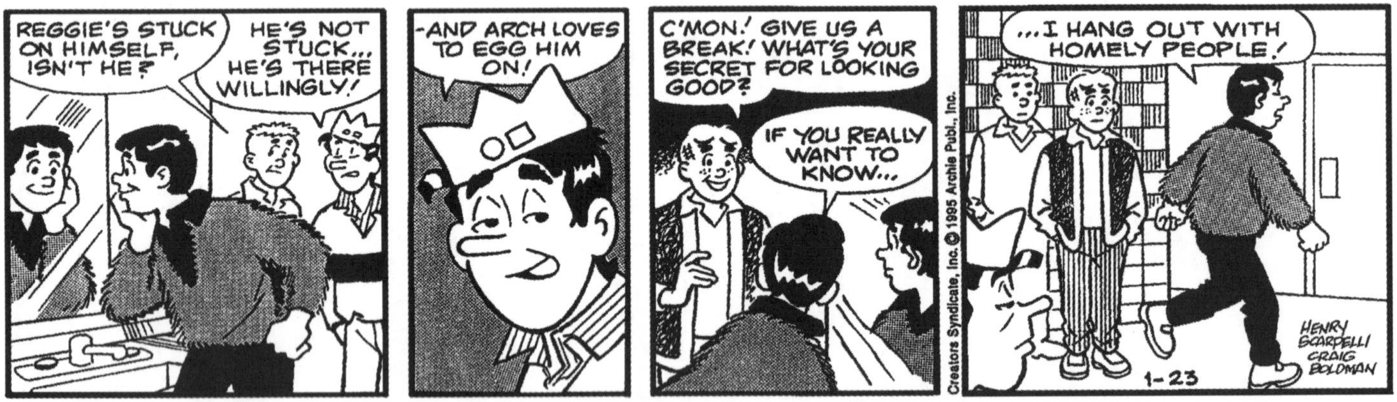
REGGIE'S STUCK ON HIMSELF, ISN'T HE?
HE'S NOT STUCK... HE'S THERE WILLINGLY!
-AND ARCH LOVES TO EGG HIM ON!
C'MON! GIVE US A BREAK! WHAT'S YOUR SECRET FOR LOOKING GOOD?
IF YOU REALLY WANT TO KNOW...
Creators Syndicate, Inc. © 1995 Archie Publ., Inc.
...I HANG OUT WITH HOMELY PEOPLE!
HENRY SCARPELLI CRAIG BOLDMAN
1-23

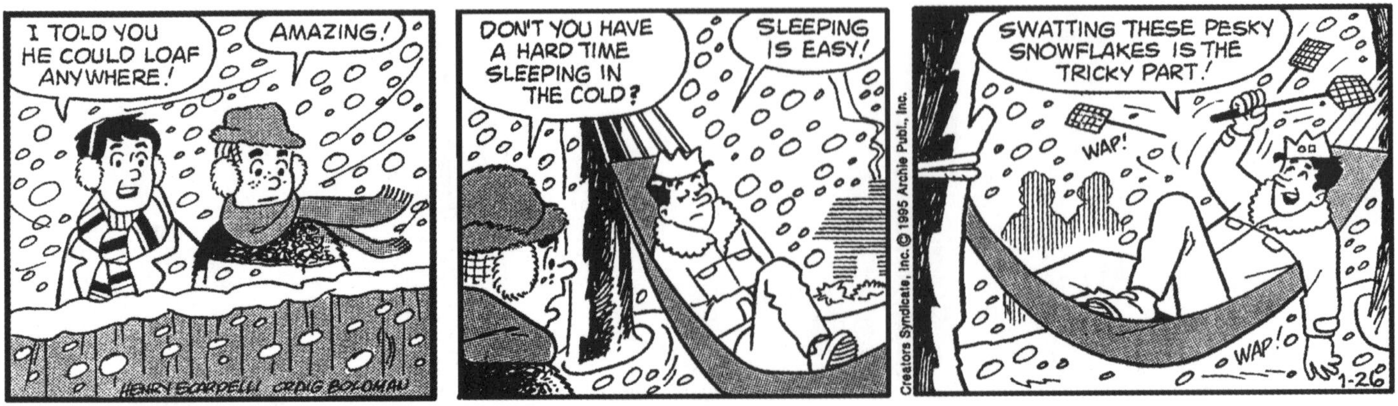
I TOLD YOU HE COULD LOAF ANYWHERE!
AMAZING!
HENRY SCARPELLI CRAIG BOLDMAN
DON'T YOU HAVE A HARD TIME SLEEPING IN THE COLD?
SLEEPING IS EASY!
Creators Syndicate, Inc. © 1995 Archie Publ., Inc.
SWATTING THESE PESKY SNOWFLAKES IS THE TRICKY PART!
WAP!
WAP!
1-26

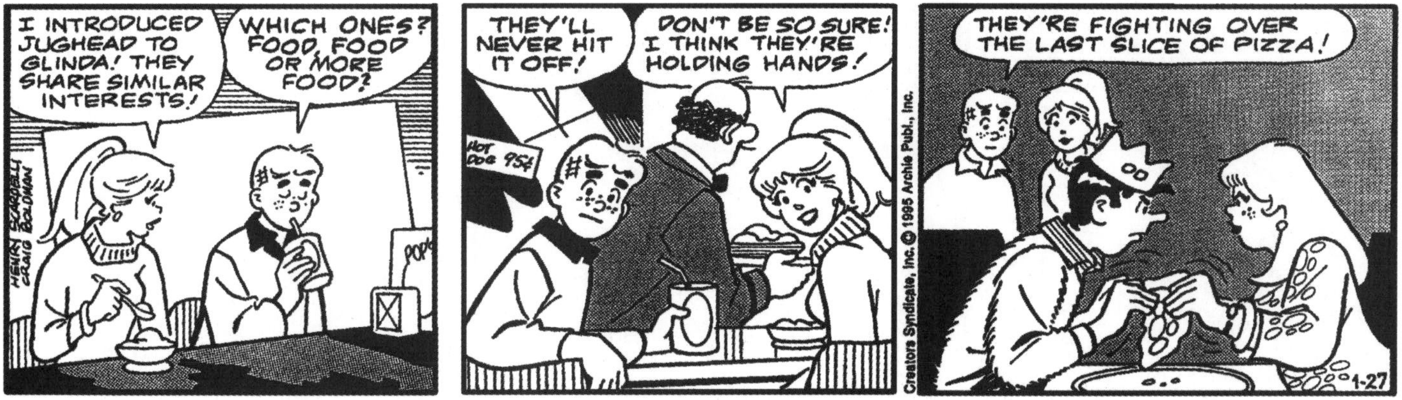
I INTRODUCED JUGHEAD TO GLINDA! THEY SHARE SIMILAR INTERESTS!
WHICH ONES? FOOD, FOOD OR MORE FOOD?
HENRY SCARPELLI CRAIG BOLDMAN
THEY'LL NEVER HIT IT OFF!
DON'T BE SO SURE! I THINK THEY'RE HOLDING HANDS!
HOT DOG 95¢
THEY'RE FIGHTING OVER THE LAST SLICE OF PIZZA!
Creators Syndicate, Inc. © 1995 Archie Publ., Inc.
1-27

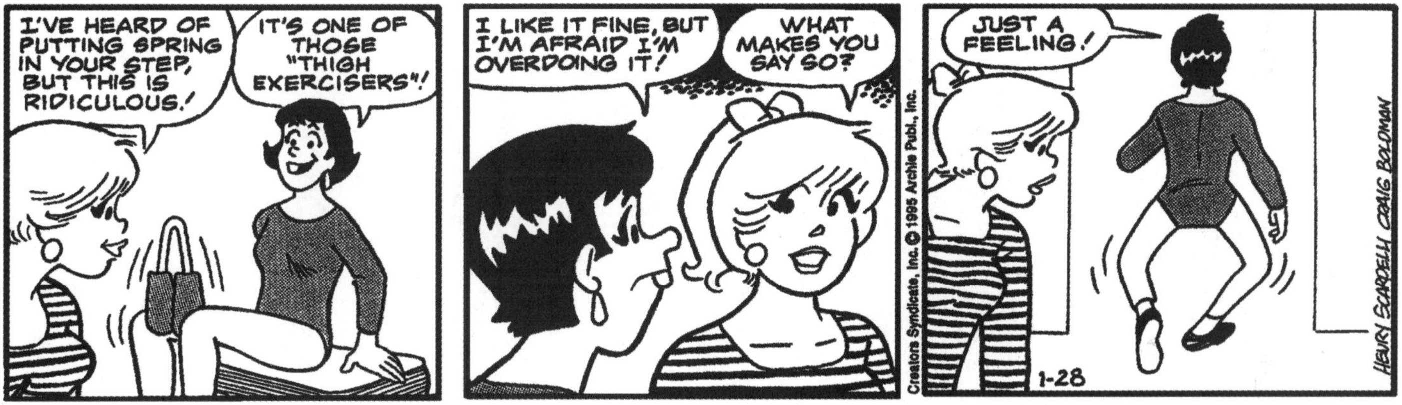
I'VE HEARD OF PUTTING SPRING IN YOUR STEP, BUT THIS IS RIDICULOUS!
IT'S ONE OF THOSE "THIGH EXERCISERS"!
I LIKE IT FINE, BUT I'M AFRAID I'M OVERDOING IT!
WHAT MAKES YOU SAY SO?
Creators Syndicate, Inc. © 1995 Archie Publ., Inc.
JUST A FEELING!
HENRY SCARPELLI CRAIG BOLDMAN
1-28

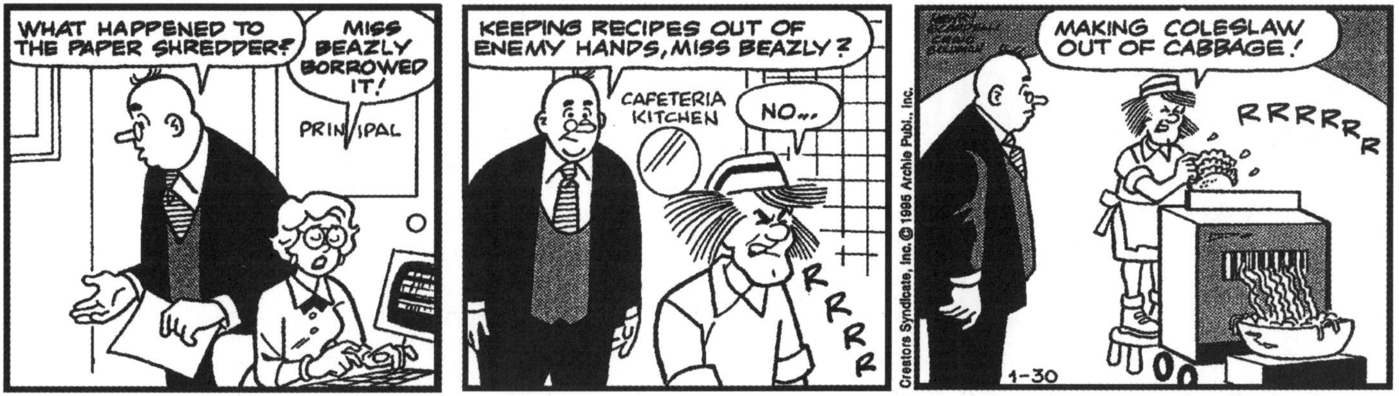
WHAT HAPPENED TO THE PAPER SHREDDER?
MISS BEAZLY BORROWED IT!
PRINCIPAL
KEEPING RECIPES OUT OF ENEMY HANDS, MISS BEAZLY?
CAFETERIA KITCHEN
NO...
RRRR
Creators Syndicate, Inc. © 1995 Archie Publ., Inc.
MAKING COLESLAW OUT OF CABBAGE!
RRRRRRR
1-30

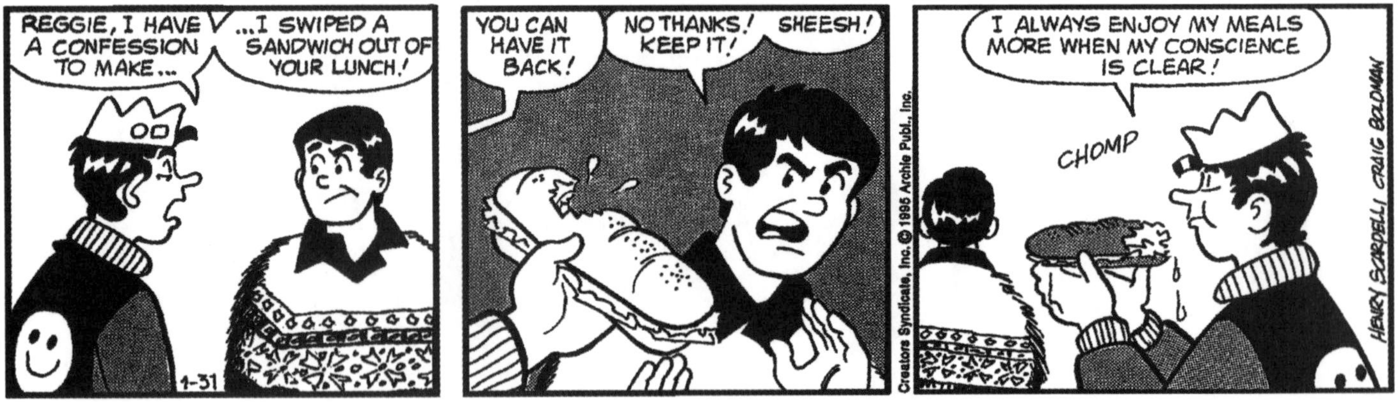
REGGIE, I HAVE A CONFESSION TO MAKE...
...I SWIPED A SANDWICH OUT OF YOUR LUNCH!
1-31
YOU CAN HAVE IT BACK!
NO THANKS! KEEP IT!
SHEESH!
Creators Syndicate, Inc. © 1995 Archie Publ., Inc.
I ALWAYS ENJOY MY MEALS MORE WHEN MY CONSCIENCE IS CLEAR!
CHOMP
HENRY SCARPELLI CRAIG BOLDMAN

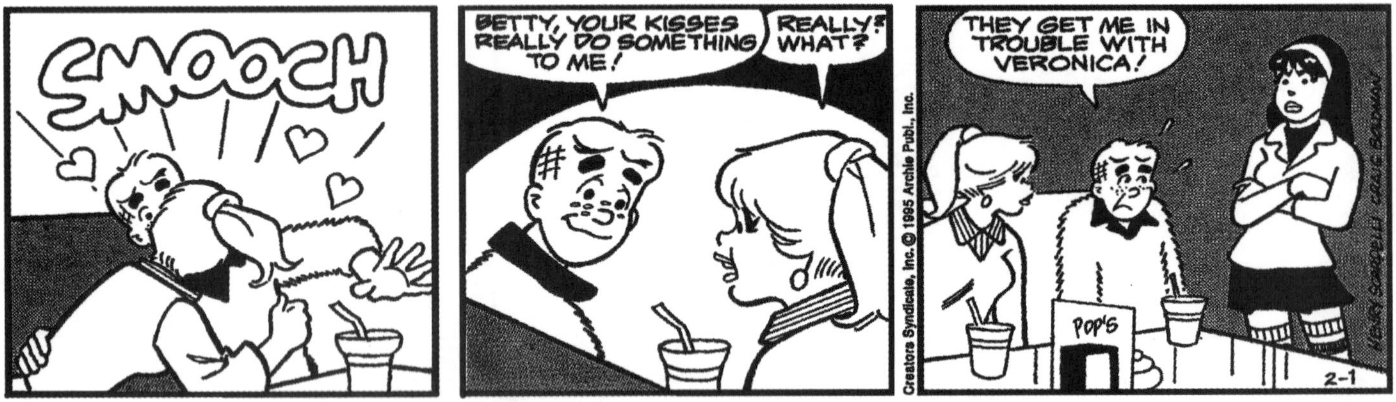
SMOOCH
BETTY, YOUR KISSES REALLY DO SOMETHING TO ME!
REALLY? WHAT?
Creators Syndicate, Inc. © 1995 Archie Publ., Inc.
THEY GET ME IN TROUBLE WITH VERONICA!
POP'S
HENRY SCARPELLI CRAIG BOLDMAN
2-1

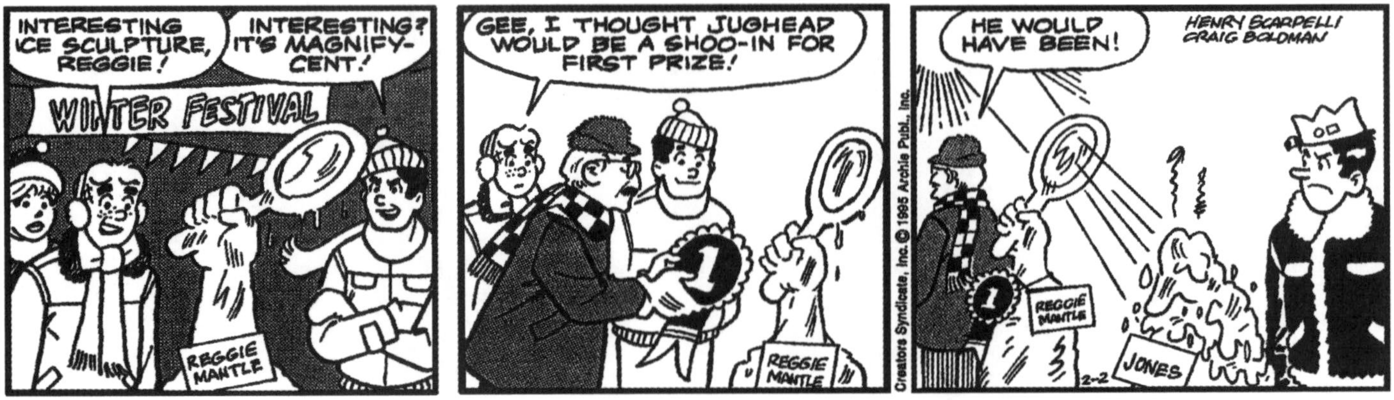
INTERESTING ICE SCULPTURE, REGGIE!
INTERESTING? IT'S MAGNIFY-CENT!
WINTER FESTIVAL
REGGIE MANTLE
GEE, I THOUGHT JUGHEAD WOULD BE A SHOO-IN FOR FIRST PRIZE!
1
REGGIE MANTLE
Creators Syndicate, Inc. © 1995 Archie Publ., Inc.
HE WOULD HAVE BEEN!
HENRY SCARPELLI CRAIG BOLDMAN
REGGIE MANTLE
JONES
2-2

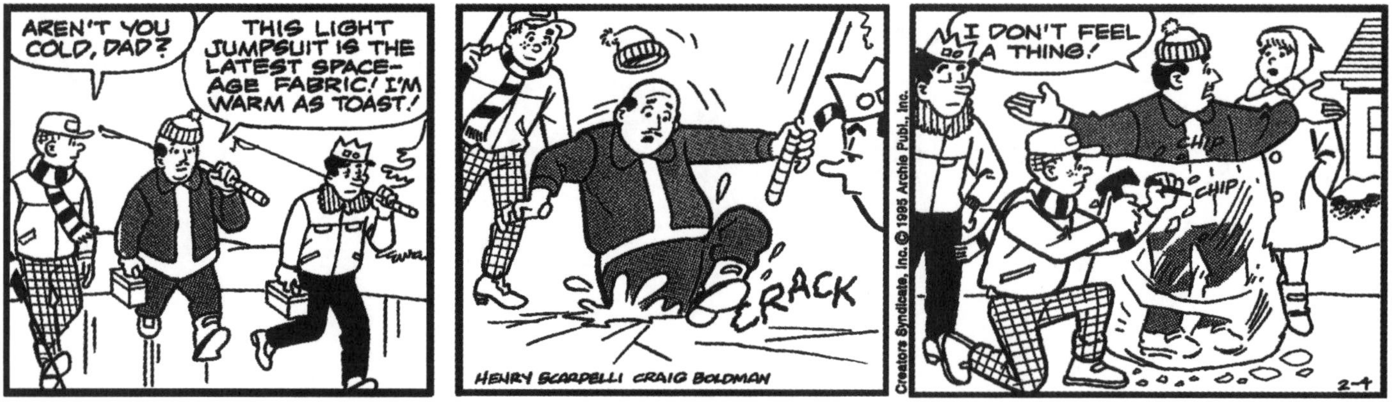

AREN'T YOU COLD, DAD?
THIS LIGHT JUMPSUIT IS THE LATEST SPACE-AGE FABRIC! I'M WARM AS TOAST!
CRACK
HENRY SCARPELLI CRAIG BOLDMAN
I DON'T FEEL A THING!
CHIP
CHIP
Creators Syndicate, Inc. © 1995 Archie Publ., Inc.
2-4

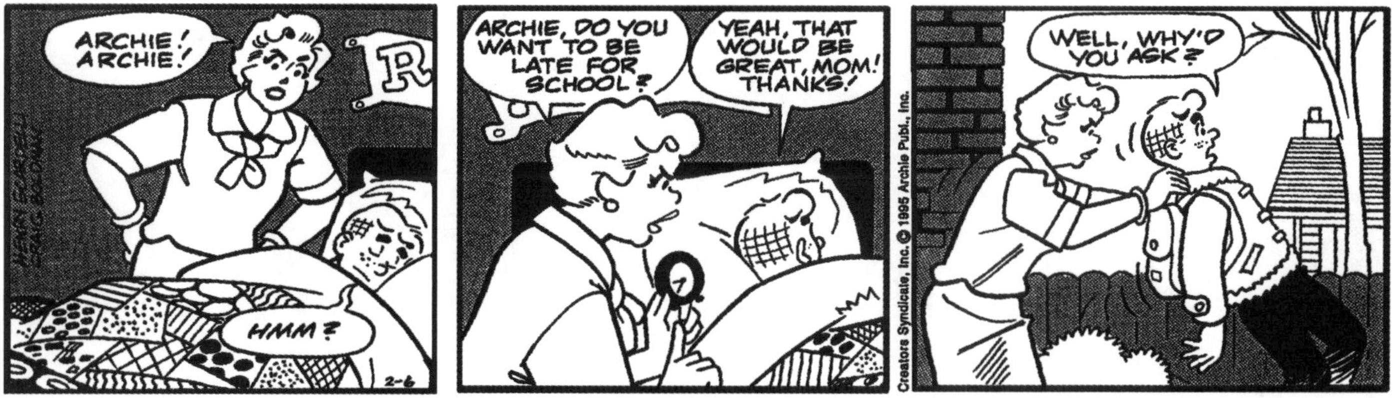

ARCHIE! ARCHIE!
HENRY SCARPELLI CRAIG BOLDMAN
HMM?
2-6
ARCHIE, DO YOU WANT TO BE LATE FOR SCHOOL?
YEAH, THAT WOULD BE GREAT, MOM! THANKS!
WELL, WHY'D YOU ASK?
Creators Syndicate, Inc. © 1995 Archie Publ., Inc.

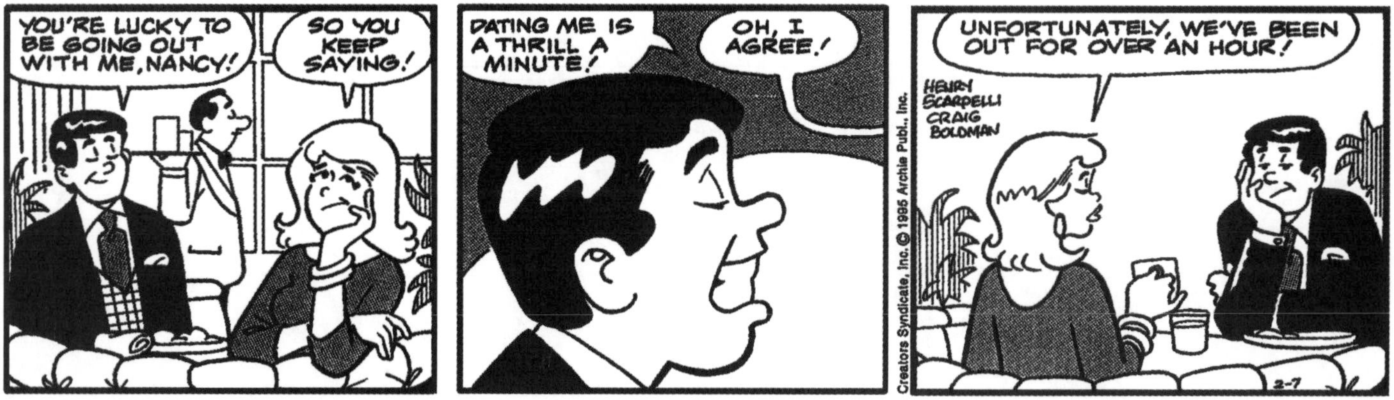

YOU'RE LUCKY TO BE GOING OUT WITH ME, NANCY!
SO YOU KEEP SAYING!
DATING ME IS A THRILL A MINUTE!
OH, I AGREE!
UNFORTUNATELY, WE'VE BEEN OUT FOR OVER AN HOUR!
HENRY SCARPELLI CRAIG BOLDMAN
Creators Syndicate, Inc. © 1995 Archie Publ., Inc.
2-7

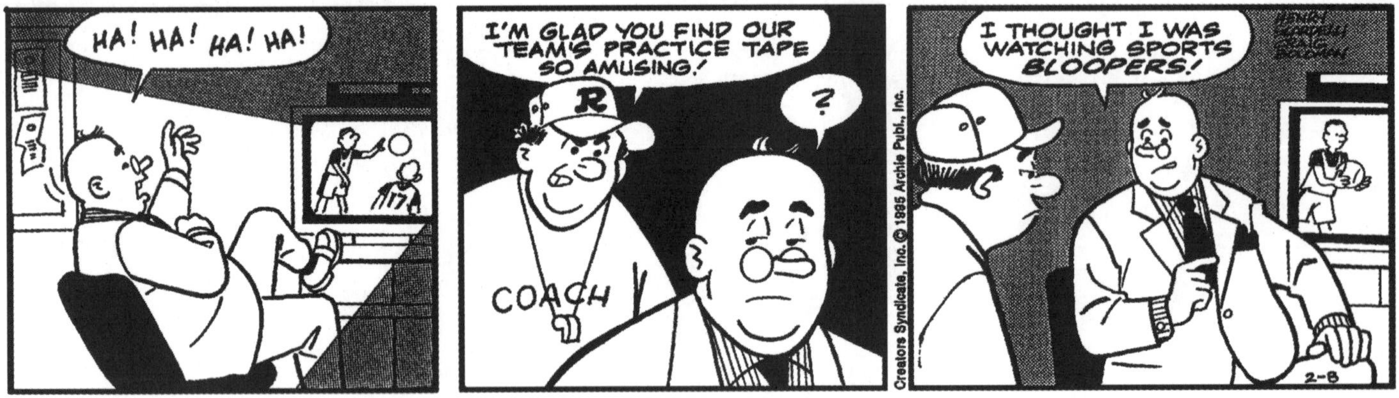
HA! HA! HA! HA!
I'M GLAD YOU FIND OUR TEAM'S PRACTICE TAPE SO AMUSING!
COACH
?
I THOUGHT I WAS WATCHING SPORTS *BLOOPERS!*
HENRY SCARPELLI CRAIG BOLDMAN
Creators Syndicate, Inc. © 1995 Archie Publ., Inc.
2-8

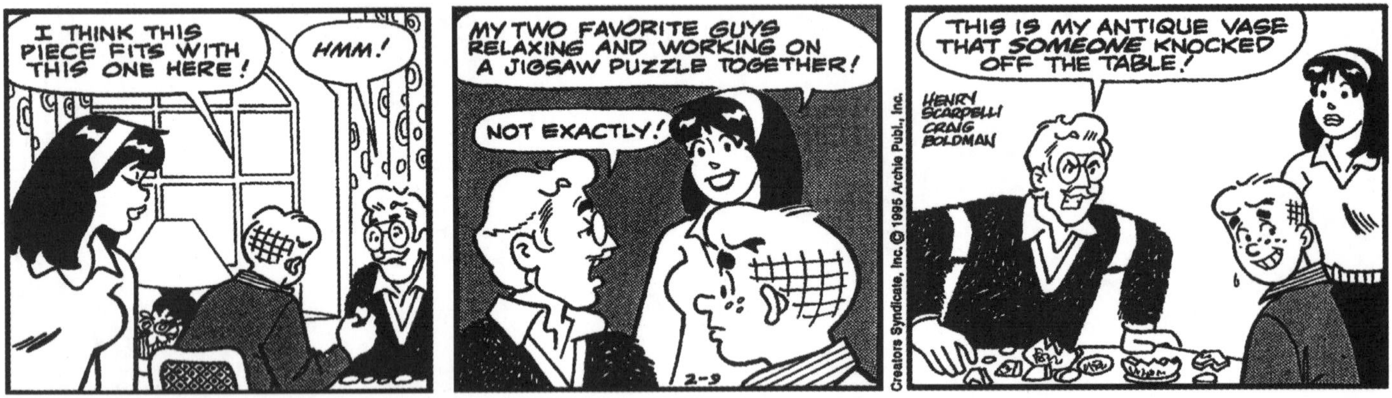
I THINK THIS PIECE FITS WITH THIS ONE HERE!
HMM!
MY TWO FAVORITE GUYS RELAXING AND WORKING ON A JIGSAW PUZZLE TOGETHER!
NOT EXACTLY!
2-9
Creators Syndicate, Inc. © 1995 Archie Publ., Inc.
THIS IS MY ANTIQUE VASE THAT *SOMEONE* KNOCKED OFF THE TABLE!
HENRY SCARPELLI CRAIG BOLDMAN

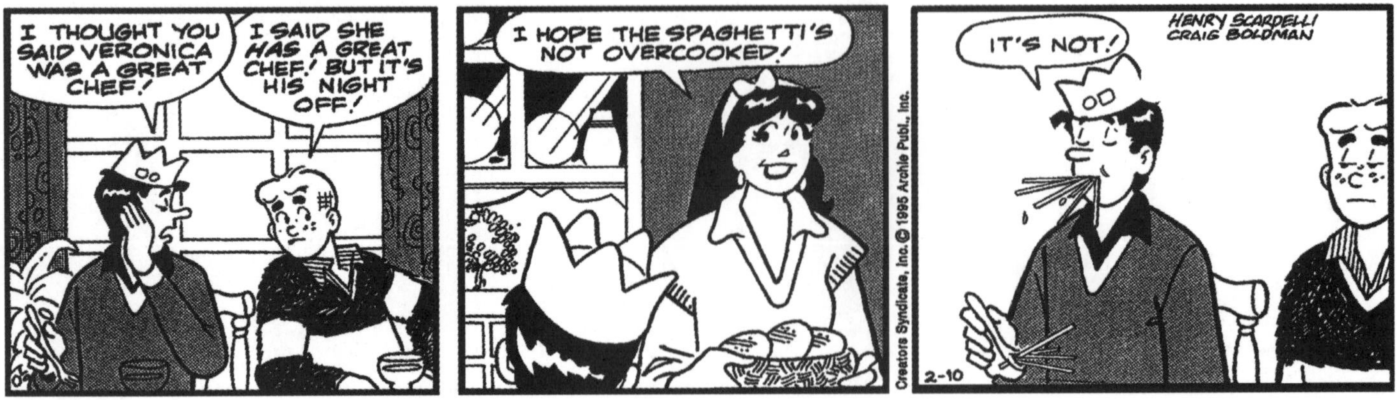
I THOUGHT YOU SAID VERONICA WAS A GREAT CHEF!
I SAID SHE *HAS* A GREAT CHEF! BUT IT'S HIS NIGHT OFF!
I HOPE THE SPAGHETTI'S NOT OVERCOOKED!
Creators Syndicate, Inc. © 1995 Archie Publ., Inc.
IT'S NOT!
HENRY SCARPELLI CRAIG BOLDMAN
2-10

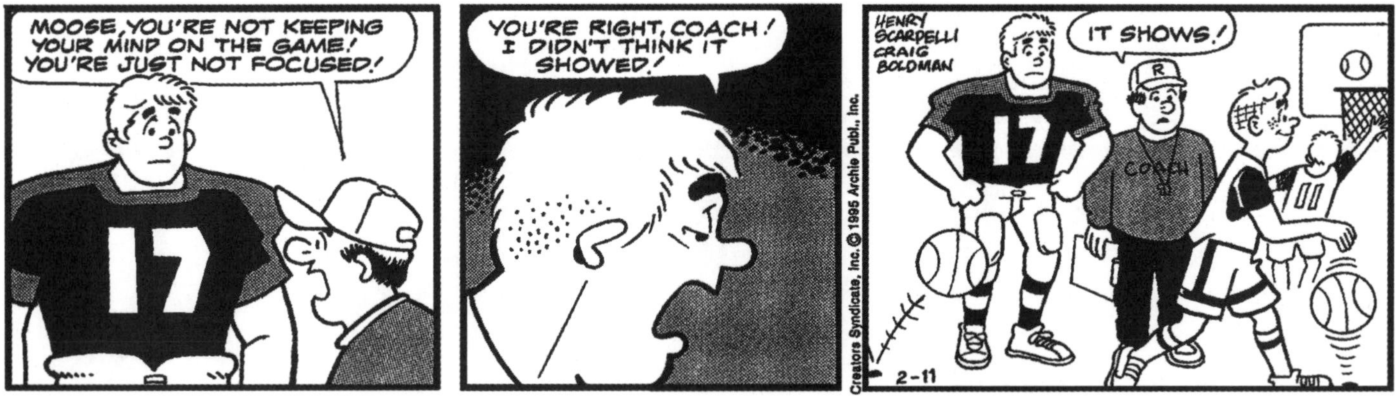
MOOSE, YOU'RE NOT KEEPING YOUR MIND ON THE GAME! YOU'RE JUST NOT FOCUSED!
YOU'RE RIGHT, COACH! I DIDN'T THINK IT SHOWED!
HENRY SCARPELLI CRAIG BOLDMAN
IT SHOWS!
COACH
Creators Syndicate, Inc. © 1995 Archie Publ., Inc.
2-11

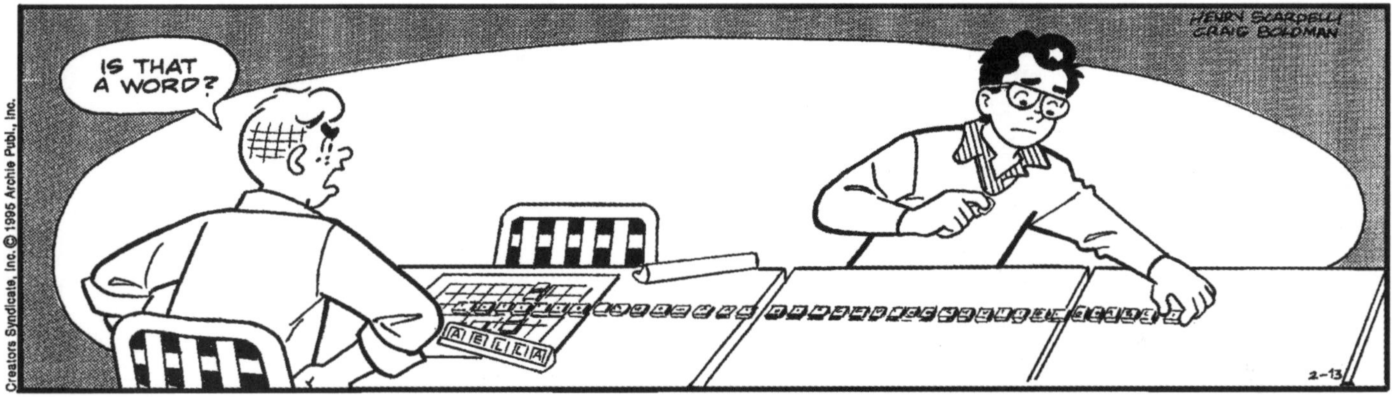
HENRY SCARPELLI CRAIG BOLDMAN
IS THAT A WORD?
Creators Syndicate, Inc. © 1995 Archie Publ., Inc.
2-13

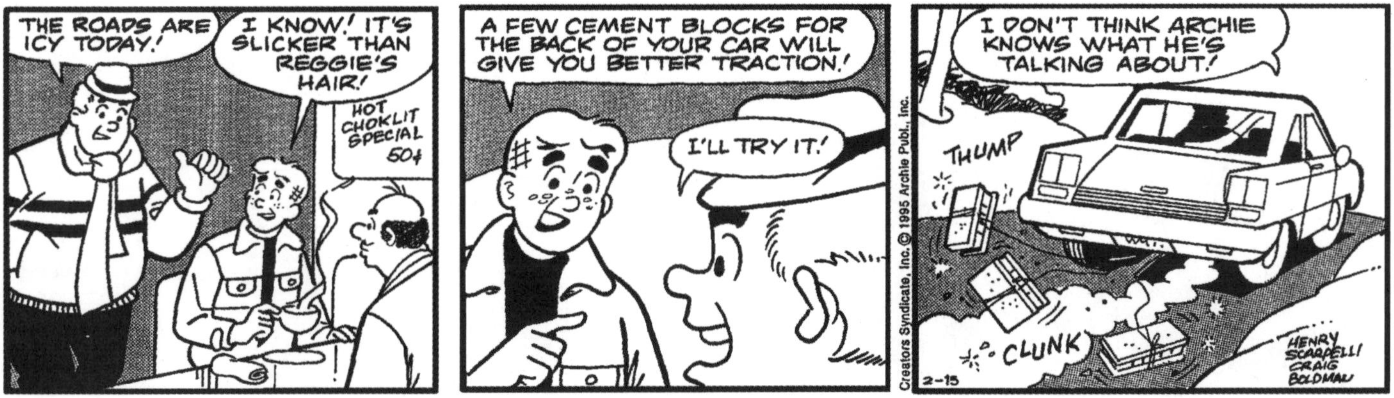
THE ROADS ARE ICY TODAY!
I KNOW! IT'S SLICKER THAN REGGIE'S HAIR!
HOT CHOKLIT SPECIAL 50¢
A FEW CEMENT BLOCKS FOR THE BACK OF YOUR CAR WILL GIVE YOU BETTER TRACTION!
I'LL TRY IT!
I DON'T THINK ARCHIE KNOWS WHAT HE'S TALKING ABOUT!
THUMP
CLUNK
HENRY SCARPELLI CRAIG BOLDMAN
Creators Syndicate, Inc. © 1995 Archie Publ., Inc.
2-15

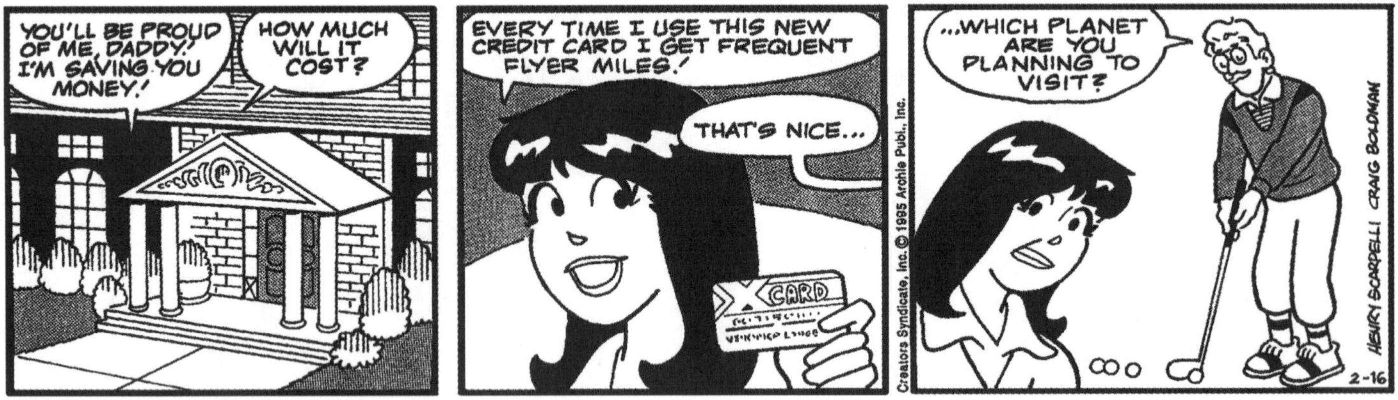
YOU'LL BE PROUD OF ME, DADDY! I'M SAVING YOU MONEY!
HOW MUCH WILL IT COST?
EVERY TIME I USE THIS NEW CREDIT CARD I GET FREQUENT FLYER MILES!
X CARD
THAT'S NICE...
...WHICH PLANET ARE YOU PLANNING TO VISIT?
Creators Syndicate, Inc. © 1995 Archie Publ., Inc.
HENRY SCARPELLI CRAIG BOLDMAN
2-16

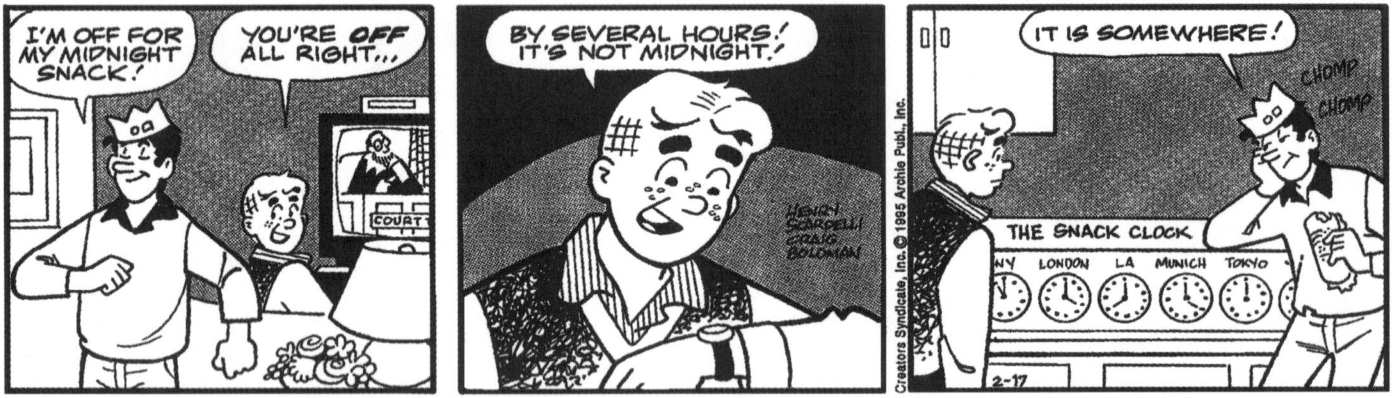
I'M OFF FOR MY MIDNIGHT SNACK!
YOU'RE OFF ALL RIGHT...
COURT
BY SEVERAL HOURS! IT'S NOT MIDNIGHT!
HENRY SCARPELLI CRAIG BOLDMAN
Creators Syndicate, Inc. © 1995 Archie Publ., Inc.
IT IS SOMEWHERE!
CHOMP
CHOMP
THE SNACK CLOCK
NY LONDON LA MUNICH TOKYO
2-17

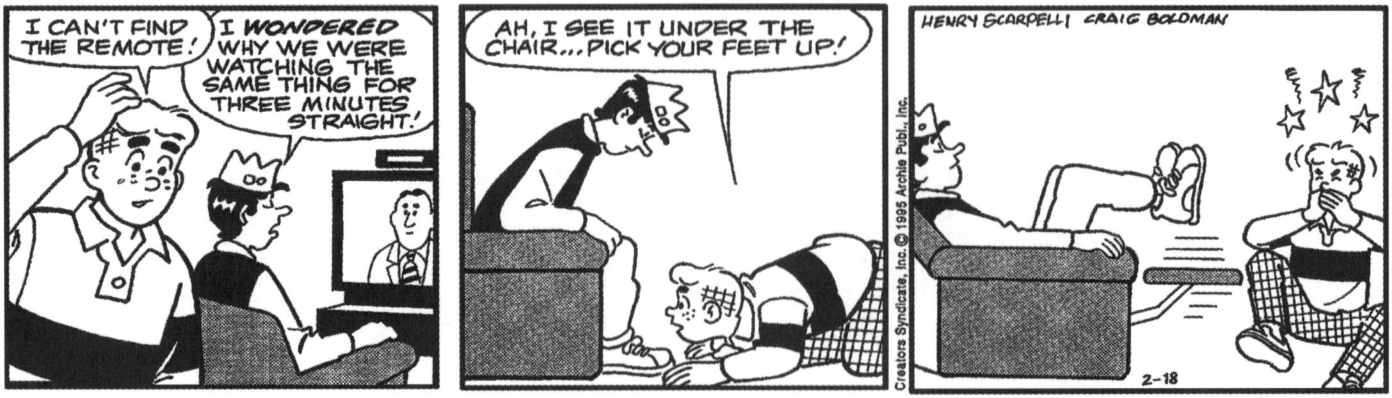
I CAN'T FIND THE REMOTE!
I WONDERED WHY WE WERE WATCHING THE SAME THING FOR THREE MINUTES STRAIGHT!
AH, I SEE IT UNDER THE CHAIR... PICK YOUR FEET UP!
Creators Syndicate, Inc. © 1995 Archie Publ., Inc.
HENRY SCARPELLI CRAIG BOLDMAN
2-18

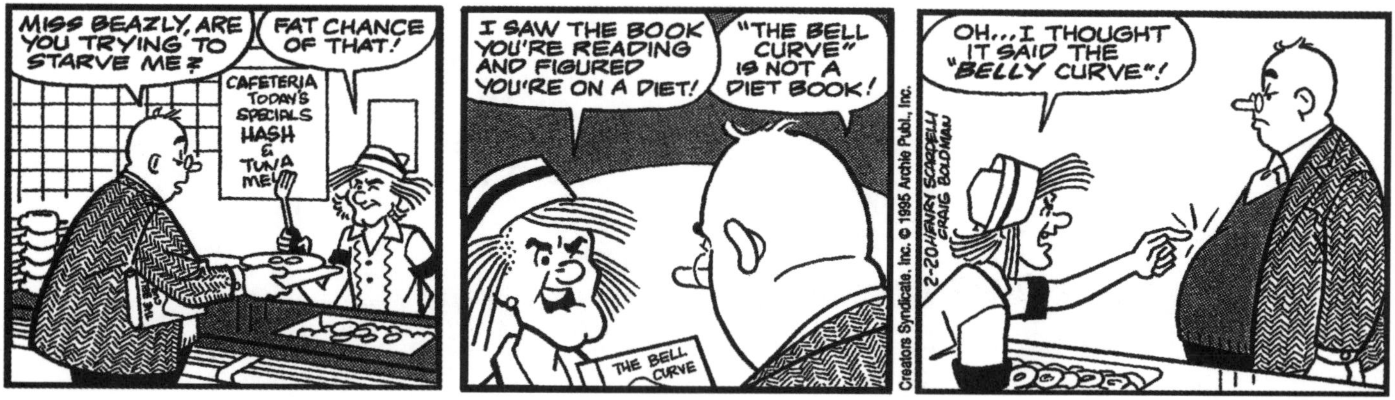
MISS BEAZLY, ARE YOU TRYING TO STARVE ME?
FAT CHANCE OF THAT!
CAFETERIA TODAY'S SPECIALS HASH & TUNA MELT
I SAW THE BOOK YOU'RE READING AND FIGURED YOU'RE ON A DIET!
"THE BELL CURVE" IS NOT A DIET BOOK!
THE BELL CURVE
OH...I THOUGHT IT SAID THE "BELLY CURVE"!
2-20 HENRY SCARPELLI CRAIG BOLDMAN
Creators Syndicate, Inc. © 1995 Archie Publ., Inc.

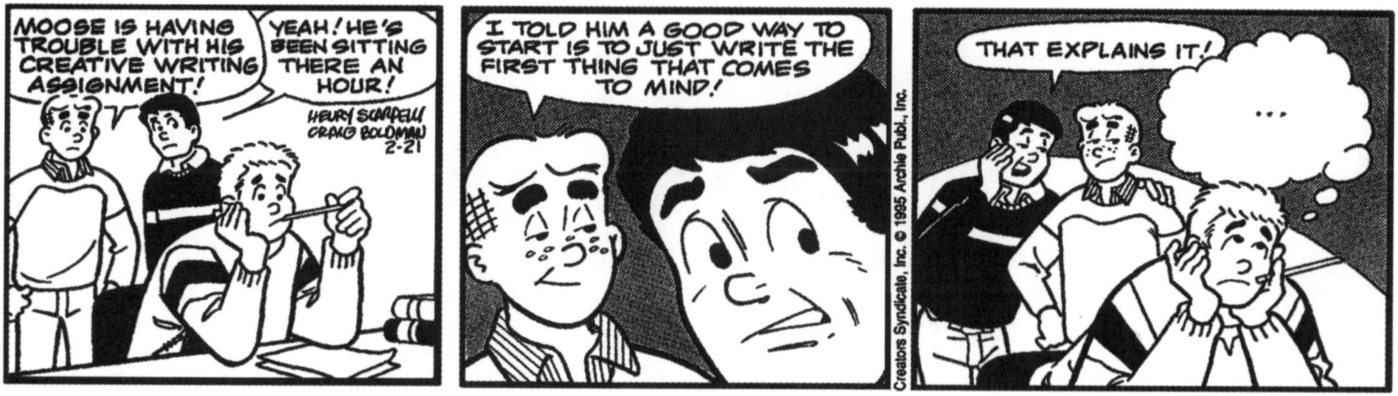
MOOSE IS HAVING TROUBLE WITH HIS CREATIVE WRITING ASSIGNMENT!
YEAH! HE'S BEEN SITTING THERE AN HOUR!
HENRY SCARPELLI CRAIG BOLDMAN 2-21
I TOLD HIM A GOOD WAY TO START IS TO JUST WRITE THE FIRST THING THAT COMES TO MIND!
THAT EXPLAINS IT!
...
Creators Syndicate, Inc. © 1995 Archie Publ., Inc.

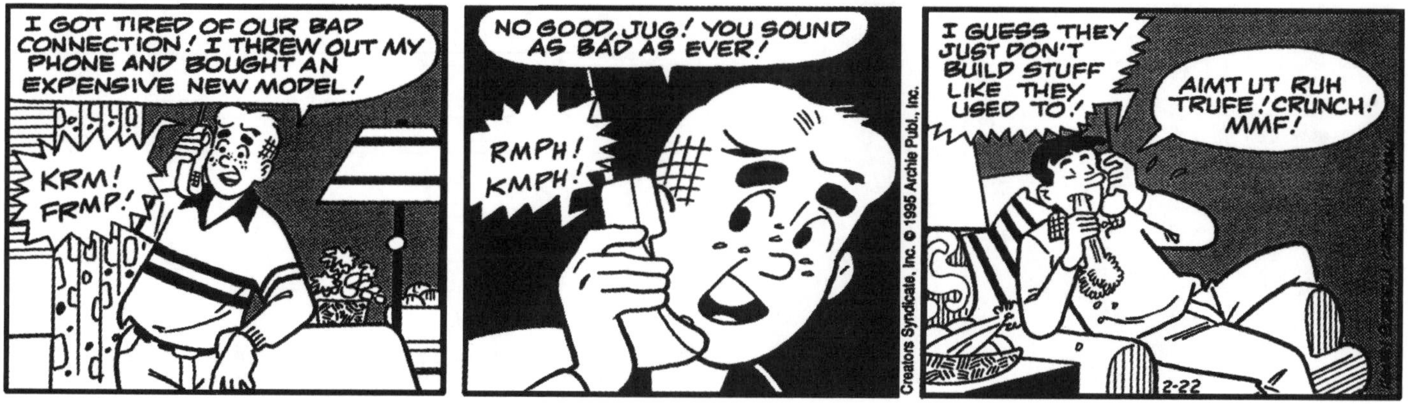
I GOT TIRED OF OUR BAD CONNECTION! I THREW OUT MY PHONE AND BOUGHT AN EXPENSIVE NEW MODEL!
KRM! FRMP!
NO GOOD, JUG! YOU SOUND AS BAD AS EVER!
RMPH! KMPH!
I GUESS THEY JUST DON'T BUILD STUFF LIKE THEY USED TO!
AIMT UT RUH TRUFE! CRUNCH! MMF!
2-22
Creators Syndicate, Inc. © 1995 Archie Publ., Inc.

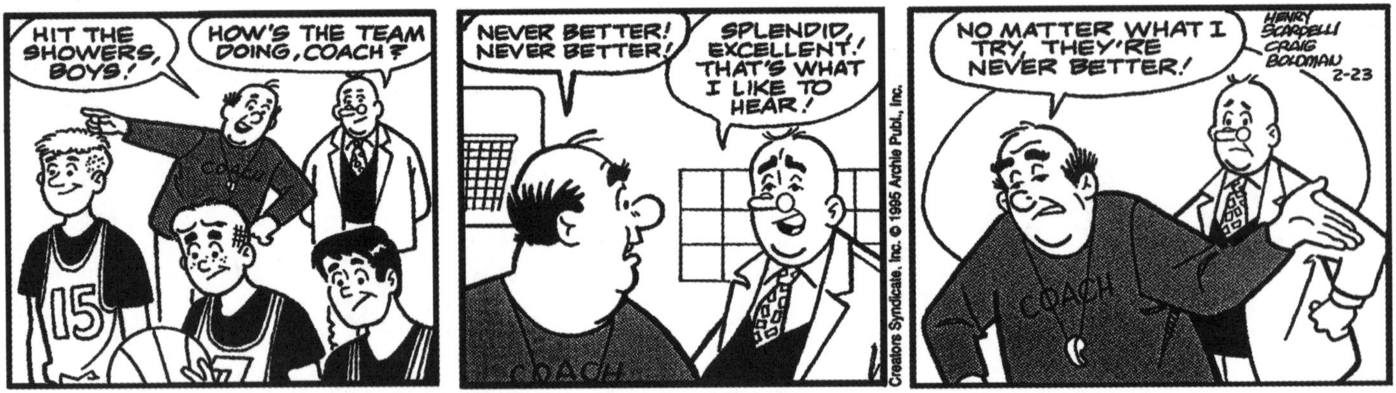
HIT THE SHOWERS, BOYS!
HOW'S THE TEAM DOING, COACH?
NEVER BETTER! NEVER BETTER!
SPLENDID, EXCELLENT! THAT'S WHAT I LIKE TO HEAR!
Creators Syndicate, Inc. © 1995 Archie Publ., Inc.
NO MATTER WHAT I TRY, THEY'RE NEVER BETTER!
HENRY SCARPELLI CRAIG BOLDMAN 2-23

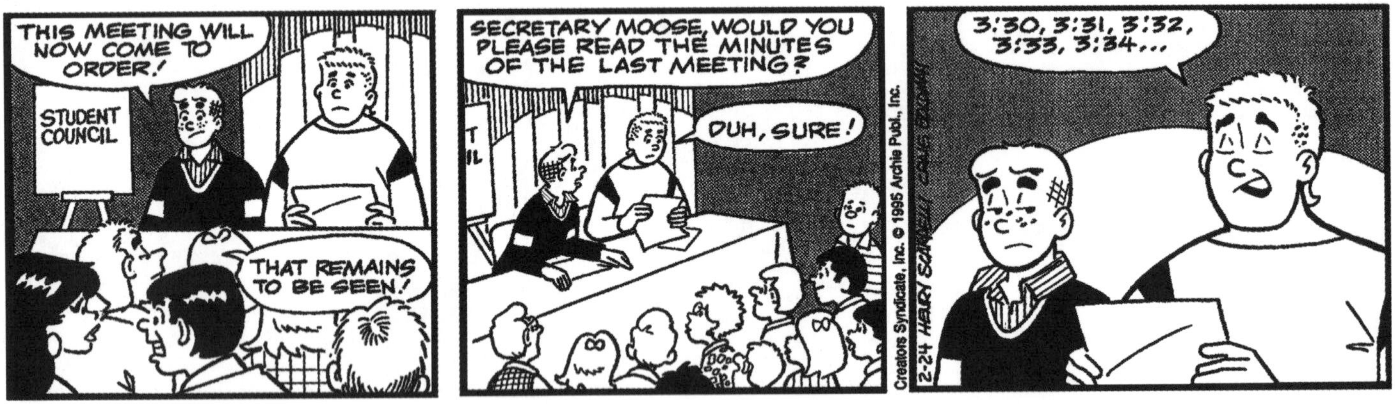
THIS MEETING WILL NOW COME TO ORDER!
STUDENT COUNCIL
THAT REMAINS TO BE SEEN!
SECRETARY MOOSE, WOULD YOU PLEASE READ THE MINUTES OF THE LAST MEETING?
DUH, SURE!
Creators Syndicate, Inc. © 1995 Archie Publ., Inc.
2-24 HENRY SCARPELLI CRAIG BOLDMAN
3:30, 3:31, 3:32, 3:33, 3:34...

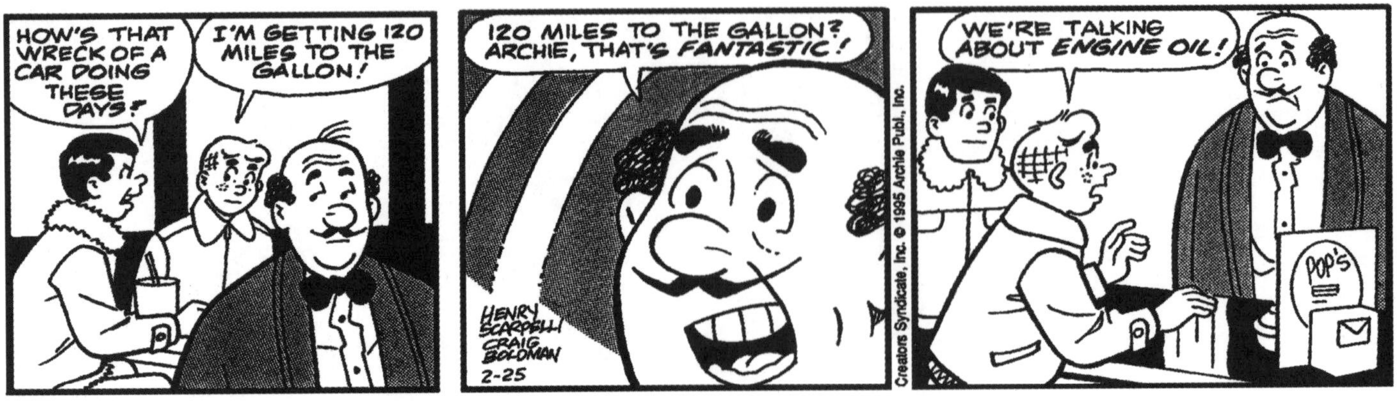
HOW'S THAT WRECK OF A CAR DOING THESE DAYS?
I'M GETTING 120 MILES TO THE GALLON!
120 MILES TO THE GALLON? ARCHIE, THAT'S *FANTASTIC*!
HENRY SCARPELLI CRAIG BOLDMAN
2-25
Creators Syndicate, Inc. © 1995 Archie Publ., Inc.
WE'RE TALKING ABOUT *ENGINE OIL*!
POP'S

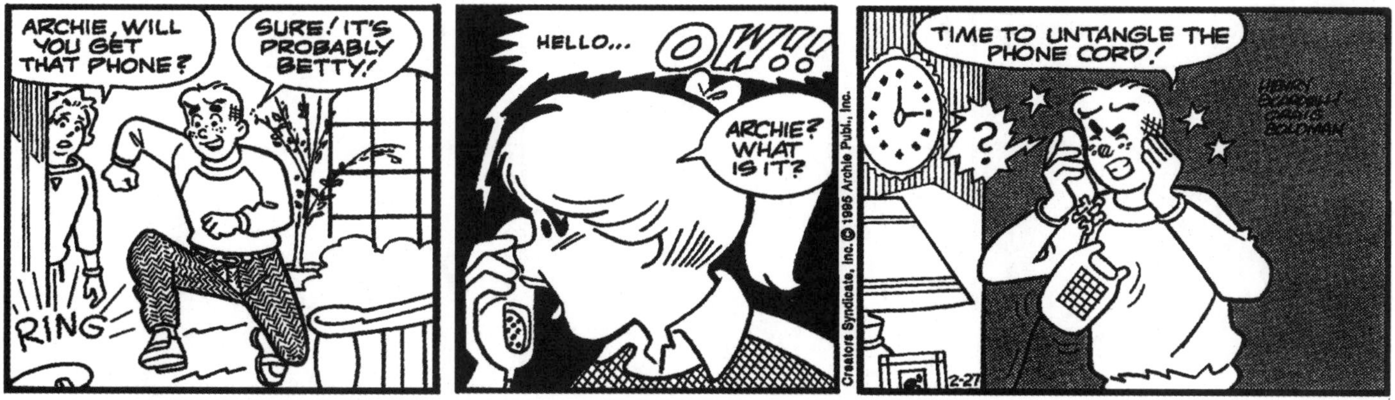
ARCHIE, WILL YOU GET THAT PHONE?
SURE! IT'S PROBABLY BETTY!
RING
HELLO...
OW!!
ARCHIE? WHAT IS IT?
Creators Syndicate, Inc. © 1995 Archie Publ., Inc.
TIME TO UNTANGLE THE PHONE CORD!
?
HENRY SCARPELLI/CRAIG BOLDMAN
2-27

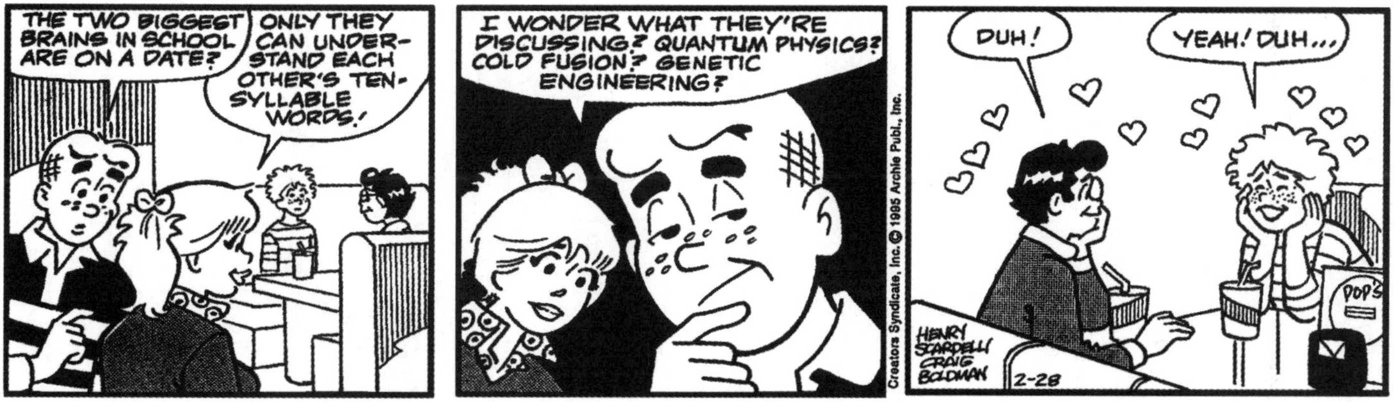
THE TWO BIGGEST BRAINS IN SCHOOL ARE ON A DATE?
ONLY THEY CAN UNDERSTAND EACH OTHER'S TEN-SYLLABLE WORDS!
I WONDER WHAT THEY'RE DISCUSSING? QUANTUM PHYSICS? COLD FUSION? GENETIC ENGINEERING?
Creators Syndicate, Inc. © 1995 Archie Publ., Inc.
DUH!
YEAH! DUH...
POP'S
HENRY SCARPELLI/CRAIG BOLDMAN
2-28

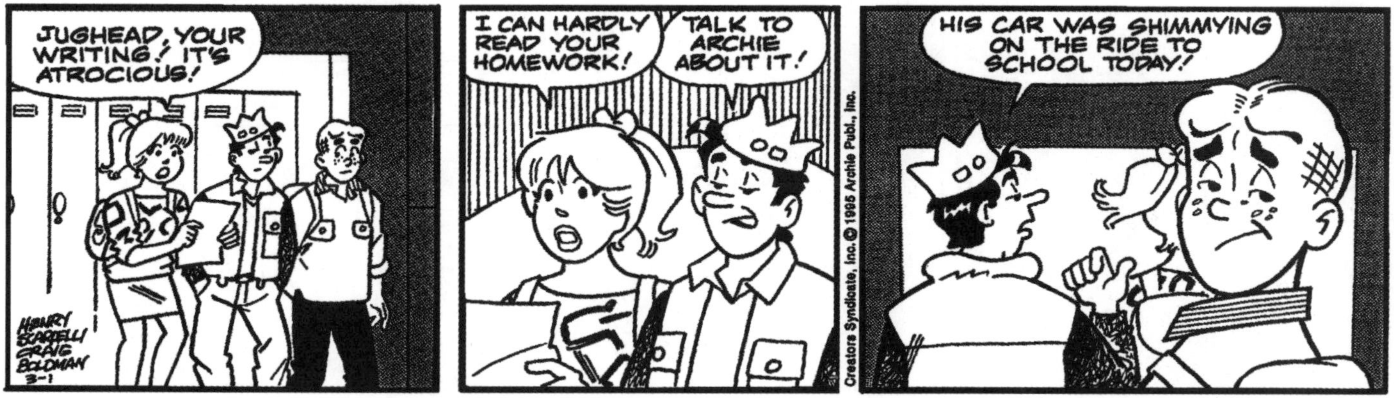
JUGHEAD, YOUR WRITING! IT'S ATROCIOUS!
HENRY SCARPELLI/CRAIG BOLDMAN
3-1
I CAN HARDLY READ YOUR HOMEWORK!
TALK TO ARCHIE ABOUT IT!
Creators Syndicate, Inc. © 1995 Archie Publ., Inc.
HIS CAR WAS SHIMMYING ON THE RIDE TO SCHOOL TODAY!

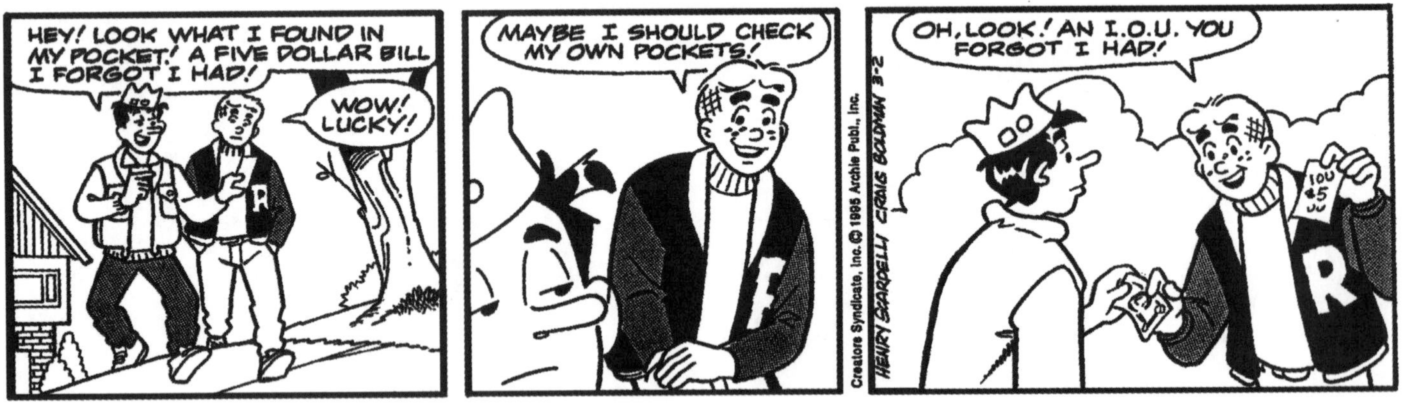
HEY! LOOK WHAT I FOUND IN MY POCKET! A FIVE DOLLAR BILL I FORGOT I HAD!
WOW! LUCKY!
MAYBE I SHOULD CHECK MY OWN POCKETS!
Creators Syndicate, Inc. © 1995 Archie Publ., Inc.
HENRY SCARPELLI CRAIG BOLDMAN 3-2
OH, LOOK! AN I.O.U. YOU FORGOT I HAD!
IOU $5 JJ

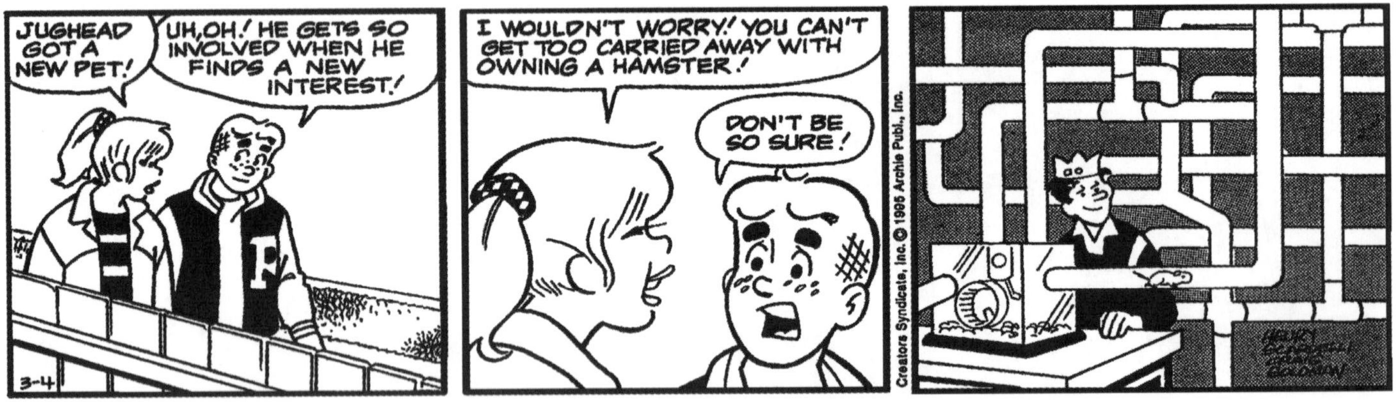
JUGHEAD GOT A NEW PET!
UH, OH! HE GETS SO INVOLVED WHEN HE FINDS A NEW INTEREST!
3-4
I WOULDN'T WORRY! YOU CAN'T GET TOO CARRIED AWAY WITH OWNING A HAMSTER!
DON'T BE SO SURE!
Creators Syndicate, Inc. © 1995 Archie Publ., Inc.

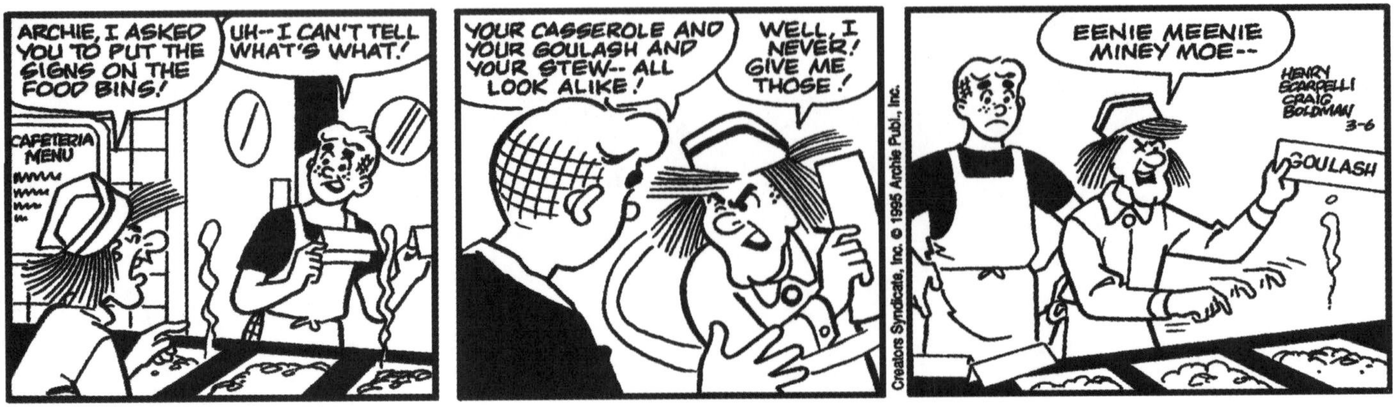
ARCHIE, I ASKED YOU TO PUT THE SIGNS ON THE FOOD BINS!
UH-- I CAN'T TELL WHAT'S WHAT!
CAFETERIA MENU
YOUR CASSEROLE AND YOUR GOULASH AND YOUR STEW-- ALL LOOK ALIKE!
WELL, I NEVER! GIVE ME THOSE!
Creators Syndicate, Inc. © 1995 Archie Publ., Inc.
EENIE MEENIE MINEY MOE--
HENRY SCARPELLI CRAIG BOLDMAN 3-6
GOULASH

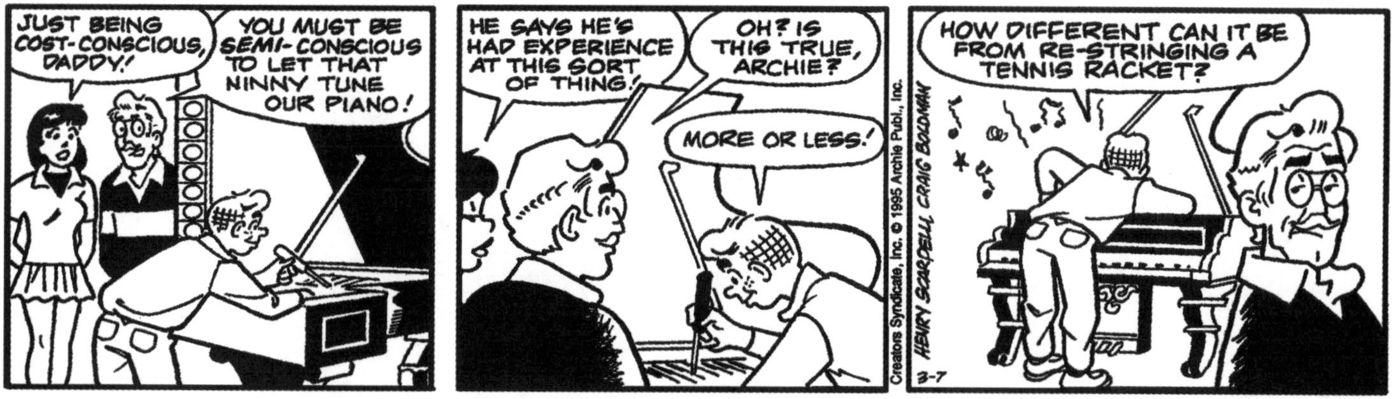
JUST BEING COST-CONSCIOUS, DADDY!
YOU MUST BE SEMI-CONSCIOUS TO LET THAT NINNY TUNE OUR PIANO!
HE SAYS HE'S HAD EXPERIENCE AT THIS SORT OF THING!
OH? IS THIS TRUE, ARCHIE?
MORE OR LESS!
Creators Syndicate, Inc. © 1995 Archie Publ., Inc.
HENRY SCARPELLI CRAIG BOLDMAN
3-7
HOW DIFFERENT CAN IT BE FROM RE-STRINGING A TENNIS RACKET?

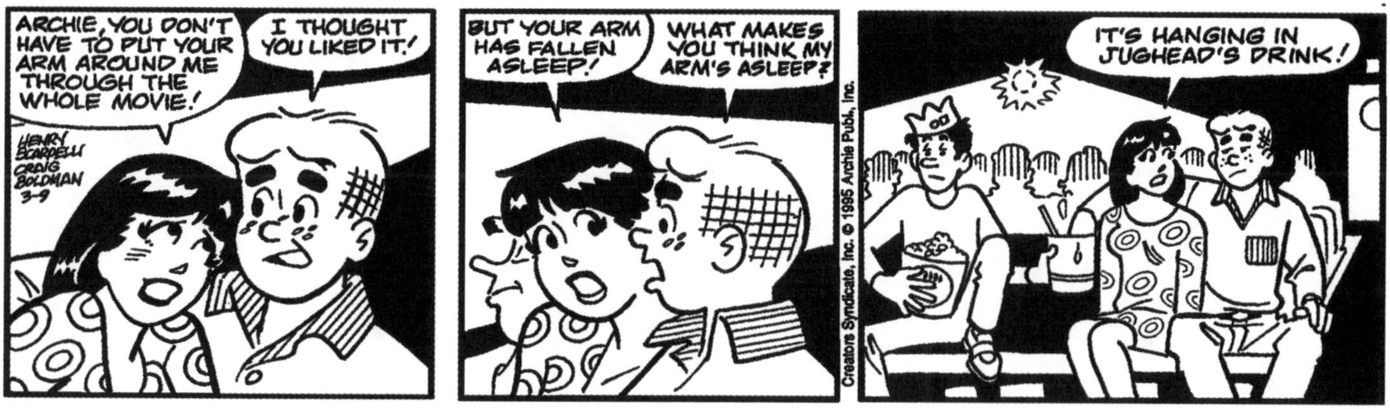
ARCHIE, YOU DON'T HAVE TO PUT YOUR ARM AROUND ME THROUGH THE WHOLE MOVIE!
I THOUGHT YOU LIKED IT!
HENRY SCARPELLI CRAIG BOLDMAN 3-9
BUT YOUR ARM HAS FALLEN ASLEEP!
WHAT MAKES YOU THINK MY ARM'S ASLEEP?
Creators Syndicate, Inc. © 1995 Archie Publ., Inc.
IT'S HANGING IN JUGHEAD'S DRINK!

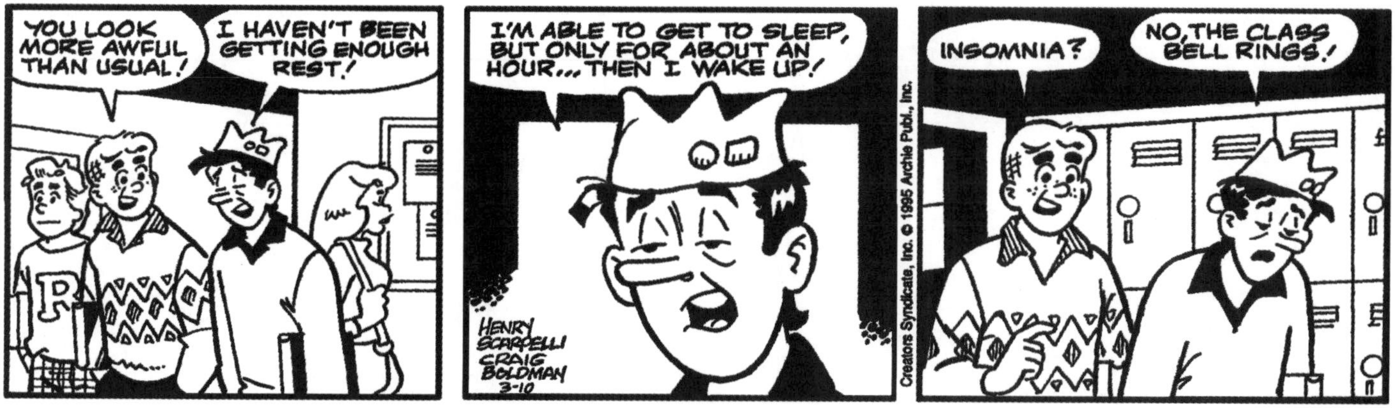
YOU LOOK MORE AWFUL THAN USUAL!
I HAVEN'T BEEN GETTING ENOUGH REST!
I'M ABLE TO GET TO SLEEP, BUT ONLY FOR ABOUT AN HOUR... THEN I WAKE UP!
HENRY SCARPELLI CRAIG BOLDMAN 3-10
Creators Syndicate, Inc. © 1995 Archie Publ., Inc.
INSOMNIA?
NO, THE CLASS BELL RINGS!

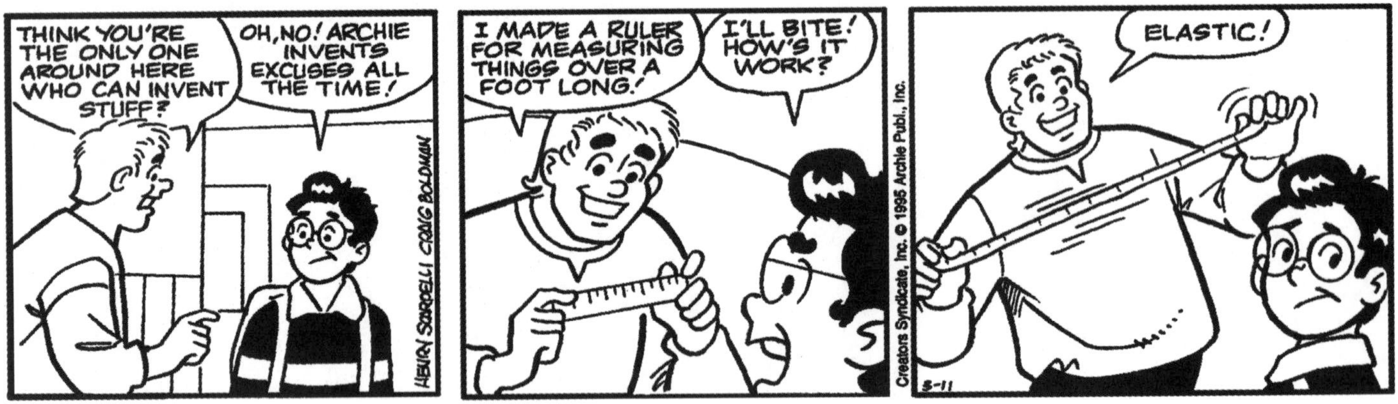
THINK YOU'RE THE ONLY ONE AROUND HERE WHO CAN INVENT STUFF?
OH, NO! ARCHIE INVENTS EXCUSES ALL THE TIME!
HENRY SCARPELLI / CRAIG BOLDMAN
I MADE A RULER FOR MEASURING THINGS OVER A FOOT LONG!
I'LL BITE! HOW'S IT WORK?
ELASTIC!
Creators Syndicate, Inc. © 1995 Archie Publ., Inc.
3-11

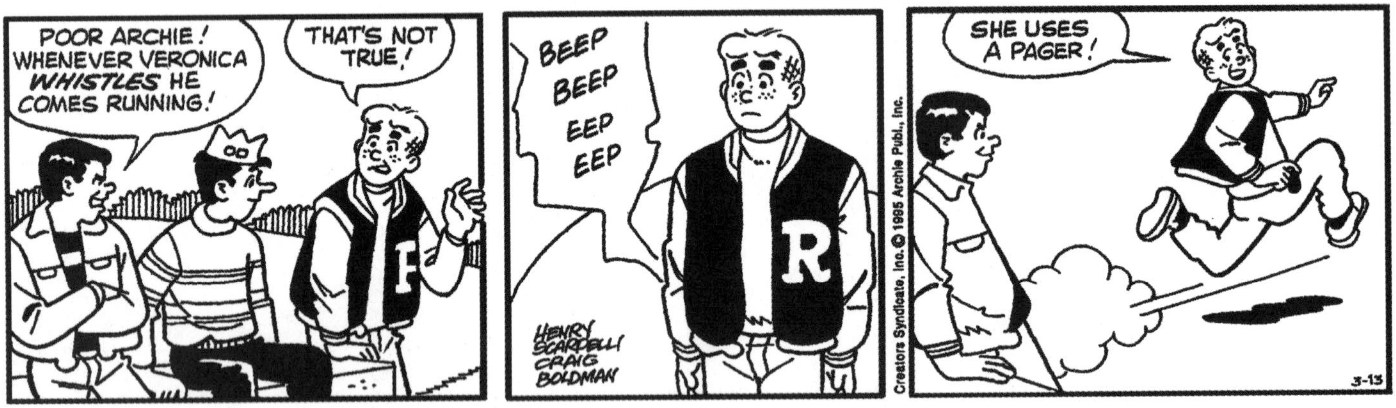
POOR ARCHIE! WHENEVER VERONICA *WHISTLES* HE COMES RUNNING!
THAT'S NOT TRUE!
BEEP
BEEP
EEP
EEP
HENRY SCARPELLI / CRAIG BOLDMAN
SHE USES A PAGER!
Creators Syndicate, Inc. © 1995 Archie Publ., Inc.
3-13

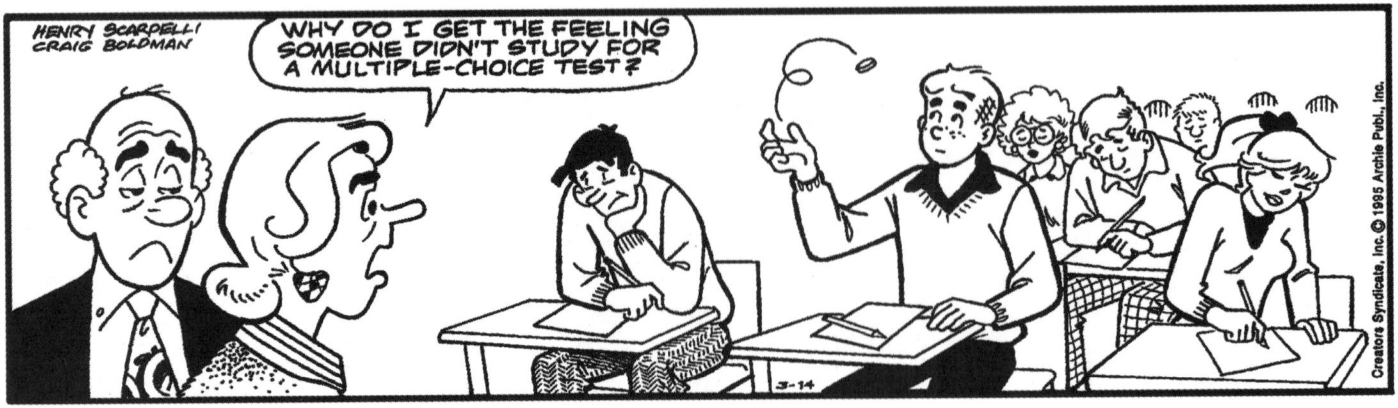
HENRY SCARPELLI / CRAIG BOLDMAN
WHY DO I GET THE FEELING SOMEONE DIDN'T STUDY FOR A MULTIPLE-CHOICE TEST?
3-14
Creators Syndicate, Inc. © 1995 Archie Publ., Inc.

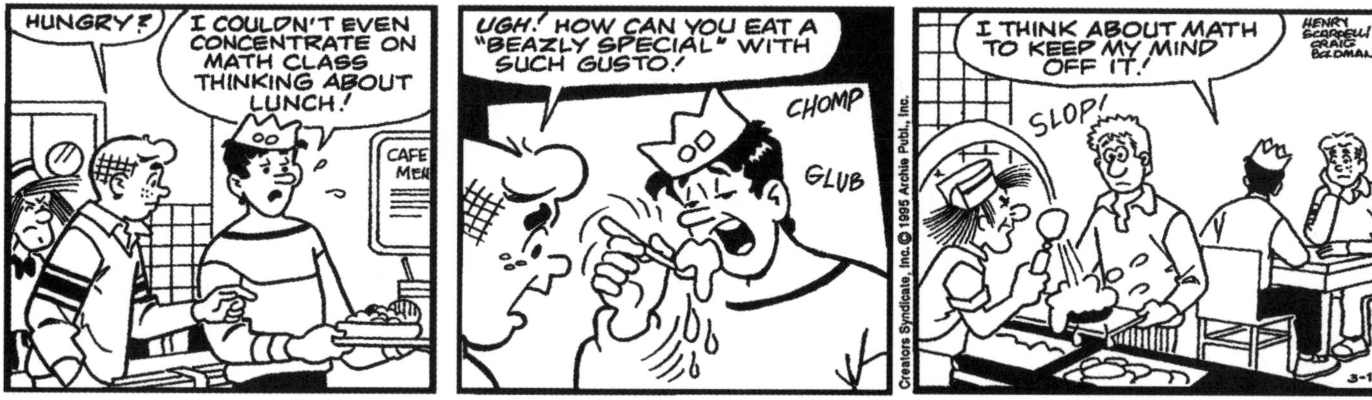
HUNGRY?
I COULDN'T EVEN CONCENTRATE ON MATH CLASS THINKING ABOUT LUNCH!
CAFE MEN
UGH! HOW CAN YOU EAT A "BEAZLY SPECIAL" WITH SUCH GUSTO!
CHOMP
GLUB
Creators Syndicate, Inc. © 1995 Archie Publ., Inc.
I THINK ABOUT MATH TO KEEP MY MIND OFF IT!
HENRY SCARPELLI CRAIG BOLDMAN
SLOP!
3-15

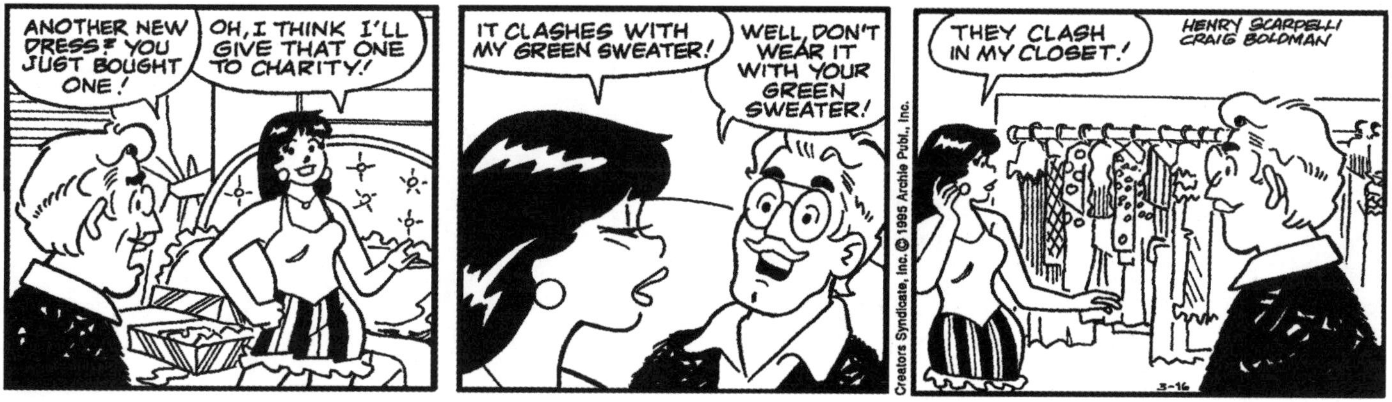
ANOTHER NEW DRESS? YOU JUST BOUGHT ONE!
OH, I THINK I'LL GIVE THAT ONE TO CHARITY!
IT CLASHES WITH MY GREEN SWEATER!
WELL, DON'T WEAR IT WITH YOUR GREEN SWEATER!
Creators Syndicate, Inc. © 1995 Archie Publ., Inc.
THEY CLASH IN MY CLOSET!
HENRY SCARPELLI CRAIG BOLDMAN
3-16

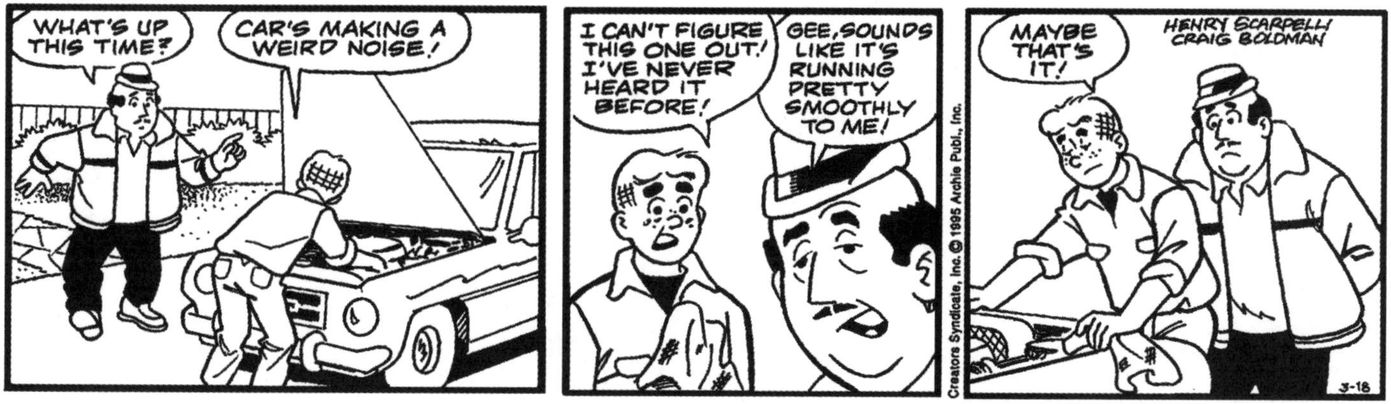
WHAT'S UP THIS TIME?
CAR'S MAKING A WEIRD NOISE!
I CAN'T FIGURE THIS ONE OUT! I'VE NEVER HEARD IT BEFORE!
GEE, SOUNDS LIKE IT'S RUNNING PRETTY SMOOTHLY TO ME!
Creators Syndicate, Inc. © 1995 Archie Publ., Inc.
MAYBE THAT'S IT!
HENRY SCARPELLI CRAIG BOLDMAN
3-18

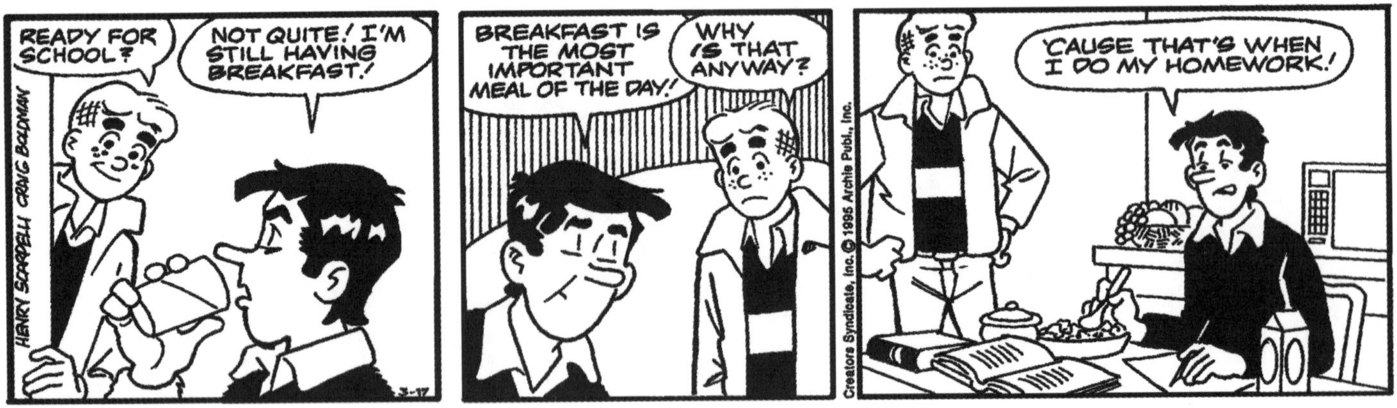
READY FOR SCHOOL?
NOT QUITE! I'M STILL HAVING BREAKFAST!
HENRY SCARPELLI CRAIG BOLDMAN
3-17
BREAKFAST IS THE MOST IMPORTANT MEAL OF THE DAY!
WHY IS THAT ANYWAY?
Creators Syndicate, Inc. © 1995 Archie Publ., Inc.
'CAUSE THAT'S WHEN I DO MY HOMEWORK!

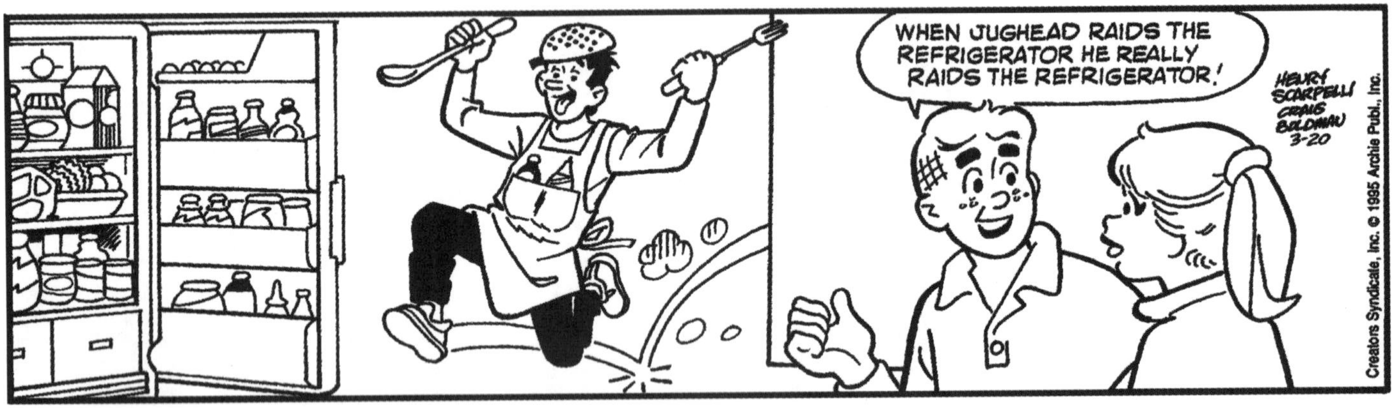
WHEN JUGHEAD RAIDS THE REFRIGERATOR HE REALLY RAIDS THE REFRIGERATOR!
HENRY SCARPELLI CRAIG BOLDMAN 3-20
Creators Syndicate, Inc. © 1995 Archie Publ., Inc.

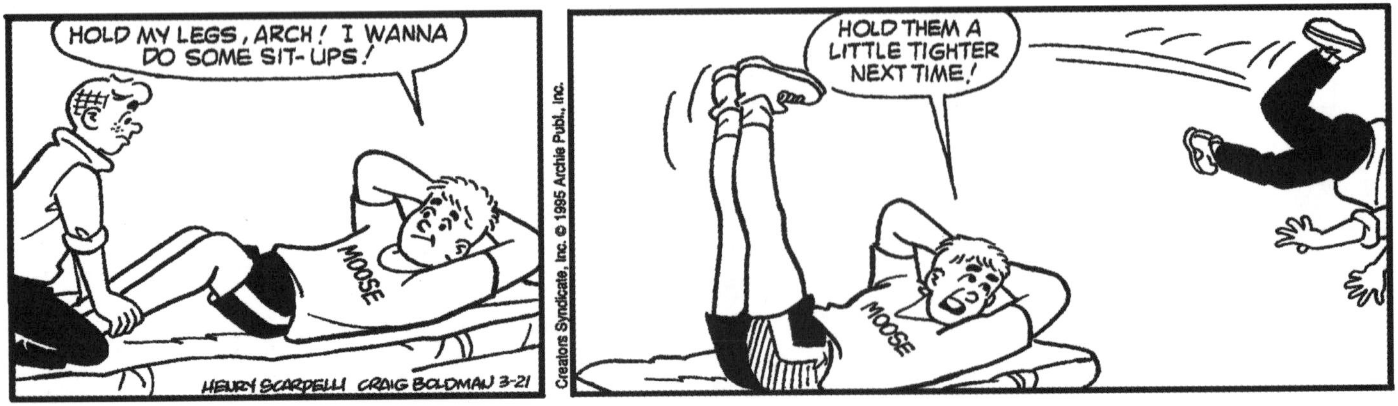
HOLD MY LEGS, ARCH! I WANNA DO SOME SIT-UPS!
MOOSE
HENRY SCARPELLI CRAIG BOLDMAN 3-21
Creators Syndicate, Inc. © 1995 Archie Publ., Inc.
HOLD THEM A LITTLE TIGHTER NEXT TIME!
MOOSE

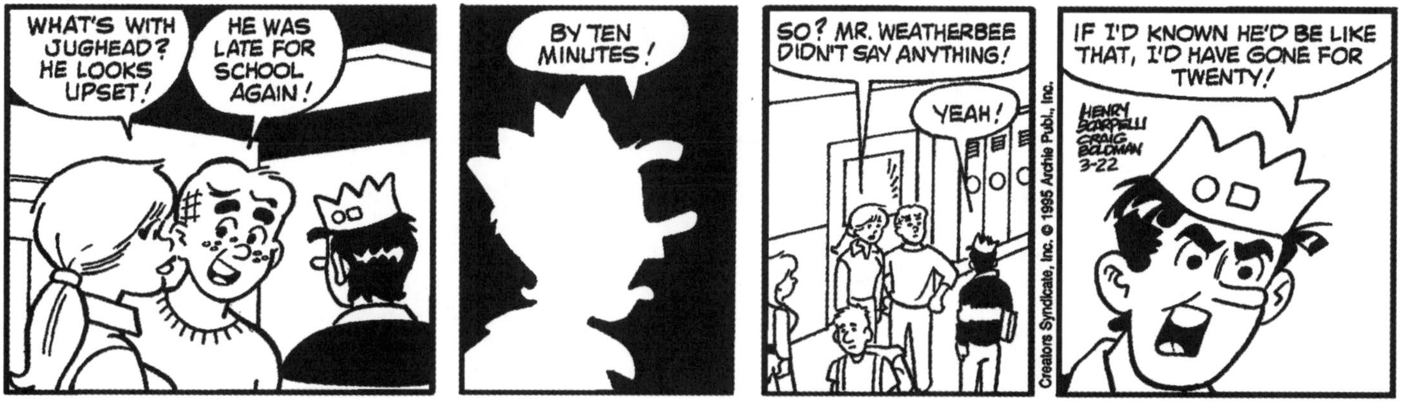
WHAT'S WITH JUGHEAD? HE LOOKS UPSET!
HE WAS LATE FOR SCHOOL AGAIN!
BY TEN MINUTES!
SO? MR. WEATHERBEE DIDN'T SAY ANYTHING!
YEAH!
Creators Syndicate, Inc. © 1995 Archie Publ., Inc.
IF I'D KNOWN HE'D BE LIKE THAT, I'D HAVE GONE FOR TWENTY!
HENRY SCARPELLI CRAIG BOLDMAN 3-22

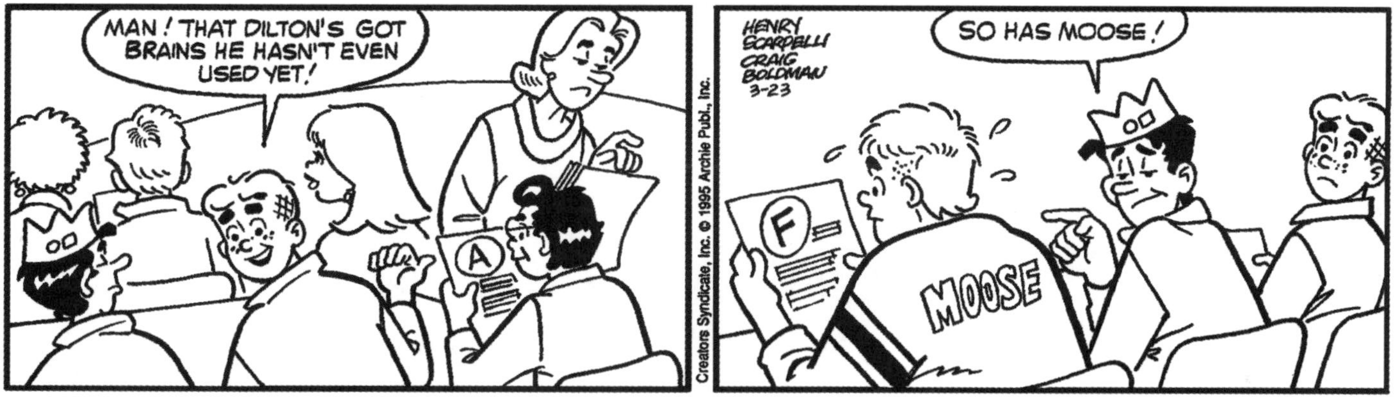
MAN! THAT DILTON'S GOT BRAINS HE HASN'T EVEN USED YET!
A
Creators Syndicate, Inc. © 1995 Archie Publ., Inc.
HENRY SCARPELLI CRAIG BOLDMAN 3-23
SO HAS MOOSE!
F
MOOSE

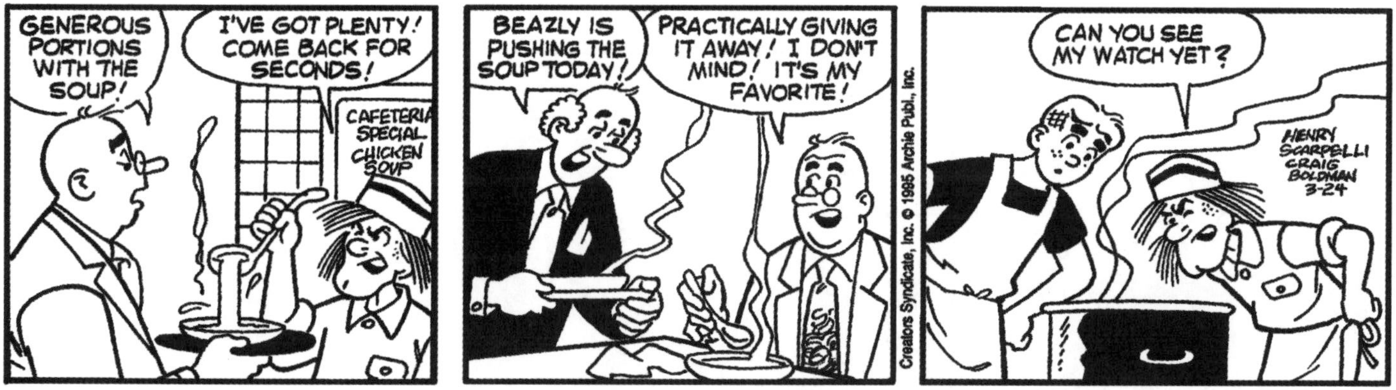
GENEROUS PORTIONS WITH THE SOUP!
I'VE GOT PLENTY! COME BACK FOR SECONDS!
CAFETERIA SPECIAL CHICKEN SOUP
BEAZLY IS PUSHING THE SOUP TODAY!
PRACTICALLY GIVING IT AWAY! I DON'T MIND! IT'S MY FAVORITE!
Creators Syndicate, Inc. © 1995 Archie Publ., Inc.
CAN YOU SEE MY WATCH YET?
HENRY SCARPELLI CRAIG BOLDMAN 3-24

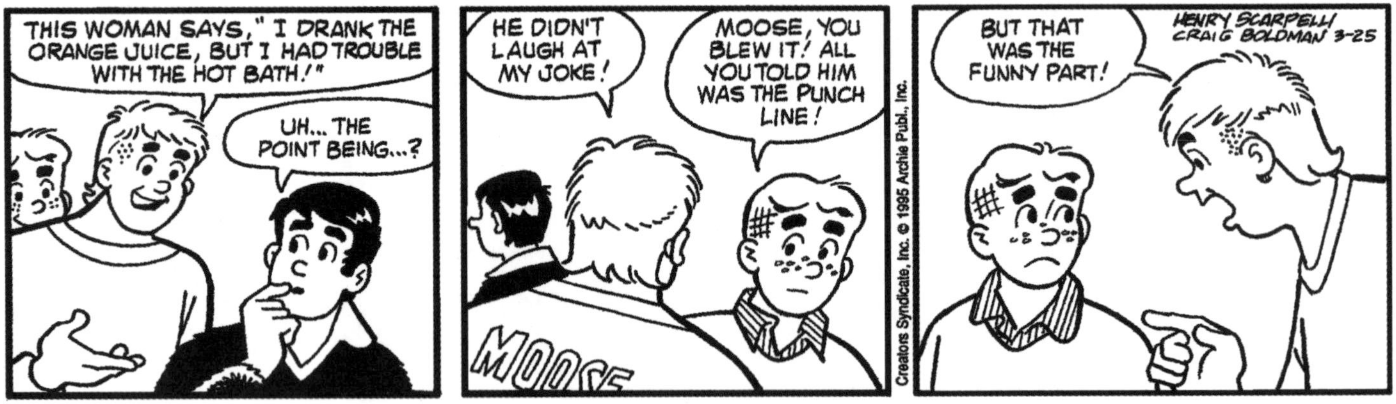
THIS WOMAN SAYS, " I DRANK THE ORANGE JUICE, BUT I HAD TROUBLE WITH THE HOT BATH!"
UH... THE POINT BEING...?
HE DIDN'T LAUGH AT MY JOKE!
MOOSE, YOU BLEW IT! ALL YOU TOLD HIM WAS THE PUNCH LINE!
MOOSE
Creators Syndicate, Inc. © 1995 Archie Publ., Inc.
BUT THAT WAS THE FUNNY PART!
HENRY SCARPELLI CRAIG BOLDMAN 3-25

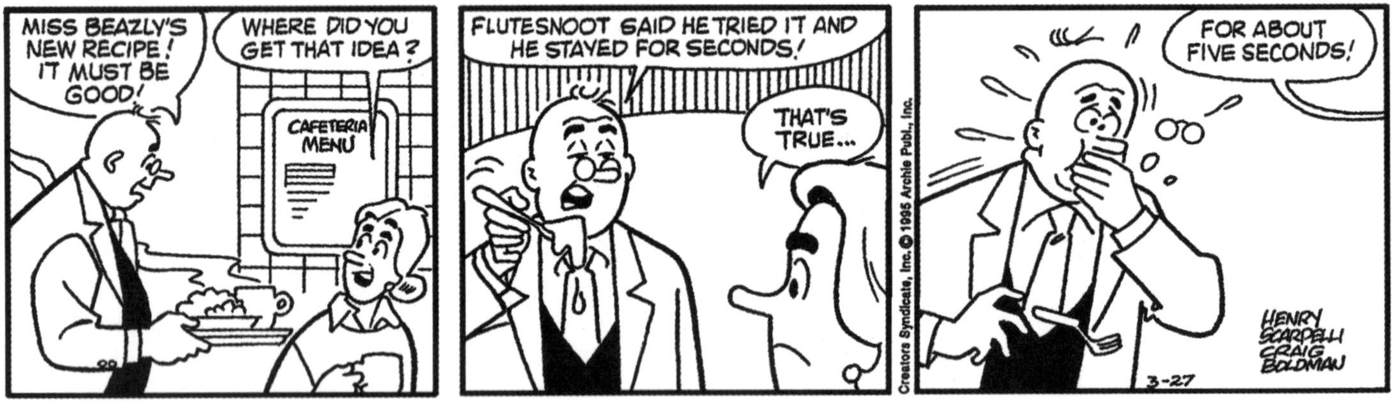
MISS BEAZLY'S NEW RECIPE! IT MUST BE GOOD!
WHERE DID YOU GET THAT IDEA?
CAFETERIA MENU
FLUTESNOOT SAID HE TRIED IT AND HE STAYED FOR SECONDS!
THAT'S TRUE...
Creators Syndicate, Inc. © 1995 Archie Publ., Inc.
FOR ABOUT FIVE SECONDS!
HENRY SCARPELLI CRAIG BOLDMAN
3-27

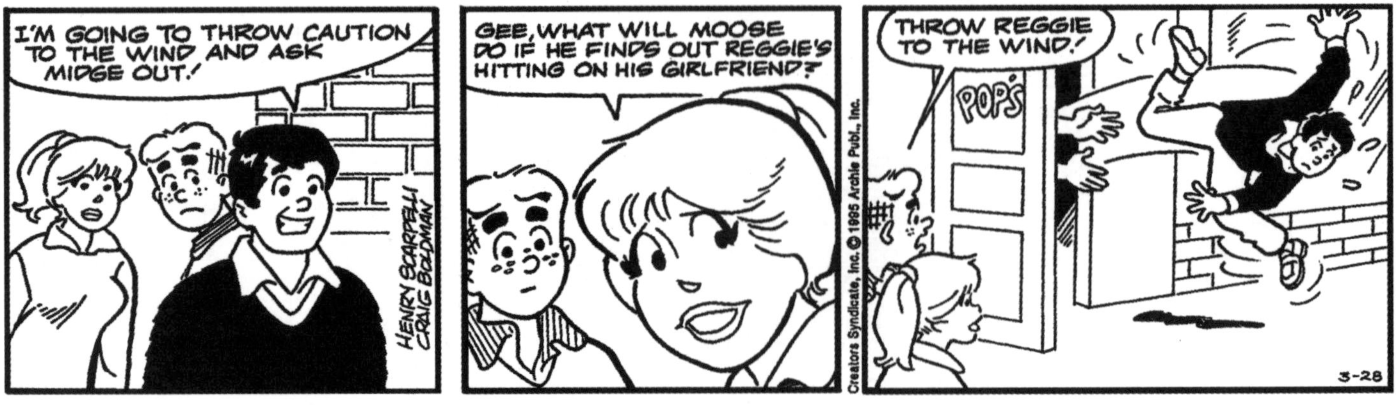
I'M GOING TO THROW CAUTION TO THE WIND AND ASK MIDGE OUT!
HENRY SCARPELLI CRAIG BOLDMAN
GEE, WHAT WILL MOOSE DO IF HE FINDS OUT REGGIE'S HITTING ON HIS GIRLFRIEND?
Creators Syndicate, Inc. © 1995 Archie Publ., Inc.
THROW REGGIE TO THE WIND!
POP'S
3-28

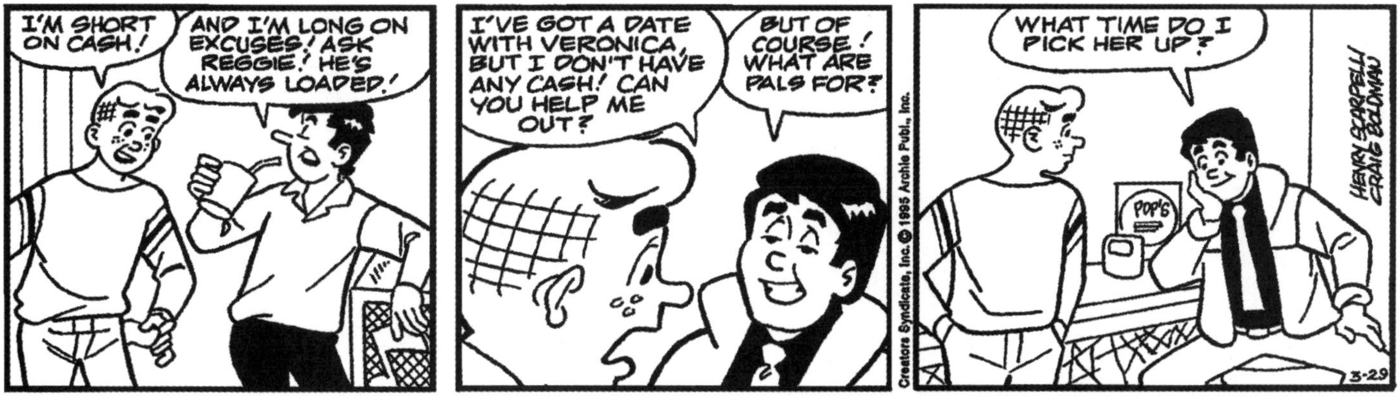

I'M SHORT ON CASH!
AND I'M LONG ON EXCUSES! ASK REGGIE! HE'S ALWAYS LOADED!
I'VE GOT A DATE WITH VERONICA, BUT I DON'T HAVE ANY CASH! CAN YOU HELP ME OUT?
BUT OF COURSE! WHAT ARE PALS FOR?
Creators Syndicate, Inc. © 1995 Archie Publ., Inc.
WHAT TIME DO I PICK HER UP?
POP'S
HENRY SCARPELLI CRAIG BOLDMAN
3-29

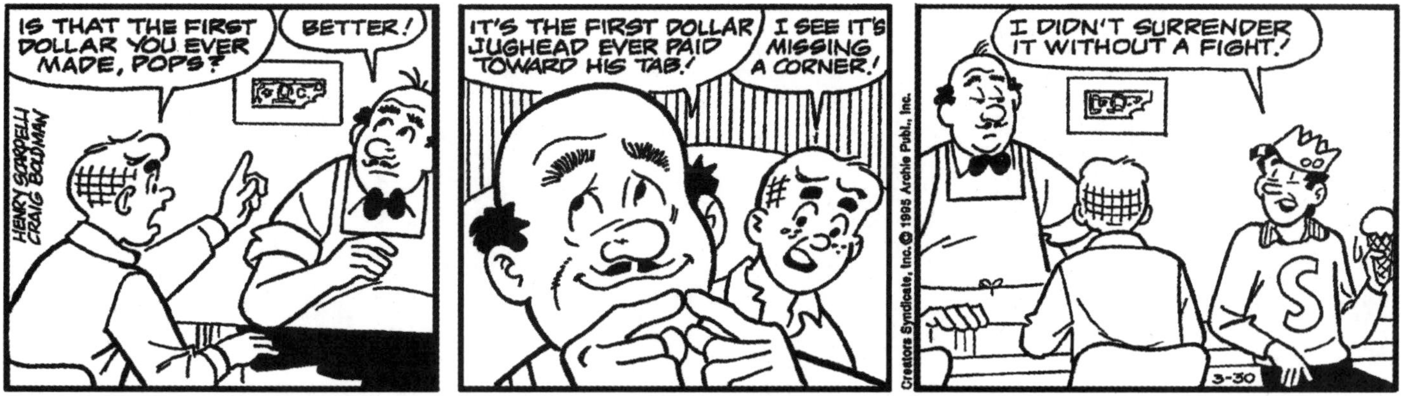

IS THAT THE FIRST DOLLAR YOU EVER MADE, POPS?
BETTER!
HENRY SCARPELLI CRAIG BOLDMAN
IT'S THE FIRST DOLLAR JUGHEAD EVER PAID TOWARD HIS TAB!
I SEE IT'S MISSING A CORNER!
Creators Syndicate, Inc. © 1995 Archie Publ., Inc.
I DIDN'T SURRENDER IT WITHOUT A FIGHT!
S
3-30

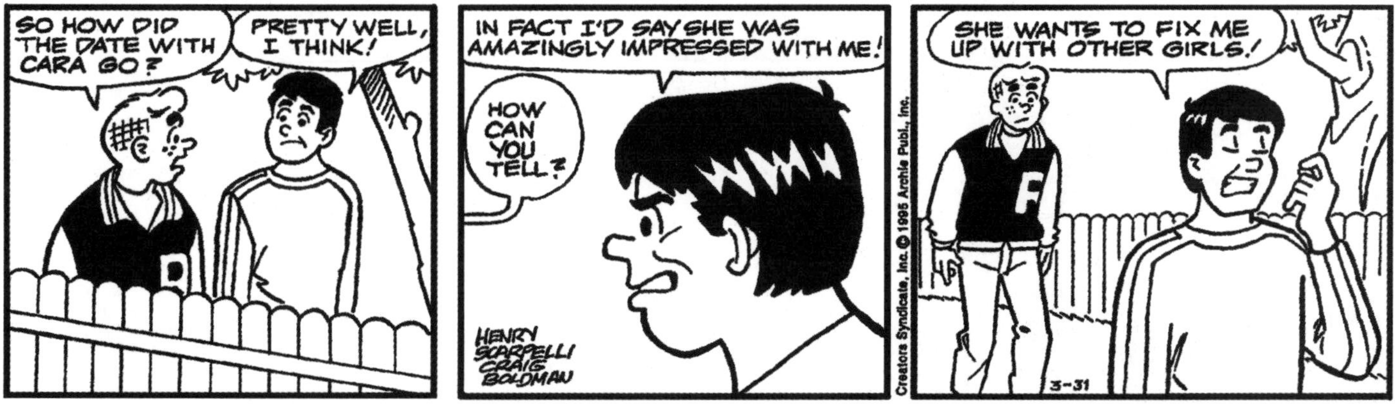

SO HOW DID THE DATE WITH CARA GO?
PRETTY WELL, I THINK!
D
IN FACT I'D SAY SHE WAS AMAZINGLY IMPRESSED WITH ME!
HOW CAN YOU TELL?
HENRY SCARPELLI CRAIG BOLDMAN
Creators Syndicate, Inc. © 1995 Archie Publ., Inc.
SHE WANTS TO FIX ME UP WITH OTHER GIRLS!
F
3-31

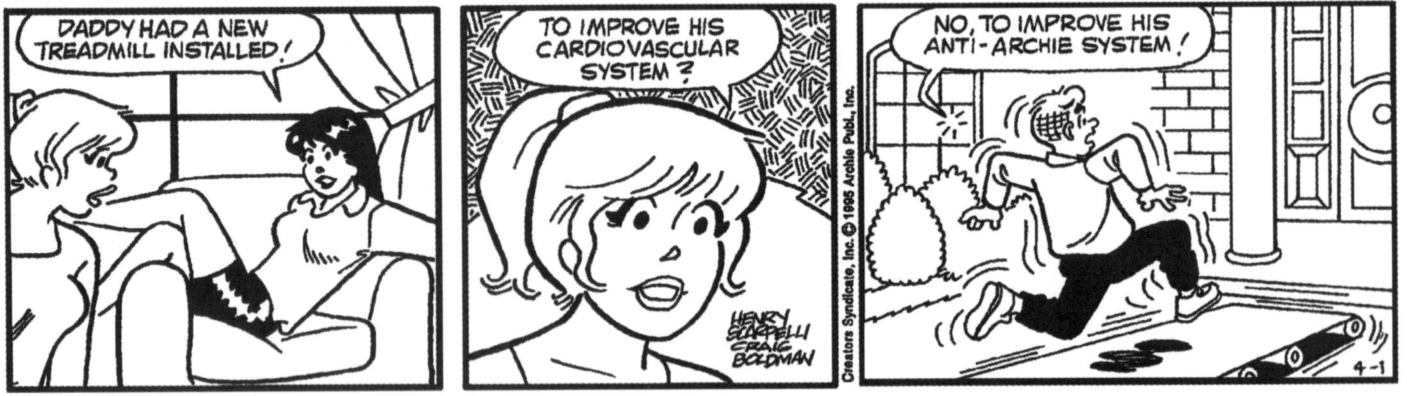
DADDY HAD A NEW TREADMILL INSTALLED!
TO IMPROVE HIS CARDIOVASCULAR SYSTEM?
HENRY SCARPELLI CRAIG BOLDMAN
Creators Syndicate, Inc. © 1995 Archie Publ., Inc.
NO, TO IMPROVE HIS ANTI-ARCHIE SYSTEM!
4-1

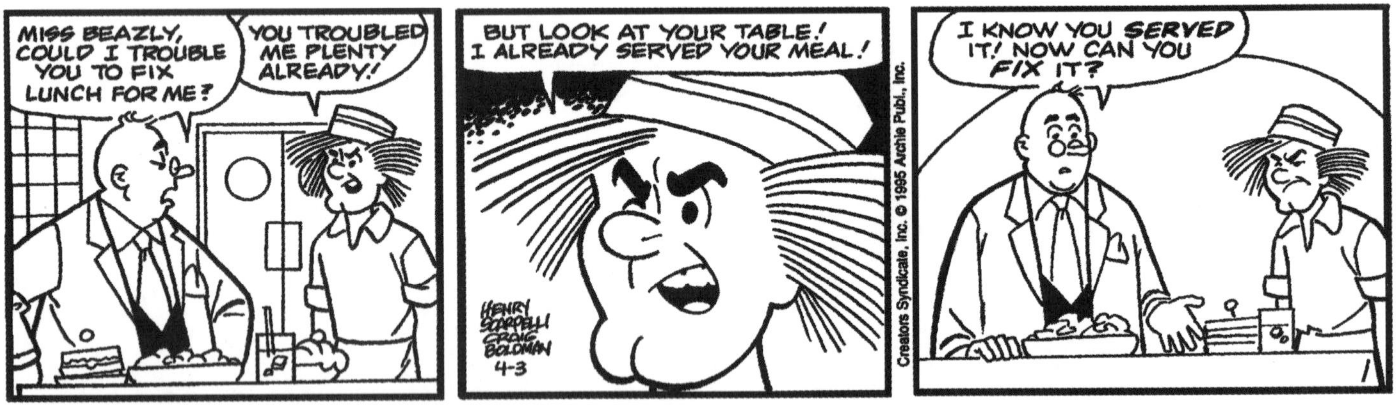
MISS BEAZLY, COULD I TROUBLE YOU TO FIX LUNCH FOR ME?
YOU TROUBLED ME PLENTY ALREADY!
BUT LOOK AT YOUR TABLE! I ALREADY SERVED YOUR MEAL!
HENRY SCARPELLI CRAIG BOLDMAN
4-3
Creators Syndicate, Inc. © 1995 Archie Publ., Inc.
I KNOW YOU SERVED IT! NOW CAN YOU FIX IT?

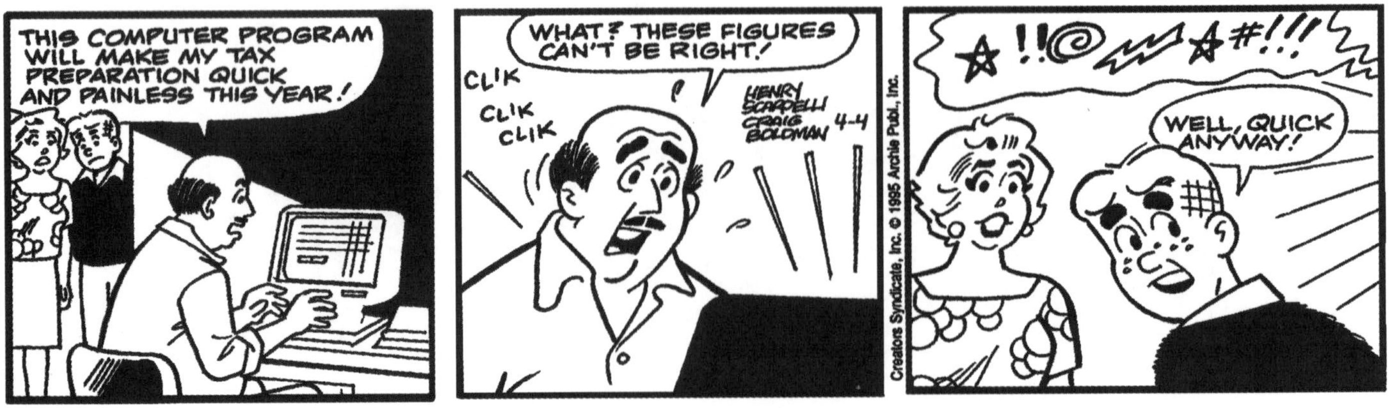
THIS COMPUTER PROGRAM WILL MAKE MY TAX PREPARATION QUICK AND PAINLESS THIS YEAR!
CLIK
CLIK
CLIK
WHAT? THESE FIGURES CAN'T BE RIGHT!
HENRY SCARPELLI CRAIG BOLDMAN
4-4
Creators Syndicate, Inc. © 1995 Archie Publ., Inc.
WELL, QUICK ANYWAY!

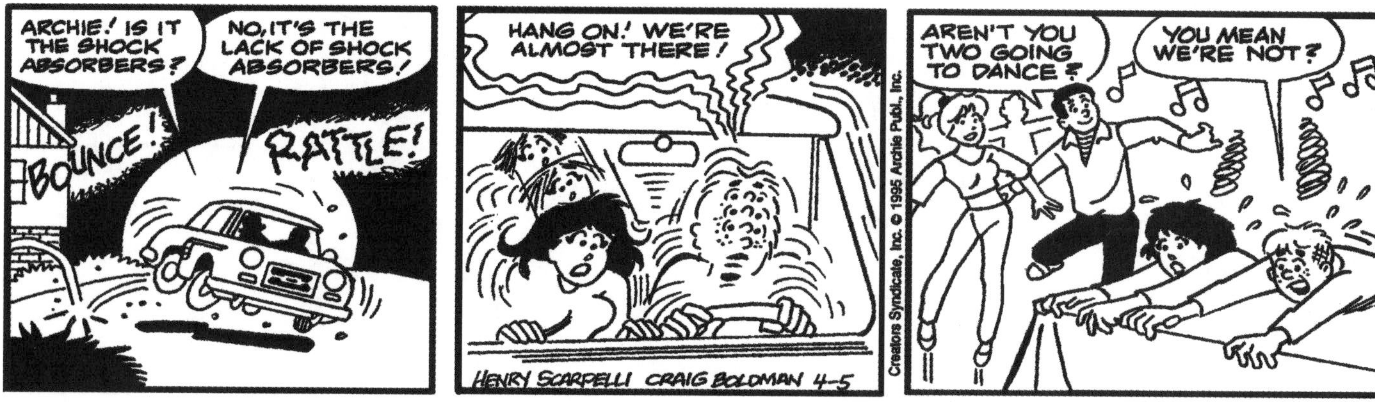
ARCHIE! IS IT THE SHOCK ABSORBERS?
NO, IT'S THE LACK OF SHOCK ABSORBERS!
BOUNCE!
RATTLE!
HANG ON! WE'RE ALMOST THERE!
HENRY SCARPELLI CRAIG BOLDMAN 4-5
Creators Syndicate, Inc. © 1995 Archie Publ., Inc.
AREN'T YOU TWO GOING TO DANCE?
YOU MEAN WE'RE NOT?

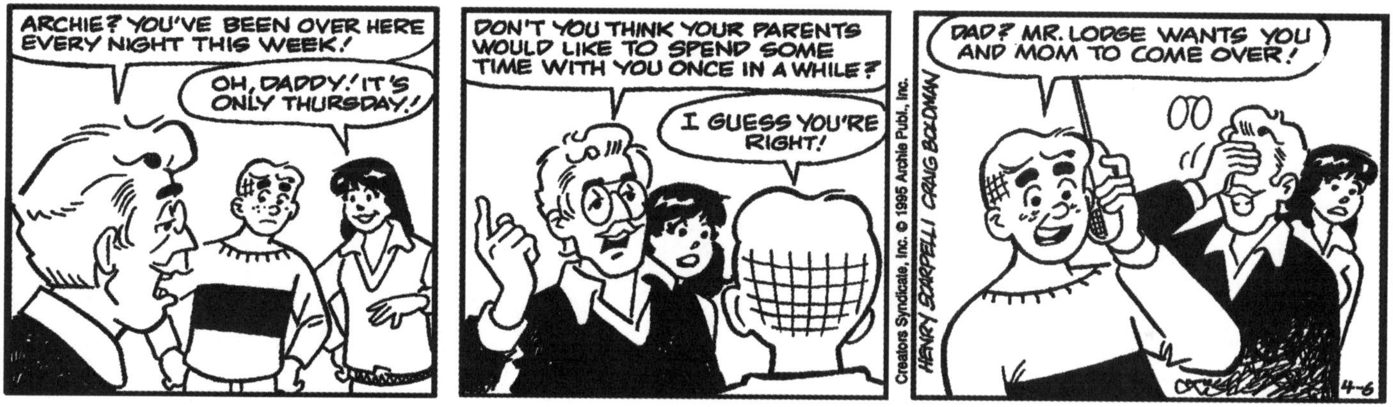
ARCHIE? YOU'VE BEEN OVER HERE EVERY NIGHT THIS WEEK!
OH, DADDY! IT'S ONLY THURSDAY!
DON'T YOU THINK YOUR PARENTS WOULD LIKE TO SPEND SOME TIME WITH YOU ONCE IN A WHILE?
I GUESS YOU'RE RIGHT!
Creators Syndicate, Inc. © 1995 Archie Publ., Inc.
HENRY SCARPELLI CRAIG BOLDMAN
DAD? MR. LODGE WANTS YOU AND MOM TO COME OVER!
4-6

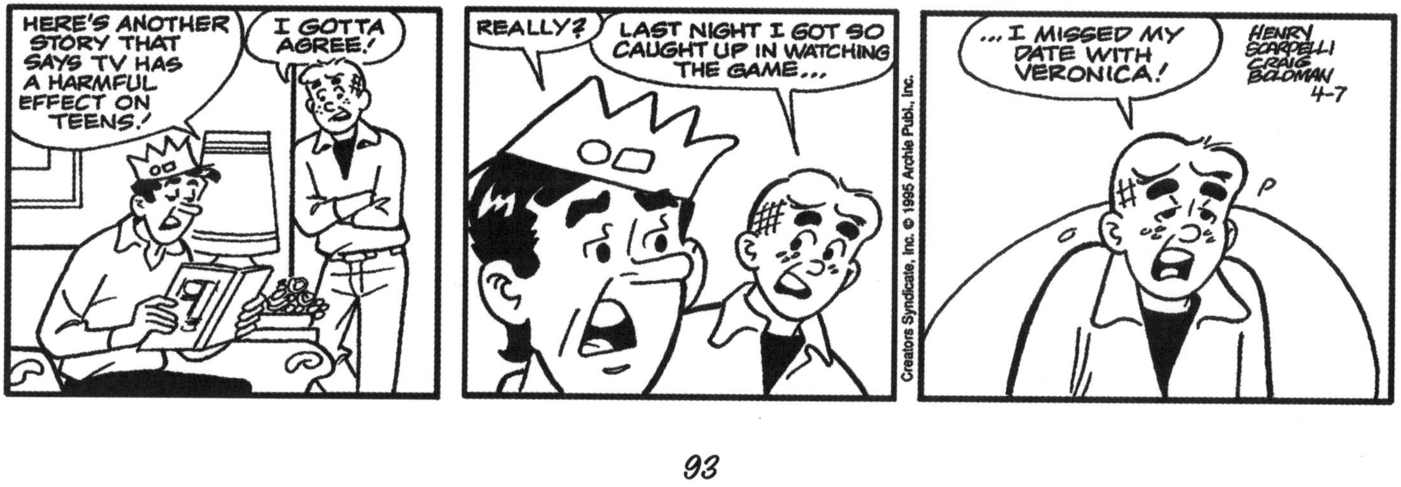
HERE'S ANOTHER STORY THAT SAYS TV HAS A HARMFUL EFFECT ON TEENS!
I GOTTA AGREE!
REALLY?
LAST NIGHT I GOT SO CAUGHT UP IN WATCHING THE GAME...
Creators Syndicate, Inc. © 1995 Archie Publ., Inc.
...I MISSED MY DATE WITH VERONICA!
HENRY SCARPELLI CRAIG BOLDMAN 4-7

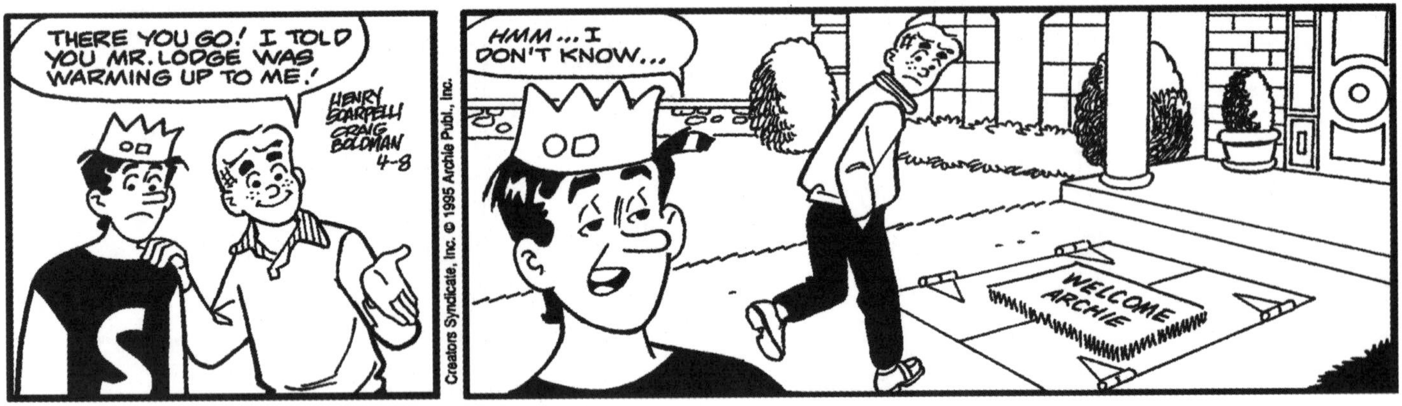
THERE YOU GO! I TOLD YOU MR. LODGE WAS WARMING UP TO ME!
HENRY SCARPELLI CRAIG BOLDMAN 4-8
Creators Syndicate, Inc. © 1995 Archie Publ., Inc.
HMM... I DON'T KNOW...
WELCOME ARCHIE

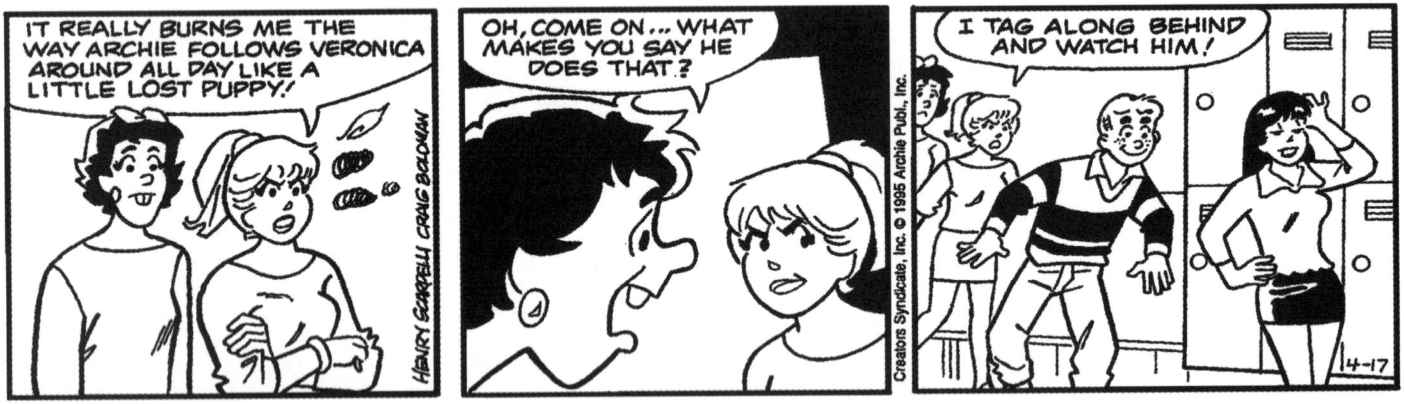
IT REALLY BURNS ME THE WAY ARCHIE FOLLOWS VERONICA AROUND ALL DAY LIKE A LITTLE LOST PUPPY!
HENRY SCARPELLI CRAIG BOLDMAN
OH, COME ON... WHAT MAKES YOU SAY HE DOES THAT?
Creators Syndicate, Inc. © 1995 Archie Publ., Inc.
I TAG ALONG BEHIND AND WATCH HIM!
4-17

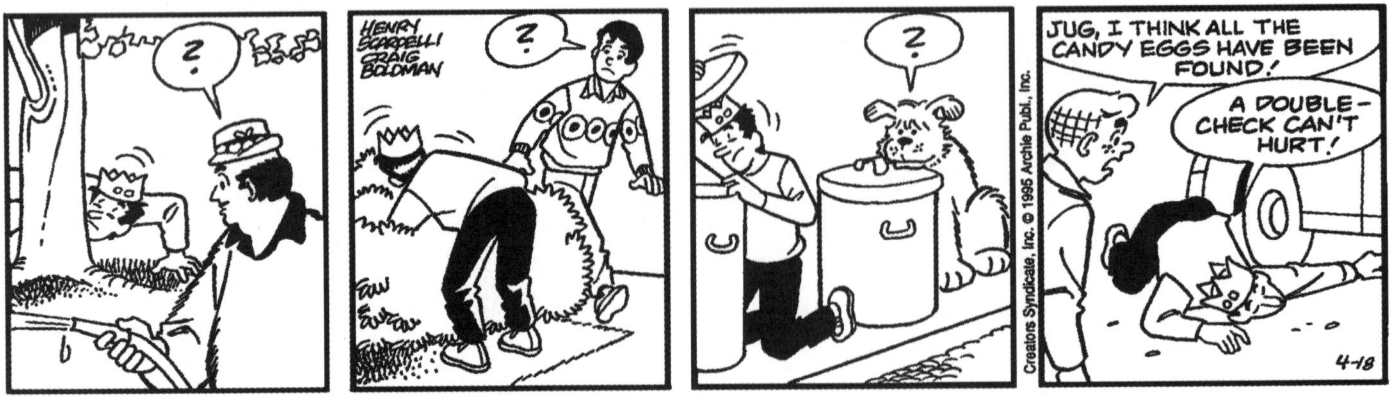
?
HENRY SCARPELLI CRAIG BOLDMAN
?
?
Creators Syndicate, Inc. © 1995 Archie Publ., Inc.
JUG, I THINK ALL THE CANDY EGGS HAVE BEEN FOUND!
A DOUBLE-CHECK CAN'T HURT!
4-18

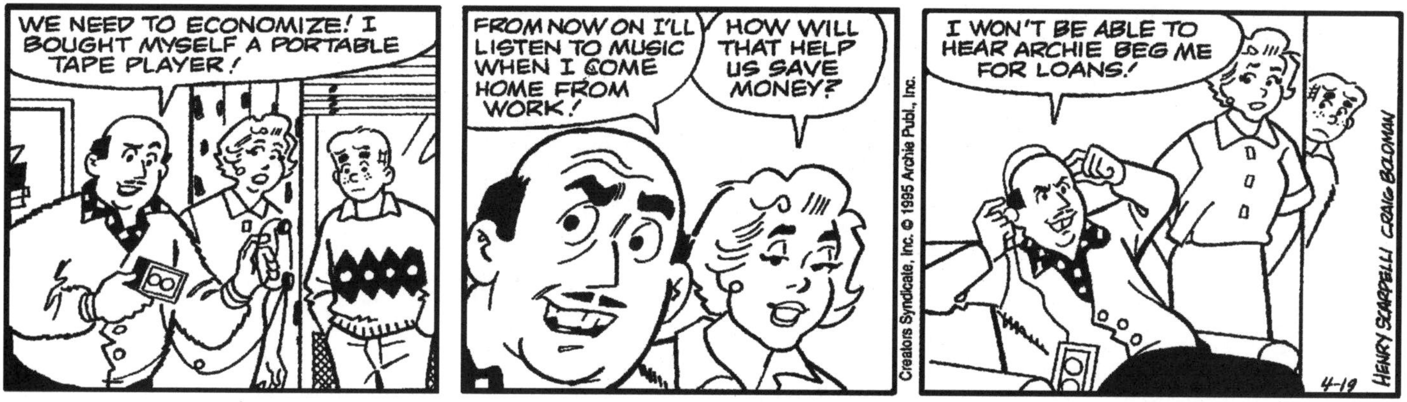
WE NEED TO ECONOMIZE! I BOUGHT MYSELF A PORTABLE TAPE PLAYER!
FROM NOW ON I'LL LISTEN TO MUSIC WHEN I COME HOME FROM WORK!
HOW WILL THAT HELP US SAVE MONEY?
I WON'T BE ABLE TO HEAR ARCHIE BEG ME FOR LOANS!
Creators Syndicate, Inc. © 1995 Archie Publ., Inc.
HENRY SCARPELLI CRAIG BOLDMAN
4-19

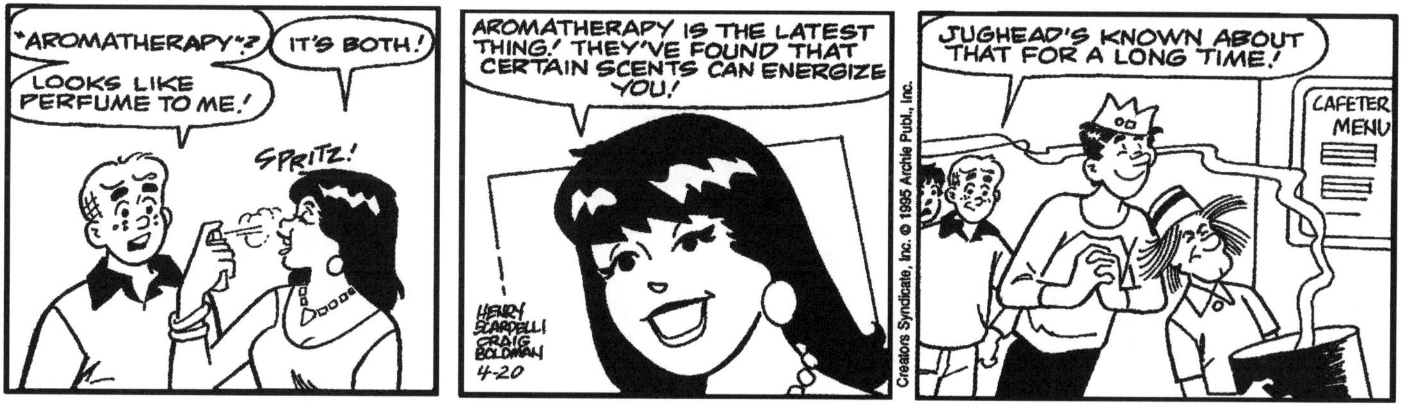
"AROMATHERAPY"?
LOOKS LIKE PERFUME TO ME!
IT'S BOTH!
SPRITZ!
AROMATHERAPY IS THE LATEST THING! THEY'VE FOUND THAT CERTAIN SCENTS CAN ENERGIZE YOU!
HENRY SCARPELLI CRAIG BOLDMAN
4-20
JUGHEAD'S KNOWN ABOUT THAT FOR A LONG TIME!
CAFETER MENU
Creators Syndicate, Inc. © 1995 Archie Publ., Inc.

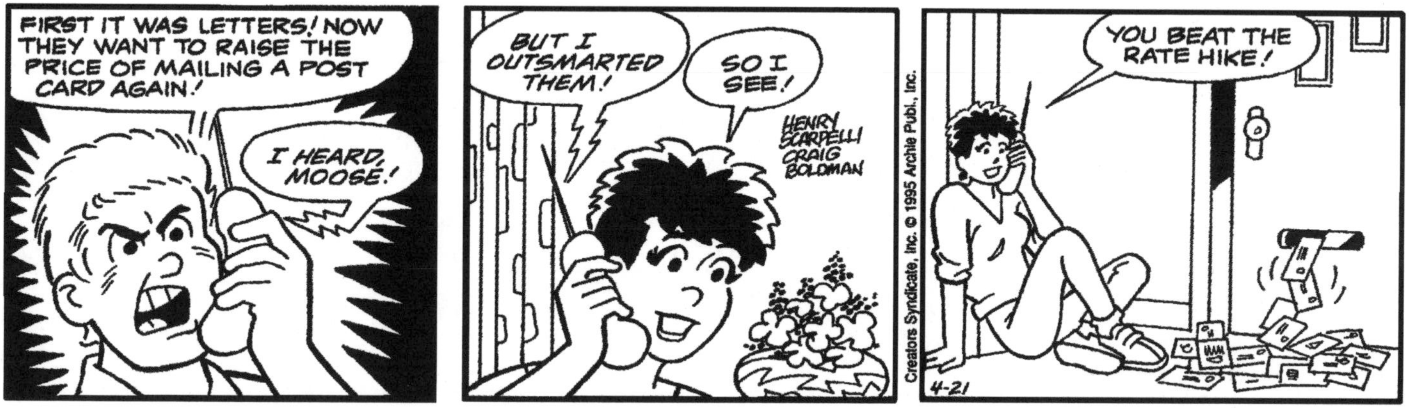
FIRST IT WAS LETTERS! NOW THEY WANT TO RAISE THE PRICE OF MAILING A POST CARD AGAIN!
I HEARD, MOOSE!
BUT I OUTSMARTED THEM!
SO I SEE!
HENRY SCARPELLI CRAIG BOLDMAN
YOU BEAT THE RATE HIKE!
Creators Syndicate, Inc. © 1995 Archie Publ., Inc.
4-21

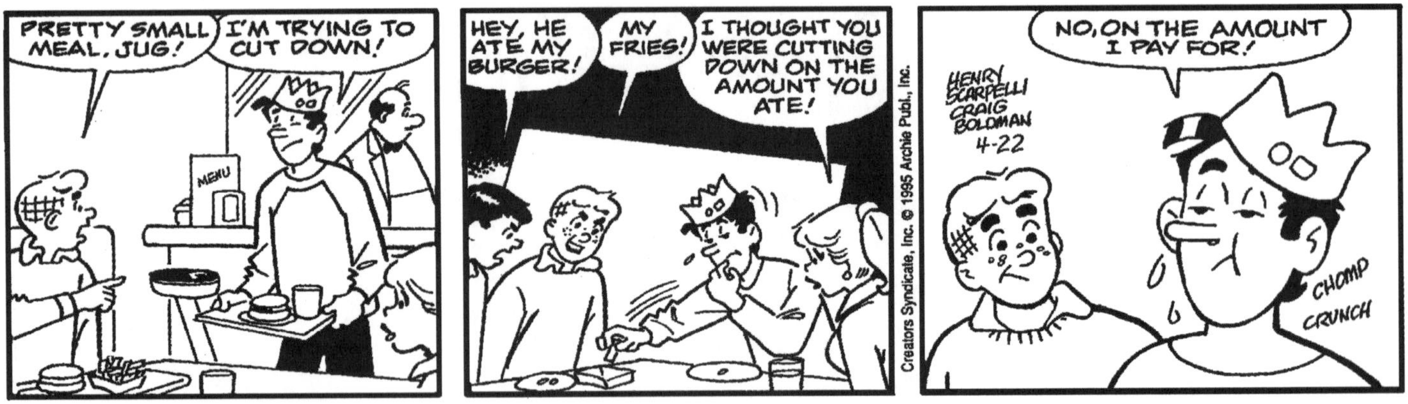
PRETTY SMALL MEAL, JUG!
I'M TRYING TO CUT DOWN!
MENU
HEY, HE ATE MY BURGER!
MY FRIES!
I THOUGHT YOU WERE CUTTING DOWN ON THE AMOUNT YOU ATE!
Creators Syndicate, Inc. © 1995 Archie Publ., Inc.
HENRY SCARPELLI CRAIG BOLDMAN 4-22
NO, ON THE AMOUNT I PAY FOR!
CHOMP
CRUNCH

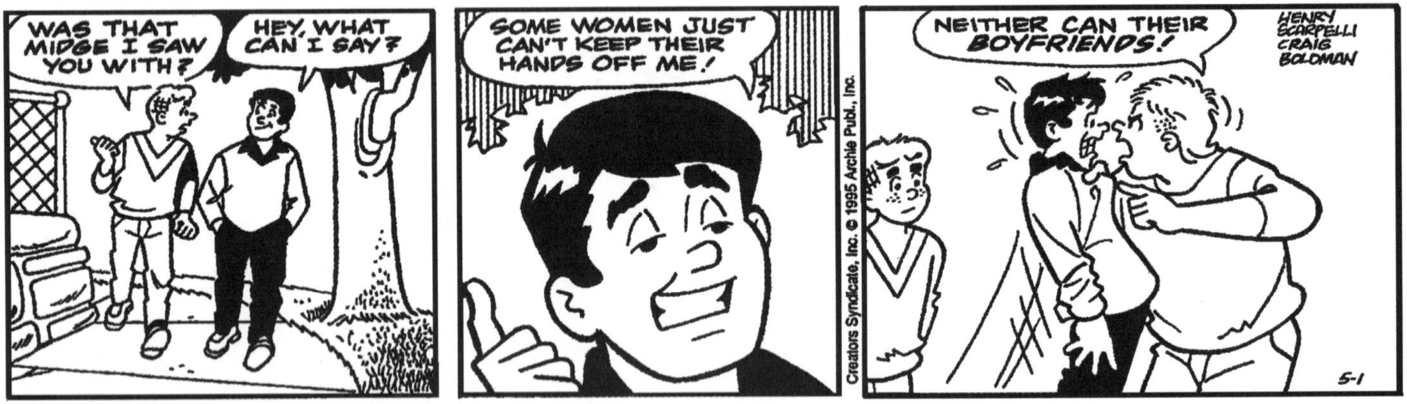
WAS THAT MIDGE I SAW YOU WITH?
HEY, WHAT CAN I SAY?
SOME WOMEN JUST CAN'T KEEP THEIR HANDS OFF ME!
Creators Syndicate, Inc. © 1995 Archie Publ., Inc.
NEITHER CAN THEIR BOYFRIENDS!
HENRY SCARPELLI CRAIG BOLDMAN
5-1

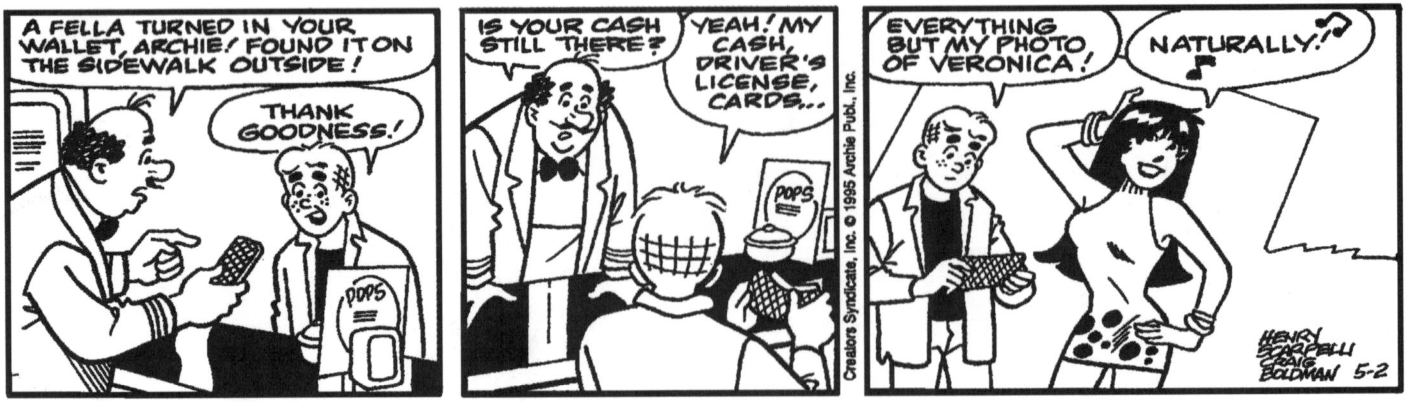
A FELLA TURNED IN YOUR WALLET, ARCHIE! FOUND IT ON THE SIDEWALK OUTSIDE!
THANK GOODNESS!
POPS
IS YOUR CASH STILL THERE?
YEAH! MY CASH, DRIVER'S LICENSE, CARDS...
POPS
Creators Syndicate, Inc. © 1995 Archie Publ., Inc.
EVERYTHING BUT MY PHOTO OF VERONICA!
NATURALLY!
HENRY SCARPELLI CRAIG BOLDMAN 5-2